Katharine McMahon is the author of six novels. She has taught in secondary schools, performed in local theatre and worked as a Royal Literary Fund fellow teaching writing skills at the Universities of Hertfordshire and Warwick. She lives in Hertfordshire.

By Katharine McMahon

The Rose of Sebastopol
The Alchemist's Daughter
A Way through the Woods
Footsteps
Confinement
After Mary

THE
ALCHEMIST'S
DAUGHTER

Katharine McMahon

PHOENIX

A PHOENIX PAPERBACK

First published in Great Britain in 2006
by Weidenfeld & Nicolson
This paperback edition published in 2006
by Phoenix,
An imprint of Orion Books Ltd,
Orion House, 5 Upper St Martin's Lane,
London WC2H 9EA

An Hachette Livre UK Company

A CIP catalogue record for this book
is available from the British Library.

Typeset at The Spartan Press Ltd,
Lymington, Hants

Printed and bound in Great Britain by
Clays Ltd, St Ives plc

The Orion Publishing Group's policy is to use papers that
are natural, renewable and recyclable products and
made from wood grown in sustainable forests. The logging
and manufacturing processes are expected to conform to
the environmental regulations of the country of origin.

www.orionbooks.co.uk

For Mark Lucas

THE
ALCHEMIST'S
DAUGHTER

Chapter One

THE ALCHEMIST'S DAUGHTER

I

True it is, without falsehood, certain and most true
1st Precept of the Emerald Tablet

In one of my earliest memories I walk behind my father to the furnace shed. He wears a long black coat that gathers up fallen leaves and his staff makes a little crunch when he stabs it into the path. My apron is so thick that my knees bang against it and the autumn air is smoky on my face. Suddenly I trip over the hem of his coat. My nose hits ancient wool. He stops dead. My heart pounds but I recover my balance and we walk on.

When we reach the shed I take a gasp of fresh air before being swallowed up. Gill is inside, shovelling coal into the arch of the furnace mouth, which roars orange.

My father's finger emerges from his sleeve and points to a metal screen Gill made for me. There is a little stool behind it and at just the right height a couple of peepholes covered with mesh are cut into the metal. I must not move from this stool in case something spills or explodes. We are boiling up vatfuls of urine to make a thick syrup which eventually will become phosphorus. After a while the stench of sulphur and ammonia is so strong that it almost knocks me off my stool. I can't breathe properly and my throat is hot but I hold firm and don't let my back slump. Gill is like a black shadow moving back and forth; a twist of his upper body, a jerk of the shovel, a stooping out of sight, another turn, the racket of falling coal, then the flames roar fiercer until I think the furnace will blow apart and the shed, Selden, the woods, the world will all fly away in pieces.

But my father isn't worried so I feel safe too. He stands at his high desk by the door and puts his left hand to his forehead as he writes. The only bit of his face I can see under his wig is his beaky nose. This black and orange world is crammed with a million things that he knows and I don't. I want to be like him. I will be soon, if I can only pay attention and learn fast enough.

2

I have no memories of my mother because she is a skeleton under the earth all the time I am a child. When I was born she died and though I appreciate the symmetry of this I'm not satisfied. It's hard finding out more about her because I'm not allowed to ask my father and Mrs Gill, who looks after me, is a woman of few words.

However, on my sixth birthday, 30 May 1712, I ask Mrs Gill the usual questions about what my mother was like and she suddenly sighs deeply, puts down the great pot she is carrying – it is the week for brewing up the elderflowers – and takes me on a long journey through the house past the Queen's Room, through a series of little doors and up a flight of narrow stairs until we come to a low room with a high lattice window and a sloping floor. She says, 'That's where you were born.'

The only furniture is a rough-looking chest and a high bed shrouded in linen, which I look at with wonder. The bed is surely too small and clean for such an untidy event as a birth. 'Why?' I say.

'Because everyone has to be born somewhere.'

'Why this room and not a bigger one?'

'Because it's quiet and ideal.' She leans over the chest in that Mrs Gill way of not bending her back or knees but just lowering her upper body. I go closer as she brings up the lid and I see that the inside is lined with white paper but otherwise nearly empty. It smells like nothing else on earth, a dusty sweetness of folded-away things. And out comes a cream-coloured shawl like a spider's web, a tiny bonnet, a baby's tucked nightgown and a coil of pink ribbon with a pin in one end to keep it rolled up. 'These were your things that I made you,' she says, patting the clothes, 'and this was your mother's.' She hands me the ribbon, which I rub and sniff. 'You can have that if you like. And now those elderflowers will be boiled half dry so down we go.'

Later she tells me the story of my parents' marriage. My mother, Emilie De Lery, was from a family of Huguenot silk weavers who had been driven out of France in 1685 and settled in a district of London called Spital Fields. Competition in the silk market was fierce but my grandfather De Lery decided that fashionable London wanted colour so he went to the Royal Society to see if he could find someone who knew about dyes.

When Grandpère De Lery knocked at the Royal Society's door my father, Sir John Selden, was giving a paper about the green mineral, malachite. Grandpère De Lery listened rapturously, collared my father afterwards and insisted he dine *en famille* in Spital Fields. There John Selden met the daughter Emilie, twenty-two years old to his forty-nine, and his old bachelor heart was won by her dark eyes and shy smile. Within six months a new shade, De Lery green, had swamped the silk market; within a year my father had abandoned his fellowship at Trinity College Cambridge and carried Emilie off to his home, Selden Manor, in Buckinghamshire.

Of course, all that happiness didn't last long. My mother died nine months later on a May morning crowded with blossom and birdsong. She, Emilie the elder, was buried under a stone in the churchyard of St Mary and St Edelburga, while I, Emilie the younger, was wrapped in the cobwebby shawl and committed to the care of Mrs Gill, housekeeper.

My father never went back to Cambridge but devoted himself to his own researches and my education. Mrs Gill said he was so sad when my mother died he burnt all her things. The pink ribbon was saved because Mrs Gill thought I should have something as a keepsake.

Until the age of nineteen I never left our estates, which included acres of woodland, a sprinkling of neglected farms and the two villages of Selden Wick and Lower Selden.

Seldens had lived in Buckinghamshire at least since the eleventh century when the first Sir John Selden was buried in the north transept of the new church of St M. and St E. Selden Manor was a long, low patchwork of a house, part stone, part brick, part timber-framed with wings and roofs and chimneys tacked on here and there whenever a new generation could afford to make a mark.

As an infant I met the scuffed chair legs which had supported centuries of restless Selden backsides, and door panels pitted by the spurs of passing boots. My fingers clutched the fat balusters on the staircase and traced the grooves in the carving of the family motto round the newel post: *Vide Mira Domini*, my first Latin, 'Behold the wonderful works of the Lord'.

By the age of five I was eye level with the battered cuisses of a suit of armour worn by a John Selden at Bosworth – Seldens were not politicians, said my father, they always picked the losing side in a war. The groan of joints when I shook the rusty gauntlet had me squirming with pleasure and I sucked my fingers to taste the metal. The rest of my Selden ancestry, each frozen in a portrait, had only two dimensions. Selden women were hung in the alcoves of upstairs passageways. They had oval faces with semi-circles instead of eyebrows.

'Where's my mother?' I asked Mrs Gill.

'There was no time to have her painted.'

'How long does it take to paint a portrait?'

'Too long.'

'More than nine months?'

'Most like.'

'If there had been a portrait what would she have looked like?'

'Like you, of course.'

Mirrors were in short supply at Selden. My father had given me a piece of polished obsidian and if I peered in a good light I could see the shadow of my face, and there was an ancient looking-glass in a disused bedchamber where I climbed on a chair and saw distorted little features: thin nose, slanted black eyes under thick brows, hair that didn't lie flat. I translated these into one of the upstairs portraits and gave my mother a long neck, white bosom and jewels in her ears like the other Lady Seldens. I dressed her in silk, of course; there was a farmer's wife in church who sometimes wore black silk and it went hush-hush like wind in the leaves, but my mother didn't wear black, oh no, she wore green, lovely shifting green, De Lery green to match the emeralds on her throat.

Selden men were lined up in the great hall. I liked the detail of their pleated ruffs and spindly thighs, and even better I liked the fact that they were part of me. Their eyes were elliptical and full of mystery and learning. Mrs Gill taught me to look for a symbol inside each picture. One Selden had a globe, another a set of compasses, a third an exotic plant, and these were clues to the fact that Seldens were driven by the pursuit of knowledge. Some had been explorers, others astronomers, astrologers, scholars or plant collectors. But all Seldens had one thing in common which didn't show up in their portraits. They were puffers, or as my French mother would have said, *souffleurs*, dabblers in alchemy.

My father was no dabbler but a true alchemist though he had received an orthodox education at Trinity and was fascinated by all branches of natural philosophy. He had become a fellow of the Royal Society on the strength of his expertise in minerals and investigations into the nature of fire but still his vocation remained alchemy. Like most alchemists he was largely self-taught though he was in secret correspondence with other practitioners, notably his former teacher at Cambridge, Isaac Newton, now president of the Royal Society.

As he had no male heir, my father passed on every speck of knowledge to me. Very few girls in the history of the world had been given the chances I had, he said. 'You are an empty flask and I am filling you up as fast as I can. You are my daughter and I will make you into me, just as if you were my son. And at the end of each day I will write down your progress so that when you become a great alchemist, greater perhaps than Mary the Jewess, people will see how I did it. And when you lapse I will write that down too and try to discover what has caused the weakness.'

This Emilie Notebook of his was a source of great anxiety to me. At Selden the written word was sacred. Ink was measured drop by drop and paper was kept in a locked drawer. A word committed to paper was regarded as a little explosion of energy. I had access to the notebooks on plants, minerals and alchemy but not to the Emilie Notebooks, which he wrote after I had gone to bed and were kept locked away in a hiding place I never saw and therefore haunted me with their ghostly authority.

4

To the world beyond Selden, say to the blacksmith's daughter brought up on the other side of the gates separating our manor house from the village, our life must have seemed very strange. Had the girl poked her head through the bars to take a closer look she would have seen a quiet house unchanging from season to season except for varying quantities of smoke coming from the chimneys. I know we were talked about in the village because when Mrs Gill took me to church or visiting in the cottages people stared.

The church was named after St Edelburga, a saint so fond of books that she'd built an entire abbey so that her niece could be educated in it. A window in the side chapel had a stained-glass picture of Edelburga who had black brows like my own and therefore, I assumed, my mother's. The Selden pew was at the front under the pulpit so I had an excellent view of Reverend Gilbert's chin and nostrils, and was expert at dodging a spray of spittle. After the service his damp fingers clung to my hand as I argued some point in his sermon. My father and I did not believe in the Trinity. Only God was God, not Jesus and not the Holy Spirit, whereas Gilbert preached the 'three in one'. Meanwhile everyone else hung about and listened. At the time I thought it was because they were amazed at how much I knew. Actually I must have been an odd little black-haired, pale-faced thing, full of long words but no girlish charm.

Sometimes church saddened me because I couldn't help but notice that most other children had mothers. The blacksmith's wife held a baby against her shoulder and another on her hip as she thrust her way down the aisle with the rest of her brood tagging on to her skirts. What was it like, I wondered, to have a mother who let you plait her hair, kept crusts in her pocket in case you were peckish, hauled you off the gritty floor if you fell, kissed your tearful face and let you play with her string of blue beads?

My own mother was in a corner of the churchyard. Sometimes Mrs Gill and I went and had a look at her grave. My anatomical education was such that I could picture the arrangement of her bones and the hollow of her pelvis, wide enough for my baby head to slide through, but there was no reaching her. I was very critical of my mother's grave. All the other Seldens were under slabs in the church or had grand memorials in the wall. The Bosworth Selden even had a tomb on which his stone replica lay with a sword at his side and a book in his hand. Some Selden women had little oval plaques like afterthoughts but at least they were inside out of the rain. 'So why is she out here?' I asked Mrs Gill.

'Lord knows. I suppose because she loved the fresh air.'

But I knew there was no fresh air under the ground. I had scooped up handfuls of earth and discovered that it smelt of cellars and tasted of coal. I had watched a fat worm writhe across my palm. 'Was she wearing a silk dress when you buried her?' I asked Mrs Gill.

'What a waste that would have been,' she said.

As we left to go home we passed villagers huddled in groups, nodding and smiling. I thought they envied me. I thought every girl in the village must want to be me and spend her days as I did, distilling and calcifying and learning the myriad qualities of sulphur, the works of Maier and Paracelsus and the Twelve Keys of Basil Valentine. Anyway, usually I was too busy, too fascinated by the dramas of our investigations to pay much attention to the world beyond. My vision was so filled with books and fermentations and hypotheses that I had no time for the study of human beings other than of their anatomy and the circulation of their blood.

Selden Manor was the crucible in which my father, the Gills and I lived together. I peer into it now with the respectful caution with which I was taught to approach any volatile experiment. I am searching for a day to illustrate our life before 1725, the year when everything changed. And, unlike the blacksmith's daughter, I am an expert in observation. I know what I am looking for – bubbles of gas, a rise in temperature, an alteration in texture – small indications of chemical change that mean something significant is happening.

5

It is October 1721. I am fifteen and my father and I are at the very beginning of our phlogiston phase. I wake at dawn and the room smells of the spicy woods outside. The clock in the church tower is striking six, which means I am late. I leap out of bed and crouch over the chamber pot. We are still very interested in urine at Selden. Gill uses it to fertilise his wife's herbal beds and as a moistening agent in the making of cement linings for alchemical vessels which have to withstand intense heat.

Next I examine my body for smallpox symptoms. A week ago my father told me that he had discovered a method that would protect me from ever having the disease. 'I shall engraft you with the pus taken from the pox of a child with a very mild form of the smallpox. You will probably feel unwell, but that's all. Afterwards you will be safe for ever from the infection. This is a method that I saw tried last year on six condemned convicts. Each was inoculated with the disease, recovered and pardoned. I shall offer the same treatment to anyone in the village who wishes to accept.' He made me roll up my sleeve, scratched my skin with a needle and dropped a yellowish liquid from a phial on to the wound. My arm felt sore afterwards but nothing worse has happened yet.

Once I've established that I don't have the smallpox I put on a bunchy woollen dress sewn by Mrs Gill, then a canvas apron. When I have stuffed my hair into a cap I am ready to make the journey to the kitchen where my breakfast is on the table.

Mrs Gill and I grunt to each other. She has staring eyes, a lumpy nose and thin pink skin stretched tight over her cheeks and forehead. She smells of cotton, pastry, sweat and above all her own cottage tang of fermenting herbs and dried flower heads. She is not only housekeeper at Selden but the local midwife and herbalist. I wasn't very pleased when I first realised this. I thought she was mine, that her hands existed only for my needs, to force my face down into the wash bowl, to cook my dinners, to empty my chamber pot, and that the reason for her cottage was so I could go there when my father was angry or away. But I am old enough now to be reconciled to her dual life. Besides, I don't need her much any more.

The household is running to its autumn timetable and I have to be in the laboratory by half past six so I set off again in my lisping felt slippers back along the flagged passageway to the quiet chambers at the front of the house: the screens passage, the hall and the library, which is an ante-room to the laboratory. On the far side a brocade curtain, double thickness, hangs over a door. Inside is a little cavity, then yet another door which opens inwards to the laboratory.

I close it softly behind me. Sunlight streams through the lattices of a two-storey bay window and the air is dancing with gold dust. Now I am back it feels as if the hours I have spent away have been wasted time. I am at the hub of the world and am filled up with excitement and dread.

My father is at his desk, and his wig, a vast, fuzzy affair, already hangs on the back of his chair. It helps him think and is worn so that it can be snatched off when he gets excited. He is sixty-four but he still has lots of silver hair, which he strokes from time to time with his left hand. He takes up very little space but burns so fiercely that he has only to lift a finger for everything to change. I think of him as the sun and me as a little planet held in place by the force of his intellect.

He is writing a paper for the Royal Society entitled 'The Nature of Fire'. Nobody on earth knows what fire is or even whether it is a state or a substance. My father has been in correspondence with Sir Isaac Newton, who suggests that fire is caused by a vibration of the ethereal medium in hot bodies, but we don't like this explanation because we can't prove it.

I sit at my desk, which is pushed up close under my father's, and open the tract he has given me to read: Robert Boyle's 'New

Experiments Physico-mechanical, touching the Spring of the Air, and Its Effects'. I already know about Boyle's investigations into the vacuum and his analysis of air but I don't mind the repetition because I am fascinated by anything to do with air and fire.

As I read I am alert to what else is happening in the laboratory. I hear the tick of our three clocks – we measure everything accurately, including time – and the scuffles of mice in their cages. My father is breathing heavily, particularly when he inhales, and his pen squeaks. I can smell ancient wool and tobacco. Beyond him the room flies away filled with things I know as intimately as my own hands.

A late fifteenth-century Selden who loved praying – very unusual for our family – built this room as a chapel but his son had other ideas and knocked out the walls and ceilings to make a laboratory. There's plenty to distract me, large and small furnaces, benches, shelves, barrels, vats, boxes, a globe, barometers, scales, a variety of bellows and receptacles of every shape; retorts, cucurbits, crucibles and alembics. We use some of these things every day, others are too rare and precious except for the most advanced stages of alchemy.

The latest member of our little menagerie is a barn owl that Gill found in the attic. She had hurt her wings by dashing them against the window frame. He thinks she is one of a pair that nests in the church tower. We keep her in the laboratory while she recovers so that we can study her habits, though the mice aren't happy because we feed them to her one by one. I can just see her from my desk. She seems to be asleep.

I read a bit more about Boyle's corpuscular theory of matter. Boyle used his vacuum pump to test the possibility that there is a substance called aether which fills up the spaces between corpuscles of air, of the type described by M. Descartes . . .

The owl has opened her black eyes. She stares at me. I stare back.

'Emilie.' I jump. 'Repeat the line you have just read.'

I can't. I have been lost in the owl's gaze.

'Your concentration is very poor. Why is that?'

'The owl, I suppose.'

'You were a better scholar when you were five. You are slipping.'

'Slipping, Father?'

'I'll make a note in the book.'

The clocks strike the half-hour. He blots his work, takes off his spectacles and puts on his wig, which shrinks his face until he is all nose and glinting eyes. 'Gill tells me we should release the owl,' he says. 'We'll take her up to the roof after supper.'

He has taught me that it is wrong to have feelings for any animal so I say nothing. The owl has closed her eyes.

'Phlogiston,' he says. 'New heading, Emilie. Today we will replicate Mayow's experiment with gases as described in the *Tractatus Medico-Physico*.' His voice, like everything else about him, is worn thin. I spring into action though I am still hurt about the owl.

In the laboratory we are always on the way to somewhere else and I struggle to keep up. My nerves are on edge. Not only must I take in all that my father teaches me about what he already knows but I must keep abreast of our new experiments. I have to anticipate, predict and hypothesise. Alchemy takes less than six months of the year and in all the rest of our work we follow Sir Isaac Newton's experimental method rigorously. I must not break things. I must not say anything foolish. I must not forget what I have already been taught. I must not ask stupid questions. Above all I mustn't cry. If I do any of these things my father will be angry and then he doesn't speak. Depending on the offence, the silence can last for hours or even days while he sits at his desk with his forehead in the fingertips of his left hand until he is ready to write what I've done in the notebook.

He is just back from his annual visit to London. Each year he spends four weeks there so he can buy the latest books and equipment, and give or listen to papers at the Royal Society where he is thought to be a very great person. At the moment he is full of news, not only about inoculating the smallpox, but about a Bavarian, Georg Stahl, and phlogiston. Thanks to Stahl we now have to rework all our experiments on the nature of fire to see if the phlogiston theory works.

We suspend a little platform holding camphor over a lighted candle placed in a trough of water, and invert a glass bulb over the top. I use a siphon to draw off the air inside the bulb until the water levels are even inside and outside, then carefully pull out the siphon tube. As we expect, the candle goes on burning for a while, then flickers and dies. The water level inside the flask rises. Stahl says the candle goes out because the air has become phlogisticated, packed with the substance phlogiston – from the Greek *phlogizein*, to set on fire – released by the burning wax.

Then I take the experiment to the window and try to ignite the camphor by using a magnifying glass to concentrate the rays of the sun. It won't burn because, according to Stahl, the air in the glass is already full of phlogiston. My father grips the workbench. He is excited by this new theory of fire and makes little popping noises with his lips. His hands are covered by the sleeves of his topcoat which is of a thick, dark-grey worsted, shiny at the elbow and rear. It has a deep collar and sags beyond his knees at the front and almost to the floor at the back. Underneath he wears an assortment of waistcoats, shirts and breeches all in colours between brown and grey. His mouth is pulled inwards, the lower lip tucked under the upper – it's got stuck like that because of the thousands of pipes he's smoked – and his eyes are fixed on the candle.

My father says, 'I believe there is something in this phlogiston theory which may shed all kinds of light on the behaviour of metals when heated or burnt. We will next try the same experiment on iron and lead. Make a list.' He pulls off his wig, throws it on the bench, puts it back on his head.

I write what he dictates but I am not happy with the idea of phlogiston. I think that the results of our experiment support Stahl's theory to an extent but don't prove it. I wish we could catch the air inside the glass and do more experiments to see how it really differs in quality from what Stahl would call the dephlogisticated air around us but I say nothing of this to my father. I do as he says and after a while I feel peaceful again. I love the flow of ink from my pen, the smells of sulphur and camphor, dusty wig and tobacco, and the satisfaction of watching an experiment go as predicted. Out of the corner of my eye I notice that my father's hands are trembling more than ever and that after a little while his knees sag and he perches on a stool.

At one o'clock I go back to the kitchen for my dinner. My father eats alone in the dining parlour and then rests while I study.

6

In the late afternoon we go outside to learn about the natural world. My father wears a tricorn hat pressed firmly down on his wig and a trailing cloak that flattens the grass. We both have stout boots sent from Buckingham and I carry a leather satchel and a jar with a cork lid in case we find anything of interest. His staff has a plain brass handle and he waves it in front of him as if he needs to push aside the air. He walks too slowly for me and I rein myself back to keep one step behind.

We have embarked on the collection and classification of tiny organisms – creatures that can only be seen through the lens of our latest microscope, an instrument so precious that I'm afraid even to nudge it with my eyelid We come to a round pond within a dank circle of trees and I scoop up a sample. A transparent shrimp coils in the muddy water. 'Chirocephalus,' I say.

The water shakes when my father holds the jar. 'Tell me, Emilie, what can we expect to see when we place this creature under the lens?'

But suddenly I don't care. I think of the hours I'll have to spend drawing and labelling the wretched little shrimp and I want to smash the jar against a stone. I see the tiny creature cling to the glass and think I can make out its soot-like speck of an eye.

'I'm sorry, Father.' I rub my belly with my hand. 'I believe that I am . . . I must.' He gives me a cold look and turns away. There is an unspoken understanding that my growing female body has functions I may not discuss with him and I know he disapproves.

I run, crashing through the trees to the oak which Gill taught me to climb. I hitch my skirts, clamber up as if it were a ladder, straddle a branch and watch the leaves rise and fall above me. Each one is dappled with the shadow of another. A shaft of sunshine warms my wrist and I think about heat. Is it a state or substance? How is it passed from one object, the sun, to another, my arm?

The wind stirs the leaves. There is movement in the air. The air moves. Air is not a state but a substance.

The passage of blood through my veins beats in my ears. I grow calm. I belong in the tree, the greenwoods at Selden, on the twirling planet as it makes its elliptical journey round the sun. I am Emilie, part of the plan. But as I sway in the tree I think about the shrimp and how my father controls my knowledge and every movement of my day. I want to know much more than he will ever tell me. Each year I beg to be taken to London so I can hear more music than the dissonant chords in the church organ and the thin piping of the minstrels at the annual fair. I want to know what people look like in other worlds than mine but he won't show me them. And above all I want to know about that other woman, my mother, who bled and had breasts and soft inner thighs like mine. I'm certain she would understand the yearnings and complications of what it is to be me. The older I get, the more I long to see her. Just one glimpse of her face, brush of her skirts or whisper of her voice would do. I am no longer satisfied with fantasies of her. But if I ask about her my father turns his head away and there's an end to it.

7

In the evening when my father and I eat supper together by the library fire, the torment of the afternoon is forgotten. Afterwards I kneel by his chair to fill his pipe. He takes a leather pouch from his pocket and gives it to me – the leather, still warm, is old and criss-crossed with wrinkles like his skin but the tobacco inside is moist and fragrant. I pinch it up with my finger and thumb and drop a few strands into the bowl of the pipe.

'Well, Emilie.'

'Well, Father, I have been thinking about the phlogiston theory in the light of Boyle's investigations and our own experiments today.'

His eyes go warm. The little breaths he huffs through his nose are the closest he comes to a chuckle. I must not waste a single flake of tobacco so I take my time with the pipe. 'On the one hand Stahl's theory is beautifully simple because it allows us to accept the ancient view that air is a fixed state, a constant. Our experiment supported Stahl's theory. Phlogiston is released from the candle wax during combustion until the air can take no more. Later, when we tried to ignite a piece of camphor we couldn't, though we know that the camphor would have caught fire outside the flask because camphor is highly combustible, or as Stahl would say, rich in phlogiston.'

He doesn't take his eyes from my face as I light a taper from the fire, hand him his pipe and watch him suck until the tobacco catches.

'But I am still not ready to discount Mayow and Boyle. Mayow says the flame goes out because nitro-aerial particles are used up from the air – what Boyle would call aether – and though plenty of air remains in the flask, it is these particles that are needed for combustion.'

'Sir Isaac also supports this view,' puts in my father. He pats his lips against the stem of his pipe and blows out a perfect smoke ring, a sure sign of contentment.

'I am not satisfied with Stahl's theory for all its simplicity. Surely it can only be true if substances lose the weight of phlogiston during combustion. But we know that metals gain weight when they are burnt.'

He nods and hiccups softly – he loves argument as long as it is well-founded and leads to further experiment.

'And if the air became phlogisticated, why did the water level rise in the flask?' I ask.

'We will make a note of all these questions in the morning, and we will not be content until we have dealt with them.'

The clock strikes nine. It is time to release the owl so I creep into the laboratory and pick up the cage. I am not used to being alone here at night and I sniff old wood, old minerals, old chemicals. Old is the most normal state of things at Selden. The bird is wide awake and its huge eyes are eerie in its white face. Mrs Gill says barn owls are birds of ill omen but my father and I pay no attention to superstitions of that nature.

When I pick up her cage the bird adjusts her claws on the perch. My father and I study her for the last time. 'She is a killing mechanism,' he says, 'ideally suited to her task because she strikes from above, in the dark.'

And yet her feathers look so soft I long to bury my hands in them. I can easily see the hand of God in the owl's perfect symmetry, perfectly hooked beak and claws, perfect heart-shaped face.

We carry her up through the house. It is my privilege to hold the cage. My father lights the way and Gill follows at a distance. He never gets too close to me these days. Gill is my father's alchemical assistant and does the heavy tasks like feeding the furnace and lugging crates of minerals. When not needed in the laboratory he is supposed to be steward to the estates but I have never known him go out of earshot. He is ubiquitous. The bird shifts on her perch and swivels her head from side to side. I am afraid that she will suddenly panic and crash against the bars but she seems calm. At the top of the great staircase we turn right on to the landing designed for the reception of Queen Elizabeth, though in the end she never visited Selden. On the other side of the queen's bedroom we pass through a low door to the oldest wing where the boards creak and even my narrow skirts brush the walls. The second floor is reached by a winding staircase and now we are outside the room where my mother died and I was born. My heart beats faster. It always does. Her door is very low and made of oak planks.

My father gives the lantern to Gill and we climb yet another staircase to the roof. A breeze catches my father's coat-tails and hollows the wind funnel we set up last year for our meteorological studies. The night is mild and fine and a segment of moon sits over my oak tree in the woods. The owl's feathers ruffle and her eyes are blacker than ever. Gill comes up behind us and stands with folded arms.

Twelve hooks fasten the cage to its base and I release them gently one by one until she is free. She doesn't move from her perch though there are no longer any bars between her and the night sky.

My father whispers, 'She is letting her eyes adjust to the dark and the distances she must travel. Remember what Georg Bartisch says about the properties of the pupil.'

'I wish we didn't have to let her go,' I say.

I expect him to be harsh with me but instead he tucks his hand through my arm and holds my wrist. He's never done this before and I am absolutely still in case he moves away. His touch fills me with joy and makes me feel powerful, with my skirts blown backwards and the woods at my feet rolling away to the river that snakes through our land on its way to London.

The owl lifts her wings suddenly and drops them again. My father's hand trembles against my arm and he holds tight to his staff. And then as the wind blows in a sudden gust over the parapet the bird takes flight. One minute she is still, the next she soars away and her pale, beating wings are like the pages of a great book. For a moment or two I strain to follow her but she is gone.

My father takes his hand away. I kiss his bony knuckles and urge him not to stay too late writing in his notebook, then I light a candle from Gill's lamp and walk down through the quiet house past my mother's room. For once I don't stop at her door because I am too happy.

I go to my bedchamber, take off my outer clothes and climb into bed. Soon Mrs Gill looks in to make sure that I have snuffed the light.

I lie in the dark. My mind at the end of the day is a beehive. I visit various cells putting new facts in order, sorting and tidying away the phlogiston theory. I still haven't developed any symptoms of the smallpox but then it is only eight days since the engrafting. I remember my father's hand on my wrist and I smile.

Chapter Two

A PUFF OF SMOKE

I

At the end of November 1724 Reverend Gilbert went to join his Maker – or Makers, as he would have it – and by the beginning of the new year my father had appointed a new rector, one Thomas Shales, formerly of Middlesex. This Shales was a fellow of the Royal Society and had written a book entitled *The Qualities of Plants and Aires* that we had read and admired. He and my father had been joint witnesses to the experiment in which convicts were engrafted with smallpox and had corresponded on the matter of phlogiston. Both were disciples of Sir Isaac N. so it was hardly surprising that Shales should be my father's first choice.

The prodigy soon arrived to pay his respects to my father. I was very excited at the thought of meeting him but instead was set a lengthy piece of study from Paracelsus and told to stay in the laboratory.

The next Sunday Mrs Gill and I went to church where the pews were unusually full and the chancel decorated with snowdrops. When the frail organist struck his first discordant note the vestry door opened and I saw the new rector bend his head to avoid cracking it on the lintel. So the first shock was his height, the second his youthfulness; I judged him barely thirty. He wore a crisp alb and his well-combed wig framed bony, severe features. His speaking voice was firm and he addressed God as if talking to a trusted friend, very different from the mournful intonations of Reverend Gilbert.

During the sermon Shales didn't climb into the pulpit but stood quite near me under the chancel arch. I couldn't stop looking at his face, which consisted of unusual planes and angles. His brow jutted over deep-set eyes, his jawbone was pronounced and his lips pressed together in a firm line. He spoke without reference to notes about his pleasure in finding himself at Selden, and he praised the woods and rolling hills. There was already a connection between him and Selden, he said, because his former parish had also been on the Thames though much nearer London. When, at the very end of the sermon, he smiled the harsh lines in his face broke up and he looked directly at me. I felt excited to be singled out like that but I noticed afterwards how in moments of silent reflection his eyes were bleak and at one point he leaned against the wall as if afraid of falling.

I was so intrigued by Reverend Shales that I was surprised to find the service over. The last hour had changed me. I was wider awake and my skin was tingling. I fretted about the fact that I had never been taught to curtsy properly and that I would make a fool of myself when I met him in the porch. But he smiled at me with considerable sweetness, kept tight hold of my hand for a moment and said he'd heard great things of me from my father. My cheeks grew hot because I had no idea how to respond to a compliment and I hurried away full of anxiety about how I should behave next time we met.

2

As it was he took me by surprise. On the last day of January my father and I set out for our walk early in the afternoon. Gill had lit a bonfire in the orchard so the air was pungent with woodsmoke; frost clung to ruts in the path and cold seeped through the soles of my boots. I thought wistfully of the kitchen where I had left Mrs Gill tucked close to the hearth with her skirts pulled up and her calves exposed to the blaze.

My father never registered extremes of temperature though his nose was purple. Sometimes he paused, cocked his head and listened for small movements in the woods while I shifted from foot to foot and folded my arms tight across my chest. When we turned off the path he halted altogether and stared down at a couple of mushrooms capped with ice. With the brass tip of his staff he upended one so that its white stalk was exposed. 'Lepista Nuda. Name the parts, Emilie.'

'Umbo, velum, gills . . .'

'The Latin.'

'*Lamellae, stipe, volva* . . .' The words dropped like stones into the silence.

My father sighed. 'You name the parts of the mushroom, Emilie, as if you cared nothing for them. Now tell me how even the study of a fungus illustrates the existence of an intelligent and powerful God.'

I looked at the mushroom. It was . . . a mushroom but I remembered a time not long ago when a mushroom would have filled me with wonder because I knew that God permeated everything, every inch of space, each particle, water drop or spark. I chanted, 'Because the mushroom perfectly performs its function.'

'You sound irritated. You think you know everything but you are only at the beginning of knowledge. We must never rest, Emilie, until we have understood it all. A mushroom is easy to study – we can cut it up and look at it under our microscope, and if it withers we can pick another next day. But the essential secrets of life, fire, air, water still elude us despite the astounding efforts of Sir Isaac.'

I had stopped listening because there was a commotion of cracking twigs and then Reverend Shales appeared, muffled in a vast topcoat, the lower part of his face hidden in its high collar, a sack slung over his shoulder and his fingertips white with cold. 'Forgive me,' he said, removing his hat. 'I heard your voices.'

This was the first time I could remember that my father and I had been disturbed on our walk although we sometimes came across village children or heard the rustle of hastily retreating footsteps. Father was bound to resent the intrusion but when I looked into Shales's face I was startled. Although he was smiling there was the same look of bleakness in his eye that had been there in church. It occurred to me that he actually needed us to talk to him.

'What's in your bag?' I asked.

He fumbled with the rope. Inside was the scent of newly cut wood, curls of bark and specimens sliced from fallen branches. 'I have been studying bark,' he said, 'and its purpose in the respiration of plants. Since coming to Selden I have found great riches in these woods.'

'I'm relieved to hear it,' said my father. 'I tell Emilie that there is a lifetime's study within a mile's radius of Selden,' and he set off, leaning heavily on his staff to steady himself on the frozen ground.

The path was too narrow to walk side by side but Shales kept close to my shoulder and at one point reached forward to lift a bramble out of the way. 'I read your book,' I said. 'The detail of your observations into plant respiration is extraordinary. And the illustrations – are they your own?'

'All my own. I'm afraid those drawings were a distraction. I spent so long on them that I neglected my research.'

'They are very clear. Delicate.'

'Plants have such complicated arrangements of leaves that a great deal of simplification is needed. Do you draw, Mistress Selden?'

My father, a few steps ahead, would be listening hawkishly. 'I do draw but not well. I haven't much patience.'

'Your father tells me that you have been assisting him in his investigations into the nature of fire. Will you publish your findings?'

I stopped so suddenly that he put his hand on my elbow to prevent himself colliding with me. His eyes were the greenish grey of still water but his face was alight with interest. He really did think I might be capable of writing a paper on the nature of fire.

My father turned back and peeked at us from under his wig. 'Our ideas are half formed so we are in no position to publish.' Then he pointed among the trees with his staff. 'This is our way home, Shales.'

Shales bowed. I tried to find words that would keep him with us a little longer but Father was moving away. All I could do was offer my gloved hand. The light had faded and when I glanced back Shales was already just a shadow among the trees.

My father didn't speak to me all the way home. I had no idea what I'd done to annoy him and in any case I was too preoccupied to care. I longed to run after Shales, to invite him to Selden and prolong a conversation that had opened up the most unexpected possibilities. Instead, when we reached the bottom of the steps leading to the terraces I said I would go and warm myself at Gill's bonfire. So while my father toiled up to the house I skirted the lower lawn and ran to the orchard, a half-acre or so of apple trees planted last century by a plant-loving Selden favoured by Charles I (a Selden on the winning side but not for long). In one corner of this orchard was an apiary, including one hive with a glass side so that we could study the habits of the bees. At the far end, nearest the house, was the patch of ground where Gill lit his bonfires. He was there still, feeding the flames with brushwood and old cuttings.

When he saw me he stopped work, leaned on his fork and stared from under his wild eyebrows. He was the darker side of vegetable, the inner leaf of old cabbage, the earthy root of parsnip. He and his clothes had a density that repelled me now that I was grown up, though when I was small and he used to carry me to bed I'd snuggle my face into his shoulder and delight in his muddy smell. For a while I stood on the opposite side of the fire, turning my hands to the heat and lifting my face to the light of a rosy winter sunset. I knew that Gill was watching me because he always did.

The heat on my hands and face made the rest of me colder so after a few minutes I moved towards the house but he blocked my way to the gate and when I tried to get past him took a step towards me. I stood my ground, shivering. There was a heaviness in his small eyes that I had noticed quite often recently. At some indefinable moment he had ceased to be the third great prop of my life and instead had become elusive, even shifty. But most of my mind was still on Shales who was walking alone in the woods and who had brushed my shoulder as he hooked the bramble aside. Then I became aware that Gill was breathing heavily and had raised his hand, ingrained with sixty-odd years of Selden dirt, and brought it close to my breast.

Before he could touch me our eyes met and I saw that his were moist, as if he had been drinking. I came to my senses at last and realised that unless I acted something terrible and irrevocable would happen so I spoke the two words that would put a stop to it all: 'My father.' Then I added more gently, 'My father will need a good fire in the library. Our walk has made us very cold.'

His hand fell as he took a step back then turned, opened the gate and walked away. The bonfire whispered as I crouched to draw the last warmth from the embers. My heart ached but I wasn't sure why.

3

Within a month my father had fallen out with Shales once and for all and there was no further communication between us. I was even forbidden to attend church. The disagreement was fundamental and concerned alchemy.

In the spring of that year we began preparing for our most ambitious project ever. Our plan was to grow a rose from its own ashes. My father had been reading the work of the French physician Joseph Du Chesne, who says that each living thing has its own signature which exists for ever and makes it utterly unique. Du Chesne said he had once seen twelve sealed vessels in which flowering plants had been grown from their ashes. His view was substantiated by the great Paracelsus, by Daniel Coxe, by Jacques Gaffarel and others. After all, transmutation is at the root of all alchemy, and if a metal such as tin can be dissolved in acid and restored by the action of an alkali, or water become steam and then water again through condensation, why couldn't the same principle apply to the recovery of a plant?

My father was sixty-eight years old and I suspect all too conscious of his own mortality. He had a persistent cough and his breathing was laboured. I was so terrified by the prospect of being left alone that I would have sold my soul to prolong his life. This process of regeneration seemed to me a matter of great urgency. If we could restore a rose what else might be possible?

So we set about devising a method that would apply the most ancient art of alchemy to the most modern discoveries about plants. We would take the ashes of a rose and restore it to life by adding the fundamental ingredients of life itself, heat, water and the alchemical elixir. The latter we would brew in our laboratory; for advice on the former we needed a modern authority and who better than the new incumbent Reverend Shales who, according to Mrs Gill, had already impressed freeholders in the village with his knowledge about fertilising and resting the soil?

He was invited to call at eleven o'clock one morning. Presumably he had to show himself in through the kitchen passage because he appeared suddenly at the library door. I had been told to make a record of the interview and was seated at a little table by the window. Instead of ignoring me, as any of my father's other visitors would have done, Shales came up and bowed. I pushed back my chair, stumbled and was supported by his steady hand. Before I could do more than glance into his eyes, my father had called 'Shales' and directed him to an upright chair by the fire.

Shales folded his long frame on to the narrow seat and held himself well back from the blaze. A copy of his book lay between them.

'I am very pleased with this volume, Shales,' said my father, 'and wish to question you further about your findings on the purpose of sap, and the properties in sunlight that enable a plant to grow. I note from your introduction that you see the *signature of the hand of God in each plant*. I wonder if you could expand on that.'

'Only that the more I study even the smallest, humblest part of Creation, the more I marvel at the detail and ingenuity in the design.'

'I thought you might be referring to another kind of signature – the signature that is the key to uniqueness – the key to life itself.'

A long pause. A sigh. I couldn't see Shales's face, just his cheekbone. 'I wonder if you are referring to the alchemical meaning of signature.'

My father leaned forward on his staff, which was propped between his knees. 'You know of it then?'

Another pause. 'When I accepted this living at Selden, I made it very clear that I would have nothing to do with alchemy.'

'I am hoping to convert you. This year I am conducting an experiment with plants, the first, I believe, of its kind since the work of Du Chesne on regeneration.'

'Regeneration. Palingenesis. Sir, I cannot support you in this.'

'I don't ask for support. Merely for co-operation.'

'I cannot. I regard this kind of experiment as a form of blasphemy. Nature renews life. There is no need for any kind of meddling.'

My pen faltered. *Meddling*. I couldn't write that.

My father's hand approached his wig, a dangerous sign. 'You sound like the Church fathers who condemned Galileo. The old system with the earth at the centre suited them so they wouldn't look at any other. Galileo couldn't prove his alternative theory so they won their case.'

'I am not relying just on observation or on what suits me. I know that nature already restores itself. When a rose dies a new rose grows from another part of the stem. If you come to my house, and I hope that both you and your daughter will be frequent visitors, I will show you any number of extraordinary experiments. I will show you how to graft a rose and how a plant takes in water through its branches as well as its roots but I will not participate in alchemy.'

My hand trembled as my father plucked his wig from his head, replaced it, banged his staff, would not look at Shales. 'So. So we stop at what we know and see. We look no further. Very good, Shales.'

'In this case, yes. We are not dealing with objects or even stars. In this case we are dealing with death itself.'

'What we observe to be death.'

'Sir, there are many iniquities in this life. In my work I meet the dying and bereaved every day. I have seen young children fail and women and their newborn infants die in childbed. I would do everything in my power to restore them but in the history of mankind only Jesus Christ had that gift. There is much we could do to improve life – decent food, medicine, clean air, warm homes. Let's concentrate on what sustains life, not on some fruitless attempt to bring life back.'

'So you won't help me?'

'In anything else, yes. In this, no. I can't assist you, Sir. I believe alchemy to be counter to both the laws of my religion and the laws of nature.'

'Laws of nature. Religion. How can any natural philosopher work within the bounds of religion? I won't be contained by such pettiness.' By now both men were on their feet and my father's head was level with the middle button on Shales's coat but he was powerful; hands clenched on his staff, eyes on fire. 'I am surprised by your lack of faith, Shales. At Selden we believe that there is more to natural philosophy than experimentation and calculation. Do you think Newton would have uncovered the laws of the universe if he had been bound by what he could measure or by what men thought to be the laws of nature? He began by searching; he applied his great mind to his observations but he had the courage to believe that the very process of looking would lead to enlightenment. He knew that a phenomenon does not exist until man has found it.'

I willed Shales not to be so rigid. Surely he could show a little compassion to an old man even if he disagreed with the principles of his research. After a moment he said quietly, 'I will consider your arguments of course and if I find that they convince me I shall change my mind. In the meantime I regret that in this one area I cannot help you.'

My father was stuttering with rage. 'In the meantime . . . There is no other time, Shales. I won't ask you again. I won't have you blighting my work. Good day to you, Sir.'

Shales was still, then bowed and turned suddenly to me: 'Mistress Selden, if you ever have time to call I should be delighted to show you my most recent work with plants and airs, and to hear your views.' He crossed the room a few paces towards me but I wouldn't look at him or offer my hand for fear of my father. After a moment the door closed and I heard the sound of his feet on the bare boards in the entrance hall.

I finished my transcript and blotted my work. Neither of us spoke. As usual when my father was in a rage I tried to obliterate myself by keeping quiet and anticipating every demand but I was stricken by the loss of a potential friend. In the end I couldn't decide who had been most at fault, Shales or my father.

No more was said about that meeting though I thought about it often, especially when I heard the ringing of the church bell on a Sunday morning. When Shales came to the house, and Mrs Gill told me that he did call from time to time, my father refused to see him. I don't even know if Shales would have remained long in the parish afterwards had it not been for the arrival late that summer of Robert Aislabie, in a puff of smoke.

4

Each year we began our alchemical phase on 3 August, my father's birthday. On that morning I was sent out to find a perfect rose.

The rose garden was south-facing and very hot, sheltered by the high wall of the terrace. Neglected bushes scrambled into each other, a wasp pestered, my skirts snagged and all the roses were overblown or diseased. My search seemed hopeless. In fact, there was a part of me that wanted to fail. Since Shales's visit the prospect of palingenesis had seemed impossibly far-fetched. If there was no rose there could be no experiment. It had to be a perfect rose, a tough-stemmed, fragrant, mystical flower. But as I came to the further corner, I saw a pink gleam in the shadows. I pushed aside one thorny branch after another until my cheeks and hands were scratched, reached to the very back of the bush and uncovered a perfect rose.

I thought of my father huddled over the fire in the laboratory. In this most imperfect of rose gardens I had found a perfect rose, just as he ordained. It was on the cusp of being full blown and had a bead of dew on an inner petal. I held its stem and made a clean cut, let the branches fall back and stood up with the sappy knife in one hand and the perfect rose in the other. Its fragrance was intense and I threw back my head to draw a deeper breath. Then I saw a puff of smoke on the London road.

The hillside was scorched, the hedgerows tinder dry. A fire would destroy the wheat crop. I was about to shout for help when I noticed that the smoke was following twists in the lane. Not smoke then, but dust kicked up by a horse's hooves.

Apart from Shales, Selden rarely had visitors capable of riding a horse let alone galloping. Occasionally an elderly scholar came to call, or a tradesman, or a neighbouring squire on a mission: 'Weeds do spread, Selden, have you thought of turning over the long field by the river?' This energetic horseman would doubtless gallop through the village and away so, to cheat myself of disappointment, I walked briskly back to the laboratory where my father's delight in the rose was sufficient reward. He got to his feet and took the flower reverently in his hand, placed it in a jar of water and turned it round and round, sniffing with admiration. Then he nodded at me: 'Good, Emilie. I'm pleased,' and began calling out its various characteristics for me to record: the measurement and number of its petals, the exact appearance of each stamen and leaf. But after a few minutes we heard hoof-beats at the gate, the rasp of metal on gravel and then a brisk knock on our redundant front door.

I laid down my pen though my father didn't even look up. There was nobody to answer the door but me – neither of the Gills would bother – so I trekked through the library and across the entrance hall. The door was so unused to being opened that I cut my knuckle on the rusty bolt. White sunlight poured over me. I put up my hand to shade my eyes and there, smiling down from beneath the shade of his hat, was an astonishing young man.

'Good afternoon, Mistress,' he said and bowed so deeply that he swept the step with his turquoise plumes. 'I'm told that this is Sir John Selden's house?'

I couldn't reply, just went on staring. He shone. The sun touched glossy curls, flushed cheeks and silver buttons. Warmth spilled out of his eyes. He raised his brows but I still couldn't speak. Instead I turned and walked towards the library. He and the scorching light followed so that between them they burnt the back of my dress. In the library I pointed with my bloody hand to a chair by the window, ducked under the curtain covering the door to the laboratory and told my father that a stranger had come.

5

My father and his visitor spent the rest of the day in the library while I worked on the rose. We intended to let it dry in a sealed container so that it would not be contaminated by insects or dust. After listing, measuring and sketching the flower's various parts I dried its stem and placed it in a clean flask. Then I inverted another identical flask over it and pasted the necks together with a seal made of pipe clay and freshly cut clippings from my own hair.

After it was done I put the flower on the window seat where it had an untouchable sheen in its glass prison, like a pebble in water. I was guilty of neglect. As I worked I should have willed myself inside the rose to blend my spirit with its sap but one look at that stranger had blown away my concentration. I was listening for his departure. I had to catch another glimpse of him before he left.

In the end I escaped through a little door used by Gill, which led to a stone staircase down to the cellars. From there I ran to the stables and checked that the stranger's horse was still tethered inside, then raced to the orchard where I was safely hidden but would still hear him go. For two hours I strode about or flung myself down in the shade with my ear to the ground. My pulse throbbed. I saw everything with startling clarity: the calyx of the daisies, flecks on the peeling membrane of bark and the bees on their aerial pathways to the hives by the hedge. But I was impatient with all this familiar detail and my body refused to behave, rolling itself over until my legs were tangled in my skirts.

Of course I had put up with uncertainty before. When my father bought me a prism and told me to repeat Sir Isaac's experiment with white light my stomach was full of butterflies. We closed the shutters except for a chink and turned the prism until the light shone directly through and there on our screen of paper was a rainbow. But until that moment I had been afraid just in case it didn't happen and Newton was proved fallible. And then there was the smallpox episode when I'd woken each morning expecting to find myself ill or disfigured. In the end, on the tenth day I had felt hot, then cold and rather sick, but only for a few hours. About twenty spots appeared but left no scars. I was relieved not just because I'd survived but because my father was right as usual.

This experience in the orchard was much worse because it was quite possible that after the young man had gone my father wouldn't mention his visit at all. The episode with Shales was still a sore point in my memory; relations with him had been so ruthlessly severed. But the arrival of the stranger had hooked me clean out of my old self and made me something else. Not even my father could keep me away from him. I must see him again. I couldn't breathe for wanting it so much.

Meanwhile I branded the memory of him on to my inner eye. Again and again I opened the door and discovered him in the porch, his forehead dewy with sweat and his eyes a light blue. He was so broad-shouldered that I couldn't see past him though his stamping horse had been somewhere in the background.

I gave up at last and went back inside. The kitchen was hot as a furnace with the oven lit and a village girl, one of the blacksmith's daughters, tossing peeled potatoes into a pot. A mess of gutted poultry was heaped on the table and the air was filled with bloody vapours.

'It's a pity your father never made the stirring of soup part of your grand education,' said Mrs Gill. 'We've a guest to supper and you're to eat with them in the dining parlour.'

I gawped at her while my heart did cartwheels. I saw him again with the sun on his curls, his silver buttons, his polished boots. And here was I with damp armpits, tangled hair, hands caked with clay. I flew back to the stable yard, loosened the neck of my dress and plunged my head and shoulders under the pump. From the stables behind me I heard a restless movement of hooves and the tossing of a bridled head. His horse. None of our old work-horses had the energy to stir on such a hot day. I scraped the dirt from under my fingernails, pulled up my skirts to wash my feet and calves, wrapped my hair in my apron and ran up to my room, dripping along the passageways.

Mrs Gill had given me a better mirror for my eighteenth birthday, extracted from a stack of furniture in some distant room. I peered into its spotted glass and despaired. Black rat's tails. Black eyes. Black brows. White skin. Too much contrast. Then I unhooked my best gown – pale-green calico and not one

32

of Mrs Gill's most successful efforts. She'd copied a dress worn by the modish farmer's wife and unlike my other gowns it had an open bodice pinned to a quilted stomacher. The edges of the bodice were so uneven and the stomacher cut so low that I had to hold one shoulder higher than the other to keep myself decent. My bosom bulged over the top. What would my father say? I chewed my lip as I fixed the bodice in place and covered myself up with a muslin neckerchief. I had nothing else to match the visitor's gorgeous plumes, no necklace, no rings, just my mother's pink ribbon which I pulled out of a little drawer, held to my face, then wound through my hair and tied in a bow, just visible behind my ear.

6

In the dining parlour a pearly mist floated through the open lattices and candlelight made soft shadows amidst the folds of our visitor's cravat. Fortunately my father barely glanced at me. He was already scooping up soup, pursing his lips after each mouthful to ease it down. 'Robert Aislabie,' he said, waving his dripping spoon at the stranger. 'Come to talk to me about phlogiston. My daughter Emilie.'

I took little sips of Aislabie along with my soup, which I spooned up by leaning forward from the waist – I couldn't bend my neck in case I fell out of my gown or jabbed myself with a pin. He rippled on the edge of my vision in lustrous splashes of colour, and his snowy cuffs and cravat had a radiance unknown at Selden. He wore a turquoise waistcoat embroidered with pink and cream butterflies and flowers, and a jacket of peacock-blue to match the plumes in his hat. My mother, I thought with amazement, would have worn silks like his, iridescent and gorgeous. His brilliance scattered over everything else like pollen. The room, which had always seemed dull, was mellow with the textures of ancient wood and pewter. Even the plain food was spiced by the presence of Robert Aislabie.

Meanwhile he told us his story. He was the younger son of a Norfolk farmer, had studied for a brief spell at Cambridge with a view to the Church but found himself too liberal in his views and had instead gone into trade with an uncle. By the time he was nineteen Aislabie had so successfully invested spare income in the import of molasses and cotton, the export of refined sugar and cloth, that he was able to buy South Sea Stock. While others lost heavily when the Bubble burst, Aislabie sold out in the nick of time and transferred his funds into coffee, tea, chocolate and silk. But business was still precarious. Recently he had lost an entire cargo during a shipboard fire. Fire was the scourge of shipping because it could wipe out profits in half an hour. So, having read my father's recent paper on phlogiston during one of his frequent visits to the Royal Society, of which he hoped soon to be admitted as a fellow, Aislabie had come to Selden seeking advice on how ships might best be protected against fire.

While my father and Aislabie discussed the combustible nature of shipping materials, I risked a few peeps at Aislabie's face. His nose in profile was straight and long but quite broad at the tip with prominent nostrils, and an intriguing little hollow beside his mouth came and went when he smiled. Beside him my father was like a dry twig next to a young birch. My father's crabbed hands had yellow nails, his neck was wizened, his gums nearly toothless and his table manners, I now realised, disgusting. He carried dripping lumps of meat to the centre of the table to dip them in the salt, sopped his bread in the sauce, stuffed his cheeks with food and wiped his mouth on his sleeve. If asked a question he never answered immediately but scrutinised it as if it were a bit of moth-eaten cloth. Aislabie meanwhile, who had surprisingly well-manicured hands for a farmer's son, used fork and knife with careless ease, cut his meat very small and pressed his lips together after each new mouthful.

Towards the end of the meal my father picked up his staff, heaved himself away from the table and went to piss in the pot behind a curtain. I suffered as I heard him fart and sigh and release a trickle.

For perhaps three minutes Aislabie and I were alone. At first he didn't speak but then he said, 'Mistress Selden. Your ribbon has come loose and I'm afraid you're about to lose it altogether.' His voice had many layers; a throatiness and soft sibilance that made me shudder. I glanced up and saw that his eyes were brimming with laughter because of the activities behind the curtain.

The ribbon had fluttered over my shoulder. When I tugged at the end more and more slid away and my hair fell down. I pulled out the ribbon and tried to pin up my hair but now I was in a worse state because by lifting my arms I had strained the precarious arrangement of my neckerchief so that I had to cover my bosom with my hair and thrust the ribbon into my pocket. Fortunately when I glanced at Aislabie he seemed unaware of my discomfort, only smiled so that the dimple came in his cheek.

My father sat down again and began his night-time yawns. Once started they went on and on, contorting his face until he was like an ancient lizard. Aislabie leapt to his feet, apologised for keeping us too long and asked permission to come back soon in case my father had any further thoughts on the application of the phlogiston theory to shipping. My father said that he was about to leave on his annual trip to London but Aislabie could call again in two days' time.

I followed Aislabie across the entrance hall and waited with him in front of the house while Gill brought his horse. The top of my head was level with his upper arm and we stood so close that the tip of his boot almost touched my uneven hem. We said nothing but when he'd mounted I stepped away and looked up at him. At first he gave me a polite smile of farewell but then his eyes filled with heat and I thought I saw into his soul, pure as gold itself. He pulled the reins, the horse reared its powerful front legs and they were gone.

When I got back to the dining parlour my father peered at me. 'Well?'

'Father?'

'What are your observations?'

Since the Shales episode, I had learned to be cautious. 'I don't have any.'

'You must. What did you see?'

'I saw a young man, Father.'

'What else?'

'He held you in a great deal of esteem.'

He laughed through his nose and jabbed his staff at me. 'He

had no more respect for me than for a barrel of good sherry. He'll give me as much attention as he needs until he gets what he wants, then he'll drop me – except for the fun he'll have at my expense in his coffee house. So think again, Emilie. Tell me what you saw.'

'I saw a young man who travelled a long way to ask your opinion. He has a problem and he thinks you can solve it. Where is the harm in that? You've always taught me that one of the keys to success is knowing where to look for answers.'

'There is no harm, Emilie, so long as you're not taken in. But you were. You missed all the signs. You think that the man is after knowledge when what he actually wants is profit. Tell me how I know.'

I was as close to tears as I'd been in years. I had rarely seen my father so virulent in his attack on anyone except Shales, who had dared challenge the validity of alchemy, and various charlatans guilty of publishing rubbish. M. Étienne-François Geoffroy, for instance, had devised a table that ordered chemical substances according to their affinities for each other but had made the mistake of mixing up physical and chemical properties, an error so fundamental that my father had spent weeks muttering that it was beneath his dignity to publish a rebuke.

'Tell me.' His eyes had gone cold.

'His clothes were very fine,' I said at last.

'Ah yes, they were. But don't you go confusing the quality of what a man wears with the quality of his soul. Anyone with a bit of money can pay for expensive tailoring.'

'He dressed with care. What's wrong with that? He wanted to impress you.'

'No. He wanted to overwhelm me because he knew that I was a reclusive old man. If he'd wanted to please me he would have dressed plainly. Now what else?'

'Nothing else.'

He tore off his wig and ran his hand across the stubble of white hair. 'Emilie. Observe. Think. What did he talk about?'

'Himself mostly.'

'Money. He talked about money. The making of money. What else?'

'Nothing. I saw nothing else.'

'Then you're a fool. I've wasted my time on you. One step outside the laboratory, one glimpse of finery and all I've taught disappears. You've been dazzled. I'll made a record in my notebook. He pretended to be interested in phlogiston, Emilie, and I suppose he might be, if it will save him a few hundred pounds. But he took no notes or references. His eyes glazed when I talked to him. He's gone away no better off than when he came.'

'Then why was he here? Why did he travel such a long way?'

'That's the only reason I'll let him come back. I want to find out.'

7

For the next two nights I scarcely slept while I thought about Robert Aislabie. My father had seen him in a false light, distorted by the lens of age and prejudice. Aislabie was perfect. Every corpuscle in my body shook at the memory of his smile, his sideways glance, the quirk of his lip, the voice which was mined from a secret place inside him. I wanted to see him again so much that it was all I could do to stop myself rushing to the gates every ten minutes. The ground under my feet was wafer thin and I thought I might fall into a pit of despair if he didn't come back. And all the while I had to pretend that nothing had changed. My father was getting ready for his trip to London and there was work to be done copying papers and putting the laboratory in order.

Time behaved with extraordinary waywardness – crawling minute by minute or springing forward in leaps and bounds until at four o'clock on the second day I heard his horse and a brisk knock. I was ready, of course, had been for two days, with my hair brushed under a clean cap. When I opened the door I allowed myself one glance only, any more and he would see how my whole being was on fire with longing, but that glance was enough. His eyes looked directly into mine, smiled, went misty. We said nothing as I led him as before to the library. This time he spent only half an hour with my father while I walked up and down the screens passage, passing and repassing the two open doors to the entrance hall. I was carrying a straw hat so that when he came out I would seem to be on my way to the garden.

The door opened and he caught me on my twentieth trek down the passage. I curtsied. He bowed. 'Mistress Selden.'

He leaned his shoulder against the doorway with his hat tucked under one arm, the other raised to grasp the lintel, but he was not at ease. His voice was low and his colour high. My father must have been unkind. My ancestors stared past him from above their starched ruffs and I was struck by the contrast. There was nothing two-dimensional about Aislabie. He was breathing and muscular, with stray hairs floating loose from his rippling wig and soft fabrics tumbling at his throat and wrists.

'That hat looks very purposeful,' he said.

'I am on my way to the orchard.'

He nodded, glanced at the closed library door, transferred his own hat from right hand to left and raised his elbow in a gesture I was too ignorant to understand. 'Perhaps you will show me?'

Instead of taking his arm I walked down the kitchen passage and through the stable yard to the orchard where we stood apart from each other. I had no words. I was like my father pissing into the chamber pot, utterly exposed. Bees probed the clover, butterflies clung together mid air, a blackbird called throatily from its perch on a medlar. Aislabie asked about the trees and whether they cropped well. I managed a yes and was silent. He bowed abruptly and turned away. I ran after him until we were in the shade of the stable yard where desperation at last put words into my mouth. 'Did my father tell you what you needed to know?'

His face, now I dared look at it, was sad. The light had gone from his eyes. 'Your father said he couldn't help me any further.'

'But I could. I know everything he knows. More.'

I swayed closer but he took a step back and bowed. 'Thank you, Mistress Selden.' Then he called for his horse. For one more moment I was close enough to touch him – I reached out and put my finger on the back of his arm so lightly that he couldn't possibly have known but I felt his heat and the hardness of muscle. Then Gill brought his horse and Aislabie swung himself into the saddle, raised his arm in farewell but didn't look at me again.

8

My father was leaving for London the next day. Usually our last meal together was full of his instructions and my reassurances but at supper that night I was so agitated I couldn't speak to him. In my mind I was following Aislabie along the road to London. My father, this obstinate, wrong-headed, filthy old man, was the reason for our separation.

He handed me his pipe but I spilled a few strands of tobacco so he snatched it back and lit it himself.

'While I am away, Emilie, you are to give the rose a quarter turn every eight hours so that its petals dry evenly. In the meantime translate the *Principia*, 1723 edition – at least to the end of Book One by the . . .'

For the first time in my life I interrupted him. 'What did Mr Aislabie want, Father?'

He sucked his pipe and stared blankly.

'Did you talk about phlogiston?'

'He was no more interested in phlogiston than is Mrs Gill.'

'Well, what then?'

He jabbed the bowl of the pipe into my face. 'He pretended to have a broad interest in the nature of fire but he is an impostor. Alchemy, that's what he was after. He's been sniffing around in London and found out my reputation. But of course he's not after knowledge, only gold. The next thing he'll be asking about is the philosophers' stone. He calls himself a modern man but just in case there's an easy fortune to be made he's willing to make himself charming to me. He's already tried to wheedle his way into the laboratory by asking me if I would demonstrate the theory of negative air. Of course he was trying to impress me so I tested him by mentioning Gassendi's *Syntagma* and the theory of the atom but he had never heard of either so I said if he had any more questions he could call on me at the Society in Crane Court. I won't have him here again. Alchemy is what he wanted and he wasn't even honest enough to say so.'

I sat in silence for a while. Then I said, 'Take me with you to London, Father.'

'Whatever for?'

'I want to see what it's like there. I want to see where mother was born.'

He knocked his pipe against the side of the hearth. 'There's no place for you in London.'

'I wouldn't be a nuisance. Please, Father.'

'Who would take care of the rose?'

'Gill.'

'No, no, it has to be you.'

'Don't leave me, Father.'

He groped for his staff and got up. 'It's all that man. You were satisfied before.'

'I don't think I was. I think I was impatient. I was waiting for something to happen.'

'The notebook,' he said suddenly. 'I'll write this in the note-book.'

'Yes, you must. But in the meantime, please let me go to London.'

We stared at each other. He looked baffled and furious, and I knew it was hopeless.

He didn't put out his hand to be kissed so I walked away with my head high. In the morning I watched Gill drive our ancient carriage out of the stable yard. My father was shut up tight inside. It was my job to fasten the gates behind them. Once I had dropped the iron latch I turned to face Selden. I would rather die than go back to the laboratory where I had worked all yesterday with such high hopes of seeing Robert Aislabie, so instead I lay on my bed and relived again and again the minutes with him in the orchard. He had been bored. My father had offended him. He had been eager to leave. I would never see him again.

9

The following evening Gill returned with the empty carriage. In a month or so, when summoned, he would drive back to London and collect my father. This period of his master's absence was traditionally one of holiday for him and he was rarely to be seen. Mrs Gill, by contrast, was even busier than usual and disappeared into the kitchen of her own cottage where she brewed up potions for the coming winter. In the past I would have helped her but now I was too restless and impatient. Then she was called out to a difficult birth in Selden Wick. She thought I was studying but actually I roamed down to the river, dabbled my feet and watched the water flow busily towards London and Aislabie. It seemed to taunt me by touching my feet and rushing on and on. Water couldn't be held back and restrained. Water, like fire, was awesome; a servant one moment, a force of destruction the next.

On the way home through the woods I noticed that some leaves had already fallen and the nettles were dusty. I leaned on the papery trunk of a silver birch and closed my eyes. My neglected studies, the rose in the laboratory and the prison that Selden had become dragged at me like a heavy cloak. Then there was movement on the track behind me and suddenly Aislabie walked out of my longings and into the Selden woods as if I had conjured him up. He had slung his red coat over his shoulder and his boots shone. I clutched the tree and stared stupidly up at his smiling face.

There was a little crease between his brows as if he was unsure of how I might react, then he bowed with what I took to be a London flourish – I could see London in every complicated stitch of his clothing. 'Mistress Selden, I want to apologise for my rudeness. Last time I came your father was so brusque that I was somewhat offended. He was suspicious of my motives and disparaged my business interests. I'm sorry that in my anger I treated you so coolly and I have come to take you up on your kind offer. Perhaps you and I could have a conversation about phlogiston.' His smile slanted from the corner of his eye to the dimple in his cheek and his elbow was bent towards me like last time. I realised that I was expected to slide my hand through the space between his arm and his body and this procedure drew me up so close I could scarcely breathe. My fingers skimmed the material of his sleeve and the slightest movement brought his flesh hard under my fingers.

He tightened my arm against his side. 'Phlogiston,' he said.

Freshness returned to the leaves and I seemed to fly beside him as I gabbled in my attempt to impress. 'We've been working on phlogiston for four years and although in one way the theory does much to explain how fire happens, there are problems. The main difficulty is that metals gain weight when heated to a calx – you would expect them to lose weight because of the phlogiston lost to the air. Some people support a theory called "negative weight" – they think that bodies lose their porous nature when they're burnt and therefore the air presses down harder on them and they aren't so buoyant and seem heavier. We think this theory is unsupportable.'

We perched on either side of a slimy pond in the sunken garden and gazed intently into the jungle of water lilies as if we really cared about the fish that came gasping to the surface. But actually all I saw was our faces reflected dimly in the green water.

'Fire is one of the four elements,' I said, 'the *Prima Materia* from which all matter is formed. The ancients believed that fire was masculine.' I was hearing words for the first time and they made me quiver. *Fire. Masculine.* Aislabie was the personification of masculinity and heat. 'Fire is present in sulphur and phosphorus. It is a transforming force. But we don't know what fire is or how it is made.'

His reflection nodded. And now I couldn't stop. I wasn't used to an audience and thought my only chance of keeping his interest was to impress him with what I knew. So I spilled out information on common air, elasticated air, geometry and mathematics. The only subject I daren't mention, of course, was alchemy.

We walked on along the mossy terraces up to the jungle of the rose garden. I was enchanted by a new, double consciousness: Emilie the watcher of Emilie the girl in the midst of this extraordinary experience. There was Aislabie, the incarnation of an impossible dream, and here was Emilie, so excited she must be physically shining, like phosphorus. My Selden world was utterly transformed. The neglected garden was now full of beautiful secrets: a stone bench hiding behind a shower of full-blown roses and a tangle of briars wrapped round the throat of a lichened dryad.

I was much too shy to ask Aislabie about himself. He was a novelty, from the fine cloth of his coat to the texture of his wig. I saw him as a perfect equation, like Kepler's third law of celestial harmony which states the proportion between the time taken for a planet to orbit the sun, and its distance from the sun. He stayed for an hour and then we walked back to fetch his horse from the woods. 'So, Mistress Emilie, we have established that the phlogiston theory won't save my cargoes or my pocket but what have you offered instead? A blank.' The touch of his lips on my hand connected disturbingly to nerves in my breasts; the heat of his breath and the way he smelt of flowers and evergreen made my thighs ache. My hand stayed in his.

'I can warn you not to ventilate your precious cargo too much because one thing we do know is that fire loves the air and won't burn in a vacuum,' I said.

'Thank you. But of course I must have some ventilation in my hold or the rot will set in. Anything else?'

I shook my head, dumb with misery. He was slipping away from me.

He kissed my hand again and while his head was dipped I risked a proper look along the slope of his back but he glanced up and caught my eye. 'Mistress Emilie. I may stay just a little while longer in Buckinghamshire. If I do, would I perhaps find you again some day in this wood?'

'You might.'

'Would you mind?'

I shook my head. He nodded thoughtfully, gave a deep bow, untied his chestnut horse and led it away. His stride was easy, his hips narrow, his shoulders straight and strong. This time he wasn't in a hurry and where the track bent he turned and waved. My heart swayed on the palm of his hand.

IO

I never knew when he would come or what mood he'd be in. Sometimes he was light-hearted, offered his arm and teased me, sometimes he was distant and clasped his hands behind his back. He talked of places, politicians, writers, countries, clubs, sports I'd never heard of and my total ignorance of the world was laid bare. After he left I spent the evening foraging through our library. An ancient map of London taught me to place Lambeth, Southwark, Vauxhall, Leadenhall and Lud Gate but it couldn't help me with Lloyd's or Jonathan's, with Addison, Gay, Defoe, Pope, Walpole, Whigs and Tories. Before I met Aislabie I thought I knew almost everything. After a couple of hours in his company I found I knew next to nothing.

And what I was most ignorant about was myself. I knew the Emilie who had lived at Selden for nineteen years with her father but I had no knowledge of this person who woke each morning with throbbing wrists and beating heart because she wanted more, more, more of Aislabie. He changed my image of myself. On the day I told him about my French mother he put his hand under my chin and said, 'Yes, that accounts for it. I have never in my life seen eyes like yours. I lie in bed at night wondering how anything so black could be so bright.'

I stored up the wonderful thought that at the same time I was awake thinking of him, he thought of me. 'My mother died on the day I was born. Her window was on the second floor – there, four from the end.' I pointed to the most ancient part of the house, grey stone with crooked windows. And suddenly, for the first time in my life, I felt pitiable. Under the molten gaze of his blue eyes I felt that I should have a mother.

'Tell me about her,' he said.

'I wish I could. All I know is that she was French and that her family were silk weavers.'

'Their name?'

'De Lery.'

He shook his head. 'Don't know of them.'

Another locked door swung wide open. Was it possible that this man could knit his brow, run through a few names and come that close to knowing my mother's family? 'How would you know them?'

He laughed. 'I've dabbled in silk in my time. Most merchants do but it's a cut-throat old world.'

'There is a dye named after my mother's family called De Lery green.'

He shrugged. 'Perhaps there's family left.'

'I doubt it. Mrs Gill says there was a fire in my grandfather's house and after that the family went back to France. I never met any of them.'

'Which part of France?'

'I don't know.'

'Maybe Paris. Beautiful city. You'd like it. You should go looking for your mother's family. You never know, they might have flourished.'

'I've never even been to London.'

'You shall. You shall go to London. You'd take London by storm. You are so different. People are quickly bored in London. You'd amaze them.' He kissed each fingertip except for the little finger which he held between his lips and caressed with his tongue, thereby doing astonishing things to my insides. 'My motherless girl. My sleeping beauty.'

II

When I returned to the house I found an unexpected and not very welcome visitor in the entrance hall. Reverend Shales was hanging about by a window with the air of one who had been there a long time. He had removed his coat and wig, revealing a head of cropped, curling hair. He hastily replaced the wig but not the coat, then bowed. 'I hope you're well, Mistress Selden.'

I had intended to lie on my bed and suck Aislabie's hot kisses from my fingers. Instead I stood at another window and smiled dazedly at Shales who seemed very austere in his plain waistcoat. It was months since I'd seen him. The heat had glazed his skin and he was less gaunt than I remembered.

'I'm aware that your father is away and wondered if you were lonely. Perhaps I could encourage you to come to church,' he said.

I nearly laughed. 'It's a kind thought, Reverend Shales, but I'm not lonely.'

He shot me a surprisingly keen look. 'There are few in Selden who share my love of natural philosophy. I should like to discuss my researches with you and especially explore the issue of combustion. Everywhere I go in the parishes I hear of your reputation for learning. I have been prevented from calling by my sense that it might be disloyal to your father, in view of his quarrel with me. What do you think?'

This time I did laugh. 'I think you're right.'

There was a long silence during which he pressed his lips together and stared out of the window. On our previous encounters he had not seemed unsure of himself and his struggle to find words was unsettling. I was struck by how crowded my life had become what with Aislabie in the garden and Shales in the entrance hall.

Shales suddenly slapped the wall and plucked his hat off a nearby chair. 'Mistress Selden, I wish I knew you better. If I did you might do me the honour of listening to me.'

'I am listening to you, Reverend Shales.'

'There is word in the village that you have been receiving a visitor. Indeed, I have seen this visitor myself and tried to speak with him but he had urgent business elsewhere so our conversation was brief and unproductive. I beg you to be careful.' I was speechless but in any case he hadn't finished. 'At least wait for your father to come back before you commit yourself to some irreversible step.'

'I have no intention of committing myself to an irreversible step.'

'Of course. No. But sometimes it is hard to see the danger. People can be very persuasive.'

'I think you forget who I am, Reverend Shales. I am not some stupid village girl.'

He nodded several times, turned his hat in his hands and gave me another searching glance. 'Of course. Well, thank you for hearing me.'

I folded my arms and waited for him to leave but he only got as far as the door before turning back. We stared at each other and I was disconcerted by the contrast between this man and Aislabie, and understood that Shales would not have come in defiance of my father unless strongly provoked. He seemed trustworthy – there was an urgency about him, a clarity in his eye that was hard to doubt – whereas Aislabie was all light and shade, quirky, mischievous, unpredictable.

Shales said, 'I think your father would forgive us if we were to read a book or two together. I'm sure we could make great progress. You after all are an authority on fire and my book is about air. And we could keep away from the thorny subject of alchemy.'

'The trouble is, Reverend Shales, I think as my father does about alchemy. How could I talk to you if I knew that secretly you were disapproving of me and despising me for the work I do with my father?'

'Despise. No.'

'Nevertheless.'

The entrance hall was a large low room, unfurnished except for some ancient chairs, the Bosworth armour, a few pictures and the oak staircase. Dusty sunlight fell on the scratched and tarnished boards. Shales suddenly came across and took my hand, the same hand that had been caressed so ardently by Aislabie a few moments before, and touched it briefly with his lips. 'I beg you to take care of yourself, Mistress Selden.'

'Thank you, Reverend Shales, be sure I shall.' And then he did go at last although he turned back at the door and I had another glimpse of his troubled face. I watched him from the window as he crossed the lawn and let himself out, clanging the side gate shut behind him. By that I understood that he was informing the village that *his* visit, at least, was not clandestine.

I paced from window to window and wished he'd never come to spoil the enchantment of my afternoon with Aislabie. He was ridiculously tall and prim. And how dare he listen to gossip? But there was a part of me that was flattered and just for a moment I imagined discussing the nature of fire with a fellow of the Royal Society other than my father. Then I remembered how Aislabie had kissed my fingertips and I ran up to my chamber, lay on my bed and relived climbing the terrace steps at his side, my arm resting on his and my fingers interlaced in his warm hand.

12

Selden was loosening its grip on me. I never went near the laboratory any more because I was too busy throwing open all the lattices that weren't sealed up with damp, and bringing armfuls of flowers and branches into the house. I saw them now not as specimens but as part of a shifting green and gold world I shared with Aislabie. The time he wasn't there was full of longing and excitement. Where would he touch me next? Once, while asking the name of a little bird, he stood behind me and laid his hand on the back of my neck as if to support himself. My knees buckled. His thumb moved an inch upwards and a thread tugged at my stomach and thigh, and went on tugging long after he had gone. My body, it seemed, had functions and responses that were not covered by Vesalius or any other author in our library.

I understood that this was love. My father had used Homer to teach me Greek so even I knew that it was natural for a woman to yearn for a man. And alchemical literature is full of couplings. One of my favourite books, the *Mutus Liber*, or *Wordless Book*, shows fifteen figures, among them a man and woman working together at their alchemy. In one picture the man clutches a child to his bosom, in the last they join hands in joy of the completed work. I thought about my extraordinary transformation and decided that I was ready to be part of a pair. I was half of Aislabie now, incomplete unless we were together.

On his fifth visit I led him to the orchard where I wanted to show him the glass-sided beehive Gill had built under my father's instruction. 'We think the bees have a different signal to show whether food is far or near,' I said. 'And bees observe geometrical patterns because they move in circles and semicircles.'

Aislabie pretended to be nervous of the bees so we sat under a distant apple tree. As I lay back on my elbows and looked up at the bubbles of apples and the burning sky I thought my desire for him would come gushing out and drown us both so to hide my longing I started talking again: 'When Isaac Newton stared at the sun through a glass he blinded himself for months afterwards.'

'What a lot you know about Newton.' He leaned on one elbow and smiled into my eyes. His full-lipped mouth fascinated me because it was so pliant – it could smile or frown or tease with the merest twitch of a muscle.

'The image of the sun was scorched into his retina but even from his pain he made deductions. He studied the image within his head and noted that there are spots in the sun.' Aislabie brought my hand to his lips, kissed each knuckle and played the tip of his tongue across the scar from when I first opened the door to him. My throat went slack but I babbled on. 'Newton even pressed a bodkin between his eyeball and the socket in order to distort his vision and understand the play of light on the retina . . .'

He untied my hat and pushed it off, pulled out the pink ribbon and wound his hand through my hair. Then he kissed my mouth. 'Emilie. Silence, Emilie.'

I had barely been kissed in all my nineteen years except for dry little pecks on the cheek or hand from my father and the occasional bosomy hug from Mrs Gill, so I was entranced by what that kiss did to me and thought it the loveliest thing I knew to have my mouth fastened to his. When our tongues touched my knees fell apart and I thought: Why have I been wasting my time all these years not being kissed?

The kiss, which went on and on, unhinged me. I started to cry and shrank away in shame but Aislabie seemed not to mind. Instead he gathered me into his lap and sat with his back to the tree, stroking my cheek and shoulder, kissing the tears, pressing his mouth to my neck and whispering, 'My Emilie. Emilie.' I clung to his neck and kissed him harder.

Love, I thought, was more powerful than alchemy. It had transformed us both. Aislabie had come to our house the self-assured London gentleman buttoned up in his lovely waistcoat but now he was all loose cravat and floating shirtsleeves. I heard his heavy breathing and thought that I, Emilie, had done this, touched him so that he was no longer himself but a panting creature whose mouth and hands searched my flesh, exposing my breasts and knees almost without him knowing what he did. I sank under him and clamoured for more.

But as we rolled among the daisies and bobbles of fallen fruit my education, which had included the dissection of plants, fish and mammals, reasserted itself a little. My father and I in our desire to get to the essence of things had studied the sac of tiny eggs in the body of a female trout and made detailed observations as to why a flower needs the bee to reproduce itself. It dawned on me that my body had changed its behaviour in such a radical and clamorous way during the past few minutes because it was priming itself not just for love, but for reproduction.

I cried, 'No,' but Aislabie's tongue filled my mouth. I pushed his shoulder and jolted my knee but he was a stranger and strong, and I was feeble as a reed under him. Dark shadows came to my sunshiny mind. A tiny creature, perhaps a bee, alighted on my bare calf. Fear tightened my stomach and dried the tears on my cheek.

'No,' I said more insistently but he threw my skirt up to my neck and caged me in my petticoats. I flung my head from side to side, first towards the tree, then to the hive where the bees carried on their business as usual but he took hold of my chin and pulled my mouth back under his. The sun burnt my thighs. I locked them together but he had finished fumbling with his own clothes and suddenly pressed his hand on to my pubic bone.

I went still and quiet and stared up into his eyes as his fingers worked their way inside me until I was helpless as a frog spread out for dissection. Then he took his hand away and lifted himself up, never taking his eyes from my face as I felt a nudge and then the pressure of a long slow lunge that pushed my head against a root and split my insides apart. Emilie, the Emilie I had known, the clever, irritable, longing, knowing Emilie, sank away into the lush grass leaving only a gaping vessel for Aislabie.

The inside of my head fogged with curiosity and the need to please. He lowered himself until his thighs connected to mine and my mouth was covered and I was all Aislabie, filled up by Aislabie, drinking him in as he worked his knees between mine, took hold of my buttocks and pushed harder, harder until I felt the knock on my womb and little red flames inside my thighs. Then he lifted himself out, kissed my wet belly, covered me up and drew me back on to his lap.

I pulled up my knees like a child, buried my face in his crumpled neckcloth and thought: It is over, I am different.

'We will be married, Emilie,' he said.

When my father came home ten days later I didn't meet him at the gate as I had every other year because I thought he was bound to see Aislabie staring out of my eyes.

After supper my tired, shrunken father sank deep in his chair, put his hand to his forehead and peered about as if to reassure himself that he was actually home. There was a brown-paper package on the table. 'A gift, Emilie,' he said.

He had brought me things from London before, my prism, for example, but he had never called them gifts. I could not bear to open the parcel, to see the gleam of anticipation in his eye or to think that he had perhaps remembered our argument and racked his brains for a way of making things better between us. 'Open it,' he said. 'Go on.'

I untied the string. It was a volume of lectures, in Latin, by the Dutchman Boerhaave. 'Hot off the press,' said my father and his eyes sparked with rare humour. 'Unauthorised, I think. You will be one of the first in this country to read him, Emilie, and you will find so much to interest you. He thinks as you do on phlogiston and he is eloquent on the subject of fire. He has weighed it and concluded that although it is an element, it is weightless.'

I opened the book for the sake of showing a little interest and found a diagram of a thermometer but I couldn't take in what I saw. My father began a long speech about what he had seen in London and for the first time I realised that he was not just telling me things for the sake of my education but to relive each new experience for himself. 'I visited Sir Isaac in his Kensington house. He's getting more and more infirm, I thought, terrible cough.'

I had never been less interested in the state of Newton's health but I said, 'What did you talk about?'

'He mentioned the possibility of a translation of the *Principia* into English. Of course he has mixed feelings about that – doesn't want it to fall into ignorant hands. How is your own translation, Emilie?'

'I didn't have much time, after all.'

'Nor for the laboratory,' he said sharply. 'I found the rose as I'd left it.'

We had lit his pipe so I was kneeling at his feet. 'I should like to marry Robert Aislabie, Father.' His head jerked back and he fumbled for his staff, which instead fell to the floor with a clatter. I picked it up and gave it to him. 'What do you think?'

'I think you will not marry anyone, especially not him.'

'I believe I must.' I thought of the weight in my breasts, my lack of appetite, my desire to avoid scrutiny by Mrs Gill. 'I believe I may be carrying his child.'

The effect of this news on my father was so terrible I could almost have wished the last month undone. He seemed to shrivel before my eyes until he was yellow and ancient. His hand came up and covered his face.

'Please, Father, I know I shall be happy.'

He wouldn't speak to me though I knelt there for some minutes stroking his coat and hand, pleading with him, then retreated to the window. 'Father. Please give me your blessing. I am sorry if I have hurt you. But please, Father. You know how it is to love. I believe you loved my mother. Don't you remember? So you must know how it was. Father. Father.' My voice faded. Outside it was almost dark but I could still see the bars of the old gates. I wanted to be on the other side of them, driven by Aislabie into a painless new life.

After half an hour I crept away and from that day I was shut out of the laboratory and the library. If we happened to meet in the passage my father ignored me and though every few hours I went and knocked on the door he never answered.

I dreaded to think what he wrote in his notebook that night.

Chapter Three

THREE LETTERS
IN BETWEEN

I

On the day after my father's return Mrs Gill found me in the screens passage where I was keeping watch on the library door in case he came out. 'Follow me,' she said.

I followed. There was no disobeying Mrs Gill when she used that voice. She stood me under the high kitchen window and took hold of my shoulders so she could study my face. 'What have you done?'

I couldn't speak for dread of what she'd say next. Suddenly she cried, 'While your father was gone you were in my care, Emilie.' I stared at her. I had never seen her weak or incapable but now she was both. Her skin was clammy and her lips trembling.

'I love him,' I said.

She pushed me away, picked up the corner of her apron and rubbed her eyes. 'Love him. Love him. You know nothing about it. I should have seen. I should have known what was coming. I should have been here.'

'It's not your fault,' I said.

'It's too late for fault. Or so it seems. Sit down, Emilie. Listen very carefully. You don't have to marry this Mr Aislabie. There are other choices. The baby, if indeed there is a baby, might miscarry.' She looked me hard in the eye.

'What do you mean?'

'I mean you do not yet know if the baby will survive to full term.'

'I want to marry him,' I said, 'baby or not.'

'Your father will relent in the end, I'm sure. We could keep the baby here. Or you could marry him in time, when you know him better.'

'I'll marry Aislabie soon,' I said.

'You don't know him. What do you know of him except that he is the type of man who seduces a girl the moment her father's back is turned?'

'Seduce.' I considered the word. Se-ducere. To lead. 'No. I wanted him.'

Suddenly she took me in her arms and pressed my head to her shoulder. 'Oh my lamb. We have failed you.'

'No. No.' I drew back and looked at her in horror. Why was I pitiable because I loved Aislabie? I hurried out of the kitchen and there was Gill hanging about at the scullery door, well within earshot. He looked blindly past me as if terrified of meeting my eye and admitting the truth of what had happened.

2

A pall of silence fell on Selden as the four of us crept about, miserably isolated. I had fractured the rhythm of our lives. Every few days I wrote a letter to Aislabie. My writing covered both sides of a page crossways and down as if by writing I would forge an inky chain between us. I told him every last detail of my life at Selden, including my father's grief, and when I was sure of it I told him about the baby. His letters in reply were brief but ardent. *A child*, he wrote.

> *Dearest, dearest Emilie.*
>   *You can have no idea how happy I feel. All my life I have been working towards this. It even makes me believe after all that there is some providence which responds if we want something enough and labour hard enough to achieve it. To have you, Emilie, as my wife, and to be the father of our child . . . I will come very soon, within a fortnight, to make arrangements with your father.*

Despite the evidence of these letters, loneliness and exclusion made me wonder whether I had dreamed Aislabie but exactly at the agreed hour I heard hoof-beats through the village and there he was at the gates, horse steaming, hat whipped off for the blacksmith's daughter who happened to be passing. I emerged from the porch as Gill put his shoulder to the rusty iron. Aislabie wore dark clothes except for a jaunty yellow cockade and was more solemn than I remembered as he leapt down and kissed my hand and cheek. 'You are pale, my dear love.'

He was a stranger and I had an instant of pure terror. His face was more fleshy, he seemed altogether weightier, less boyish than before and his blue eyes looked eagerly past me to Selden. Then he held me tight in his arms, buried his face in my neck, kissed my mouth so that I felt the shock of sudden intimacy and fell against him thinking I love him, I do love him. He held me at arm's length and studied my face, then my waist. 'Are you well? What about our child? Is he thriving?'

These were beautiful words to me, especially the 'our'. They closed the gap between us and made me feel that after all I did have a place somewhere, even if not at Selden. 'All is well.'

'How is the old man?' he whispered.

'I hardly know. He won't speak to me. He won't let me near him though I knock on his door every day.'

He kissed my hand again. 'Never fear, my love. I'll find a way round him.'

I led him across the hall, tapped at the library door and stood aside to let him through. My father stayed out of sight but I heard a board creak under his foot. The door was left wide open and I glimpsed the glow of firelight on the laden shelves and smelt tobacco. I wasn't invited in. It was a sunless day and the hall was cold. I had no doubt that the open door was a deliberate ploy and that I was supposed to overhear this conversation. I was hoping for a miracle, that Aislabie would find precisely the right words to soften my father and readmit me to the old life. His cultivated London voice was very low and I missed the beginning of his address: '. . . daughter's hand.'

There was a long silence during which Aislabie twirled his hat and I tiptoed closer. '. . . rent and furnish a house by the end of November and have the banns read,' he said.

My father was probably huddled under cover of his everyday wig, refusing to speak or meet Aislabie's eye. There was another silence after which Aislabie said much more abruptly, 'So we come to the terms of the marriage settlement. Of course I understand that it may be difficult for you to make more than a token payment now so I am prepared to accept an entailment after your death, Sir.'

I retreated a few steps. I had never heard my father spoken to so curtly. There could be no hope of reconciliation now. '. . . land already entailed,' came his frail voice at last.

'I think not, Sir. I believe the land is entailed to Emilie and once she is married it will be my privilege to have charge of her property. All I ask is that you add a clause to the effect that in the event of her early death the estates should be passed to me in trust for any children, or if we are unfortunately without a living child . . .' Aislabie, glancing up, had seen me standing in the shadows. He sprang forward and shut the door.

Silence. I clutched a ridge of panelling. How had a few sunlit walks and half an hour of lovemaking in the bee orchard led to such cold-blooded bartering?

When, after another ten minutes, the door opened again I was standing in the same place, shaking. I saw Aislabie but not my father who was hidden by the door. He said very distinctly, 'I don't regard Emilie as my daughter so much as a woman for whom I have some responsibility. I have brought her up and therefore must attend to her future well-being. Though I am sorry she has fallen into your hands I am sure that whatever the afterlife contains for me I shall be indifferent to the fate of both Selden and Emilie, and therefore I agree to your terms provided I am spared any further meeting with you.'

Aislabie waited a moment longer, then bowed, came swiftly across the hall, took my cold hand and led me into the porch. He had lost colour and his eyes were dark. Cupping my face, he pressed hard kisses on my lips and eyes. 'Dearest woman. Dearest girl. I'm coming for you soon. You must not worry. You must take care of yourself and the baby. That is your only concern. I'll send you a firm date. Take care, my love.' He patted my back and whispered more endearments but I could feel that his muscles were taut. Gill brought his horse and went to open the gates while Aislabie kissed me one last time, mounted and rode away with a stab of his spurs and a pounding of hooves.

3

There was a great deal of time to be got through before my wedding and I passed most of it in my mother's bedchamber. Each day I made the pilgrimage along the creaking passageways, lifted the latch, ducked my head and closed the door behind me. Silence. Or perhaps a loose pane stirred in a lattice.

I knelt by the box and lifted the lid with extreme caution as if she might come flowing out in a sigh of silk. Inside there was that lovely papery whiff of trapped air. If cobwebs had a smell this was it, musty and sweet. Next I unfolded the shawl, the bonnet and the nightgown and tried to imagine them worn by a real baby, my own child with a warm, heavy head and strong little limbs. Afterwards I lay on the bed which Mrs Gill had made up for me with quilt and pillows. The floor sloped down towards the window so I could see into the sky above the woods, as my mother must have done. I watched the racing clouds and listened. She too would have heard birdsong, a rush of movement in the trees when the wind blew and sometimes the barking of a dog in the village or the scuffle of a creature in the eaves.

I tucked myself up in the quilt and felt my body grow slack with drowsiness. As my mind misted she came so close that she hovered outside the door and even once hung over me. I swear I felt her breath on my cheek. But when I woke I was always alone and I felt sick and chilled in the unheated room. At those times I would have been glad to speak to anyone but there was little company to be had at Selden.

One afternoon when I went down to the kitchen I heard unfamiliar footsteps, then the closing of the stable-yard door. 'Who was that?' I asked Mrs Gill.

Relations between us were strained. I thought she might show a little more interest in my condition, perhaps sew some garments for the baby, but beyond making me potions for my nausea or suggesting that I take more exercise she rarely spoke to me. Now she never even looked up from peeling shallots for the pickle jar. 'Reverend Shales. That's the second time he's called and been turned away.'

My first instinct was to thank whatever passed for God these days that at least I didn't have to meet him. Then I dashed along the kitchen passage and flung wide the door. It was drizzling and the yard was empty except for Gill who was standing in the doorway opposite, arms folded as if he had been expecting me, and a couple of hens who pecked round his feet. I ran across the wet cobbles and looked under the arch. 'Is Reverend Shales gone?'

He nodded.

'What did he want?'

'Sir John says he's not to come in.'

Gill lived by a simple, unswerving rule: what Sir John says, goes. We looked at each other for a moment. His clothes were dark with damp and as always he appeared to have nothing in the world to do except what he was engaged in at that moment. I had an odd sensation of displacement, as if I didn't know him any more because I was no longer part of his particular system of existence. And the look in his eye was defiant; he was daring me to question his loyalties.

I went back to the kitchen. I had no idea what I might have said to Shales but I felt a mix of disappointment and relief that I'd missed him. 'I suppose Shales knows what's happened,' I said. 'I suppose everybody does.'

'They will not have heard it from us.'

But of course the whole parish would know. Every move Aislabie had made since his first gallop through the village would have been noted and discussed. 'I don't regret what has happened,' I said. 'I'm sorry to have made you all unhappy but I can't regret it. I chose Aislabie.'

She laid down her knife at last. 'Then you chose. And you must bear the consequences.'

'But why? I don't understand why you are all punishing me.'

'It's not a matter of punishment. It's a matter of coming to terms with losing you when sometimes it seems to me you've barely arrived.'

Suddenly I saw her life as a long passage of years in which

every autumn she had stood at this table peeling shallots, then nineteen years of Emilie, then nothing again but the shallots. 'I will come back,' I said.

'Of course you'll come back.' She nodded towards the block where the knives were kept which I took to be an invitation to join her at the chopping board, though I could only peel half a dozen onions to her twenty.

4

On 1 December I got up at four and called goodbye to my father through the library door. He didn't answer though I knocked and spoke his name three times. In the kitchen passage Mrs Gill clutched me tight for a moment while Gill turned away, put the flat of his hand on the door frame, leaned his forehead against it and would not look round at me. Then I, and a small bag containing the baby clothes from the box in my mother's room, were enclosed in Aislabie's hired carriage and bounced from the soft seat as the horses sprang forward. Aislabie rode alongside and as my last glimpse of Selden was hidden by a view of his spurred boot I had no idea whether or not my father came to the library window. Anyway, I was too busy clasping my stomach and trying not to be sick. This was my first long journey anywhere but I was too ill and frightened to take it in. By the time we reached London I was huddled in a corner, faint with cold and bewildered by the lack of sky.

We were married in a church on the Strand so new that it smelt of paint and plaster. Shivering and nauseous, I swayed beside my new husband and held tight to his hand. I asked if any of his family would be present but he said Norfolk was much too far for them to think of coming; in fact, none of them had ever set foot more than half a dozen miles beyond the farm. So the wedding was witnessed by a business associate and afterwards we drove to the new house in Hanover Street which seemed large as Selden until I realised this was not one house but many and that each in the row was narrow and high. I couldn't see anything green.

My new husband had furnished the house with staggering attention to detail; he showed me a dining room equipped even to the smallest salt spoon and a caged parrot hanging in the window. 'Watch what you say, Emilie,' he whispered, feathering the back of my neck with his fingertip. 'That bird will copy every indiscretion.'

I was still reeling from the shock of change. Selden Manor had been a hellish place of silence and isolation but still I couldn't take in the tumult and enclosure of the city. When I saw the parrot I found myself thinking, my father will be interested in that bird. He will test its green feathers to discover the nature of their pigment, measure its cranium to see how it compares with other less able birds and when it dies slit its little throat to examine its larynx.

Upstairs in a drawing room prepared especially for me a fire burnt briskly, translucent cups were laid out on a frail-looking table and a teapot was warming over a spirit burner. The room smelt of orange peel and rose petals. I sat carefully on a cream satin chair as a carriage rolled by outside and the house shook. The chair was my anchor. When a maid appeared and removed the tea tray I clutched the seat and smiled blindly at her.

At supper Aislabie fed me titbits from his fork and I felt a little more of myself arrive in London. The rest was still lurching about in the carriage. But later, when I lay under a canopy of flowered damask and watched him shut the bed curtains I panicked and begged him to let me see the window. 'Nonsense, Em, you don't know London. We wouldn't sleep for the noise.'

He lay down beside me and buried his face in my neck. 'You're my peach, my plum, all mine now, Emilie.' His fingers and mouth played on my skin but I lay wide-eyed with shock, peering through the darkness at the canopy above and drawing up my legs to protect our child from the enthusiastic weight of its father. Aislabie kissed me fearlessly: 'We have a tough little Aislabie in here, no need to worry.'

So my legs wrapped themselves round him, my body pulsed with desire and my face streamed with tears of relief and love. But I was still two Emilies. One Emilie ran her hand shyly over the contours of her husband's back, buried her fingers in his hair and drank in his kisses, the other flew across the chimney tops and along the river to Selden where my father sat alone in the library, head in hand. Would he remember to go to bed or would he sit up all night thinking about me? And then I tasted the salt of perspiration on Aislabie's neck and smelt the musk of his skin as he plunged into me and sent ripples across my belly and thighs until I drifted away from my father into a hot elemental world of tangled sheets and muscular spasms that contracted my abdomen and drew Aislabie deeper and deeper.

I was woken in the small hours by a woman screaming in the street outside. There was a rhythmic ache in my womb and warm liquid surged down my legs. By morning I had given birth. I made them uncover the bowl and show me the perfect fourteen-week foetus floating in a puddle of blood, a curved little thing with transparent hands and ears like shells and I thought this is my punishment for breaking my father's heart.

5

A fortnight later I wrote to my father and told him that I had arrived safely in London, married Aislabie but miscarried the child. These last two events seemed dangerously inter-changeable with only the three letters between them. My father didn't reply. After that I wrote once a week but there was never any response from him or anyone else at Selden. Mrs Gill couldn't write and though Gill was literate he was hardly one for letters.

In the meantime I spent three months a prisoner in the Hanover Street house, first because of illness, then clothes. As neither of these matters had been relevant at Selden, I was very ignorant of both.

The doctor said I must stay in bed for at least six weeks so my first experience of London was from the horizontal. I felt rather than saw the proximity of hundreds of thousands of people as our house swayed to the thunder of carriages and the slamming of doors, and voices came from above and below, and either side of my bedchamber. If I peeped between the drapes I saw a row of houses opposite and people disappearing suddenly round corners rather than slowly receding, as they did in the country. How would I ever find a place for myself amidst such confusion? I longed for Aislabie to come but he was engaged in important negotiations and could only spare me half an hour at a time.

His visits were worth the wait, though at first we were nervous of each other, as if afraid of this new-married but childless state. But in fact it didn't altogether dawn on me to begin with that I had lost anything because those early weeks in London were so similar to my last days at Selden except that I lay in a warmer bed and there was a great deal more going on in the house around me. At the back of my mind was always the thought that soon I would get up and carry on with being pregnant. So when Aislabie crept up to the bed and held my hand with great tenderness, as if my fingers were porcelain rather than flesh, I drew his face down to mine, delighted by the smell of him and his willingness to lie beside me and told me tight. After he'd gone I'd curl in the emptiness he left behind, sniff the pillow where his head had been and remember baby mice in the cages at Selden and how they'd coil together in such a bundle of pink flesh that it was impossible to tell where one creature ended and another began.

Aislabie brought me presents of books but had no idea how much I already knew. *The Castle of Knowledge*, for instance, I had read from cover to cover when I was eight. I tried a book of poetry and a play by Shakespeare but the words would not form themselves into sensible ideas. I read for an hour and then discovered that I had taken in nothing but the page numbers. All the time my mind had been ranging instead along the bookshelves at Selden and leafing through volumes of natural philosophy.

On Christmas Eve Aislabie arrived with a huge box containing a gown of pink embossed silk, which he whirled about and threatened to wear himself if I didn't get up soon and put on. Next he produced a matching hat, a fan and a pair of slippers. I couldn't resist his antics with the fan so I tried on the dress but the seams writhed round my arms, the bodice wouldn't join at the back and my head poked from a froth of lace. My legs were feeble and there was no strength in my spine. Altogether the gown seemed to have won a battle against me. Aislabie sent for a maid, who stood by the door, bit the edge of her thumb and awaited instructions. I had none to give her. She looked longingly at the heap of silk but I said I felt faint and that I wanted to go back to bed. Aislabie kissed me and stroked my hair, and told me that in a couple of weeks I'd take London by storm in that pink dress.

The doctor said I should begin to take a little exercise, though I must stay inside and not expose myself to the infected airs of the winter city. Obediently I crept out of my room and poked my head round doors, cautious as a housebreaker. The servants, who were never fully out of earshot, intimidated me. I found a bedchamber furnished in burgundy velvet and a little back room reeking of stale alcohol, with a round table in the centre and heavy drapes at the window.

There were other worlds to discover without setting foot outside the house. Aislabie had a taste for French paintings, which were arranged around the walls of the first-floor salon. I peered into one and found delicate ladies in pastel robes, a copse of birches and a little stone temple. The painting reminded me of Selden because of its cloudy sky and silver river running into a distant forest, but of course there was no old man in an ancient coat thrashing his way through the undergrowth, no Emilie with restless eyes and creased apron. So I searched deeper and deeper until I was lost in the picture and instead of roaming through that unknown French landscape I was at home in Selden, skirting past Gill in the bee orchard, darting into the kitchen to scoop up a fistful of peas, standing at the window in my mother's room to watch the top of my oak tree blowing deep in the woods. And then at last I came to my senses because the pain of thinking of that window in that room where I used to lie in the early months of pregnancy was too much to bear.

Every day I studied a different painting and then had a whispered conversation with the parrot who cocked its head and gave me a piercing glance from one eye. I thought it a poor excuse for a bird compared with our owl which had so much confined energy. This parrot made no effort to fly, just sat in stony silence but I wrote about it again to my father and enclosed a green feather.

By the beginning of February Aislabie's visits had become more frequent. He said he couldn't stand the smell of enclosure in the room so he threw open the window, then rang the bell and ordered wine to be brought and the fire to be heaped with coal. When the maid left he blew out all the candles but one, climbed into bed beside me and held the wine glass to my lips. I lay against his shoulder and watched the roar of the flames as the draught got to them. The wine warmed the back of my throat and made me sleepy and light-headed. 'What have you been doing all day?' I asked.

'I have been hither and yon. To the club and the Exchange and the river.'

'Why were you at the river?' In my mind's eye I saw the gush of water under the bridge at Selden and my father leaning on his staff to watch the flight of a heron.

Aislabie took hold of my chin and kissed my mouth. 'You shouldn't lie here looking so beautiful and so sad and expect small talk, my Emilie. Those black eyes and this soft skin does not invite conversation,' and he kissed me again and covered my breast with his hand. When he stroked my stomach I flinched at the thought of my empty womb and my treacherous legs which had allowed the baby to slip away but he was too much for me. 'Dearest Em, this is the way to make another child, you'll see, easy as the last. And even more fun.' He nuzzled my ear and pressed his leg against my thigh until despite myself I ached for him.

The trouble was he never stayed long enough. I had imagined that marriage to him would be like a perpetual walk through the gardens at Selden but in London Aislabie was always in a hurry. He'd make love to me for half an hour, then dash away to dress and go out again. I grew restless with the time I was forced to spend alone. I still couldn't bear to read because books reminded me of the library at Selden, and I obviously had no place in the kitchen with the servants. The pink dress hung in the closet but I knew I could never squeeze myself into its tiny bodice and my only other garments were the Selden frocks made by Mrs Gill – even I could tell that the lowliest London kitchen maid would turn her nose up at them. So I sat at the window and watched all those strangers on their way to somewhere necessary, and I waited for Aislabie.

7

One evening he announced that he had a present for me, which would arrive in the morning. 'You won't know yourself after that, Em. Silk purse from sow's ear.'

The present was a young woman called Sarah Holborne, who knocked vehemently on the door and brought in my tray of chocolate. What with her pastel frock and lawn apron she looked as if she'd stepped from my husband's painting by Watteau. She had a pointy chin and disturbing eyes, one uptilted more than the other under fly-away brows.

I spilt chocolate on my shift while she flitted about the chamber touching every surface. 'How shall we begin, Madam?' She picked up a garter, rubbed it between finger and thumb and brushed it against her cheek.

I tucked the sheets tight round my neck and waited for her to go. Instead, she sat down on a chest and adjusted the laces on my corset with such fierce concentration that I thought she was mad. The back of her neck was fragile as the stem of a poppy.

'Mrs Aislabie, get up now,' she said. Her voice was husky but authoritative and there was no disobeying her. I stood quaking. When she came close and put her fingers on the top button of my shift I saw how soft her hair was, pulled back in an arc from her forehead. The shift fell to the floor and she walked round me, studying my body with the same air of intent expertise I would once have given a dissected dog's brain. I accepted her scrutiny because I had no idea what passed for fashionable behaviour in London. My tousled hair fell to my waist and she picked up a strand, held it to the light and let it fall. The top of her head was level with my nose and her little face frowned with concentration as if she was committing the curve of my hip and the shape of my toes to memory. Meanwhile I looked past her to my crumpled bed and shivered.

'Stand straight,' she ordered, 'and hold the bedpost. Put your feet apart. Look.' She pushed me aside and demonstrated. Then she made me thrust my arms into a corset, stood behind me and worked so fast on the laces that I didn't have time to draw breath. My lungs were deflated when she pulled the strings and I couldn't fill them up again. The ends of my ribs jabbed internal organs and my back went ramrod straight.

She tied on a hoop and flung lakes of petticoat over my head. They smelt of the wooden shuttles that had woven them, steel needles, starch. My mother, I thought, would have recognised that smell of new silk. When she pressed me into a chair my body shrieked with pain. She coiled my hair round her fist, dragged it up by the roots and jabbed pins through it. My scalp burnt and my hands clutched at the silken waterfall of my lap.

'Now you can look,' she said.

My hidden feet took me and the cartload of pink fabric across the room and stood us in front of the mirror. A beam of sunlight fell on the blue and cream rug. I took a step back, then forward, turned to left and right, stood side on to the glass and put my hands on the sloping shelves of my skirt. Then I looked myself in the eye.

Emilie Aislabie. Do I know you?

A black-eyed stranger, inserted correctly into her gown, stared back. Sarah had given me a new, definite shape. I could have drawn with a ruler the slashing lines for each side of the bodice and the folds of the skirt. When I turned sideways I saw that I was flat from breast to navel. She had taken away the last flicker of doubt that the baby was gone. Behind the mistress stood the new maid, Sarah Holborne. Our eyes met briefly in the glass and her disconcerting gaze was full of satisfaction, not with me, but with what she had achieved.

8

I was now declared to be in good health and Sarah provided me with both a veneer of fashion and a chaperone so there was no excuse to stay inside. She buttoned me up in a vast mantle and hustled me down to the waiting carriage. I hovered on the Hanover Street steps like a fledgling. London, as glimpsed on the day of my marriage, had seemed like some hideous evocation of Gill's compost heap except that whereas life in the heap – writhing, sucking, flitting, crawling – hummed softly, London screeched. It had no form, no beginning and no end, no wide lid of sky, no soft earth beneath my feet.

'Where shall we go, Madam?' asked Sarah.

I knew of only two places in London, the Royal Society's headquarters and my mother's birthplace, Spital Fields, so I gave the name of one of them – Crane Court, home of the Royal Society. She raised her crooked eyebrows, gave an order and off we lurched.

I thought the carriage would be crushed like a bird's egg. How could it withstand the pressure of so much traffic? But it was the faces outside the window that made me shudder. I hadn't been trained to interpret faces. There seemed to be no pattern to them though my father said that everything in nature has a pattern. They turned on me or away from me, opened their gaping mouths, wept, laughed, glowered, shouted, cursed, scolded: haggard, pocked, pretty, flyblown, button-nosed, handsome, childish or simple. None of them had anything to do with me. I had never met indifference before.

Crane Court had such a narrow entrance that the driver refused to take the carriage through. I leaned out and saw the usual dirty paving stones and high buildings. This was a deep disappointment. I had expected white marble pillars at least, and Sir Isaac Newton enthroned amidst a host of acolytes. I wasn't bold enough to go into the yard alone and there was no question of asking Sarah because she had suddenly shrunk down in the corner of the carriage. 'Are you ill?' I asked. 'Do you want to go back?'

She had an astonishing repertory of shrugs and curls of the lip. 'I don't mind, Madam.'

'Then we'll go on, and perhaps you could point out the names of streets and churches so I get my bearings.'

She intoned a few names but as we reached Ludgate Hill folded her arms across her chest and went stony silent until St Paul's. I wished my initiation into the mysteries of London had been with Aislabie, or with my father – whose carefully planned education, I noted, had failed to prepare me for any of this – but for the first time since the miscarriage I was really excited. It was so easy, after all these years, to be carried towards Spital Fields and my mother. I leaned forward thinking *she* will have seen that inn, those houses, that warehouse. But of course I had no idea of the De Lery address so once in Spital Square I was at a dead end. I decided that one day soon I would come back by myself and knock on doors to see if anyone remembered my mother's family but for now it was enough to look at *her* square, the wedge of sky that *she* had known, the topography of *her* childhood. Meanwhile a little crowd had collected round the carriage.

Sarah sighed pointedly and rolled her eyes. 'My mother was brought up here,' I said. 'Her name was De Lery. Her family made silk.' She looked a bit more interested, even peered out. 'De Lery green. Do you know it?'

'Green's unlucky.'

'Nevertheless.'

She puffed air through her nose as if to say if she hadn't heard of such a colour it couldn't exist.

'So where would I find silk of that colour?' I asked.

'A silk warehouse.'

'Where might one be?' She stared at me for a moment, then stuck her head out of the window, yelled up to the coachman and off we lurched until we came to a vast building with large windows and an imposing front door. The proprietor gave Sarah an obsequious bow, called her Miss Holborne, led us in and allowed us to wander among rolls and swathes of cloth. For once Sarah's face was animated as she fingered and sniffed the silks, which shimmered in every possible shade from black to white, cherry to gold, buttercup to azure; silks with the dense lustre of my obsidian; silks woven with leaves and flower heads or entire vases of blooms; striped silks in blue and pink; silks embroidered with butterflies and birds; silks so thick they could have stood alone, and silks like gossamer. But it was the greens that drew me, moss green, leaf green, the green of my oak tree at Selden.

I asked the merchant, 'Have you a silk called De Lery green?'

'De Lery, Madam. Not that I know of.'

I was disappointed but realised that of course there must be fashions in silk. De Lery green might have been sought after twenty years ago, but not now. So I called Sarah away from some creamy translucent stuff and we went back to the carriage, dazed by so much splendour.

It seemed to me, despite the lack of De Lery green, that I had come another step closer to my mother and I was sufficiently moved to ask, 'Where were you brought up, Sarah?'

She shrugged and turned down the corners of her mouth. 'South of the river.'

'In London?'

'Of course.'

'Far from here?'

She stared at me. 'Not far. Nothing is far in London.'

'So where are we now?'

'Now we are on Gracechurch Street.'

'And how would we get to your home from here?'

'What do you mean?'

'If we were to go to the place where you were born.'

'You mean down across the bridge. Stoney Street. But why would we go there?'

'If we wanted to visit your parents.'

She fixed me with expressionless eyes. 'Parents?' And then it dawned on me. Sarah had been spawned like a tadpole. Her history was short as her own memory and at the thought of this I suddenly yearned to be back at Selden. What family did I have, come to think of it, except for Aislabie?

9

Now I was better we were to host a party in my honour but first I had to be trained. I couldn't help being interested in any new procedures and was an expert pupil. Aislabie told me to choose the colour for a gown which duly arrived – emerald green as a tribute to my mother – with a plunging neck, a cascade of lace at the elbows and a petticoat of buttery satin.

Sarah handled the gown as if it might poison her fingers. 'I told you. Green's unlucky.'

'In the country everything's green and yet it is not an unlucky place.'

'I shouldn't like to go there.' I watched in the mirror as she hooked up the bodice and I could tell from the set of her jaw that she really meant what she said. The gown pinched under the bosom and burst like a seedpod below the waist. For a moment I thought it hideously ill-fitting but she knelt down and began a series of adjustments to the hem, pulling and tucking, inserting pins at the waist and under the arm, dragging at the sleeves until suddenly the dress and I looked as if we belonged together.

'Where would my husband have found such a gown?' I asked.

'Benjamin Cole,' she said through a mouthful of pins, 'for the fabric.'

'Who is Benjamin Cole?'

'Merchant. St Paul's Churchyard.' She ran her pearly little nail under a strip of lace and her eyes were full of yearning. 'And that lace is from Gostlin's. It's the best.'

'If you like you can try the dress on,' I said.

She recoiled as if I had hit her and bustled about folding my shift and lifting my shoes from their box. 'These are from a new shoemaker on Pall Mall. French. See the embroidery. I'd say forty stitches to the inch.' She spoke with great respect as she inserted her fist to mould the fabric, arranged them on the floor and held my hand gravely so that I would keep my balance when I stepped into them. 'Now I'll show you the curtsy,' and, picking up her skirts, she put her right foot behind the left and performed a wonderful little bob with her head inclined in such a way that she could still peep at herself in the mirror. When I tried of course I staggered, crumpled my skirts, caught my heel on a petticoat hem. She laughed and I glimpsed her little teeth, a sudden, childish merriment in the eye, even malicious satisfaction that she could curtsy and I couldn't. But when she caught me looking she sobered immediately. 'You must do it again,' she ordered. So I tried again and again until she was satisfied. 'We will practise again tomorrow.'

It struck me, as she left, that my father would have applauded Sarah's determination to get things absolutely right. Like Sir Isaac, he would have said, she is an expert.

A dancing master was hired to show me how to wield a fan and dance a few simple sets and, best of all, Aislabie set aside an hour each day to teach me hazard, backgammon, ombre and cribbage. I loved the intimacy of those lessons held in the smoky little back room with the velvet curtains drawn and candles lit. He sat me on his knee so he could look at my hand and show me how to hold the cards close to my chest, and interspersed each instruction with kisses on my shoulder or the back of my neck so that more often than not our games ended in the bedroom.

Then one morning Sarah pressed me into a chair, bit her lip, took my ear lobe between finger and thumb and pushed a needle into me. In the mirror I saw her absorption and the flash of excitement as blood trickled along my jawbone. She picked up a pearl droplet and forced it into the hole. Dizzy with pain I laid my head on my arm but she turned my neck and took hold of the other ear. Only when it was all done and she had wiped away the blood did she lean forward and breathe a word in my ear: 'Good.'

10

On the night of the party my waist was corseted to a couple of hands' span and my hair piled high under a speck of lawn but I resisted paints and patches. When Aislabie saw me he lifted me off my feet, kissed my mouth, pushed a silk nosegay between my breasts and gave Sarah a nod of approval. My feet in their two-inch heels went clip-clop as he led me downstairs.

Our house was transformed. The furniture, paintings, rugs and parrot had disappeared behind a dazzling crowd of people. We stood above them and there was sudden quiet, a bloom of upturned faces, then applause and I felt a twinge of anticipation, even pleasure. At last I had a function in the antheap of London. Aislabie held me tight to his side as he waved and bowed with mock grandeur before leading me among them. 'This is my Emilie. My little philosopher. She can sing you the music of the spheres and argue the case for Newton's fluxional method against Leibniz's differential calculus . . .'

Hands caught hold of mine, lips kissed my skin, eyes roved my face and body. A quintet was playing and the noise confused me.

I had spent nineteen years in near silence except for the groaning church organ and I couldn't hear music without trying to work it out.

'So this is the alchemist's daughter,' said a man with a complicated wrinkled face under a toppling pile of curls. The alchemist's daughter? But I wasn't. The alchemist had cut me off. I turned in panic to my husband but somehow my hand had been passed on to someone else's arm. For the first time it occurred to me that Aislabie was not unique but one of a kind. There were other Aislabies, none so playful and desirable, but dozens of young men in sumptuous wigs and elaborate waistcoats, heads full of ambition and knowledge.

A woman called Lady Essington with a bold face and wide blue eyes pulled me into her group. 'We have to know, how did you entrap our Aislabie?'

Leaning against her leg was a little page-boy. His skin was all black and his eyes as dark as mine. 'Entrap?'

'We all wanted him. So tell me, did you cast a spell?'

'I don't know any spells.'

'We don't believe you. We hear you were up to all sorts in your enchanted castle.'

'Not a castle.'

'What did you do there all those years? Is it true you never went anywhere? Tell us what it was like living alone with your father.'

'What it was like?'

'Weren't you bored? Didn't you long for variety?'

'I learned mathematics and natural philosophy.'

'You must be very clever,' said Lady Essington, smiling with her crimson lips. 'Tell us what you know.'

'Very little compared with some.'

The ladies bent their heads seductively and the movement of their fans slowed. I lifted my chin and felt a rush of confidence. The chance to talk about my lost studies was irresistible, especially as the fair, blue-eyed lady gave me such an encouraging nod while her black servant boy fixed me with his huge eyes. 'My own special interest lies in the nature of fire.'

'Fire. Fire. How passionate and extraordinary. And what is the nature of fire?'

'I don't know. I wish I did. I can only tell you what other people have said. Sir Isaac Newton, for instance, believes that light communicates heat to bodies by the vibrations of a medium he calls aether, hundreds of times more elastic than air so that it can penetrate even solid bodies. Robert Boyle, on the other hand, thought that fire is due to fiery corpuscles which exist in the air. And then the latest theory from the Continent is phlogiston.'

The ladies were eyeing each other across the top of their fans. I knew they weren't interested but I didn't have the skill to extricate myself.

'And what does your father, the alchemist, say?' asked Lady E.

'You'd have to ask him. I have my doubts about the phlogiston theory. My own belief is that the clue to fire lies in the air. I have noticed that only part of air is used in combustion – the same part that perhaps exists in substances such as gunpowder, which will burn under water or in a vacuum. So I think that it is not air itself, but part of air that causes fire.' As I spoke I felt a great welling up of hunger for the old life, but I had lost the attention of most of my audience – one or two were whispering behind their fans, others swayed their hoops or allowed their gaze to drift past my face.

Then they suddenly straightened up and sparkled again because Aislabie had come back, brilliant in shades of green and primrose. He kissed my nose and took my hand. 'Vultures,' he whispered, 'watch your back,' and swept me away past the first-floor drawing room where silk-clad feet were dancing a measure far too complicated for my limited experience. Instead, we paused at the door of the little room where I had learned to play cards, now full of men drinking punch and smoking. They grinned and waved at me through a thick haze.

'Will you play, Mistress Aislabie?' asked my husband. He drew up a chair and stood with his hand on my shoulder. Lady E. was opposite, her blue eyes hard as sapphire as she looked above my head to him. Her black servant boy leaned his head on her arm and his lids sank half shut over his liquid eyes. Aislabie squeezed my shoulder and kissed my hair and at the end of half an hour I had won three guineas. The other players called it beginner's luck but actually I owed my success to my mathematical education. The winning and losing of money meant little to me because I knew nothing about its value. I felt only a cold-blooded enjoyment in numbers added up and taken away. But I was soon exhausted, hemmed in by the hoops of other women, showered with extravagant compliments, shot through with the strange compulsion of the gaming table.

At four o'clock, when the first birds were already shouting in the eaves, we went to bed. For once Aislabie left the curtains open and a streak of moonlight fell on my pillow. He lay above me and traced the moonbeams across my face with his tongue.

I thought of Selden where the same moonlight would be falling through the uncurtained windows of my empty bedchamber, on the silent passageways and into the library where my father sat by the fire, writing and writing in his secret notebook.

Chapter Four

JOURNEY HOME

I

Aislabie had three ambitions: the first was a son, the second was to buy a ship, the third was to know and be known by everyone. I was necessary for the first, redundant in the second, a useful partner in the third because my educated brain and narrow French nose made me a novelty. As long as I kept my language simple everyone wanted to talk about natural philosophy. They plied me with questions as if I were the authority on everything from gravity to gases.

The more I talked, the more homesick I became. My hand twitched for the touch of an alembic or a pair of scales. I longed to wrestle with calculus or argue about phlogiston, and anxiety for my father was like a tumour gnawing away at me. The knowledge that by just one letter he might have given me weeks of happiness made me furious with him. All that we had done together apparently counted for nothing compared with his disappointment in me. I was as bewildered now as I had been when he first locked the library door against me. He despised conventional religion so why did he hate me simply for getting the usual order of marriage and conception wrong? My waist narrowed by the month as I grew thin with confusion and by autumn the pink dress had so many darts in the bodice that Sarah scolded me. 'You don't eat,' she said.

'I'm not often hungry.'

'You should eat. And you should carve. A woman should be proud to carve at her own table.'

'I don't know how.'

'I could teach you,' she said. 'I have watched enough ladies in my time.'

I put my hand on her wrist. My fingers were long, bony and scarred by too many encounters with acids and sparks; hers were small, well-formed, white. 'What else should I do?' I asked.

'How do you mean?'

'As a lady. What else should I do?'

'To be a proper wife you mean?' She withdrew her hand. I had been teasing her but she was in deadly earnest. 'You should take an interest. We should go out to the Old Exchange to buy fans and ribbons. We should be walking in St James's Park. We should go to concerts and plays and card parties. We should not be forever waiting for him.'

'I don't want to go anywhere without my husband.'

'Surely, Madam, it's clear to you that husbands and wives are not always seen together.'

She spoke coldly, as if she despised my lack of knowledge. And perhaps, I thought, as I sent her away, one of the things a lady should not do is ask her maid for advice, perhaps that's yet another mistake.

2

On the first day of January 1727 I dreamed I was lying on my mother's bed, so heavily pregnant that I couldn't get up to close the window though leaves were blowing in from outside. When I woke my first feeling was of overwhelming grief for the miscarried child, then disappointment that I wasn't at Selden after all. I nudged Aislabie awake and told him that I had to go home.

He nuzzled against me sleepily. 'Then you shall.'

'Will you come with me?'

'Would love to, Em, but can't leave business just now. Delicate stage. I have found a ship called *Flora* – wonderful little frigate going cheap because her owner's finances have come adrift. But don't let me stop you going.'

'Will you take me to see *Flora* first?'

'Nothing to look at yet, sails in shreds, masts broken, a rotten little hull, but just wait 'til we get her under way. She'll be a beauty. My God she'll be halfway round the world and back before the rest have left port.' I loved his exuberance and sudden enthusiasms. His capacity for delight was completely alien to my cautious Selden bones. 'Take Sarah with you to Selden. You'll be safe enough with her. All mouth and nails, it seems to me, that girl.'

'Sarah will hate Selden. I don't think she's ever set foot outside the city.'

'It's not Sarah's job to have feelings. She's your maid.'

'But she makes me feel awkward, as if she is doing me a favour by looking after me.'

'That's the way of London maids. They know that good servants are hard to come by so they give themselves airs. It is for you to impose discipline. What you order is what will happen. If she doesn't like it, she's free to leave. But she won't leave.'

For a moment I contemplated life without Sarah. My feelings about her were very mixed. On one hand she was a constant reminder of my shortcomings as a fashionable lady, on the other she smoothed my path and unravelled the mysteries of London life. And anyway I need not have worried. When next I saw her my husband had already spoken to her and though she made it clear by the set of her mouth that she hated the idea of leaving town, she said not a word in protest. So the trunks were packed and sent ahead, and a boat ordered to take us to Selden, much safer and quicker than by road at that time of year. I didn't give my father notice in case he ordered me to stay away.

3

Two days later we set out, rowed by a couple of boatmen hired by Aislabie who must have tamed them with threats or bribes because they hardly spoke a word all the weary journey home. Sarah and I sat at either end of the boat, I in my velvet mantle, she in grey wool. At first she stared longingly over my shoulder, then shrank down in the shelter of her hood. Her stormy face made it quite plain that she would rather be anywhere else but in that boat with me and once I thought I saw a tear welling in her eye.

London from the river was a much more manageable city than London from the streets and we slid through it as easily as rats in a gully. The river traffic soon thinned, as did the number of buildings clustered on the bank. Then there were only winter trees and bedraggled reeds, the bare earth of ploughed fields, the great houses of the rich and the little villages huddled up tight for winter. We spent the night in the inn at Chertsey but I was so chock-full of fear and anticipation I could neither sleep nor eat.

Next morning as we rowed further upstream the river narrowed, the bones of the countryside pressed in on us and the sky sank closer until our boat was the blade of a knife slitting the river from the clouds. Behind us the two closed up like mercury. And now the banks were heavily wooded and so quiet that if a bird moved even so much as a claw a branch cracked and my heart leapt. He was there. I strained my eyes to see between the trees. Was that him, with his hat pulled far down and his coat trailing? If he saw me he would surely raise his staff in welcome and a joyful spark would gleam in his eye.

It was dusk when we drew near Selden. Mist shrouded the boat and stifled the dipping oars. The quiet was shocking after the racket of London. The boat coiled to the right, the boatman leapt ashore and with a creak of his leather breeches and a twist of the rope bound us tight. He put out his bare hand, I took it in my gloved one and sprang out. My foot in its silver-buckled boot ached with recognition of the boards on the jetty. I looked down at the slick water and quivered like a cat.

The only sign of the inn at Lower Selden which lay a couple of hundred yards away was a faint glow of rush-light and a drift of smoke. I gave the boatmen a purse of money and told them I would send Gill for the boxes in the morning. Then Sarah and I began the long walk through the woods to the house. She kept close to my shoulder as we went deeper into the trees and the darkness fell. I knew every inch of these woods, even in the dark. Under that oak my father and I had studied a clump of mushrooms and here was the split ash tree where Aislabie used to tether his horse. Sarah was so close that sometimes she trod on my hem. The tables had turned. If I left her alone she would be utterly lost, just as I was lost in her talk of fashion, gowns, manners, shows and shops.

At last, when I saw a glimmer of light through the trees, I could no longer stand her dragging presence. 'Follow at your own pace,' I said. 'See the light? Keep to the left of the house and you'll find a door leading to the kitchen.'

I plunged away through the trees. At first I blundered from trunk to trunk but I soon grew more sure of myself and headed in a straight line towards Selden, breaking the silence with the gush of my skirts and the crushing of leaves, my stride so long and fast that my petticoats couldn't keep up and got tangled with my knees. I was a kind of dervish, mixed up in my silks with no form of my own.

A lighter shade of grey marked the edge of the woods and I came out on the lower lawn. Above me sprawled the house with candles lit in one window, the rest dark. I paused. Now that I was here the house seemed neutral, neither welcoming nor resisting, exactly as in the past. Suddenly I was a girl again, late home after a long walk in the woods. My father would be waiting for me in the library. Up I climbed past the sunken garden and the rose garden with my skirts slipping over worn steps and the ends of my veil flying. Faster and faster I went until my silks fled from me like sails and the skeletal rose bushes floated by as vapour.

On the terrace I turned sharply to the left, dodged round the side of the house and entered by the door leading to the kitchen passage. The smell of the house was exactly as before. My father. Chemical, pungent, old. I picked up a candle left burning in a bracket by the door, crept past the kitchen where someone clashed a pan on to the hearth and entered the screens passage. The blank eyes of my ancestors urged me across the hall to the library, which was in darkness. He must be in the laboratory. I put my candle on the floor and pulled back the curtain. The door was locked. I tried the latch twice, then threw my shoulder against it and hammered on the door: 'Father. Father.'

We kept spare keys behind a volume of Democritus so I climbed on a stool, pulled out the book, found the key, inserted it into the latch and opened first the outer, then the inner door. The room was empty and unlit. 'Father,' I called and this time was answered by a shuffling behind the door that led to the cellars: Gill holding a lantern. He was much bulkier than I remembered with bags of flesh under his staring eyes.

'Where's my father?' I didn't wait for a reply but ran through the library to the hall, shielding my candle from the draught and taking the stairs two at a time. Though Mrs Gill called my name I didn't stop but went on up to his room which was also in darkness, very austere with bare boards and uncurtained windows, a whiff of old man's sweat in the air and everything in place: wig-stand, brushes, books. 'Father.'

I was drowning. The water was almost over my head but I went on running along passages and stairs to my own bed-chamber, back to the landing, down to the entrance hall again, and there was Mrs Gill with Sarah hanging back, white-faced. They had lit half a dozen candles that dazzled me.

Mrs Gill had aged and her brow was now bare as a puffball right up to the edge of her cap. 'Where's my father?' I cried.

'Emilie . . .' I was ready to run again but she took hold of my arm. Her eyes were full of sorrow. 'My dearest Emilie.' This was an outrage – she never called me dearest. When she tried to hug me I held her off. 'Your father is dead.'

I wrenched away and headed for the library past Sarah whose head was down and face hidden. Mrs Gill followed me. 'He died on the last day of the year. He'd been ill for some time of a disease that affected his lungs. We buried him two days ago.'

I could have struck her for being so ponderous and stupid. 'I would have been told,' I said.

'No. Your father was very insistent. He said Reverend Shales wasn't to write until after the burial.'

'Father hated Reverend Shales.'

'Not at the end. The rector came often.' Something had happened to Mrs Gill's face. It was blurred and wet. We stared at each other. There was a rushing in my head and I thought I'd faint so I walked away very straight-backed, got myself into the laboratory, set my candle down and locked the doors.

Smell first. The smell had changed, the brew not nearly as rich as before. Old wood, yes, alcohol, a hint of sulphur, but a softness in the air of too much dust. And then silence, not even the stirring of a mouse in straw or the ticking of a clock.

My candle reflected on the smeared surface of a flask. When I moved light fell on a disorderly bookshelf, an empty cage, the mouth of our smallest furnace, my father's desk, which looked as if its surface had been stirred with a giant ladle; notebooks left open, the inkstand rusty with dried ink, books piled up anyhow, the contents of his tobacco pouch spilling on to the floor. On the nearby workbench a pestle was stuck into some dried-up substance, there was a powdering of spilt crystals, bottles were unstoppered and instruments dirty.

'Father.' My voice was faint. I sniffed the contents of the mortar. Clay, hard and useless, mixed with a black powder which was in fact hair cuttings, the clay I had used on the day Aislabie came to Selden. I crossed to the window. More glass, two flasks, one inverted over the other containing a dead rose.

'Father.'

I blundered back across the room and looked at the writing in his notebook: uneven, spidery, no attention to straight lines. He had written the same title over and over again with different dates attached, the last *18 September 1726. Palingenesis.* And above that *3 August 1726. Palingenesis. 9 June 1726. Palingenesis.* In the book beneath I found a little more coherence: *4 October 1725. Palingenesis. To begin with the purification of our instruments, and the grinding . . .'* The alchemical process, as regular to me as the coming of snowdrops in spring, was set out in precise detail; observations, repetitions, explanations. But the last date with any detailed notes attached was March 1726, then the new notebook and a new title.

My father never wasted paper. Every sheet he wrote was covered in minute script, both sides. Not these.

My own desk was completely bare. Where were my things? I opened drawer after drawer, tearing my nails in my frantic rush. Where were they, my treasures bought for me by my father? I found them at last buried under a pile of papers and pulled them out one by one: the prism so I could see for myself how Sir Isaac had split light, the magnifying lens, my collection of rocks, my piece of obsidian. My foot hit something that rolled backwards and went on swaying from side to side, metal on wood, his staff with its heavy brass knob at one end and casing to protect the tip at the other. Never in my life had I seen my father stray more than a foot or two from this staff. My hand closed over its globed handle and my shadow flew up the wall, flickered along the shelves of bottles, the balances, notebooks, globe, clock and hourglass.

The house enclosed me: the attics, the labyrinthine cellars, the kitchens, dairy, furnace shed, stables and gardens. I clutched the staff tight to my breast and rested my chin on its handle.

The planet turned.

Sir Isaac N.'s law of inertia. Things will go on moving unless prevented by an opposing force. Death, in this case.

4

When I went upstairs at last Sarah was waiting for me. She'd lit a row of candles and a blazing fire, unheard of in a bedchamber at Selden. After she'd undressed me she fussed with the sheets, brushed my hair for five minutes, then sat in a corner and fiddled with the laces on my stays.

'Have you found somewhere to sleep, Sarah?'

'In here with you, since you've had bad news.' I thought this show of concern was in part due to her terror of the profound darkness beyond my room. To get rid of her I blew out every candle except one which I thrust into her hand, then showed her the room next door which Mrs Gill had used when I was a child.

After she'd gone I lay in my old bed and watched the cushiony shadows cast by the firelight. At first I heard her creep about, then, when she was settled, a shifting and cracking of boards as the house rearranged itself. From somewhere deep in the woods came the screech of an owl.

Hush, Emilie, hush. There is no great change after all. I strained to see into the night sky beyond the lattice. Where was the girl I had left behind at Selden? Just out of reach – I had heard her rustle and sigh as I picked up my father's staff. She circled the house in her stiff linen apron, sniffed a dribble of sap from a yew tree and tasted its sweetness, stared at the moon and plotted the stars. Her hands trailed the river bed and picked up fistfuls of mossy stones.

Emilie Selden, natural philosopher and alchemist.
Where are you now?

5

Gill must have driven early to Lower Selden and fetched our boxes because in the morning Sarah brought me chocolate, a substance unheard of at Selden. I was full of determination. It had occurred to me that the person to blame for my father's disappearance was Reverend Shales, who had taken it upon himself to bury him without permission. Such highhandedness could not be allowed. If I confronted Shales the past would surely unravel and my father come back.

Sarah laid out a plain gown and worsted stockings. 'No, silk,' I said. 'I am paying a call today.' I would give Reverend Shales a dose of London finery. In my black-work bodice, white quilted petticoats, veil and glazed kid gloves I would descend upon him like an avenging angel.

While Sarah dressed my hair I risked a glance at her face in the mirror. Her brows were drawn together and her teeth clenched so I took pity on her and said, 'You can come with me if you like. It's up to you.'

'Whatever you want, Madam.'

How did she manage to make even the simplest phrase so insolent? Nothing on earth, she seemed to suggest, would please me less than a walk with you. 'I shall be perfectly all right on my own, if you prefer to stay here,' I said weakly.

'Then I'll stay.'

There was a maid in the scullery, one of the blacksmith's daughters. 'What is your name?' I asked.

She stared at me with rabbity eyes. 'Annie.'

'Annie. Do you know Reverend Shales?'

She nodded.

'I assume he'll be at home in the rectory?'

She gaped until I walked away. 'No,' she called after me. 'Then where?'

'He don't choose to live at the rectory. He chooses to live at the church cottage in Lower Selden.'

'What on earth for?'

She went on gaping. Curse the man, I thought, and set out across the stable yard and through the bee orchard where mortar crumbled from the walls and the trees were crooked and bare. I didn't pause to look at the beehives or remember what had happened there. I held it all at bay.

6

My father owned the living of two parishes, Lower Selden on the other side of the river and Selden Wick, the cluster of cottages, rectory and church built up close to the manor. Reverend Shales for some reason had not chosen to live in the comfortable modern house in Selden Wick but had settled instead for the ancient church cottage at Lower Selden, a three-mile walk through the woods and across the river. My gown had a short train, ideal for cutting a swathe in a crowded salon but hopeless in a swampy lane, and my boots were designed for brief strolls across London cobbles. The sky oozed and branches dripped in the morning thaw. Gill's cart had worn deep ruts, which were so filled with water I was often calf deep.

I slowed down. I couldn't help it. Where a pool had collected in a felled tree trunk I leaned forward, lifted my veil, touched the water with my tongue and watched a little creature flit across its surface. If you don't look up, Emilie, Father will surely come treading carefully along the track, take a test tube from his coat pocket and capture some of these water insects to study under the microscope.

Mrs Gill said he had a disease of the lungs but hadn't she noticed that his breathing was always laboured – probably because he sniffed and tasted chemicals with a reckless disregard for what Von Helmont called 'gas' released by their interaction with each other? Perhaps in the end he got so ill that every breath was a struggle until his lungs collapsed altogether. I knew what that must have been like. We had experimented on the lungs of a live dog by tying it down and cutting open its windpipe just below the thorax because we wanted to try the effect of different types of air, first by allowing it to breathe only its own expired air caught in a bladder, then by driving fresh air into it through a tube. I had seen the light come and go in the dog's eyes, the inflation and deflation of its abdomen as it gasped for breath, the failure of its pulse whenever we stopped blowing in the clean air. Then it lay quietly, concentrating on each next breath.

Finally my father had demonstrated what happened when a creature drowned. He trickled water into the tube and filled the dog's lungs until it choked. Death came too quickly for us to rescue it, though my father had wanted to pump out the water and try to recover the dog with a different type of air, possibly the fumes produced by burning brimstone.

These memories of the dog's suffering and our frantic efforts to revive it worked me into a fury. Had I been told my father was ill I would have made him recover. This was all Shales's fault.

I stopped on the bridge and looked down at the empty jetty. Our boat had gone. Yesterday when I stepped ashore I was full of hope and fear, now I was scrambling to undo the past. Don't look there, I thought. Concentrate on Shales. He is the cause.

A lane ran up the main street to his house opposite the church. Heaps of grit had blown into the corners of well-worn steps. I lifted the knocker and tapped sharply. Nobody answered. Across the lane a steep bank supported the graveyard. The church was squat, had no tower and the flags inside were so uneven that during a sermon the congregation slid together along the tilting pews. Shales must have a sort of pretend humility, a desire to lower himself in order to seem more pious. After all he might have lived, like all rectors before him, in the shadow of St M. and St E., Selden Wick, a proper church with stained glass, a ring of bells and a spire.

I was about to tap sharply on the window when the door was flung open by a bleary-eyed servant.

'I want to speak to Reverend Shales. I'm Mrs Aislabie.'

'Step in.'

The doorway wasn't wide enough for my hoop. She showed me into a room so small that I stood crushed against the wall by the volume of my own clothes and for a moment surprise made me forget why I was there.

Every available inch was filled with instruments: a barometer, a globe, an armillary sphere to demonstrate the Copernican system by which the planets revolve round the sun in circles, an air pump, a microscope and a telescope. On the table in the centre was an orrery, a model of the sun and planets supported by wires with a mechanism underneath to turn each in its individual orbit. The machine had been made by a true craftsman, every tiny part polished and balanced to perfection. The beams of light cast by these instruments – brass, glass, varnish – shone dimly through my veil and for a moment it was as if I had entered a pod of my childhood: the stillness of the air, the fragility of precious things, a web of ideas interlocked by steel wires of learning and experiment, the presence of my father like a flashing blade at rest one minute, lethally aroused the next.

'Mrs Aislabie.'

I turned abruptly. Shales was in the doorway, his head on one side to avoid the lintel. We stared at each other. I was conscious that the last time I saw him was when I had run in from the garden all damp with heat and desire after an afternoon with Aislabie. I had forgotten the peculiar intensity of his eyes.

'I had not expected you yet,' he said.

'Yet?'

'I wrote two days ago and here you are already.'

'I didn't get a letter. I came because I had heard nothing from my father. In the end I couldn't bear the silence.'

The maid popped her head up behind him in an effort to see what was going on while he peered into my face, trying to penetrate my veil. At last he remembered his manners. 'Please, Emilie . . . Mrs Aislabie, won't you sit down,' and backed into his study, trampling the maid. He ordered tea and I squeezed myself and my skirts into yet another little room while the maid went out and closed the door.

He drew up a chair for me near the hearth but I wouldn't sit down. I thought I must stay in charge and quickly get what I'd come for – an admission of guilt – so I intended to keep my face covered, rap out a few questions and leave. But I was already thrown off balance by what I had seen in the other room, by his courtesy and the unexpected ordering of tea. After the horror of the previous evening the sudden tranquillity of this study was shocking and I had such a longing to weep that I drew breath sharply and allowed myself to be distracted by what was on the desk: an arrangement of retort and receiving flask, an open ledger, a candle. I threw back my veil for a better look and had a sudden whiff of hot wax and fermentation, saw the lovely gleam of polished glass, the invitation of blank paper. In all my months in London I had not been so homesick as in that moment.

'I have been heating plant matter – in this case peas – to see how much air is produced. I measure the liquid in the tube over a number of days,' he said.

I moved round the desk to look at his meticulous measurements, every six hours over four days. There were thread markings on the tube to show how the water had been forced down. The neatness of the experiment and his records, the measured ticking of his clock, the soft fall of a coal in the hearth opened a wound in me.

'I have repeated the experiment several times with different plant matter. I can show you my findings if you like.'

'What do you do with the air once you have collected it?' I asked.

There was a pause and I glanced up impatiently. He was gazing down at my face with the same expression I had noticed in church when he lifted the host – absorption, fascination even. 'Well?' I demanded.

'Well, I shall release it.'

'What a waste.'

'What would you suggest I do, Mrs Aislabie?'

But I had remembered why I was here and would not be drawn into a conversation about airs so I sat down in his chair behind the desk, folded my hands and tried to stop my gaze straying back to the retort.

He arranged the other chair so he could face me. 'I'm sorry your father is dead,' he said.

'Why didn't you write to me?'

'Your father ordered me not to.'

'Why? Why would he do such a thing?'

'I can't say.'

'Didn't you try to make him change his mind?'

'I did.'

The door burst open and in came the maid with the tea tray resting on her bosom. The room was so small that her skirts flurried the flames in the hearth and the candle almost blew out. She stooped down with a lot of huffing and puffing, poured us each a cup and then disappeared, somewhat reluctantly. The quiet came back and I thought: I must sort this out quickly before I lose control of my voice. 'Did he not mention me at all before he died?'

'Yes. He spoke about you.'

'What did he say?'

'I'm very sorry that I can't tell you. We talked in the absolute confidence of a dying man to his priest.'

'My father was not religious. What did he care for priests?'

'Nothing in the conventional sense, I'm sure. No. But he was suffering and very sad.'

I got up so violently that my hand knocked over the dainty teacup, breaking its handle and spilling tea on the desk. 'I wrote to him month after month and he never replied. It was his choice to suffer.'

'He never mentioned to me that you wrote to him.'

'Would it have made a difference? Was the reason you didn't tell me about his illness that you thought I deserved punishment for not being a dutiful daughter?'

'I was carrying out his wishes. Of course I tried to persuade him to let me write. On the occasions when I visited London I wanted to call on you but felt I would be breaking my word. He was very sick for quite a long time. Do you remember how we had quarrelled about alchemy? I think he would not have allowed me back into his study if he weren't desperate. We spent a great deal of time discussing phlogiston, which interested us both for different reasons, him because of his observations on fire, me because of what I had discovered about air. But although we grew quite used to each other in the end, when it came to persuading him to send for you he wouldn't listen and became so agitated I stopped trying.'

'Then you did wrong. You should have convinced him to see me. What could be more important?'

He was silent for a moment. Then he said in the same measured voice, but softly, 'I thought it most important to give what little comfort I could to a dying man.'

'I wonder how you managed that, Mr Shales. I hope you didn't pray over him. He hated prayer.'

'No, I knew better than that. I read to him. I had a book by Sir Thomas Browne that he coveted. It became a little joke between us that I possessed that book and he didn't.'

'Did you talk about anything else? Did you talk about my mother?'

Another pause. 'We did.'

'What did he say?'

Silence. He picked up his pen and pressed it into the blotter. I nearly snatched it from his hand to stop him damaging the nib. He was pale and his lips were compressed. I knew it was no use arguing with him.

'Mistress Aislabie . . .'

'You won't tell me.'

'I can't.'

'Did you ever talk about alchemy?'

Shales put his hand to the back of his head and patted his wig as if arranging his thoughts in better order. All the time he watched me closely, perhaps wary of my next outburst, and I didn't take my eyes off his face because I wanted to pounce the moment I saw weakness. 'We talked about alchemy. Yes.' Silence. Another long look at me. A deep sigh. 'He was a very disappointed man. He felt that alchemy had failed him in the end. He could get nowhere with his project on regeneration though he had spent his last year on it. He seemed very bitter and afraid that he had been pursuing a futile dream.'

'I'm sure you were happy to agree with him, given your views on alchemy.'

'I was not happy at all. I would have given a great deal to have seen the old man satisfied with his life's work. I tried to persuade him that many of his more fruitful investigations, into dyes and phlogiston for instance, had emerged through his alchemical work.'

'Do you believe that?'

'I do in a way. I believe nothing is wasted, that there is no real failure in natural philosophy.'

'But I was a failure. He saw me as something of an experiment and I failed him.'

Another long, considering look. His eyes had grown darker, I noticed, and warmer. 'Mrs Aislabie, I think he believed that it was he who failed in his proper understanding of you.'

'I know I failed him. He used to write me down each night in his notebook. He wanted to see if a girl was capable of learning but I proved as weak as all the rest. So yes, I failed him. I'm sure that's what he told you.'

Silence.

'Did he show you the notebooks?'

He shook his head.

And it was in that silence, broken by the faintest shuffling of coals and the song of a thrush on a branch outside, that the truth of my father's death struck me. I felt it like a hollowing out, an absence of hope, an ending made a thousand times worse because I hadn't been there. I thought of the dust falling and falling on the glass containing the dead rose, my father's abandoned staff, his coat on the hook behind the door. 'Have you any idea how it felt for me to come home and find him gone?' I cried. 'I wonder when you would have written to me. After a month, a year, never?'

'As I said, I wrote two days after the burial, as instructed.'

'Mr Shales, I loved my father. You can have no idea how much. If you had an ounce of humanity you would have thought not only of him but of me. I know him. He was rigid. He wouldn't know how to change his mind but if I could have seen him we might have been reconciled.'

'I thought about all that. But I reasoned that he might have ended up forgiving neither of us, and then he'd have been left with no one.'

'You reasoned. But what did your heart tell you, Mr Shales, if you have one? If you had ever lost someone without any opportunity to say goodbye or to ask for forgiveness you would never have treated me like this.'

I didn't look up to see his reaction, though I think he covered his face with his hand. I twitched my veil over my face and said fiercely, 'Were you there when he died?'

'We all were. The Gills and me.'

'Tell me how he died.'

'He stopped breathing. After each breath there was a silence and then he simply failed to draw another breath.'

'Did you pray over him then?'

'We did.'

I imagined the sheet drawn up over my father's beaked nose, the flesh tight on his little bones, and to escape these images I got myself round the desk and walked into the hall. With my hand on the latch I said, 'Why are you living in this ridiculous house when there is a spacious rectory at Selden Wick?'

'My curate has six children. I thought his need for space was greater than mine.'

'Well, I think you are a fraud, Mr Shales, when you claim to be a natural philosopher. You know nothing about the experimental method. You're wasting your time with those plants and that apparatus.'

'I hope not. It has taken me months to perfect. I am simply trying to measure the quantities of air generated by distillation of plant matter.'

'And you are going to do nothing with the air you have collected in the tube?'

'I have no further use for it but if you have a suggestion I'd love to hear it. Please stay and drink some tea, or let me accompany you home.' He had followed me and I was conscious that he was struggling to find some word or gesture that might comfort me but I swept up my filthy skirts, got out on to the step and slammed the door shut behind me.

A flurry of icy wind blew me away down the street, back across the river and into the woods. And behind every tree, at every twist in the path I looked for my father. Only yesterday his living self, his beating heart, his resentment, rage and cruel exclusion had been the truest part of me.

7

When I got back to Selden I locked myself in the laboratory, mixed some ink, sharpened a quill and wrote to Aislabie that my father was dead. There was nothing else to do. Nothing happened. No one came. No clock ticked.

I waited for some other feeling to strike me than this absence of feeling. Nothing. Then I thought of my mother and how my father had given all her belongings to the fire after she died. Should I do that with his things?

The laboratory was cold and dark. It never used to be but now it was. I went to the window and flung back the shutters one after another until the room was revealed in all its complicated vastness. Then I sank down on the window seat. Everything was wrong. The laboratory had been the hub of my universe, its wheels turned by fire and water, the instruction of our notebooks, the recording of our processes. I had indexed and labelled its contents myself because my father, fanatical about order and economy, depended on being able to put his hand on a book, a substance, a crucible, the instant he needed it. And every instrument had to be maintained to a perfect level of utility: scales balanced, chisels polished, irons scrubbed clear of rust, chemicals redated and replenished. Even while the hedges on our land were broken and our roses mildewed our laboratory had remained airy, well-oiled, constant. But now the room was furred by a kind of violent neglect.

Next to my hand was the rose. I held it up to the light. Its desiccated leaves rattled faintly against the glass and its petals had only a ghostly tinge of pink. I saw how roughly the flasks had been sealed, quite unlike my usual neat work. What a frenzy I'd been in that day when Aislabie came.

The thought of my energetic husband revived me somewhat. When he got my letter he would come and take possession of both me and Selden. Thank God for Aislabie.

I turned the glass roughly in my hands. After all it was only a long-dead flower plucked at the command of an arrogant old man who believed he could find the secret to immortality. What right had he to inflict such pain on me? I drew back my hand and hurled the flasks the length of the laboratory where they smashed against the wall and showered themselves in a million splinters.

The door to the cellar flew open and in came Gill, blank-eyed with consternation as the breaking of glass rang on and on. It occurred to me that since my father's death he must have suffered too, like a drone without a hive. I pointed to my desk: 'That letter is to be sent to my husband.' For a moment he didn't move except for a clenching and unclenching of his thick fingers. Then he blew a long gust of air and crossed the room, his feet soundless as ever, though he walked from the hip because his knees had long since ceased to bend. 'Why is this place so dirty?' I demanded.

He looked sideways at the shattered glass but said nothing.

'Well?' I shrieked. 'The fire hasn't been lit for months. He must have been so cold.'

He picked up the letter and hung his head. 'He locked me out.'

'It was your job to keep him warm.'

'Shall I be lighting you a fire then?'

'No, no fire.' And then, as he moved towards the cellar I asked, 'Gill, where are my father's notebooks?'

'On his desk and shelves.'

'Not those. The other notebooks he kept at night.'

He looked round blindly, like the mole that he was. 'I said. They'll be on his desk.'

'No, no, the others.' But he had disappeared on to the dark staircase.

8

I sat in front of a plate of supper in the kitchen where flames roared in the hearth and not a pan, ladle or dish had altered. Mrs Gill stared at me from her gooseberry eyes. 'You are grown so thin and grand I would scarce have known you.' I laid my arms along the surface of the table and put my head down, sniffing the grain for the faint smell of flour and onions, connecting my cheekbone to the ancient wood. After a moment her hand fell on my neck and she spoke more gently than I had ever known. 'He never stopped punishing us for not keeping more of an eye on you that summer. It was not just you that had to suffer.'

'I was determined to be with Aislabie. It wasn't your fault.'

'He thought so. He would scarcely speak to me until he was at his very last breath.'

'What did he say then?'

'I could hardly hear. I think he thanked me for my care of him.'

'Did he talk about me?'

'Ah yes. He was sorry you had lost that child.'

'Did he say that?'

'He did. Most unfortunate, he said.'

'Did he talk about my mother?'

'No, his thoughts were on you.'

'Did he give you the notebooks he kept about me?'

'I know nothing about those. He spoke most to Reverend Shales.'

'I went to see Shales and told him he took too much on himself. He should have written to me.'

'Your father wouldn't have it.'

'Shales should have guided him.'

'Your father was so sick, Emilie, the smallest upset had him failing and choking. Reverend Shales was very patient sitting up with him night after night, reading. I think he brought some comfort.'

'He seems a cold man.'

'It's not how it appears to the village. They like him. And he has their pity because he had a wife who died in the year before he came to Selden. He's always courteous to me and when I've seen him with a sick mother or baby he's been very kind and appropriate.'

It had not occurred to me that Shales might have a history. I closed my eyes, ground my cheek against the table and thought I'd stay there for ever.

9

B ut I was alive and had to pass the time so I roamed the house looking for distraction. My father's notebooks became something of an obsession. They at least would bring him back to me in some form. I couldn't find them in the laboratory or library, though I unlocked every cupboard and searched each shelf. Next I crept up to his bedchamber where I opened every shut chest and drawer but found no books.

When I visited this room as a child to fetch his spectacles or handkerchief I took a deep breath and dashed in and out, afraid of glimpsing something too intimate. Now that he was gone I realised that what I had feared was the unknown in my father. In the laboratory I saw the natural philosopher, alchemist and teacher who at night presumably removed his wig and outer garments and slept for a few hours on this bed. But there must have been a different man altogether once, although I simply could not imagine him losing himself in a woman as Aislabie did in me. I couldn't imagine him in a moment of abandon.

There was no sign of the notebooks. It was quite possible he had burnt them before he died. Though I didn't give up looking for them my search lost momentum for the time being. Then I had nothing else to do. In my own room Sarah sat like a pink and white spider repairing my clothes. She got up and curtsied but I was too weak to drive her away and claim the space for my own use. The wintry gardens meant nothing because there were no lessons to learn and no collections to be made. Once I went up to my mother's room but when I reached the door I didn't have the heart to press down the latch. Inside would be nothing but emptiness, the old absence. And last time I lay on her bed with the child growing inside me I had been sad and sick and hopeful all at the same time. What richness of emotion that now seemed compared with this horrifying blankness.

In between my ramblings I went back to the laboratory time after time, like a doe I had once watched from my oak tree, grieving her dead fawn. She had recoiled in terror, then gone back to sniff and paw at the little corpse as if simply by repetition she might bring him back to life. Each time I went there I felt a glimmer of hope that I would find it miraculously restored with my father standing over the furnace and all the clocks ticking.

On my third visit I picked up the rose, intact in its bed of broken glass but light and brittle as burnt parchment. Then I found a long jar with a cork plug, polished it with my petticoat, slid in the rose and replaced it on the windowsill. This small act cheered me a little because at least I had put something back together again, and afterwards I sat in my father's chair by the hearth and dared to hold his staff in my lap. The brass handle was so tarnished I couldn't resist buffing it to a sheen.

A dull knock came from behind the double thickness of the library doors. 'Mrs Aislabie. Emilie. Reverend Shales is here.'

I couldn't face him, had probably behaved badly – I would not have been quite so harsh if I'd known his wife was dead – and I had no idea what to say to him. Shales disturbed me. Perhaps it was that he had been there at the start of palingenesis or that I couldn't forgive him for warning me against Aislabie. Either way, he knew too much.

Mrs Gill rattled the handle, called again, then went away but the incident made me restless. I remembered the atmosphere of purpose and contemplation in Shales's study and here was I in the neglected laboratory, doing nothing. So I got up and wound the clocks. Each had stopped at a different hour and as I had no idea of the real time I left them to march on, one from three thirty-eight, another from five eleven, the third from three minutes past twelve. Suddenly, it seemed, the laboratory hiccuped into life and the old pulse was re-established. Then I took my apron from its hook, fetched Gill's broom from the top of the cellar steps and began to sweep. The restoring of the rose to its glass prison had inspired me. If I could not have my father back, I could at least return the laboratory to a state that would please him. I began with the shards of glass which I heaped together, raising clouds of dust from the cracks in the boards. Then I extended the circle of my sweeping and collected mouse droppings and ash into my pile, tobacco, dead insects, flakes of rust and wood shavings. As I swept I grew more ambitious and went to the kitchen to ask for quantities of hot water, soap, rags, beeswax and vinegar.

Sometimes, when I had raised a lot of dust or made a great deal of noise I held still and listened. In the old days when Gill came to clean the hearth or sweep the floors my father vanished to the library until everything was back to normal. So I leaned on the handle of my broom and peered through the dust cloud, sure that at any moment I'd hear the key in the latch and in he would come with his shuffling gait and his coat-tails pinned up. His staff would tap across the damp floor and his head tilt to one side as his beady glance took in Gill's work and checked that I had performed the tasks he'd set.

I stood waiting for several minutes then moved on to the next cupboard and took down a row of bottles one by one, sniffed their contents, wrote fresh labels, brushed the shelf, busy, busy, until it was time to listen again. And as I cleaned, I searched for the notebooks, testing the boards for a hidden door, a hinge, a cavity. The more I couldn't find them, the more I wanted them.

Chapter Five

PILLARS AND
PORTICOES

I

An affectionate letter arrived from my husband full of sympathy and assurances that he would come to Selden just as soon as he had found a captain for *Flora*. There was no time to lose – she must start paying for herself immediately and would set sail in May. Not much of a refit was needed, just a little carpentry and a few adjustments to the hold. This letter brought Aislabie very close but the thought of his vibrant presence at Selden made me quake; I simply couldn't imagine what it would be like living in these austere rooms with him.

I told Mrs Gill that he had ordered servants to be hired and rooms aired. She said, 'Extra staff will need paying. I hope he knows that,' but I chose to ignore this uncomfortable subject and walked away. 'Reverend Shales called again,' she added. 'He left you this.' There was a book on the table, a brown, leather-bound volume with a slip of paper between the pages. I kept my distance. That book was a reminder of the years I had spent with my father, the life I had not chosen. Besides, the book was from Shales, a peace offering maybe. Well, I wouldn't touch it. I couldn't. It had nothing to do with me.

In any case, the task of restoring the laboratory was vast and all absorbing. I soon grew tired of carrying hot water from the kitchen so I relented and called Gill. He was an expert at making fire and within a few minutes flames were blazing in the hearth. The heat transformed the room: first colour, yellow, blue, orange licking through the tinder, then the smell of sulphur and spirit of salts. After half an hour shadows and light gave the hearth definition and flames licked cleanly under my cauldron of water.

I worked from the outside in, beginning with windows and ceiling. Earwigs, woodlice, beetles scurried from the cornices and my hair was tangled with cobweb. A moth the size of a small bird beat against the window until I released it into the frosty air. Then I took down more and more precious alchemical volumes, dusted the spines and pages and replaced them in order, un-stoppered each bottle, threw away the contents or relabelled it, polished it and returned it to its proper place, cleaned our instru-ments and turned out the drawers of my desk. And all the time I was avoiding the root cause of the mayhem – my father's desk and workbench which I could not bring myself to touch.

2

The house beyond the laboratory was full of strange faces; a maid on her hands and knees brushed the hearth in the great hall and another girl ran up a back staircase with an armful of pressed linen. When I passed the kitchen the blacksmith's daugh-ter was washing windows.

All these girls lived within a few hundred yards of the house and went home at night. Only Sarah stayed. Instead of mixing with the others she lurked in my bedchamber with her back to the door and stitched my father's death into a petticoat, exquisitely quilted and embroidered with black leaves climbing up white satin. She seemed dug in, had already colonised my room and hers by scattering herbs and ribbons, hanging up my clothes, importing rugs from other chambers. It was as if by the ferocious thrusts of her needle she might sew herself into the fabric of the house.

3

After a fortnight or so I heard the commotion of rusty gates scraping on stone which heralded the arrival of my husband. I took off my apron, locked the laboratory doors and ran through the library, the great hall and the kitchen passage. Outside the still room I careered into Mrs Gill who had a jar of pickles clutched to her bosom and together we crossed the grey flag-stones past the distillery to the stable-yard door. A cluster of girls blocked the way, their untidy heads haloed by a shaft of sunlight. Even Sarah was there, arms folded. Whispers and giggles filtered back to me as I stood on tiptoe and saw that my husband had already dismounted. His horse, the chestnut stallion, steamed and bucked while Gill hung on to the reigns. I smelt leather and manure, and glimpsed a metallic flash on my husband's hat.

The girls nudged each other and let me through. Aislabie, in mourning for my father, wore a black coat and brilliant white gloves, and his head was flung back to survey the tottering archway, bowed roof, barley-twist chimneys and wormy timbers of his new possession, Selden Manor. Sunlight gleamed on his throat and the folds of his necktie.

The stable yard had never seen such brilliance. Usually the pace here was slow: a carthorse was led clip-clop across the cobbles, hens pecked between the paving stones, a dairymaid's pattens went tapping from door to door, and water was pumped into a pail with a grind and a gush. Colours were mellow, uneven russet brickwork, cobbles shaded grey on grey, the faded blue of a servant's jerkin.

Time stood still for one beat while my husband's gaze flicked across our faces. When they met mine his eyes were turquoise bright. He smiled – that wicked widening of the mouth, the dinting of the cheek. There was a moment's disjointedness as I left the twilit world of the laboratory behind me and then some-thing inside me that had been out of time clicked into place, my blood leapt with delight and I knew I was very glad to see him.

Selden's new master flung out his right arm and made an expansive gesture with the flat of his hand. 'There will be guests soon,' he told Mrs Gill, who was gawping at him over her jar. 'I have invited two gentlemen to stay.'

The servants trampled each other as he sprang towards us and Sarah slid backwards into shadow. 'Now then, Mrs Aislabie,' he said, pulling off his glove and taking first my knuckle then my palm to his lips, 'show me our kingdom.'

The house was too low for him. He had to duck when he climbed a stair or walked under a beam and quickly grew bored with the chill of unused rooms, with peering through opaque glass at the wintry garden and with asking about some staring ancestor in a painting. Through his eyes I saw how tarnished and broken everything was. In the dining parlour there was a stale smell of a hundred thousand dinners. Chairs sagged, tapestries were faded and a marble bust of Caesar had a chipped nose.

When we came to the library where our marriage negotiations had taken place Aislabie didn't drop my hand but strode about as if claiming every dusty inch. While he was sharply etched in black and white everything else in this room was brown and muted. Our entire library, that vast repository of knowledge, was made finite by his presence: an ancient room filled with unfashionable books.

He threw his cloak over a chair with such force that its weight drove the legs a few inches along the floor. A book lay on the table. Aislabie read the spine with some difficulty: 'Thomas Browne. *Pseudodoxia Epidemica.*' His left eyebrow disappeared into his wig. Then he opened the book and picked up the marker. '*Mrs Aislabie, perhaps this will interest you. T. Shales.* And who is T. Shales?'

'The rector here. A friend of my father's. I believe he spent a great deal of time reading this book to my father before he died.'

I was transfixed by the book which now, perversely, I longed to read but Aislabie dropped it dismissively on to the table. 'I trust Shales's motives are pure. You never know with a clergyman.'

His gaze fixed on the curtain covering the door to the laboratory. He kissed the inside of my wrist and the many textures of him were brought up close: the ripples of his wig, the stubble on his chin, the puckers of velvet on his arm. 'Poor Em. Dearest Em. How have you managed without me?' He smelt of the outdoors, of horseflesh, salt and smoke, and his eyes were very bright as they glanced over my shoulder at the locked door. He kissed me again and stroked the back of my neck with his fingertips until I dipped my fingers between my breasts and took out the key.

He was looking down at me under his eyelids, smiling but inexorable, and I felt a shudder of loss. The laboratory was my dominion and he was going to take it away. Then panic, just for a moment, that it might not have been me that he'd wanted after all, but this. I drew back the curtain, unlocked first the outer then the inner door and stood with my back to the wall to let Aislabie through. He was unusually hesitant. I peeped over his shoulder and saw that although most things were now in order they were also diminished. I thought I had recreated clear, airy spaces but in fact the laboratory was no more than a muddle of crooked cupboards and shelves, piled books and ancient glassware.

He didn't go in, just looked about him. 'Well, you must teach me what all this means.'

'It doesn't mean anything. It's a place of work.'

'Not at all as I expected. I thought it would be mysterious . . . fiery, full of potions and smells.'

'Much of our work was very dull and painstaking.' He began to wander about, pointing to things and asking their purpose. Then he flicked through my father's notebooks and some alchemical texts but they were all in Latin so he drummed his fingers on the pages and after a while looked up and smiled. 'You'll have to translate for me. My Latin is somewhat of the schoolboy variety.'

'If I did, you wouldn't understand. Most of it's in code. It takes decades.'

Next he went to my desk, picked up my prism, squinted first at the fire, then at me before replacing it carefully. When he touched my father's staff I couldn't prevent a hiss of indrawn breath. He glanced at me sideways, gave it a twirl and began a tour of the room, leaning on it from time to time to read the title of a book or the inscription on a bottle even though the staff was too short for him and he had to stretch out his arm to balance himself. For several minutes he rummaged among the contents of the workbench, sniffing and prodding. Finally he touched my chin with the tip of the staff and ran it in a straight line down my neck to the top of my bodice.

I was nervous of him. The light of anticipation had gone from his eye. He was disappointed. 'I'll demonstrate Newton's experiment with light, if you like,' I said shakily but he took the prism from me, held it up to his face and brought his distorted eye close to mine. 'Lovely piece of glass, fine workmanship.' He tossed it from hand to hand, never taking his eyes from my face. I laughed anxiously, fumbling to understand what was happening as he placed it in my palm and pressed my fingers until they were clutched round it and his hand enclosed mine. Was he telling me that he wasn't interested in Newton's experiment with light, that he had no desire to enter my world if all I had to offer was a bit of glass and a candle? But then I became absorbed in the stitching along the neck of his coat and the way the muslin on his cravat was twisted carelessly at the throat and had floating ends falling from a ruby pin, and I thought that after all nothing mattered except that Aislabie was here at Selden.

4

Mrs Gill had prepared Queen Elizabeth's bedchamber by throwing out piles of parchments, a tapestry and a writing desk collected by the ambitious poetic Selden who had never after all received a visit from his monarch. The room was the finest in the house with silk hangings and unblemished oak panelling. Sarah was kneeling over the hearth but when she heard us she stood up and dropped a slow curtsy, bending her slender neck so far forward that I could see soft hairs rising on the nape. She flickered past, leaving behind the habitual after-smell of antagonism.

Aislabie examined with great interest the tasselled canopy over the bed and the screen on which a creamy Diana and her buxom maids bathed after a hunt. He flung open the window and looked out over the terraced gardens and the woods plunging down to the river, then pulled me close, tucked his foot under my hoop, took hold of my face and kissed me until my knees buckled. The episode with the prism still lingered but I dragged at his clothes and covered his skin with kisses. I remembered the heat of our first embrace in the bee orchard, the burning sunlight. How could our lovemaking in the stifling Hanover Street bed be a substitute for this? Here there was no hurry. In this chamber we were a dozen rooms away from the next person and beyond the windows there was only sky and forest. There were no constraints, no eavesdroppers, no events or business to take Aislabie away.

Afterwards we lay topsy-turvy on the bed. He wore one boot and half his breeches. The cold air from the window chilled my breasts. 'Tell me what you have been doing in London all this time,' I whispered.

'Plotting. Spending money. *Flora*'s a demanding mistress. She's proving to be an expensive proposition. And I still haven't paid for the cargo.'

'*Flora*. My rival.'

'*Flora* has half your beauty and no brains at all. But she is glorious. When I sniff the new paint and see her sails unfurled I am dizzy with love.'

'What will she carry?'

He took hold of a tassel from the bed curtains and dabbled it between my legs, watching the silken strands with more concentration than I'd seen him apply to anything else.

'Weapons. Tower guns mostly. Brandy. Rum. Beads. Your mother was a Huguenot, wasn't she? Or so you say. They drive a hard bargain over their amber beads, the Huguenots.'

'Tower guns. Rum. Brandy. A highly combustible cargo, I should say.'

'Precisely so. We'll have to avoid mutiny at all costs, eh, Em? That's the trick. Keep everything shipshape.'

'And organise your cargo carefully.'

'Don't worry your head. There are experts.'

'But I should love to help. I know that extreme agitation can in some cases cause combustion. If enough heat is generated.'

He rubbed his foot along my calf and licked my ear.

'And who will buy this cargo?' I whispered.

'*Flora* will sail to the South Seas. Africa. Calabar.'

Calabar. I gave a mental twirl to the globe in the library and found Calabar on the western coast of Africa. The world opened before Aislabie, easily as a nutshell. I had more questions but he kissed me again, prised my legs apart with his chin and his tongue flickered inside me until the bed was a warm red boat in which I sailed away on wave after wave.

I lay back, sated as a queen bee but Aislabie never stayed in one place for long, even the queen's bed. As he scrambled back into his clothes he said, 'We must keep this room. Imagine the fun we could have with it.'

'Keep?'

'I've got plans for this house, Em. You'll see. Trust me. Wait 'til you meet my friend Harford. The man's a genius. And I tell you what else we'll do. We'll have a party. Let the local gentry know we've arrived.'

'I can't have a party with my father only just dead.'

'Not this minute. For my birthday in May. And yours. People will come in droves at that time of year.'

I saw myself in my green dress floating down the old staircase. The entrance hall was lit by a hundred candles. There would be musicians in the gallery and a host of London people spilling out on to the terraces. Aislabie could perform miracles like this. He could marry the alchemist's daughter and recreate her, just as he could buy an old ship and breathe wind into her tattered sails.

5

Aislabie said books were the thing and he was envious of the hours my father had spent reading in the library. 'Time to read is a luxury I've never yet had,' he said. On his first morning he insisted on taking breakfast there. I knelt at his feet and toasted bread, bemused by this sudden turnabout in the ritual of life at Selden. It didn't seem right to mix the smell of old books with that of hot bread or to be half undressed in my father's library with the scent of lovemaking on my skin.

There was a scurry of footsteps and Annie appeared, inarticulate with the responsibility of showing in our first guest, Reverend Shales, who had mud clinging to his boots, a black stock at his throat and a cloak slung over his arm which she ought to have taken. I tripped over my skirts as I stood up, my lips swollen with early morning kisses and my cheeks hot with firelight.

Bows and introductions were exchanged, coffee offered and refused, then I sat primly on a hard chair by the window with my hands folded, wishing that my hair were not loose on my shoulders. Shales took the chair on the other side of the hearth. I knew that he must have spent a great deal of time here with my father and I was acutely aware of being caught out. This used to be a place of measured silences devoted to learning, my father's own space in which I was always a visitor. It was as if Aislabie and I had desecrated a hallowed shrine.

Both men were looking at me. My husband was sprawled with one leg outstretched, wigless, a satin morning robe loosely tied and his chest bare. Shales, in his dark clothes, sat slightly forward with one arm hooked over the back of the chair. I clutched the sides of my robe together and pushed my tumbled hair behind my shoulders.

Aislabie took a mouthful of coffee, licked butter from his fingers and seemed to be puzzled. 'So, Shales, I believe we may have met before.'

'We did, when you first began to call at Selden.'

'Ah yes. Indeed.' Aislabie pierced another slice of bread and held it to the fire. 'And what unpleasant advice have you come to offer this time?'

'I came simply to welcome you and to ask after Mrs Aislabie.'

'Most kind of you. Mrs Aislabie, as you see, is flourishing.'

They studied me; Aislabie as if he remembered every detail of our lovemaking an hour previously, Shales with his usual grave attention. 'I am well, thank you,' I said, glancing up and meeting his gaze for the first and last time.

Shales crossed his legs. 'Your tenants are eager to welcome you,' he told Aislabie.

'I'm sure they are.'

'The late Sir John gave me authority to experiment with different types of dressing for the soil to help improve yield. I have spent years investigating the nature of plants and how they grow and flourish. I was hoping you would allow me to continue this work.'

'By all means.'

'There is some anxiety among the villagers that a new master will mean higher rents.'

'Good Lord, I've not thought about any of this. I've barely got my feet under the table here.'

'At any rate, we will be delighted to see you both in church.'

Aislabie nodded, pursed his lips and winked at me. I felt the collusion of that wink and wasn't surprised when Shales got up abruptly. 'Thank you for lending me the Sir Thomas Browne,' I said.

'I thought it might be a distraction.'

'I expect you'll be wanting to take it back with you,' put in Aislabie.

'You are welcome to keep it as long as you like.'

'I doubt she'll get much time for reading one way or another,' said Aislabie, kissing my palm and the inside of my elbow. My neck grew hot and I looked studiously into the fire.

Shales picked up the book. 'Good day then, Mrs Aislabie. Sir.'

Aislabie had nudged back my sleeve further and was running his lips up to my shoulder. When Shales had gone he gave a shout of laughter, fell back in my father's chair, pulled me on to his lap and burrowed his hand under my petticoats.

6

Days of intense activity followed. Aislabie in the country was just as restless as Aislabie in town. He had brought a trunk of country gear, drabs, serges, camlets in shades of buff and dark green, wore his wig tied in a queue at the back and strode about in his riding boots. He couldn't be idle, hated not being among his friends, was quickly bored and once bored was off. He had horses and dogs to buy, a carriage to order, local grandees to meet, talked of becoming a magistrate, maybe an MP, and embarked on an extensive survey of the land. I went with him when I could though I didn't know how to ride and the Selden carriage was a cobwebby monstrosity abandoned in one of the stables. But we did whisk on foot through the miry high street of Selden Wick where Aislabie scattered pennies for the children, flashed admiring glances on any woman under thirty, and paused at the forge to talk to the blacksmith and an assortment of his offspring. We were invited to warm ourselves at the raging fire and Aislabie tried to hammer a bit of molten iron. The blacksmith was fearsome, with masses of bristling beard, red skin and huge forearms. I had never seen him deferential, as he was with Aislabie. 'We's hoping for great changes, now you're here, Sir,' he said.

Aislabie pounded the iron until the sparks flew and we laughed at his violence. 'You'll see changes, never fear.'

'The old master tended not to notice us much,' said the blacksmith, nodding apologetically at me.

'Well, he had other things on his mind, I don't doubt.'

'So, we've been looking forward to things getting better,' persisted the blacksmith, tapping shape into the horseshoe and dropping it into a pail of water. 'We've had a hungry winter and the estates are falling apart.'

'Don't you worry. All will be well,' said Aislabie, clapping him on the shoulder and accepting the horseshoe as a gift on my behalf.

I had never looked on the village as a possession before but Aislabie, with the expertise of a farmer's son, pointed out unenclosed common land, wild hedges, derelict barns, fields full of dock and cattle roaming freely until I couldn't help feeling that my father, Gill and I had been guilty of appalling neglect. 'But never mind,' said Aislabie, tossing the horseshoe into a ditch. 'I have plans for Selden.'

7

One morning a mud-spattered carriage arrived and out of it, clutching boxes and books, emerged two gentlemen, Mr Harford, a garden designer, and Mr Osborne, a draughtsman. I was sent away from the library and sat in the kitchen with Mrs Gill who was polishing the cutlery. After half an hour or so I saw their London-shod feet walk past the window.

'I assume you know what they're up to,' said Mrs Gill, although it must have been obvious to her that I didn't. It was her job to brush the knives with baking soda, mine to buff them with a linen rag.

'Aislabie is full of surprises. It is one of his great gifts.'

'Ah yes. There's no doubt we'll see some changes now. But then as I said to Gill,' she added after a long pause, 'where would we all have been had your Mr Aislabie not come? Your father was bound to die one day.'

Both the fact that any conversation had taken place between husband and wife and its content were so extraordinary that I stopped work. 'And what did Gill say?'

'He said there was no telling.'

'My husband is a good man,' I said. 'He is full of ideas about how to make things better. He will bring new life to Selden.' Silence. One aspect of this new life had already been extinguished. My hands shook. 'Do you think there will ever be another baby, Mrs Gill?'

'There's never any shortage of babies. But it will never be that one, Emilie. There's never any replacing a dead baby and you mustn't expect it.'

'I don't expect it,' I said hastily. 'I never think about it. Aislabie has taught me to look forward, not back.'

8

Late in the afternoon I was summoned to the terrace where a nasty little breeze scraped bits of twig and leaf along the paving stones. The sky was overcast and the only bright thing in sight was my husband who wore apricot breeches and a black waistcoat. Despite the temperature he was in his shirtsleeves. He tucked his arm round my waist and kissed me with a passion that made me blush.

The two other men averted their eyes. They were soberly dressed: one large with a jutting belly, the other too scrawny to fill his dove-grey coat.

'My dear Emilie,' said my husband, 'here are Mr Osborne and Mr Harford. Show Mrs Aislabie your sketches, Osborne.'

'It would be better inside under a strong light,' said Osborne, who looked chilled to the bone.

'No, here, here. She'll have a clear idea if she can look about her and visualise how it will actually be.' My husband rolled the word 'visualise' on his tongue. The wind ruffled his sleeves as he kicked at an uneven paving stone and scraped a smear of lichen with his fingernail. I knew the signs. He was bored with these two.

Mr Osborne darted forward and spread a large sheet of parchment on the low parapet. 'Mrs Aislabie,' he said, 'you are standing here.' He stabbed a manicured finger on to the design, which rolled up abruptly and fell into a bush in a herbaceous bed. Harford went puffing down to retrieve it. A muscle contracted in my husband's arm.

The scroll was again unrolled but this time Harford sat obligingly on one edge while Osborne held the other. I leaned forward and saw a detailed plan, drawn to scale, of the front elevation of a house or temple. The central feature was a colonnaded porch with a square wing on either side. The windows were rectangles divided by twelve panes of glass and on the roof chimneys formed regimented lines. There was even a dome, like a modest St Paul's. 'The dome is still under discussion,' said Osborne.

'I've spoken to Osborne about the Queen's Room,' said my husband. 'It could be preserved in two ways. We could dismantle it completely and reassemble it within the structure of the new house or build a shell round it. Whatever we do we cannot, obviously, spoil the line of Osborne's exterior.' Poor little Osborne looked anxiously into my husband's face to see if he was being mocked.

'What about the library?' I asked.

'All this side of the house,' said my husband, sweeping his hand across the space now occupied by the laboratory, 'will be part of a set of apartments ranged round a central, three-storey hall with a dome and gallery. There will be a library, but much smaller than the present one.' His head was tilted back and he was watching me.

'You mean you will pull the library and laboratory down,' I said.

'Remodel. That's the word.'

'What about the oldest part of the house. Where's that in these plans?'

'I've told you, Em, this will be the new house. All the old ramshackle bits will go. We'll build something modern and symmetrical, not all piecemeal.'

'But this is my home,' I said.

'Our home. Yes. We'll make it better.'

'I was born in one of these rooms. My mother died there.'

'Lord, Em, it's not like you to be so morbid. They're just rooms.'

Harford and Osborne were listening attentively. I couldn't take in what was happening so I hid my face by stooping over the plans again. Osborne had drawn two urns to mark the bottom of twin flights of steps that flew to right and left and back towards the porch. A number of triangles were thereby formed, reflecting the pediments above the porch and windows, and the regular slope of the roof on either side of the dome. In fact, the entire scheme would have made an excellent geometry lesson.

'What will you plant in the urns?' I asked, my voice unsteady with panic.

Osborne smiled politely. My husband pinched my fingers and Harford, who had been peeking eagerly into my face, laughed indulgently. 'You ladies think of every detail. Fortunately, it is my job to know what will grow in the urns, Mrs Aislabie. They will be replanted according to the seasons. In winter, evergreens, perhaps the *Phormium tenax*, and a fall of variegated ivy.'

Aislabie's hand slipped under my cloak, on to my waist and down. 'And now the grounds, Harford.'

Mr Harford, I noted as he began to unroll his plans, had been careless when powdering his wig and had speckled the back of his jacket even though he was better prepared than Mr Osborne and produced metal weights from his pocket to keep his drawing flat.

In Mr Harford's garden design the new house was represented merely as a rectangle with an adjoining set of outbuildings arranged round a central courtyard. By contrast he had drawn the gardens in bewildering detail and his plan was peppered with written explanations in minute script. To the south stretched a park with sloping lawns, artfully placed knots of trees, flowering shrubs and a lake spanned at one end by an Arcadian bridge. 'I don't understand,' I said. 'We have no lake.'

With a flourish Harford produced a brass-tipped pointer. 'If you will allow me, Mrs Aislabie.' His big face came close to mine and his instrument fell upon a tiny circle. When I bent forward my husband's hand darted between my legs. 'Mr Osborne's urn, here, is where you now stand. The lake will be built here. You see the edge of the wood – those birches, the chestnut, the line of oaks. They'll go. This temple will stand to one end, a near exact copy of Palladio's Villa Rotonda near Vicenza.' The Italian names were enunciated with great gusto by Mr Harford. 'If you'd allow me, I'll take you down and show you.'

Aislabie gave my behind a tap. 'I'll see you inside, Harford. Don't you go confusing my wife with too much detail. Broad strokes only.' He sauntered away with Osborne in his wake.

I watched him go, amazed. It could not be true that Selden with its terraces, its bee orchard, library, laboratory and ancient rooms could simply be dismantled. Harford's elbow was held out ready so I took his arm and walked with him to the lower lawn. He moved with exaggerated care as if I might shatter if he hurried. We made our stately way across the sodden grass and came to the edge of the wood where Mr Harford pointed to his brass-buckled shoes. 'Here will be the lake, and here, just about where this hawthorn is, the bridge. From where your husband is standing, Mrs Aislabie, there will be a perfect view of temple, bridge and even a small island.'

I thought my husband had disappeared inside long ago but there he was, his apricot breeches and white sleeves luminous against the dark walls. Then he waved and disappeared.

Mr Harford backed away, gesturing excitedly. He had reached the edge of the wood and entered the trees so that his neckcloth and the fall of lace at his wrists shone eerily in the gloom. 'The temple,' he said, 'will be about here. And behind it a knoll, a few trees, spring flowers. The perfect summer house for the ladies – for all sorts of assignations.' He smiled suggestively.

I moved away, peering up at the manor house through a web of trunks and branches. It sat snug to the side of the valley with its chimneys stacked randomly against a fading sky. I imagined a white mansion floating above me, our impossible terraces smoothed into an expanse of lawn, a glassy lake.

Mr Harford had followed me. 'These thrilling plans are mostly the work of your husband. He has seized the opportunity of having the river so near. Such inspiration. I have simply worked out the mechanics and put it all on paper.'

'You and Mr Osborne have done wonders,' I said, sweeping away up the steps to the house, 'considering you have had so little time.'

Harford panted behind me. 'Certainly we have not been idle although we came prepared – we had been given a sketch of what was required. And as I say, your husband . . . So clear about what he wanted. Do you remember there is a painting in your London residence, a landscape by Lorrain, an idyll of woods, sloping fields, water and human habitation in the classic style? When we saw the lie of the land, the position of the existing house, it all fell into place. I have rarely met a layman with such talent. He will created a French landscape peopled by Englishmen.'

I had reached the parapet where the garden design was still spread out so I was able to trace an avenue of trees stretching from the north of the house to a pair of gates. 'The village of Selden Wick is not marked,' I said.

'Ah.' Mr Harford scooped his weights into his fist, rolled up the parchment with a flourish and tucked it under his arm. 'The village, my dear Mrs Aislabie, will have to go.'

'Go where?'

'Out of sight,' said Mr Harford. 'It's all to do with vistas. I am known for my vistas, Mrs Aislabie. My first aim is to please the eye. When you stand at the window of your new house or take tea in the little temple or stroll across the bridge, you will be delighted by ever-changing but ever-harmonious vistas. No untidy little cottages, no intrusion from the village children.'

'Where will they all go?'

'Your husband has mentioned another village on the estate which might be expanded. Or he's talked of designing a model village. Your husband, Mrs Aislabie, has the mental energy of a truly great man. He sees problems as opportunities. A model village. Just think. Model cottages built to modern specifications. Perfect. Don't worry, Mrs Aislabie. Where there is money, there is always a solution.' He looked keenly into my face, a hint of a question in his voice. Money. Now there was the rub.

'And what of the church?' I asked, thinking of Shales. Perhaps some premonition had made him choose to live in the cottage at Lower Selden rather than the doomed rectory at Selden Wick.

'Churches can be a problem,' admitted Mr Harford. 'There are laws about churches. But this one has an attractive spire. We will plant an arbour and make it a charming feature of our landscape.'

'But how will people come to church if the park gates are kept shut?'

'I expect they can be allowed to enter the park on Sundays,' he said, 'provided they remember to wipe their boots.'

9

When Harford had gone into the house I watched silver clouds close over a marble moon. Behind me the kitchen window was lit by tallow candles and a less smoky light shone from the library and a few lattices on the first floor. I reeled under the fast-moving sky. How had this sudden and extraordinary turn of events come about? Aislabie had married me. Selden belonged to me. I was Selden. Who had given him permission to rip it open and start again?

I had been taught to look for cause and effect. Well, Aislabie had made love to me under the apple tree and now Selden was to be pulled down and a new house built instead. What was the formula that linked these events? I thought it was me, Emilie, but I seemed to have been left out of all the calculations. If only my father would come and give me the answer or show me the right book.

The clouds sped away, the moon showed half its face and the winter trees sighed. I reached with my fingertips and felt the white light ripple on my skin. The terraces beneath me were black as water and an owl undulated overhead.

There was no room for an owl in Harford's design. He had given me a niche in the shade of the temple with my mythical lady friends poised on the banks of the non-existent lake, and Aislabie's place was under the dome, but what about the owl? I saw her again, swooping lower and lower. Some poor creature in the undergrowth must be trying to make itself invisible to those extraordinary eyes.

Cause and effect. I was the cause, this the effect but what was the chemical reaction in the middle? It was a puzzle harder than all the rest. Please, please, please, Father. Tell me. What did I do that was so wrong? In the past you forgave me everything in the end. I only loved Aislabie. I only loved him first and married him second. Was that all it took to make this happen?

No answer. Not a word. No encouraging prod with the staff or instruction to go and look it up, Emilie, plunder the writings of Agricola, Paracelsus or Mayow for answers. Only the soft hooting of the owl. So I thought again. I love Aislabie. I owe him a great deal: knowledge of my body and his, the child . . . The child that came floating to the surface of my mind more and more often these days, despite my efforts to keep the memory down. I couldn't stop myself thinking if only the baby had lived and I had brought it home last summer when my father was still alive. Surely he would have forgiven me and I would have been allowed to look after him, and he would not have died.

But at Selden we never indulged in speculation. A hypothesis only had value if it could be used as a basis for experiment. No experiment that I knew would bring back either the baby or my father.

The moon came fully out. Newton had put that old moon firmly in its place, likewise the earth and other planets. He had found guiding laws for them all. And the wonder was so much was happening at the same time. I used to believe that there was only the laboratory and everything else existed so that Emilie and her father could find an explanation for it. Now I was shrunk to almost nothing by the knowledge that in some stylish London address Newton was coughing himself to death while the earth turned, my father lay in his coffin, Aislabie planned, Sarah sewed and Shales measured his plants.

How small I was. How irrelevant to all these activities.

A small night creature had been caught in its scurry between one sheltering leaf and another. The owl was as delicate in her operations as my father when he dissected a rat. She drew out the creature's entrails in a translucent slide of mucus and tissue. I knew how it felt to be torn open like that.

Sarah had built such a huge fire in my bedchamber that I thought I would faint. She laced me first into the black and white petticoat she'd embroidered for me, then an overskirt of white alamode so gauzy that it floated in the heat. That overskirt was my favourite. My mother, I thought, would have recognised its slight sheen and whisper on the skin.

Sarah breathed heavily as she rubbed colour into my cheeks. 'You are very pale, Madam. Perhaps just a hint of red on your lips?'

'No. Thank you.'

'Mr Aislabie's waiting for you in the library.' She could never speak gently, there was always a layer of aggression in her tone, but as she took strands of hair and wound them in a knot her knuckles brushed my cheeks and she watched her own hands in the mirror until the touch of her skin on mine was almost a caress. I had never known her this distracted. And she smelt different. Her sweet scent masked a change. I looked at her face in the glass and saw that she was biting her lip and her brows were drawn tight together.

'Stand up then, Madam.' Aislabie had brought a mirror from London at Sarah's request and now I could see my reflection much more clearly than ever before at Selden. Yet that night I seemed a ghostly figure in my white gown. Sarah put her arms round my waist and lifted the overskirt so that it puffed up and fell airily back.

'What do you think?' I had never asked this question before and she looked at me with a sudden flash of interest, then studied me with great seriousness in the mirror. Her head was just higher than my shoulder and she was rosy in the firelight. 'I think it will please him,' she said, which I took to be approval.

My white skirts floated up and brushed my elbows as I went downstairs. I skimmed the banister with my thumb, held my body upright and thought that all would be well. I had only to explain my point of view to Aislabie and he would change his mind. I was full of hope as I crossed the entrance hall, the fabric of my skirts flying, my ancestors hidden by the dark.

The library door was wide open and the room lit by a dozen candles so corners that had always been shadowed were now shockingly displayed. The plans for the house and gardens were laid out in a glaring display of new parchment on my father's supper table. Aislabie was pulling books off the shelves and piling them on the floor, sending little clouds of dust into the air. He bounded across and kissed my hands. 'Now, my scholar, you must guide me. Three piles. One to keep. One to sell. One to burn.'

The room smelt of dust and ink and parchment, and I saw not only the living flames in the hearth and the bright colours of Aislabie but the old library where Emilie had knelt beside her father to fill his pipe, scraped her nail on the rough bowl and sniffed the scorched wood on her fingers.

I held tight to my husband's warm hands. 'Burn?'

'We have to start somewhere. This library has too many books. The library in the new house will be much smaller and of course I have books to display – poetry, plays, novels, essays – not to mention my collection of porcelain. There'll be no room for all these.'

'You can't burn our books.' But my voice was insubstantial because I was back inside the nightmare of violent, unthinkable change.

'Well, will they all sell, do you think? What price will they fetch? Maybe we should give them away.' Even at his most tender there was always a hint of amusement and this gleam made him bigger and me smaller, as if he was constantly seeing jokes I was too ignorant to understand.

'You know I couldn't bear to have these books sold.'

'No choice, Em. We have to be practical. Look at the plans.'

'I should like that. I should very much like to look at the plans with you.'

'Of course. What would you like to know?'

'I should like to know why I wasn't consulted about the rebuilding of my own house.'

'You are being consulted. I thought we'd start by seeing what's possible, then you can say whether you like it or not.'

'There are parts of this house that must be kept as they are. The laboratory, the library and the gardens have been stocked by generations of Seldens. And my mother's room in the old wing is all that I have of her.'

He dotted kisses on my temples and cheekbone. 'Now these,

my dear old Em, my alchemical little wife, are the very parts of the house that are the most tumbledown and outdated.'

'Why do you insist on calling me alchemical? I was brought up to be a natural philosopher, a mathematician. My father was an expert on the nature of fire. Don't dismiss my education as if it didn't matter. It does. If you destroy the laboratory and all my books what will be left?'

'You'll be left, my dearest girl, and all that you are. When we have children of our own I hope they'll have Selden brains and Aislabie daring. What a combination, eh?' His little-boy-longing was disarming. 'Fact is we'll be a laughing stock if we don't rebuild this house. I'm told Selden used to be one of the most prominent manors in Buckinghamshire and I want it to be that again. Our houses are backdrops to what we are and I'm known for seizing every fresh opportunity, adapting to each new circumstance. I can't be seen in a house that's merely a dull relic of the past. We'll fill the lake with fish, woods with pheasants, stables with hunters. Selden will be crammed with all manner of good things and you're one of them, Em. Imagine smooth walls hung with exquisite landscapes, cabinets full of antiquities brought by *Flora* from far-flung continents, music, dancing on marble floors. Isn't that what you want?'

What did I want? I wanted him to love me. I wanted my father. I wanted Selden to stay the same and I wanted my child to have lived. 'I want to make up my own mind about these changes,' I said. But I'd never made a proper decision in my life. I hadn't been trained to choose.

Aislabie was delighted by this reply. His cheek dimpled and he squeezed my arm. 'Of course. You can have whatever you like so long as you choose to look forward not back. Your father was a great man but he had his feet in the past. I'm not wasting my time there and neither should you.'

'Then nothing is certain?' I said. 'It's not too late to keep some things as they are.'

He sighed. 'I've already told you, nothing ever stays the same except at Selden. You and your father were unique. When I arrived I was amazed. It's like stepping back in time. But the house isn't useful or modern. You can't keep something just because it's old. Old isn't good enough.'

'For the sake of memory. And affection.'

'But that's the past. You're my wife now. You are part of me. Selden is like an old skin. Shed it, my lovely girl, my jewel. I want to see you in a brand-new setting.'

'I don't think you understand. I have nothing at all of my mother except her room.'

'Her room. Well, show me if it's so special. We can perhaps keep the furniture. How about that? Or the curtains. Come and show me.' He held out his hand.

Of course I couldn't take him up there. I imagined him standing in the little chamber and kicking open the lid of her box. 'There is nothing to keep except the space.'

'The space?' He threw back his head and laughed. 'There'll be plenty of space in the new house.'

He was still smiling but deep in the heart of him I saw a hardness like steel. 'What about the village?' I asked more calmly. It seemed to me I must stay rational in the face of this insanity. 'You plan to change so many lives. What about the people who live there?'

'They'll have spanking new houses, never fear. And we'll reform the way we use the land. Bigger fields. Crop rotation. All sorts. In a few years' time they'll be far better off.'

'You must consult them. You must give them time.'

'Of course there's time. Nothing's going to happen tomorrow.' He glanced over my shoulder. Harford and Osborne were hovering in the doorway. 'Emilie's been talking about our plans,' he told them. 'She's afraid of change. We need to reassure her.'

They were eager to explain. 'This is the century of change, Mrs Aislabie. No one likes change at first. But this is not just a moving forward, it's a going back to the most ancient of harmonies, the Classical world . . .'

Sarah brought wine. She was a different girl in their company, sweet, flirtatious and pliant. They clutched my father's crystal in their well-kept hands, gulped the ruby liquid and drew close together. Their laughter rolled into the cornices and up the chimney.

I stood in my white alamode, watched my husband and thought: Dear God. Dear God. Do I love him? Why do I love him?

When I backed to the door nobody noticed.

II

The alchemist's daughter. That's what they thought. Emilie Selden, an irrelevance. I went to the stable bock, seized a lantern, entered the pitch-black cellars and groped my way to the winding staircase leading to the laboratory.

Let them do as they like. Let them.

I am the alchemist's daughter.

I was in a frenzy of terror. If I didn't love Aislabie. If I didn't love him.

Gill had lit the fire, sharpened my pen, dampened and swept the floors. Everything was ready.

The alchemist's daughter, that's what I was. My hands shook when I picked up my father's notebook. *Palingenesis. 5 October 1725. And so to the grinding. Four hours, for four days. Four lots of four days. And on the fifth day I rest. First to cleanse the* . . . My father had been late starting his alchemical experiment in the autumn I was pregnant with Aislabie's child; usually we began the grinding process in September under the sign of Virgo. I couldn't bear to think of it. I had made him late. While I lay upstairs in my mother's room, he hesitated.

If my father had been right about Aislabie all along . . . And after all the baby had died . . .

Usually we shared the work an hour at a time grinding the iron ore, the lemon juice and the quicksilver which began all alchemy. We believed that there is mystical power in repetition. The same action again and again and again, and on the hundredth or thousandth or ten thousandth attempt the great change would happen. So all our processes were painstaking because it was safer to stay with one phase than move on to the next, the next being closer to the end and the end inevitably resulting in disappointment.

Suppose Aislabie had stopped loving me. Suppose this episode with the house marked the end of his love? I couldn't think of any other reason why he would ignore my wishes. Unless this was how marriages always were. How would I know? In the last couple of years Aislabie had done exactly as he wanted but then I had never asked for anything other than what he chose to give me.

My father and I took it in turns to sit in the chair by the fire with the pestle between the flat of our hands and the mortar clenched in our lap, grinding, grinding. While he ground I was half immersed in my book, half aware of the chinking of the ore against the mortar, the practised chafing of his hands, the tilt of his head, the glint in his eye as he cast his wig over the fire-irons. He loved this stage, the first daub on the blank canvas of alchemy, and I loved his dedication, even though with the weighing of the ore, the turn of the pestle, came the cloud of incipient failure.

So, Aislabie, I thought. So, your mind is made up. You will take everything and transform it in your chosen image. I felt the pressure of my corset and the pinch of my brocade shoes. He had certainly changed the image of Emilie Selden. Then I picked up the piece of obsidian from my desk. Dr Dee, the queen's magician, had believed that the future was revealed in its glassy depths but I saw only the shadow of Emilie's face: blank eyes, pointed chin, features faded into blackness. Fearfully I put down the stone and pressed my hands to my cheeks. Yes, I was substantial. Yes, I existed still. Aislabie wouldn't have all of me until I had tried one last time.

In the grinding, the simple exercise of blending substances, my father's spirits were always high and the laboratory hazy with expectation.

So that's what I did. I started to grind. I ground while on the other side of two doors my husband and his cronies planned to pull Selden down about my ears.

I began the experiment called palingenesis. My aim, to regenerate a dead rose and so become once more the alchemist's daughter.

12

Aislabie went back to London because *Flora* needed his attention. Meanwhile Harford and Osborne colonised the house like ants. They broke open locked doors, inspected the cellars, examined the roofs and explored the outbuildings. Wherever I went I found one of them accompanied by an acolyte measuring, recording, sketching or scrutinising. When I appeared they stopped work and bowed, Osborne briskly from the neck, Harford with such enthusiasm that his face went red.

Only the laboratory stayed out of bounds to them because I had the key and nobody dared press me for it. My father's reputation was too potent for H. and O. and for the time being I reigned supreme there, though I knew it would just be a matter of time before they insinuated their way in. So I worked with a haste that would have horrified my father.

26 November 1725, he wrote. *The calcination. I summon Gill to light the medium furnace. We have modified the chimney with another vent . . . A grey plume of smoke above the crucible . . .* Calcination was the second phase. My father had made observations of the changes wrought by heating the alchemical paste. There was evidence of these activities on the workbench – the discarded crucibles blackened by heat, one with a perforated base through which molten metal could flow during fusion.

I was so intent on following his every move that I even looked up the references he'd made to other alchemists, though in the old days I had disliked their portentous prose. But with Selden under threat I read these alchemists with different eyes. The more Harford and Osborne tapped into the hidden cavities of Selden, the more I became committed to the alchemical process. H.'s and O.'s preoccupations were transitory. If Selden could be torn down once, it could be torn down again. But alchemy was at the heart of Selden and they couldn't touch that. It seemed to me now that the alchemists were entirely justified in their faith in a unifying spirit that transcended the material and mortal life. Thus Paracelsus on the immortal soul: *The Iliastric (uncorrupted, immortal soul) is so natured that neither cold nor heat can harm it. Rather heat is its life and nourishment, joy and pleasure. Therefore it is the salamandric Phoenix which lives in the fire and indeed this truly is the Iliastric soul in Man.*

There must be an immortal soul, I thought, or human life is absurd; my father's life had no meaning. It is my destiny to find its key. So during the day, perched beside the workbench or at my desk, I sank deeper and deeper into the old preoccupations. But at night, in the small hours, I was so restless and anxious that I decided I couldn't watch passively while Selden was torn down.

I must gain time. I must act. I must save something from Harford and Osborne.

And then I thought of Reverend Shales. Surely he would help me resist the demolition of half a village.

13

I decided that my meeting with Shales should take place on relatively neutral territory after Communion at St Mary's and St Edelburga's, Selden Wick, but the trouble was I needed a chaperone. First of all I tried Mrs Gill, who was in the pantry hanging a couple of fowl. 'If only I had time for church,' she said.

'Just the once,' I pleaded.

'Emilie, these friends of your husband make three times the work. I haven't noticed you offering much help.'

'I don't have time,' I said, wishing I'd never raised the matter, 'but I'm sure Sarah could help out more than she does.'

'I've scarcely seen that girl for weeks. Besides, what does she know of kitchens and scrubbing?'

'You could teach her.'

'She's the type who'll learn only what she chooses. She certainly doesn't choose to come near me. Sometimes I'm amazed you keep her with you here.'

'But she belongs with me,' I said.

She gave me a long stare and raised a thin eyebrow. 'That girl seems to me to belong nowhere.'

'She's my maid.'

'She's not a person to be owned. She has a mind of her own. And it'll be an entirely different mind from yours, so just you watch out.'

I thought of Aislabie and how he would say that Sarah was not paid to have a mind and was suddenly confused by the incongruity of talking to Mrs Gill about how a servant should be treated so I left the pantry rather hastily. As I reached the passage she called after me, 'I wish they would go, your husband's friends.'

I hovered a moment but in the end said nothing in reply.

*

In fact, Sarah's recent behaviour had been more encouraging than usual. She had been self-effacing and co-operative, skimming in and out of my presence as I assumed a good maid should, although she still seemed to be homesick for London. I once saw tears fall on her sewing, despite the danger of leaving rust marks. I wondered whether to ask what was wrong but thought that she would dislike it. After all, her lessons on how to be a lady had not indicated intimacy between mistress and maid.

She was the obvious chaperone to church, though I waited until Sunday morning to tell her so. In the country I wore my hair parted plainly in the centre and rolled into the nape but she still insisted on brushing until it crackled. The rhythm was hypnotic and she began to hum a slow arpeggio repeated over and over.

'We shall go to church today, Sarah,' I said into the glass. The back of the brush knocked against my skull and went clattering to the dressing table. 'It's much more expected in the country,' I added.

'I have never been to church in my life,' she said.

'It's not so bad. It's just a matter of standing still and being quiet.'

'I would rather not go to church, Madam.'

'But I need you to be there. I can't go alone. It would look very strange.' And now I was determined that she should go. It was her duty, after all, to do as I said.

She went on glaring into the mirror. Then her head went down. 'Please. No.'

'Sarah. I hardly ask you to do anything for me. Of course you will come. Why ever not?'

'It is not the church, it is the being under the eye of God.'

I laughed. 'If God has an eye, we are under it all the time, not just in church. You'll come with me to church, if only as part of your education.'

She was silent a while, then rallied. 'You can't go to church anyway, Madam, there's nothing suitable for you to wear.'

'Any of my gowns will do.'

She flounced next door to where my clothes were stored and came back with my most unattractive gown flung across her shoulder. Though I now wore my clothes with some confidence I had no idea how to choose them for myself so my gowns, gifts from my husband, arrived full-blown, swathed in muslin. I didn't mind because dressmakers terrified me but sometimes Aislabie's choices seemed very odd. This particular gown was a monstrosity of brocade trimmed with black feathers and I especially did not want to wear it to church. I doubted whether Shales knew any more about fashion than I did but even he could not fail to notice the ostentation of those feathers.

I watched Sarah's white face in the mirror as she shook out the skirts and untied the laces. 'That gown is too grand for a village church,' I said.

Her arms went limp, the dress sighed to the floor and her angry eyes stared into mine. 'Which would you like to wear, Mistress Aislabie?'

'Any other. Yesterday's.'

'Even though the skirts are full of dirt? I've taken it down to be brushed.'

'The blue silk.'

'Blue,' she repeated, flinging the word into the cross-currents of my confusion.

'Sarah, if you hate going to church, I'll not ask you again.'

She gave one of her annihilating shrugs. Though her left shoulder and eyebrow were raised only a fraction, the effect was as momentous as Sir Isaac's celebrated planetary wobble. He said that because of the varying rotational forces on the earth it had become flat at the poles and rounded at the equator. In the same way Sarah's shrug changed the shape of my morning. 'Is there nothing else black?' I begged.

'Nothing.' She picked up the gown, treating me to a glimpse of her neat little waist under the immaculate tie of her apron and her smart close cap. 'Then I shall wear the feathered gown,' I said.

14

So the black orphan bird scraped and glistened its way to church accompanied by its maid Sarah, demure in an appropriate grey cloak. St Mary's and St Edelburga's, Selden Wick, was a stone's throw from the manor. We crossed the stable yard, took a stepping-stone path over the front lawn to the iron gates, turned left past a handful of cottages and the rectory – all now condemned by our plans for Selden – across a small strip of glebe land on which a solitary goat was tethered and up three stone steps into the churchyard.

I paused, though it still rained a fine soaking drizzle. In planning this trip I had fatally overlooked the fact that my father was buried in the church and that for the next hour I would be sitting within a few feet of him.

Sarah sighed impatiently and we walked on. Inside the church I blinked through the gloom of my veil at a surprising number of backs. There never used to be such a crowd in Reverend Gilbert's day. The only sounds were the click of Sarah's nailed heels and the scratching of my feathered skirts against the little doors boxing in each family. Two years ago I had known our tenants well enough to drink tea in their cottages and tease their off-spring. Now no one turned and smiled, and it dawned on me that word must have got around already that my husband had plans for the village. When I passed by, people clutched tight hold of their children's hands and drew themselves upright. The door to my own pew was shut. I fumbled with the latch and fell to my knees but though I pressed my hands to my face I couldn't help peering sideways through my fingers. Yes, one stone stood proud of the others, not quite settled.

The organist played a chord and the vestry door opened. I stared straight ahead at the flame of a solitary candle but I saw Shales move at the edge of my vision and knew that he must be conscious of me and my monstrous gown.

At the start of the sermon Sarah went rigid, her face turned the colour of tallow and she seemed to gaze straight through the thick stone of the church walls into the moist farmland beyond. Then I forgot about her as the subject of the coming spring led Shales to reflect on the natural order of things or, in some cases, the lack of it. God had created a perfect mechanical universe working according to precise laws but some people were so full of the wonderful achievements of mankind that they had forgotten man was created in the image of God. Instead they assumed that God was created in the image of man.

I studied my clasped hands.

'For instance,' said Shales, 'consider the modern fashion for building houses in the style of Palladio. These houses are built to reflect the glory of man, not God. They are designed to imitate the symmetry of the human frame. Measurements have been taken from one side of the human body to another and it's been found that the width is a sixth of the height and the depth, from navel to kidneys, a tenth. These then are the dimensions that are considered most perfect and suddenly all our great houses must be built according to them. Never mind the real needs of those who live in or near them. All must be sacrificed for a spurious ideal of beauty.'

I looked up. As always when I saw Shales, I felt a jolt of surprise because he was never quite as I remembered. This time he seemed more substantial and confident. When his eyes fell on my veiled face there was a flicker of recognition between us. This sermon was certainly for my benefit.

'Architecture,' he said, 'is a noble art. The best architecture reminds us not of the achievements of man, but the achievements of God. Man's extraordinary skill with glass and stone, even in this little church, reflects our desire to get close to God and to express our sense of awe and delight in our world. But there are those who build purely to reflect their own sense of self-importance. They use the number of windows and the height of their walls to say, Look how much money I have, what marvellous taste, what authority. I can tame nature and keep my neighbour at bay. But it is not the houses of the rich that need rebuilding so much as the homes of the poor. The wealth of a great nation is reflected not in the prosperity of the few but in the freedom and contentment of all, and architecture can be an outward sign of this.'

I was shaken to the core. His sermon was tantamount to sedition. If Aislabie had been here he would have accused him of rabble-rousing. But more disturbing was the fact that I was on Shales's side – in fact, had come to church for the sole purpose of engaging his sympathies – but I certainly couldn't confide in him now that he had publicly criticised us.

I stayed in my pew during Communion but Sarah got up, put her hand over her mouth and headed down the aisle towards the door. As if, I thought, I have not been pilloried enough by

Shales's sermon, now my maid has to make a public display. Meanwhile Shales moved above the row of heads, 'The Body of Our Lord Jesus . . .' and presented the host before the eyes of each communicant, 'preserve thy body and soul . . .' I scorned myself for feeling left out.

At the end of the service I waited while the church emptied and the silence of stone and oak closed around me. The wintry arrangements of evergreen were aromatic and hinted at the coming spring. My ancestors lay about underground with their skeletal hands folded and their searching philosophical brains all rotted away – except for my father whose flesh must still be intact.

At last I did go over to look at the tombstone, as creamy and clean-cut as a slice of cheese.

John Selden
1656–1726
Natural Philosopher

Shales must have composed that. And what would I have written, had I been consulted? *Beloved husband . . . beloved father . . .* None seemed to fit. Only the forbidden word, *Alchemist*, might have pleased him.

Shales was still in the porch with Mrs Moore, a frail old parishioner with a pea-head on a round body bundled up in a hood and shawls. They were laughing but when the old woman saw me she backed away and wouldn't meet my eye. Shales helped her down to the gate, she half on tiptoe, he stooping to accommodate her, his stride adjusted to match hers. There was no escape. I must meet him either in the porch or at the gate where Sarah was waiting. He spoke a few words to her but she put her chin in the air disdainfully.

When he came back his wig and shoulders were misted with drizzle. A little bit of residual laughter stayed in his eyes and his features were all broken up by the flurry of rain. I slid my gloved fingers through his, exchanged greetings and moved away but he came after me. 'Mrs Aislabie, it was very good to see you in church.'

I said nothing.

'I hope you'll come again.'

'I doubt it. Not if I'm to be mocked in front of the entire congregation.'

'That was not my intention.'

'But that was the effect.'

'My parishioners are afraid of losing their homes. I have tried to speak to your husband. I have called at Selden day after day and been turned away. I have written to him and had no reply. Of course it is none of my business what happens to the house itself but people need reassurance. I thought I must get your attention.'

'You should persist in your efforts to speak to my husband rather than try to embarrass me.'

'He won't give me a hearing.'

'Then I can't help you.'

'Nothing I have heard or seen of you so far has led me to believe that you are a powerless woman. I'm sure that if you wanted to make a difference you could.'

'As you probably know, a woman seems to have no say in situations such as these. And even if a wife dares speak out, her husband will still go his own way.'

'But you, Mrs Aislabie, must have some sway.'

'Why? Why am I different? In your sermon you preached about freedom and prosperity. I only have freedom and prosperity if my husband chooses to bestow them on me.'

'I'm sure you have some influence over him. No man could fail to be influenced by you.'

I remembered that when he had called in the early morning my hair had been round my shoulders and my skin bruised with Aislabie's kisses. Is that what he meant? 'How much freedom did your wife have?' I demanded. His eyes went blank and he looked over my head but he had maddened me with his self-righteous preaching so I persisted: 'Well? Did your wife rejoice in perfect equality? Did her voice matter as much as yours?'

'She was a woman of principle, certainly. She knew her own mind. But no. You're right. I think at times she must have felt confined. Your maid is ill, by the way. You should take her home.'

We stood looking away from each other. This was his fault. His sermon had been an outrage. If only he'd kept quiet we might have had an amicable conversation about how best to restrain

Aislabie. As it was I had no choice but to side with my husband and I now found myself saying something I hadn't planned at all. 'There will be no room for a laboratory in the new house. I should hate all our instruments and books to be wasted. Perhaps you could make use of them?'

'This is terrible news, Mrs Aislabie. No laboratory. Where will you work?'

'Oh, I have nothing to do with natural philosophy these days. It would be foolish to keep so many old, disused things.'

'But how can you give it all up?'

'I'm giving up nothing except what has already given me up. My father closed the door of the laboratory to me. You can hardly blame me for not wishing to preserve our work. So will you take my father's things?'

'I can't. My parishioners are in despair. How can I be seen to profit from the demolition of Selden? It's my duty to resist your husband's plans, at least until I'm convinced that your tenants have been consulted.'

'Duty. I hate that word. Duty. Do you do nothing, Mr Shales, of your own choosing? Well, I'm asking you to do your duty by my father and take the valuable things that I am offering you.'

But he was now offended beyond measure. 'Unfortunately, as you rightly say, my parish duties are very pressing and you have seen how little space there is in my study.'

We stood apart from each other and I wondered miserably if I should stay just a moment longer and thank him for lending me Sir Thomas Browne. But the chance was gone. While I hesitated, he had turned away.

15

Sarah was still a very odd colour but I was in no mood to sympathise with her so we walked home in stony silence and found that the gates were flung wide and Aislabie's horse was being unharnessed in the stable yard. I was too flustered by my argument with Shales to face him immediately so I sent Sarah indoors and slipped through the stables to the Stygian darkness of the cellars, intending to hide in the laboratory. The cellars had been hacked directly into the chalk hillside so it was impossible to go there, however briefly, and not emerge smeared with white. Light came from unexpected sources: a vent in the ceiling, an opaque window high up under the wall of the house above, a grid let into one of the terraces in the garden. Among the empty ale barrels and apple stores Gill had a hidey-hole of his own, which had both frightened and compelled me when I was a child as it contained an enticing collection of old things: a blunderbuss, an ancient iron helmet, potato tubers, a selection of small rusty knives, nails and bee-keeping equipment – sinister leather gloves, veil and baskets.

I stumbled on him now hunched on a three-legged stool, fists resting on his knees and his few remaining hairs pricking the tips of his ears. His fish eyes roamed the powdery feathers on my gown and rested on my bosom.

'Gill, it may be that I shall soon need your help. My husband has come home so we shall have to pack away my father's things and hide them.'

My words took a while to penetrate the flaccid channels of his ears. 'Help.'

'Will you help me?'

He dropped his head and didn't reply. This sulkiness was my own fault because I had scarcely spoken a dozen words to him since I came back. I needed Gill and the only way of winning him was to conjure the past. 'I've been meaning to ask. Did my father speak to you before he died?'

No answer so I tried again. 'Where did he die?'

'In his bed.'

'How did he get ill?'

He shrugged.

'For instance, had he been working with lead or mercury? Perhaps he inhaled some bad air.'

'I saw him do no work since last winter.'

'So after I'd gone, what did he do?'

'He carried on for a while. Then he gave up. He stopped the work. And then he locked me out.' Gill was so unused to speaking that his lips were sticky with a resinous substance unlike saliva. As my father said, Gill was of the earth and had little of air or water about him.

'Gill, have you any idea where he might have kept . . . ?' Then I heard Aislabie's voice. The porous nature of the cellar walls muted sound and gave it a slight echo. 'Emilie.'

I glanced back at Gill but there was already nothing left of him except a faint earthy odour.

Aislabie cursed as he crashed into something and I saw first the glow of lamplight, then his shadow. 'Emilie. Strange woman. What are you doing down here?'

'I was hiding.'

'From me?'

'From Sarah. I made her go with me to church this morning and she was so angry she made herself sick.'

He slid his hands up my arms and murmured against my lips, 'You are the mistress. Dominate her. Beat her. Lock her in a dark room until she does nothing but smile and curtsy every time you call for her. The girl needs a thrashing.' I imagined Sarah cowering in the corner of my bedchamber as I took her dress by its laundered collar, ripped it open to expose her pearly little back and whipped her skin to shreds. What would I use? My husband's riding whip, perhaps.

His breath was very sweet and the pressure of his lips on my mouth, the nudging of his tongue against my teeth struck the old chords in my body and made me hazy with desire but I didn't know what these kisses meant any more. They seemed to be saying he loved me but what about his plans for Selden? He liked the feathery trim to my bodice and nuzzled his face to my breast while I held tight to the sides of his head and hoped that at least my gown would be so damaged by our frenzy that I need never wear it again. But there was something else that made me grip the short hair under his wig and pull it so tight that he gave a little gasp of pain. A shudder of defiance, hot, delicious, ran from my breasts to my fingertips. The cellars belonged to Gill and me. Aislabie was a creature of the city, of light and words and coins, and none of these things had currency here. We would win, Gill and I. Somewhere in the darkness Gill waited, obsessive, subversive. Aislabie didn't know everything after all.

I leaned sideways and snuffed out the lantern. The darkness was astonishingly complete and stifling.

'Little bitch,' he said, holding me tighter. I put my fist under his chin, brought up his head and pushed him back to the wall, stumbling among the bee baskets until the canes of my petticoat squeaked. Then I slid off his wig and pressed my lips to his ear. 'I want you to change your mind about Selden. I want you to let me keep my mother's room at least, and the laboratory and the cottages until new ones have been built.'

He laughed and pulled me down among the heap of baskets. I imagined dead bees trapped in the straw meshes all winter suddenly released by this battering; their airy little bodies crumbling on the stone floor. My hair caught on something rough and pulled loose as I twitched sideways and crouched down among the baskets.

'Emilie.'

I began to crawl away. I wouldn't surrender so easily this time. He must give me something in return. He was quiet too, waiting for the darkness to break apart. Our breathing rode the space between us and suddenly he pounced, grabbed first my ankle then my knee and yanked me down until I was helpless as an upturned bee. He climbed my body inch by inch, clutching fistfuls of feathers, and though I writhed and kicked he had me by the waist, pulled plumage from my bodice and slapped me back and forth across the thighs with the flat of his hand until I was whimpering with shock and the cellar echoed with the report of skin on skin.

I fought him with a deadly desire to wound and be satisfied. I tore at his clothes and thumped him with my heels and fists, grabbed his short hair and twisted, tried to bite him but he only laughed and clamped down harder, ground my head against the stone floor and bit my breast until I howled with pain. Then he drove himself inside me and my legs opened wider, wider, my body arched and I pounded my wrists in an ecstasy of sensation. But I was a divided Emilie and one half looked on at this sensuous, thrashing creature and hated her.

We spoke not a word of tenderness when we lay back to rest against the summery baskets though he massaged my stomach with the flat of his hand. 'You're not keeping anything from me,

Em. No little Aislabie brewing? Never mind. We'll keep trying. Not too much hardship in that.'

I knelt up and tried to put my clothes straight. 'I've been to church. Everyone's very angry with us.'

'Who is everyone?'

'The congregation. Shales.'

'Shales. This Shales is a troublemaker. I hope he's not been stirring things up.'

'You should talk to him. I'm sure he's not against change for the sake of it. But people are frightened. They don't know what you have in mind.'

'Well, they must wait until the plans are drawn up. Then we'll show them how they'll be much better off in the end.'

'I felt a fool, unable to explain why you have ignored him all this time.'

'Then you shouldn't have gone out. You should have stayed home and cooked up some more alchemical brews in your laboratory. When are you going to show me what you're up to, Em?'

'I'm up to nothing.'

He plucked feathers with his teeth and arranged them on my bosom. 'Not what I've been told. My friends say you're in there night and day.'

'Where else can I go? There's no peace elsewhere in the house.'

'What are you up to, Emilie?' He hung over me and planted little kisses between my nose and ear, then nipped my chin. 'What are you doing in there?'

'Working on phlogiston. It's still not resolved in my mind that fire is caused by the phlogiston in combustible materials.'

He bit again, this time my earlobe. My eyes watered. 'What else?'

'Nothing else.'

'Nothing else. Well, just you let me know when you find that old philosophers' stone because I could do with the gold.'

I turned my head aside and he suddenly kissed me softly on the nose. 'Now, don't be peevish, Em, I've brought you a present,' and he kissed me again and again on the cheeks and lips and eyes until I began to kiss him back. 'Come on, my dearest girl, come and see what I've brought you.'

The remaining feathers on my gown drooped, my hat and veil

were ruined, my hair had come unrolled on my shoulders and I smelt of sex and cellar. My rebellion, my desire to stand apart from him, was utterly defeated. He had turned me inside out; my mouth was slack with kisses, my thighs wet and bruised but even so I wanted more of him. When we reached the stables he pushed my hair behind my shoulders, squeezed my breast and kissed me long and lazy on the throat. Then he took me by the hand and led me along the kitchen passage to the dining parlour where candles were lit though it was barely noon, and Sarah, who seemed better, was unpacking his saddlebags. She lifted out a porcelain bowl glazed a buttery yellow with a design of leaf and flowers in green and orange. On the inside was a painted parrot, a replica of the real bird which perched in our dining parlour in Hanover Street. It had mossy green feathers, chocolate-brown claws and folded wings tipped with a dusting of dull gold.

'French,' said my husband. 'Paul le Riche.'

Sarah held the bowl to the candle flame so I could see every detail. When I stepped forward for a closer look she paused for a moment to take in my ruined clothes and bruised skin before placing the bowl on the table with infinite care.

Chapter Six

WESTMINSTER ABBEY

I

Aislabie returned to Selden with a new idea. He had met the designer of the gardens at nearby Hall Barn and decided that we must have a cascade that would gush down to the lake through a broad avenue in the woods directly opposite the dome. Everyone was so absorbed by the detail of this plan that they failed to comment on my long absences. I made myself visible at breakfast, dinner and supper but not in between or at the end of the day when the wine bottles came out.

I now had two lives, the life I shared with my husband, a life of violent emotions, passion one minute, despair the next, and my life in the laboratory, the one I shared with my dead father. Never before had I applied myself to alchemy with such intense devotion.

Compared with the dissonance beyond the laboratory, alchemy seemed straightforward, even rational. I simply had to follow my father's method. On 8 November 1725 he had written, *The calx obtained from prolonged and gentle heating next has to be dissolved in oil of vitriol*. At Selden we always used ethanoic for this stage of the alchemical process because we thought it purer than nitric or sulfuric acids. And we needed an outside force, concentrated white light, to consecrate the dissolution. My father preferred to work by moonlight but his diary recorded night after night of cloudy skies so by early December he had resorted to candlelight.

He must have hated this defeat but it suited me because it enclosed me deeper in the laboratory with him. I polished a lens and adjusted it in front of a candle, turning the glass until a steady beam shone on to the workbench. My father's notebook was a pressing weight in my lap and his staff rolled in my hand. If I looked up I would see the gleam in his cold, clever eye, the many layers of his clothing, each pocket with its allocated function – pipe, pen wiper, pipette, wire, string or measure – the sleeves tucked with a row of his own neat stitching and his little black slippers trodden down at the heels. I could smell him, shade on shade.

But instead I stared at the candle flame, like water in its fluidity and movement but lighter than air, tongue-shaped, blue at the base, grey and cool in the centre, then a pure yellow drawn up and up to a point as if dragging against the pull of gravity. Flame – too little air and it would go out, too much and it would blow away.

2

On 22 March Aislabie came back from a visit to London and summoned me to the library where I found him sprawled in my father's chair, surrounded by teetering piles of unsorted books. His feet were propped on a small chest with leather straps and he held a long furl of paper.

'Your friend Shales has been busy,' he said. 'Fifty names. Or rather crosses. Most of them ain't literate.' I took the paper and saw Shales's precise handwriting above the list. Aislabie folded his hands and seemed to be examining his thumbs but I knew he was weighing up my reaction. 'He's taken against the plans for the house and got the tenants to protest.'

'What will you do about it?'

'I shall have a word with Reverend Shales. I expect loyalty. He depends on me for his living.'

'I'm sure he doesn't intend to be disloyal.'

'The fact is if he wasn't stirring up dissent nobody would say a word. He's a subversive and I won't have it. But never mind, my dearest love, none of this affects you. I've brought you this.' He nudged the chest with the toe of his boot. 'Open it up, Em.'

Inside was a vast black lustring mantle that went on and on pouring into my lap. I threw it round my shoulders and the heavy gathers settled at my throat and went tumbling to a slight train at the back. The weight and coolness of it was like being caught in a deluge of rain; it had a brilliant crimson lining and the hood was so deep I had to fold it away from my face.

Aislabie slid down the chair and thrust his legs to the fire. He flashed gold and bronze in a new wig and cinnamon waistcoat with winking buttons, and his drowsy eyes watched me examine the cloak. Then he drew me down so that it shuddered into a black pool. 'You need a mourning cloak, Em. The news from London is that Sir Isaac Newton is dead. People don't talk of anything else. He's to lie in state and have a funeral at the Abbey. Good God, I bet if Walpole himself died he wouldn't get half the attention. Everybody will be there.' My first thought was that it was high time Newton died. After all, he was fifteen years or more older than my father. 'Genius,' added my husband surprisingly. 'He put the fear of God into counterfeiters. Ferreted them out and saw them hung. They were costing us a fortune in lost revenue.'

'My father was a great admirer of Newton's scientific work.'

'That's the difference between your father and me, Em. It all boils down to money in the end. I make it, he spent it. The thinkers of this world need the doers to keep their bread buttered. Newton just happened to be both. That's what I admire. He didn't limit himself to one line of interest.'

'My father's career was thwarted because of me, otherwise he would have done as much as Newton. When my mother died he chose to live at Selden with me rather than retain his fellowship at Cambridge.'

'Exactly so. What a distracting bunch you women are. Newton was eighty-four years old. Never married. A moral for us all, eh. Anyway, I expect you'd like to go to the funeral.'

This was such a surprising offer that at first I couldn't take it in. 'I thought women never went to funerals in London.'

'This woman can if she likes.'

'But I would be out of place.'

'So what's new, Em?'

'I can't leave Selden.'

'Em. That ain't very gracious when I brought you this lovely cloak and came back all this way to fetch you.'

'All the same, I'd rather not.'

'Matter of respect. Your father would have gone.'

The question I should have asked was why he wanted me in London but all I could think of was that I couldn't leave the alchemical experiment. 'It's because of my father that I can't go. I couldn't bear it.'

Aislabie had been caressing my neck and hair but his fingertips were a little less gentle as they kneaded my scalp behind my ear. 'Can't have you rotting away down here, Em. London needs a glimpse of your lovely face. So do I. We should be seen at the Abbey. It's been the devil of a job getting us an invitation. And you will be welcome because of your pa. Lord, Em, you've no idea how you're talked about in some circles. Come back with me before they forget all about you.'

I knelt in the silken folds of my new cloak and bent my head as his fingers worked my neck and breasts. I love him, I do love him, I thought, kissing his knee. He wants me in London, so to London I will go.

3

Aislabie rode while Sarah and I drove in the carriage. I thought she'd be glad to leave Selden but at first she seemed more miserable than ever with her arms wrapped tightly under her breast and her chin sunk low. Only after an hour or so did she rouse herself enough to plan my costume for the next day. She unstrapped the chest containing the cloak and ran the fabric between finger and thumb. 'With such a cloak, it will hardly matter what you wear beneath.'

'Something plain, I suppose, for a funeral.'

She shook her head. 'In Westminster Abbey you must wear your finest. And your black and white petticoat. First thing in the morning I will buy new ostrich feathers for your hat.'

'Does it matter about the feathers in my hat?'

'It matters. Of course it matters. And no veil. Veils are not worn this season.'

What a pity. A veil provided a convenient screen behind which I could hide and observe. The prospect of immersing myself once more in the fashionable world frightened me. London was not a place where I knew myself and as we drew closer I remembered vividly the bewilderment and sorrow of my wedding day. Hanover Square, for all its elegance, had a harsh symmetry unrelieved by lines of elm trees just coming into leaf. When I ran up the steps of our house I was met by the scent of potpourri and the clutter of too many fabrics: pine cones printed on to flock wallpaper, sprigged muslin, the fateful French painting by Lorrain, silk rugs, brocade, linen, lace. But I was glad to see the parrot who had been moved down to the kitchen, though he was almost as rigid as his porcelain counterpart and glared at me from one round eye.

Aislabie, who wanted to take a look at *Flora*, said he would meet me at the Abbey in time for the funeral if possible.

'Am I ever to see this ship?' I asked.

'One day. When she is scrubbed, polished and watertight. You'd fuss if you saw her all exposed in her dry dock.'

'I never fuss. And I should really like to visit her. I have never seen a great expanse of water or a large ship.'

He kissed my mouth and smiled into my eyes. 'Listen, Em, in May *Flora* sets sail for France on her first little voyage – just to try her out before we send her further, pick up a few bits of cargo. How would it be if you came with me? A maiden voyage for my maiden.'

I caressed the back of his neck in the warm place I loved and ran my thumbs under his jaw as I saw myself flying under crisp white sails across a blue sea to France, and my French mother a tiny waving figure on the opposite shore. I imagined the vastness of the sky, the creatures in the ocean, the salt of the air.

So I was happy as I set out for the Abbey swathed in my new cloak. I told Sarah that once we got there she would be free until evening and she sat pressed to a corner of the carriage, watchful as a frog on the brink of its pond. Almost before I had stepped out she was gone.

The black ripples of my mantle and the sweep of my hat made me prominent and I wished that Sarah had not forbidden a veil. My heart was pounding. Since babyhood I had lived under the long shadow of Isaac Newton and the Royal Society. Now we, the Royal Society, Isaac Newton and I, were all gathered under one roof. Only the pivot, my father, was missing.

My husband was there already, glorious in inky blue velvet and black armbands, working his way along the pews, shaking hands and making a show of boyish charm and respect. I realised suddenly that I was the only woman in sight. Surely I shouldn't be here? But at that moment Aislabie came up, ushered me into a pew and began pointing out the assembled dignitaries: 'James Thomson, see there.' He nodded to a girlish-lipped, quite young man who made no acknowledgement in return, 'Alexander Pope – you recognise him from last winter?' How could I forget tiny, crook-backed Mr Pope? 'Monsieur Voltaire, French, exiled due to some argument over a woman I expect, you have to admire the French; John Gay, playwright, artist; Hogarth, God, look at them all.' I studied French M. Voltaire long and hard, and indeed his nose was satisfactorily long, even longer than mine; his thin, upturned lips unlike those of any Englishman I knew and his eyes dark. My husband meanwhile was less pleased to note the arrival of Thomas Shales, who stepped into a pew several rows in front. I shuddered when I remembered the acrimony of our last meeting but he turned and bowed gravely as the organ struck the first vigorous chords.

The music was by the German visitor, George Frideric Handel. I feared his work and understood why my father had taught me theory and harmonics but given me no chance to play. Music tapped into a darkness that was not rational. My imagination was unleashed, I couldn't hold it back. I no longer saw Newton's coffin, draped in crimson like the lining of my cloak, accompanied by a procession of sombre scientific gentlemen: 'Sir

Hans Sloane,' whispered Aislabie, nodding to the largest and most imposing of them all, 'Lord Foley, Mr Folkes, Dr Halley . . .' Instead I was in the church at Selden Wick where the box pews were empty and shut fast except for the one belonging to the Gills who stood with their backs to me, Mrs in a dusty black shawl, Mr bare-headed. Shales was at the top of the nave in his starched surplice, book in hand, praying over my father's coffin. And I so wanted to be in that little church with Shales, the Gills and my father. Just to say goodbye.

So it was not Newton I mourned but my father. The sight of that coffin, the knowledge that the man inside would never emerge but would soon be covered by earth and stone, the howling draught that seemed to blow through my life because he wasn't there, broke over me. And then another, even keener shock, the lost baby, the perfect curledness of it, the packed potential of its being. All lost. And for the first time I dared to think: Was it lost because of Aislabie, because he didn't bother himself to be gentle with me that night?

By the end of the service the neck of my gown was wet with tears. No wonder women are not encouraged to attend funerals, I thought, if this is what happens. I touched Aislabie's arm and asked if we could leave quickly but he squeezed my hand, darted out of the pew and began to circulate, dropping a private word or two into distinguished ears. I felt a rush of despair at being abandoned among so many strangers and tried to follow him but my tears made me inarticulate.

During the past eighteen months my father's education had been shown lacking in certain vital respects and the business of crying was apparently one of them. Sobs now kicked out of my chest so violently that I had to cover them with a coughing fit, leave the pew and hide behind a pillar. I didn't know how to stop crying. Though I trembled and gasped and wiped away a stream of tears there seemed to be no reaching the bottom of my grief. I hardly knew where I was or what I should do.

'Mrs Aislabie.' I turned my head aside. Shales would surely have the sense to leave me alone. He didn't go away but stood beside me for a while, then said again, 'Mrs Aislabie,' and I saw that he was offering his arm. 'I wonder, is this your first visit to the Abbey?'

I couldn't speak.

'Perhaps you would allow me to be your guide.'

'I'm waiting for my husband,' and I reached out my hand as if Aislabie would come up and take it at any moment.

Shales glanced over his shoulder. 'Come with me until he's ready,' he said gently.

There was Aislabie on the far side of the Abbey, an arm flung round the shoulders of one of the pall-bearers. I was still shuddering with grief, and the distance between Aislabie and me threatened to overturn me again.

'Come.' Shales tucked my hand under his arm, pressed a handkerchief between my fingers and led me over to the portrait of a sober, flat-faced nobleman. 'As far as we know this is the first portrait ever painted of an English monarch . . .' The Abbey boomed in my ears. Again I looked for Aislabie but he was nowhere in sight. I mopped my face with Shales's handkerchief and was comforted by the scent of linen. He waited while I pulled my hat lower over my eyes and then we walked on. The strangeness of his coat under my fingertips, of drifting with him of all people deeper into the Abbey, soothed me. The scene was mellow: ancient oak burnished by candlelight, the scent of seven-hundred-year-old stone, the swaying of banners, the murmur of educated voices. We paused frequently to acknowledge bows and nods and he introduced me as 'Mrs Aislabie. Sir John Selden's daughter'. I kept my tear-stained face averted but I heard their respectful comments: 'Delighted . . .' 'Your father . . .' 'Luminous mind . . .' 'Great privilege . . .'

Then we left them all behind until they were a distant echo. Shales, presumably well practised in the art of soothing distressed females, kept up a steady flow of conversation: 'I suspect that though Sir Isaac would have been pleased by the numbers here, he would also have been scornful of the fact that some who picked quarrels with him or took no interest in his work while he was alive should wish to be seen at his funeral.'

A rush of air heaved up from my chest in a shuddering sigh and shook me from head to toe. I made a mental note to study the anatomy of tears so as to be prepared next time. Shales led me to the tomb of Edmund Duke of Lancaster and I moved about on the ancient paving stones, breathing deeply and thinking: This is all very well but what if Shales knew what I was up to in the laboratory at Selden? What if he knew that I was experimenting with palingenesis? In the circumstances it seemed deceitful to allow him to be so kind to me.

At last I recovered enough to speak: 'Where do you think Isaac Newton is now?'

He smiled. 'If you'd asked him that question he would probably have said, "In one of God's many mansions." He was a great one for believing in heaven for the blessed – a giant laboratory, probably, where God could share the secrets of his creation with those few mortals with wit enough to understand.'

'What do you think?'

'I have no idea what heaven contains. I like to think there is a place of rest, particularly for those who have suffered too much on earth.'

'Did my father suffer?'

'He was very ill, Mrs Aislabie. It was terrible to see him struggle for breath. But he was fighting a great many demons, I think, that tortured him more. For instance, I didn't understand at the time how much he must have fought his longing to see you.'

This was nearly an apology. Perhaps it would do. Perhaps I should forgive him. In return I tried to repair some of the damage I had done in the church porch. 'Did your wife suffer much?'

'She did. Too much.'

'How did she die?'

'Of smallpox.'

'How long ago was that?'

'Nearly three years.'

'She wasn't inoculated then?'

'No.'

'But I thought you met my father during the experiment in which convicts were engrafted against the smallpox.'

'Nevertheless. When I said the household should be inoculated she refused.'

'But why?'

'She was afraid.'

I stared up at him. I was about to say: Surely you should have persuaded her, but the look in his eye was so remote I didn't dare. I said, 'At least you can pray for her. I wasn't taught how to pray.'

He said nothing.

'Do you mind telling me what you pray?'

'I pray for the wisdom to find meaning in the . . . her death.'

'And have you?'

'No, Mrs Aislabie, I find no meaning. But perhaps that's because I'm too small to see a plan so large I rarely get anything but a brief glimpse of it.'

'Should I pray for my father's soul, do you think?'

He laughed. 'Not if you don't believe in such a thing.'

'So how should I pray for him?'

'Are you asking my advice as a clergyman?'

'Yes. As a clergyman. That's your profession, after all. Why are you surprised?'

'I wouldn't dare advise you about anything.'

'Please.'

'Mrs Aislabie, I'm sure you pray for him night and day just by keeping him in mind.'

'And if I don't pray. If I am neglectful, do you think I will be punished?'

'By what? By whom?'

'Do you think I might be struck a blow because I have done wrong?'

He was silent a long time. 'What kind of blow?'

'I lost . . . I cannot help thinking . . . I married Aislabie and then I lost . . .'

'You lost your baby, Mrs Aislabie. Is that what you mean?' Another long pause. 'No. I don't think it is a matter of punishment. I think it's a matter of recognising how frail we all are.'

'I feel punished.'

'No. No. I do not believe in a mechanism for punishment and reward.'

'So your prayer is not entreaty.'

'For what? For favours? For an assured place in heaven? I have tried all kinds of asking and am never satisfied. What I do know is that the expectation of heaven can be no substitute for what happens here. It can't be an excuse for inflicting misery on others. But sometimes I can't help hoping that heaven will contain a few shocks for those of us who are complacent or cruel.'

'What shock will be prepared for you?'

'Perhaps a series of meetings with Mrs Aislabie will be arranged, to ensure I am never complacent for long.' I looked up and was caught off guard by his smile and then a sudden change, an expression in his eye that was intense and unnerving. We walked on in silence, my hand still resting on his arm but now I was self-conscious, aware of the occasional pressure when his leg brushed my skirt. Once I glanced up at him but he was looking away. Then I saw that we had returned to the nave and that the crowd had dispersed. My husband was standing fretfully by the door and I felt a stab of anxiety.

Before we reached him Shales took the crumpled handkerchief from me and put it in his pocket. He said, 'I remember when you came to visit me in my study you asked what I intended to do with the air I had collected by fermenting those peas. Ever since, I have been wondering what was behind that question. I have struggled with my plants, with small-scale measurements and observations, but until I spoke to you it never occurred to me to go a step further with regard to the airs I had collected. It seems to me that I have been taking a very narrow view. Do you think you would have time to give me a lesson or two, Mrs Aislabie, or direct my reading?'

I was flattered and amazed but there was no time to answer. My husband sprang forward and my hand transferred itself from one arm, black worsted, to another, blue velvet. Aislabie bowed low to Shales. 'I gather you've called at the house a couple of times. We must arrange a meeting.'

'I was wondering if you have any comments on the petition we handed to you,' said Shales. His voice was clipped and for the first time I saw he could be formidable.

'Can't say I remember it.'

'You should take note. The mood is ugly. My parishioners have heard all kinds of rumours – they can't sleep peacefully in their beds for fear of losing the roof over their heads.'

'Nonsense.'

'And then there's the matter of money. They pay their rents and see no return. The land is in a poor state. Wages have not been paid.'

'Not everyone pays rents. I've been looking at the books.'

'Nonetheless . . .'

'Nonetheless. We are all having to pay for decades of neglect and mismanagement despite your commendable efforts with fertilising the soil. It will take years of careful husbandry to restore the estates. I am not a magician, Shales, unlike my predecessor.'

'People are very unhappy.'

The roguish dimple played in Aislabie's cheek. 'I hope this isn't a threat, Shales.'

'I'm no threat. It's your choice. But if you don't consult with them they will rebel.'

'I doubt if any of those peasants would have the wit to rebel without a ringleader. I shall remember this conversation, Shales.'

'As their priest, I have a duty to speak for them.'

'As their priest, I'm sure you'll explain to them the consequences of any violent or illegal action,' and Aislabie bowed deeply before whisking me away to the waiting carriage.

Once I was inside he stuck his head in after me: 'I forbid you to speak to that man again without first asking my permission.'

'But he's been so kind to me.'

'Probably part of his plan. He'll try and get you on his side. He's been stirring up all kinds of trouble. Watch yourself, Em.'

'He's no threat, he's a clergyman.'

Aislabie roared with laughter. 'As if that were a guarantee of good behaviour. Nonetheless Em, do as I say, there's a good girl.'

5

My husband was out late that night so I went to bed alone. Because Sarah hadn't returned either, I had to rely on an unfamiliar maid to untie my laces and as soon as she'd gone I snuffed the candles and got into bed. As usual when Aislabie wasn't there I left the bed curtains open so I could see the night sky and the moon if there was one. Again and again I walked through the Abbey with Shales, saw the banners and the monuments, the soot caught in the furls of stone carving, the glint of gilt, the pocks of woodworm. I listened to what we'd said to each other and wished I could relive the conversation only this time I would be more honest with him about palingenesis and I'd find the right words to comfort him for the death of his wife. Certainly I wouldn't return his handkerchief until I'd had it washed. And above all I'd say more about the quality of air. The fact that I hadn't given him an answer when he asked for my help grieved me most; it was as if a closed door had been pushed open on to my former life of investigation and natural philosophy but then been slammed shut again.

In the small hours I heard Aislabie's footfall on the stairs. He tried to open the door quietly but it banged against a chair and he cursed. Then he sat down heavily on the edge of the bed and took off his shoes. I turned my back and wrapped my arms round my knees.

'It's a cold night, Em,' he murmured. 'I'm looking for a place to warm these hands of mine.'

I heard his wig drop softly on the table, then his clothes, one by one, until at last the mattress sagged under his weight as he coiled himself round me and tucked his hand under my arm. He had been drinking and the kisses he planted on my neck were soft and wet.

I remained in a tight knot.

'Come on, Em, take pity on your poor cold man.'

'I'm too tired. Too unhappy.'

'What's to be unhappy about, now your old man's here?'

I turned on my back. 'Didn't you realise how sad I was at the funeral? It hurt me to be there.'

'You mean because of your father. But Em, he was an old man. It was time he died.'

'And our child. I was thinking about the baby we lost.'

He sighed and straightened himself so that we lay like a couple of knights on their slabs in Westminster Abbey. 'It would be a very good thing for all of us, Em, if you learned to let the past stay in the past. Lord, how would it be if we all went around tearing our hair out because at some time someone had died.'

'Who are the dead people in your life, Aislabie?'

'I don't choose to remember them and I think that is a cultivated choice. My life is crowded enough without being cluttered up with the dead.'

'Tell me about your parents.'

'They're not dead, as far as I know.'

'Shouldn't we visit them?'

'Whatever for? It's years since I clapped eyes on them.'

'That seems to me a very cold attitude. How do you know they're not in trouble and needing you?'

He propped himself on his elbow and leaned over me so that I felt his warm, wine-laden breath on my cheek. 'You've said enough. Point taken. Should not have taken Mistress Em to a funeral. Can we have an end to this now?'

'You ignored me.'

'When did I ignore you?'

'In the Abbey. I was in tears and I needed you but you ignored me.'

'Dear God. Em, I went to a deal of trouble getting you in there in the first place. All you had to do was tag on to my arm and you would have been find. But when I looked for you there was no sign because you'd gone off with the very holy Reverend Shales.'

'Not gone off. He took pity on me.'

His hand had crept down to the hem of my shift and he sprinkled kisses on my shoulder but still I lay rigid. It was not like me to resist him; I didn't recognise myself and part of me wanted to put my arms round his neck and abandon myself to the comfort of his body. But some stony Emilie had taken hold and she was waiting for Aislabie to show just a hint of regret that he had not been kinder in the Abbey. It was his lack of knowledge that was so hurtful, his inability to take my feelings into account.

After a moment he gave a little grunt then flung back the sheets, swept his coat from the floor and left the room, slamming the door behind him. I heard him stumble on the first couple of steps leading to the next floor, then turn back and go to the small bedchamber with the burgundy drapes he used when I was away in Selden. I lay in my solitary bed feeling a curious mix of triumph and sorrow. I had surely been right to tell him that I was unhappy but if he'd stayed just a few seconds longer I would have given in. I couldn't have resisted the pressure of his hand on my thigh or his penitent little kisses for long.

By morning Sarah still wasn't home, which I saw as yet more proof that she had little respect for my authority. Without her savage ministrations my clothes wouldn't fit. The maid who dressed me was so tentative about lacing my stays that my gown gaped. When Aislabie came in, affectionate as ever and apparently quite unperturbed by what had been said the night before, he laughed at my frustration and wouldn't hear of letting me go home to Selden without Sarah. Instead he took hold of the laces and gave a few sharp tugs. 'See, we don't need her. The wretched girl has probably met up with her family and been persuaded to stay an extra night.'

'She has no family. I've a good mind to dismiss her if she ever does come back.'

'I told you before to be firmer with her. You keep her on much too loose a rein. She's a London girl and she'll take everything she can.'

'Then how can I trust her?'

'You can trust her as well as any other. And do you really want to put yourself to the trouble of finding someone else?' He tossed me a purse of change. 'Give her one more chance. Amuse yourself in town today. Take another maid, go shopping and buy yourself something decorative.'

I strode about the house for a bit, spoke to the parrot and thought of my alchemy steaming away without me. And then it occurred to me that this was the first chance I'd had to visit London alone and that there certainly were places I wanted to go very badly indeed. So I asked the maid to summon a chair, told her I wouldn't be needing her, thank you, and ordered the men to take me to Crane Court, Fleet Street.

The uneven, rocking motion was quite pleasant and with the curtains shut the bustle in the streets was less intimidating, but I felt very alone and was suddenly overwhelmed by yearning for that moment yesterday when I had stood by the tomb with Shales and talked about heaven and suffering.

This time I went right into Crane Court, which was in deep shadow even though the sun was shining. At the far end was a modern double-fronted house with a flight of steps leading to the door, the home of the Royal Society where my father had come each year to read in the library and attend lectures and meetings. The windows were shuttered and there was a mourning ribbon on the door. I knocked.

'Madam.' Behind the servant I could see a broad staircase and a passage to a small garden where a birch fluttered in the sunlight. From somewhere above came men's voices.

'I wonder if I might read in the library.'

'Fellows only are admitted to the library.'

'My father was a fellow. Perhaps you knew him. Sir John Selden. He left papers. I should like to see them.'

'Sir John Selden.' His fat jowls bulged when he smiled. 'I remember Sir John Selden. Quite the recluse. Quite the character.'

At this point two gentlemen in mourning bands came up beside me, brushed past and nodded to the footman. 'Sir John Selden's daughter,' said the footman, 'come to take a look at his papers.'

They smiled politely but I realised that these younger men had scarcely heard of my father.

'Regrettably the rules on admission are very clear,' added the footman as the others disappeared upstairs.

'You could ask . . .'

'Perhaps you are unaware, Madam, that our president was buried yesterday. It is hardly the time to break the rules.'

After the door closed I retreated into deep shadow at the opposite side of the yard. Another man emerged from the alley, tall, dressed in black, Shales, was it? No. But it occurred to me that Shales might come here and that it would be shameful to be caught in the shadows of a world which belonged to him and my father but not to me.

7

I walked out into Fleet Street where coffee houses had opened up on every alley and street corner. For me London had only two real landmarks. I had visited one of them and now I turned east towards Spital Fields thinking I would have another search for my mother's house. The street was very crowded and without Sarah's protection I was knocked about and eyed up so insolently I almost turned tail. But that spare day, the day when I should not have been in London, turned out to be so momentous that afterwards I thought that some guiding hand had taken hold and was directing my feet because the next thing I saw was a notice tacked up on the side of an entrance advertising a lecture by the eminent German philosopher Hans Wepfer who would shed light on the vital force of life, the Archaeus. Everyone was welcome to attend at the Swan in Wine Office Court at twelve o'clock.

How could I resist such an invitation? I bought a pie like a true Londoner, took it down to the river, watched the mass of oars on the choppy water and looked downstream to where *Flora* must be moored somewhere among the distant forest of masts. I remembered that Shales had once given a sermon about the river and how it was a link between his past and his present. No wonder his face in repose was full of sorrow when he had lost his beloved wife so needlessly to smallpox.

I followed the progress of a little boat weaving in and out of larger vessels and discovered that I was nearly happy, with my head full of ideas and purpose. After the lecture I would go to Spital Fields and this time I would certainly find news of my mother's family. Sarah had been the problem before. Her attitude had discouraged me and made me timid.

I had to pay sixpence for admission to the upstairs room at the Swan. The rows of chairs were already packed with interested citizens of every age and calling who went quiet as a slight man in an untidy wig made his entrance, took his place behind the lectern and began with the dramatic question: 'What is life?'

He was so struck by his own profundity that he stood stock still for several minutes fixing us with his mournful brown eyes. Then, like a magician at the Selden Wick fair, he added confidentially and in a strong Germanic accent, 'I will tell you. Life is a vital force called the Archaeus. This Archaeus has a more familiar name, Nature, and is the essence of life when combined with matter in water or air. Meanwhile light shines from the sun and stars, and when dispersed through the Archaeus forms fire. Many natural philosophers, among them the greatest and the best including the phlogistonist Georg Stahl, are now pursuing this idea to its inevitable conclusion.'

I jumped at the sound of that word, *phlogistonist*, and glanced behind me in case my father was listening. But there was only the same motley audience, some already bored, others nodding wisely as if they knew all this already.

'That is why metals,' said Wepfer, 'gain weight when they are reduced to a calx; in the process of strong heating they take the Archaeus from the air and that makes them heavier. And this same spirit or Archaeus affects the fermentation of plants and the action of our own nervous system,' and here he produced a chart showing the inner workings of the human body, its veins and arteries accurately drawn but with a most improbable-looking fire in the belly.

I had never heard so much nonsense talked in so few minutes. Wepfer was undoing years of painstaking research and made no reference to the experimental method which required proof of a theory rather than wild speculation and the reckless linkage of unrelated ideas. But I did understand one truth as a result of the lecture. His high-flown foolishness was permissible because even the late-lamented I.N. had not nailed the question of whether fire was state or substance, and whether the air consisted of just one type of corpuscle or several.

By the end of the talk the room was so smoky that several ladies had to be escorted out and Wepfer said there was time for only three questions. My hand shot up and he turned to me with amusement. 'I wonder if you are familiar with John Mayow and his conclusions about fire and air?' I asked. His smile faded but he nodded gravely. 'Then you'll know that Mayow noticed that if a mouse was placed under a glass it could not live after part of the air – the part he called the nitro-aerial spirit – had been consumed, even though some air was left in the glass. Likewise with a candle flame. How does Mayow's theory that air in fact consists of at least two different parts fit your theory of the Archaeus, which you say is a force separate from the air?'

People turned their heads and looked at me with a mix of astonishment and annoyance. 'I am impressed,' said Wepfer, 'that you have read a digest of Mayow's *Tractatus Quinque Medico-Physici*, but, my dear lady, I'm afraid it never does to believe that just because one has understood a particular detail everything else will be equally clear. Behind the most simple explanation is a world of experience, a lifetime's reading, not just a wet afternoon curled up with the latest journal.' Laughter. 'The Archaeus, Madam, is a much more plausible theory than that of Mayow, who believed that the invisible air around us could be divided into various parts.' And he turned to the next questioner.

8

I stalked outside to find that the sunlight was gone and a haze had descended on the street but, spurred on by outrage, I flagged down another chair and asked for Spital Fields. The men calculated the cost and told me that I had enough for the journey there but not home afterwards. I didn't care. My good mood was all gone and I was back in the same fever of confusion and sorrow I had felt in the Abbey.

The latest periodical . . . *A digest of Mayow* . . . *My dear lady* . . . My father had told me that I knew more than any other woman alive and yet I had been patronised by a charlatan with a taste for public lecturing. If I had no voice, if my knowledge was discounted, what had all those years with my father been for? I shifted restlessly in the chair and felt the men adjust their handhold as we lurched round a corner. What was left of me if the learned Emilie was taken away? A hollow thing with no father, no mother and no child.

No child. Back it came again, out of nowhere, the memory of that little creature in its bubble of a lost opportunity.

The men dropped me in Spital Square and scrambled off. I walked up and down a nearby street, scanning each house. Mrs Gill had told me that my mother's family house was destroyed by fire so I thought there should be one house newer than the rest.

I knocked on doors. After a few minutes a maidservant would come panting up from the basement and sometimes I was shown into a back parlour where the lady of the house sat over her knitting or nursed a child or two in her lap. Some of the women spoke English, some French. 'Do you remember the De Lery family?' I asked.

'De Lery? *Non.*'

I mentioned '*un feu depuis vingt ans*'.

Shrug. '*Non. Pas un feu. Pas ici.*'

I gave my mother's married name. 'Selden.'

'Selden. *Non.*'

The more I asked the more lost I felt. My questions became frantic, people looked at me strangely, I was on the brink of tears. Someone should have known the De Lerys. I tried another tactic, peered through open doors, saw rack after rack of silk bales, carts loaded with silk thread, the confusion and commotion of the looms and the vats of dye, the lanterns of the pattern drawers, the nerve-tingling slicing of silk. Everyone had a purpose except me.

Panic-stricken, I reviewed what I did have of my mother and found it hopelessly inadequate – a strip of ribbon, a gravestone, an empty chamber. And somewhere, if they were not destroyed, my father's notebooks. The Gills never told me anything useful, Shales had talked to my father in confidence, the villagers who might have known her were alienated. A blank, in fact.

The sun was now blotted out altogether by brown smoke and I was confused by the maze of streets. I knew I should head south towards the Thames and then west but I soon found myself in an area I had never visited where houses were so crammed together that I could have stood in the middle of the street and touched the walls on either side. In five minutes I had rubbed shoulders with more people than I had met in nineteen years at Selden. Though the thick fog muffled sound and dulled colour my black silk cloak stood out by being so lustrous and densely dyed. There was a sliding of eyes, a stiffening when I passed by as though people were valuing the clothes on my back and registering that I was unprotected. It seemed shameful that I, swathed in my shimmering cloak, should ask the way of a ragged girl. She would be sure to realise that I was not a lady at all but an alchemist's daughter with the smell of acid in the folds of my petticoat and my heart full of grief.

I stumbled down yet one more alley and found that I had reached a dead end with rubbish piled against a high grey wall. The only way was back, though I dreaded the contemptuous eyes of the street children who sat on the steps and watched. For a moment I stood still, bracing myself, while the stench from the heap penetrated the scented folds of my hood. I stared abstractedly, struggling to stay calm. The rubbish heap was made of rags, dirt and bits of brick and metal soaked in the flyblown mess of emptied privies.

Something caught my eye, a purple triangle sticking out of the waste. I darted forward and put my hands to my mouth, then spun round and walked away.

Faster, Emilie. If you stop, these children will fall on you and tear you to shreds.

But the perverse Emilie, the natural philosopher's daughter, would not walk on. Instead she turned back, covered her nose with her mantle and went right up to the heap.

Now the terrible thing took shape. What I had seen was the heel of a newborn babe flung face down in the rubbish, and on top of it, so that their two knees were locked together, the baby's twin. Both infants were naked. One had its face compressed against the muck, the other's was turned sideways so that I could see its miniature profile, round forehead, tiny beak of a nose, pouting lips. Their little bellies were distended and their arms and legs stick-like.

I had never been allowed to show distaste during a dissection in the laboratory or to recoil from putrefaction so I brought my face closer, closer, and remembered the weight of my own stillborn foetus, hot like a stewed plum, and the few moments I had spent examining its petal-thin ears. When I looked again I distinctly saw the infant's mouth gape.

London was bellowing. I heard a thousand wheels turn beyond the watchful silence of the alley as I crouched down, took off my glove, reached out my hand and touched a stone-cold foot. Behind me there was movement among the spectators in the alley.

I scooped up both the little bodies and folded them in my cloak, wrapping them up tight until only their mouths were exposed. Then I strode out of that dreadful place spurred on by hope that made my instinct for home preternaturally sure so that I found my way with never a wrong turn, pushing confidently through the crowds as if my own mission was the only one that mattered.

When I reached Hanover Street Sarah opened the door. She started to say something but I took no notice. 'Fetch warm water,' I said. 'Quickly.'

I ran up to my dainty bedchamber and laid the cloak by the fire. Immediately all the room's carefully contrived perfume was blotted out by a terrible smell of excrement and rancid meat.

Sarah came in with two pails. 'Shall you be bathing, Madam?'

I was crouched over the cloak with my back to her. 'Bring the water to the fire. Hurry. Now fetch me some towels.' Gently I unravelled one infant from her sister – they were both girls. 'Look what I found on a dung heap. I couldn't bear to leave them. One of them may be alive. I think I saw her lips move. I want you to send for a doctor and a priest.'

I lifted the child with the turned head, laid her on my lap and placed my fingers over her heart. Did her hand twitch? I circulated my fingertips on the little chest and put my face to her mouth to see if she breathed but the baby was certainly dead, as dead as her sister. Her head was flung back on my lap and her perfect little nostrils were grey and useless. The soundless cry must have been an illusion. Both had probably been dead for many hours.

Then I became aware that the room was filled with noise. Sarah was standing behind me, eyes fixed on the dead babies, fists pressed into her mouth. From the back of her throat came a steady screeching.

'Stop that, Sarah. It helps no one.' I laid the babies tenderly on the lining of my cloak and folded it around them. 'You must go and fetch a priest. These poor children should at least be buried properly.'

She didn't move.

'Sarah.'

At last she came forward and shoved her face so close to mine that her saliva spat on my lips. 'You have ruined that beautiful cloak. Have you any idea how much it cost? What was you thinking of?'

9

After Sarah had gone I was triumphant at first. Good, she obeyed me. But what with the long trek home, her shrieking and the blow of finding both babies dead, I began to tremble so hard that my teeth knocked together.

To calm myself I dipped my hands in the pail of water. The sight and feel of the metal reminded me of home and Mrs Gill. Everything she touched got clean in the end. Then I had a good idea – I'd wash the babies anyway. That's what you did with the dead. So I picked up a baby and lowered her into the bucket but her head on its thread of a neck flopped on to my wrist and then down into the pail, dragging the rest of her body with it.

I shook harder but managed to haul her out though grey bruises appeared on her arm where I'd held her too tight. 'Well, Emilie. It's just as well that your own child died. What a mess you'd have made of bringing her up. A ducking like that would have killed her,' I said briskly as I soaped her downy head. I even began to hum a melody from yesterday's *Te Deum*.

Then the door burst open, my husband appeared – 'By Christ, Emilie, what have you done?' – and I was jolted back to the reality of my parlour where scum floated on tepid water in the bucket, a heap of dead flesh lay on the red lining of the cloak and lice crawled through the folds of my filthy skirts.

I clutched my hands tight together to stop them flying off my wrists. 'I couldn't leave them in a dung heap. They deserve a proper burial.'

He was pale and dull-eyed. I hadn't seen him angry like this since the day he came out of the library after the interview with my father. 'Deserve. Emilie. They're bastards. Some whore throttled 'em and slung 'em away. A hundred such are tossed into the gutters every month. Christ knows what infection you've brought into the house.'

'But they are babies. They have a soul.'

'Women have hung for less. Who's to prove you didn't kill them yourself? This is London, Emilie. You're supposed to behave in a civilised way.'

The horror of the dung heap and the blank eyes of those watching children came back in such a rush that my knee jolted one of the babies off my lap. 'I expect the priest will be here soon. A guinea or so should be enough for their burial.'

'There'll be no burial.'

'They must be buried. I could take them back to Selden if you like.' For a lovely moment I was in the grassy graveyard near my mother's little plot. Just the place. She would take care of them with her silken hands. Gill could make them a box lined with flannel to keep them warm and surely Shales would agree to bury them. He and I would try to understand why some poor woman took them to that dreadful place and abandoned them, dead or alive.

I should have been paying more attention to my husband because he lunged forward, bundled up the babies and made for the door.

'Where are you taking them?'

'Never you mind. The nearest ditch. Where they belong.'

'No.' I tried to reach him but tripped on my petticoats so that he had the door half open by the time I caught hold of his knee. My other hand gripped his heel but he kicked me aside and I was flung back on my elbow. I lunged after him again and this time his boot got my chin and sent me reeling. The door slammed shut and I heard the key turn in the lock and his pounding feet on the stairs.

I lay with my face on the Persian rug. Pain ran round my jaw and into my eyes but it seemed a welcome and definite feeling compared with the chaos in my head, swirling vortices like those described by Descartes and disproved by Newton – only Descartes's vortices or whorls of matter weren't chaotic, they moved in one direction, or he thought they did until a wayward comet was observed travelling the wrong way, thereby causing a dent in his tidy universe.

Comets. What were comets? Heavenly portents unleashed by God as a warning, according to Newton. But good old, saintly old Newton never accepted an easy answer. Instead, he went on and on looking at a problem until he had beaten it into submission. The elliptical path of the comet, for instance, had shown him the way all planets move. How wise Newton had been sometimes to study heavenly rather than earthly bodies which were so unpredictable and full of pain.

I was mesmerised by the flames in the hearth, which went on flaring and licking despite everything. Mrs Gill told me that some midwives choke unwanted babies with a spoonful of gin to finish them off. A baby was snuffed out by gin, fire by water and a rose by imprisonment in a flask.

Putrefaction, the black crow of alchemy, according to my father, was a necessary process as the decomposition of one thing gives life to another, otherwise the planet would groan under the weight of too much creation. In a year or so all that would be left of the babies apart from their immortal souls – and that seemed to be a matter of some argument – would be bone and fingernails.

For those lumps of flesh I had put my husband into such a rage that he would surely never forgive me. No wonder he kicked me. I had got it all wrong again. But what was more wrong, to bring home putrid babies, to leave them in the dung heap or to put them back there? And I'd come no closer to my mother after all. Another failure. The frustration, the pointlessness of my day's work, had me forcing my wrist into my mouth to hold back the sobs as I used to when I was a child and my father was angry with me for shattering a flask by overheating.

Chapter Seven

THE FURNACE SHED

I

The next day Sarah and I drove back to Selden. We were not on speaking terms. She never bothered to explain her non-appearance on the night of Sir Isaac's funeral and I blamed her for fetching Aislabie rather than a priest. My head still ached because of the dark bruise under my chin. Fortunately she and I were forced apart because the carriage was stuffed with bales of cloth and crates of other things needed for my husband's assembly, or party, as he chose to call it. He had been so impressed by Sir Isaac's funeral that he decided to decorate Selden Manor crimson, this particular colour being Sir I. N.'s favourite. The great hall was to be swagged in red muslin, the guests would be required to wear red and only red food would be served by a cook brought from London.

Selden was turned upside down. Aislabie shoehorned Mrs Gill out of her usual haunts and sent her upstairs to supervise the clearing of dozens of unused chambers. The party was in four weeks and after that the demolition would start. I met her on the stairs one morning with a trio of village girls and Gill in tow. They were on their way to my father's room and once there Mrs Gill took no notice of me but gave a series of rapid instructions. 'The chest is wormy and must be burnt. Likewise its contents which have been taken by moth. The bedding is to be washed. The windows must be treated with vinegar, and the mirror. You will need to sprinkle the floor before sweeping.'

'Mrs Gill.' She stared across at me. 'Mrs Gill, a word.' She finished her list before joining me on the landing. 'These are my father's things. Do you not think I should be consulted?'

'I assumed that these orders were from you since you'd not troubled yourself to speak to me.'

'They are from my husband.'

'Then with your consent, I suppose.'

'No. No. But I can't stop him. I cannot seem to make my mark with him.'

'Have you tried?'

'You don't understand. He doesn't take me into account.'

'And why should he? You are like a rock in the river. You watch us all gush past and you don't lift a finger to stop us.'

'It's because I can't. I don't know how. My father . . .'

'Your father is dead and gone. He has nothing to do with what happens now.' We stood side by side on the draughty landing, aware that there was silence from within the room where the girls stood about and listened. But I remembered the night of the dead babies and how my husband's foot had cracked against my chin, and I knew that I hadn't the strength to fight him so in the end I said, 'Well, well . . . So I'll trust your judgement.'

2

Gill presided over a bonfire in the bee orchard as day after day a procession of servants formed to carry out wormy cradles and broken-backed chairs. Anything of value was spirited over the wall and into the village. I caught Annie creeping across the stable yard with a warming pan, a footstool and a rolled carpet. She looked frightened and dropped the pan with a terrible clang on to the cobbles. 'Mrs Gill said I could have them.'

I took the footstool and examined it curiously because I'd never seen it before and wondered which of the Selden wives had worked the elaborate tapestry. 'I won't take it if you don't want,' said Annie.

'No. Have anything, have it all,' and I left her standing there with her worn trophies. What right had I to protest now, when I had never cared about these things in the past?

Meanwhile Sarah produced a skein of red silk, sat in the window of my chamber from which she had a good view of the parrot bowl on the mantel and proceeded to embroider me a fiery edge to my black petticoat.

3

Though I was sometimes aware of what was happening, just as I knew by the greening of the woods and the startling volume of birdsong that spring had come, I spent most of my time in the laboratory. When I first got back I opened the door cautiously, afraid of what changes I might find, but everything was in order. Gill had kept the fire going and completed the dissolution process.

I sat in my father's chair and tried to remember what had been in my head before I went to London. His instructions for the next, most delicate stage of the process of palingenesis were clear. The distillation. Ah, the distillation.

For this we used a bain-marie, named after our alchemical predecessor, Mary Prophetissa, the Jewess. The bain-marie was an iron pan inserted into the top of our medium furnace. We filled the pan with water, heated it to a gentle simmer and then suspended the flask of mixture in the bath to keep it at a constant temperature. The flask was one of our most precious, a cucurbit bought fifty years ago and purified annually between each alchemical experiment. It lay on its side at the end of the work-bench, a gritty grey solution clinging to its base, and beside it the alembic or still head which had to be cemented to the top so that the vapour from the heated mixture could collect, condense and trickle through a long, downward-pointing neck into a receiver, like a swan dipping its head. Mary Prophetissa's preferred seal was a mixture of clay – my father and I had fine white clay brought from London – chopped human hair, my own, and a little dried cow dung.

My father's alchemical notebook did not go beyond this stage. He had prepared the bain-marie and cucurbit but gone no further. His notes stopped on 28 March 1726 and I knew why. In recent years his fingers had grown so stiff that I had to perform the delicate operation of sealing the neck of the cucurbit to the still head for him. It had been my job to mix the paste, handle the glass and suspend it over the bain-marie, his to record the operation. He had stopped work because he simply hadn't the heart or the physical skills to go on without me.

Hence the last heading: *28 March 1726 The Distillation*. And nothing more. Defeat.

But I was determined not to be defeated; I knew exactly what to do now. So I summoned Gill and told him to light the medium furnace, then I chopped off a fistful of hair and snipped it smaller, smaller until I had a heap of black filings. Gill lifted a lump of clay from its moist nest in the cellars and fetched a scoop of dung from the stable yard, and I mixed the paste with gobs of spittle until I had a perfect glue, reeking of the earth. Next I added my own alchemical mixture to the dried-up remains my father had left in the cucurbit. The contents would surely be much more potent if I used both.

The trouble came when I picked up the delicate vessel and tried to add a measure of distilled water to the alchemical brew. Since Sir Isaac's funeral and the dead babies my nerves were in such a state that I scarcely trusted my fingers to hold such a precious thing. There seemed to be a constant shrieking around me and I had to shake my head and clutch my skirts to steady myself. When the equipment was at last set up and the water bath had reached its ideal temperature I perched on the stool and rested my chin in my hands. The furnace had to be watched day and night through weeks of distillation.

4

On the day before the party Aislabie sent for me to the Queen's Room to view his new outfit. The prospect of seeing him frightened me because we had hardly spoken since the day after Newton's funeral. Aislabie had spent a lot of time in town and on the occasions when he was home had been solicitous though wary, as if afraid of what I might do or say next. Once or twice after supper I caught him watching me speculatively but I always withdrew my hand if he took it or averted my face from a kiss. I was relieved that he didn't come near me at night because the incident with the dead babies was still in my head and I wasn't sure if I could bear him to touch me. Yet, perversely, all this time I had been waiting for him.

The strange thing was that he seemed to have forgotten the episode altogether and greeted me with his usual exuberance and affection. He was a vision in a waistcoat of crimson damasked satin very flared below the waist and stiffened with buckram. It had thirty or so matching buttons and was so gorgeous that the front of his coat had been cut away to reveal its full glory. His breeches were dyed amber, his buckles decorated with amber, his cravat pinned with a miniature amber dagger and he had a new cane with an amber knob the size of a hen's egg. He smiled at me from amidst all this finery in the old rakish way, brought his arm up behind me and stroked my back with the handle of the cane.

I held back at first but his mouth tasted of apples and with a few caresses of his fingertips there it was, the old magic, the promise of refuge and excitement. I fell against him with relief because it seemed that I was forgiven and the nightmare of the babies was over.

'My pale girl,' he said, 'what have you been up to? Never mind. After the party we'll be off to London and then you'll climb aboard *Flora* and we'll all sail away together. What do you think, Em?'

'Is *Flora* fit to be seen at last?'

'*Flora* is the sweetest little vessel in all the wide world. You should see her brasses and the tight coils of her ropes and the way her sails are all tucked up. I've had a cabin fitted out high up in the stern and you and I will sleep there, Em. Imagine lying together amidst the motion of the waves, the moving forward at a great rate.'

I tried to visualise the confinement of a little cabin. How would Aislabie be on board a ship with nowhere to go but a narrow deck and nothing to do but watch the waves? Perhaps I could teach him about the tides, show him the constellations, explain how Aristotle had believed the saltiness of the sea was due to the action of the sun on the waves whereas Leonardo da Vinci and later Boyle knew that all the sea is salty, not just the surface, and that salt is contained one way or another in all created things.

I was so absorbed by these speculations that I hardly noticed our lovemaking. I expect it was energetic as usual, a pulling up of petticoats and an unbuttoning of breeches, an urgent union of flesh, a great many kisses planted on my breasts and thighs while I clutched at his clothes and tried to hold him inside me for a little longer. I expect my body clamoured under his fingers but I have no memory of it, though I do remember that he was in a hurry to get downstairs and review the arrangements for the party.

It's a pity I wasn't paying attention because that is the last time I ever lay with Aislabie.

5

Sarah and I were still not quite back to normal – she contemptuous, me apologetic – so it was a relief the next day to find her much more like herself. Because of my father's death I was excused the red rule but my new black gown, an early birthday present from my husband, was hardly suitable for mourning – cut like a vast coat with a cross-over bodice that revealed most of my bosom, and skirts pinned up to display the red embroidered petticoat. Sarah treated me roughly, as if I were a clothes-horse, and when I complained about the amount of exposed flesh pinned a pleat of ribbon to my bodice so clumsily that she scratched me. She sucked her lower lip and tutted with irritation, bundled up my hair and threw row after row of jet beads round my neck.

The reason for this hurry was that she, like all the other more presentable servants, had to help serve. I saw her later, airy and winsome, slipping from room to room with a muslin apron tied above her waist and a tiny cap perched on the back of her head. I, by contrast, was thrown off balance by the weight of my overlapping skirts. I stood in the great hall amidst vases of monstrous peonies and watched petals fall like gobbets of flesh. I picked one up and thought I might preserve it under glass like the rose but guests were arriving with splashes of red in their costumes; on caps, handkerchiefs, stockings or waistcoats. They stared at me and I knew they were thinking: There's that fright, Emilie Aislabie. Did you know she went around London picking up babies as if they were stray dogs? Their raised voices filled my head almost to the brim and the quintet from London sawed its elbows back and forth and produced music vivace, staccato, crescendo, tangling with my hair and crushing me against tables of food daubed by that same red-soaked paintbrush; glossy red jellies, dyed vegetables, berries, bleeding pink meats.

Then my hand was taken by a sharp-nailed lady who dragged me into her circle of country matrons some of whom I knew dimly from childhood glimpses at fairs and feast days and who now sat like red cabbages in their great skirts.

They interrogated me about the house: 'Is it true that the white columns will be seen from the bridge at Lower Selden? . . .' 'They say twenty acres of woodland will disappear . . .' 'And the lake will drain the wells in the village so the poor souls will be without water . . .' I saw diseased teeth like chips of resin and turkey flesh hanging from a receding chin. And on the other side of the room Aislabie stood in front of the mantel, glass in one hand, cane in the other. He'd drawn some favoured individual aside for a more intimate conversation and I couldn't catch his eye. Then he summoned a servant – Sarah – with the twitch of an eyelid. She was at his elbow in an instant, took his order, curtsied, left. Nobody would have guessed the venom beneath the surface.

Other ladies joined the group, Lady Essington, the fair woman I knew from London with the little black slave child ever in tow, and a couple of her sophisticated friends. She sat on a low stool next to me so that her skirts billowed, and smiled winsomely across at Aislabie. He blew her a kiss. I swear I saw it go wafting over the heads of the other guests like a bit of gossamer to land on her moist lips and I was sorry that it hadn't come my way. The conversation turned to childbearing; who was lying in, whose infant had lately died, the difficulty of finding reliable nurse-maids, the cost of laundry, the question of education. I knew what was going on: because I was childless there were whispers about what was or was not happening in my marriage bed.

And then they lowered their voices and put their hands on their throats and slavered over the even more delectable topic of unwanted children. It was an iniquity. These girls. When would they learn? Everyone knew that in London babies smothered at birth lay knee deep in the ditches. And this sickness had even extended to the country where you couldn't move without tripping over dead infants. A fund had been set up but should one contribute? Surely that would simply encourage these girls, who frankly couldn't keep their legs together . . .

As I hadn't kept my own legs together when it mattered I studied the speaker with some interest, Lady E.'s mother, a stately matron who'd given a disdainful nod to the red theme by tying a red ribbon to her fan.

'Could you have put a pillow over your own child's face?' I said.

'What a question.'

'So you chose life for your children?'

'Naturally.' Her eyes were the colour of iron.

'Naturally. I don't think any mother would kill her infant, unless the alternative was worse.'

Her fan worked so furiously that her cap strings blew over her shoulder. 'I'm sure. But my point is that they should not . . . The child ought not to be conceived in the first place. Every woman has a choice.'

I disappeared for a while into the bee orchard to consider whether or not I'd been given a choice and by the time I came back to the scarlet present the conversation had moved on to the disgracefully high charges made by certain midwives and I had to speak loudly to pull them back into line. 'I think that human beings are very odd. In any other species a mother, having copulated, is properly equipped to nurture her young until they can survive alone. The human species expects the woman to be respectable, married and moneyed before she can manage motherhood.'

There was a gulping behind the fans and Lady E., blushing in her pink satin, said, 'That's because we're higher than animals. Heaven forbid that we should all behave like beasts,' and she stroked the head of her big-eyed slave child who stared unblinkingly into some distant place. All that leaning forward revealed Lady E.'s entire bosom and she glanced under her eyelids across the room at Aislabie who narrowed his eyes in appreciation. 'Animals work by instinct. We humans have emotion and intellect.

If we are Christian we know good from evil. We choose how to behave.'

Bewildered by the unexpected display of intimacy between Lady E. and my husband I spoke much too sharply: 'Ah, choice, but how do we know whom or what to choose? And a girl doesn't have much choice if some man chooses to push her onto her back and pump her full of his seed.'

I don't know how they reacted to this last remark because the room had changed. There was a black pillar among the crimson: Shales of all people. I stood up and peered over the crowd to be sure it was him but there was no mistaking his trim wig and sober face, although just at the moment there was a distinct gleam in his eye.

I fought my way over to him. ' Why are you here?'

He kissed my hand like a London gentleman and the unexpected contact of his lips made me flinch. I thought I knew where I was with Shales who smiled only when he was glad and never spoke untruths. 'I was invited and I'm pleased I accepted because I couldn't help overhearing some of your conversation. You have been giving your lady friends quite an education.'

'Did you really get an invitation? My husband said I wasn't to speak to you.'

'He and I have our differences obviously, but of course he'd invite me. How could he not?'

'I'm amazed you would bother with a party like this.'

'I quite like parties. I used to go to a good many at one time. But I came because I wanted to see you. You haven't been in church and when I called at the house they said you were unavailable.'

'Who said?'

'Once your husband. A second time your maid.'

'I wasn't told. What did you want to say to me?'

'I wanted to show you the second edition of my book, which is nearly ready for the printers. I thought you might be just the person to check it for inconsistencies. And I was hoping to add a chapter on investigations into the air exhaled by plants but I need a bold mind to guide me.'

I wouldn't meet his eye in case he found out that instead of furthering my work on fire and air I had been spending week after week watching the distillation of my alchemical mixture. 'As I've said, my husband distrusts you. I couldn't have spoken to you even if I'd wanted to.'

'But you've been working, obviously. Both times I called they said you weren't to be disturbed. May I ask what you've been doing?'

'The house has been full of upheaval. I've had no time for experiments.'

'A pity. I was sure that by now you would have come close to confounding the phlogistonists.'

I was silent. On the one hand he irritated me with his questions about phlogiston, on the other I wished he would offer his arm and take me somewhere cool and quiet, like in the Abbey, so that I could tell him all that had happened on the day of the dead babies.

'So, the house,' he said. 'I gather the plans are going forward. You must be very sad.'

'I no longer care. It is just a house.'

'Mrs Aislabie, if it would help, I will take your father's things. I could store them until such time as you are able to use them again.'

'I'd hate to compromise you in the eyes of your parishioners.'

'I've decided that their good opinion matters less than that you should be able to keep these precious books and instruments. Will you let me help you?'

'If need be.'

'And the house and village – is there no hope of reprieve?'

'I believe not,' I said in a cool, light voice. 'Next week my husband and I will set sail for France. We expect work to begin during our absence.'

'What takes you to France?'

'My husband's ship has been refurbished and we will sail on her maiden voyage.'

'You will enjoy that, I expect,' he said, somewhat formally.

'Of course. I have never seen the sea. My mother was French. I have much to look forward to.'

'And who will be left here in your absence? To whom should we apply for advice?'

'You must ask my husband,' I said, deciding that he cared

nothing for me after all, only for the village. 'I believe Mr Harford has agreed to oversee the work. And now if you'll excuse me . . .' And I walked away, acutely disappointed.

6

I went to the library thinking I would go through it to the laboratory, but I'd forgotten that this was now a gambling den so fuggy with smoke and liquor fumes that I could hardly get more than a few feet inside. In one corner a swathe of red cloth had been torn down, revealing the spines of our books like sinews in a wound. Lady E. was at one of the tables, red lips smiling as she made a neat fan of her cards and tossed coins into a heap. She waved gaily and beckoned me over. I would gladly have played her – I was sure I could win against a fluffy head such as hers – but at that moment a drunken squire lurched towards me, clamped his foot down on the edge of my petticoat and pressed his whiskery face into my bosom. I gave him a shove and got myself out to the relative coolness of the hall.

Shales had now been cornered by the MP for Buckingham but he took a step towards me. 'Mrs Aislabie . . .'

I was still angry with him and certainly didn't want to speak to a fat politician so I fled along the kitchen passage intending to reach the laboratory through the cellars but the stable yard was full of coachmen leaning on their carriage wheels, and bored horses who flung up their heads to the stars. As there was no way of getting past them to the cellar door, I kept to the shadows and darted out on to the terrace where there was no moon but a breeze blew sappy perfume from the woods. One or two other guests had strayed outside, tempted by the mild evening, so I hurried on, my skirts lipping down the mossy steps until I was in the trees and could breathe all the good green leafiness of the woods. Sometimes I tore along as the wind got behind my hoops, sometimes I was buffeted back.

In the orchard, ash from Gill's bonfire powdered my face. Above me the ground-floor windows of Selden glowed red. Then I had a sign. A light was shining under the door of the furnace shed – my father's light. The furnace was only ever lit for him. Everything went away except me and the light. He is there, I thought. At last he has come back. I knew for sure that he would be stooped over the fire with his coat-tails dragging and his wig thrown impatiently to one side as he rattled the long-handled pan we used for the precious ores. I could crouch on the earth floor and watch the flames. I would smell coal, hot stone, scorched mineral.

I ran, his name stuttering on my tongue, my skirts bundled up round my hips so that my feet could move faster and faster before he disappeared again. The door was shut. I lifted the latch quietly so as not to disturb him and the first thing I noticed was that the temperature was so low that no fire could possibly be burning there and that the glow I had seen was not firelight but lamplight. Next I saw that the furnace wasn't lit by a real fire but with only a pretence of flame, a fall of crimson. And what I saw flickering were not tongues of fire but two slender white legs and between them two sturdy male calves and the skirts of a red waistcoat.

It took me a while to unravel this picture, which kept changing and re-forming. What confused me was the swathe of red that the lovers had arranged in the furnace mouth to protect themselves from the dirt. And then the picture suddenly clarified. This was my husband bent over the squirming figure of a young girl, and beneath them was my cloak, the one with the crimson lining which I thought had been ruined by the dead babies.

And now I saw things very clearly indeed and realised that the white female legs weren't at all unwilling. The knees flexed and straightened in time to my husband's working buttocks and were clad below the knee in a pair of white stockings with a familiar clocking on the heel and a pair of brass-buckled shoes once worn by me, and this proved that the woman to whom my husband was making love so energetically was none other than my maid Sarah.

My husband pumped faster and faster, and Sarah's athletic leg movements showed a familiarity with the rhythm that suggested they had done this many times before. Besides, her small right hand, which a few hours ago had pinned the pleat of ribbon to my bodice, had manoeuvred itself between his thighs and was fingering his genitals and buttocks as if it knew exactly how to please him.

The trouble was I stayed too long. It was the habit born in this furnace shed to stay and watch. I knew I had been hit but not how badly. I saw, and at first was numb. The lovers went still and there was a moment of dead silence before Sarah's white face appeared over my husband's shoulder and our eyes met. I never thought she and I meant anything to each other except that we had been thrown together as mistress and maid but that look she gave me was one of violent connection. There was a force between us, the kind of impulse that squares two cats for a fight. I saw triumph, lust and fear, and I saw her for the first time. Really her. Sarah. She entered me like the blade of a dagger.

I stepped outside and pulled the door shut, fumbled my way between the outbuildings and went back to the house where everything was much as before except that Lady Essington's mother had joined her at the table and the heap of coins between them had doubled in size. Harford offered me a place and I sat down and drank glass after glass of wine while I gambled my husband's sovereigns on three hands of quadrille and won every time.

7

A voice in my ear: 'Mrs Aislabie. I wonder if I might have a word before I go.'

I played another hand. If I spoke to Shales in this bitter mood I would wound him. But he didn't go away so in the end I scooped up my winnings and said, 'I've told you. I can't do anything for you. Speak to my husband.'

'I've been watching you. You are unhappy.' Though the crowd was dense as ever I heard him clearly as if he were the only person in the room. I always did. I could have repeated every conversation we'd ever had, word for word. But I couldn't attend to him properly. Beyond my consciousness of him and the nightmarish scene in the furnace shed was the most dreadful realisation of all: when I first saw Aislabie I was mistaken. I thought he was one thing but he was another. I remembered him so clearly standing in the porch with the sunlight falling on and round him, the image of a perfect young man, and now I knew that had been the false light of what my father used to call gramarye, his word for necromancy, and it had taken all this time for the enchantment to be lifted.

A glint of amber; Aislabie was in the doorway, flushed and breathless. When he caught my eye his defiant smile told me that he knew I'd seen him with Sarah and he didn't much mind.

I took Shales's arm. 'You wanted to take my father's things. Come then, come with me.' Clutching his sleeve I ran along the kitchen passage and across the stable yard. This time I didn't care who saw me as I plucked a lantern from its hook and plunged down into the cellars. On and on we went, kicking aside tumbled bee baskets and stooping in uneven passageways. When we reached the spiral staircase I gathered my petticoats and led him upwards to the laboratory which was occupied by Gill who'd made himself scarce during the party and was cocooned in my father's chair. He stumbled to his feet, gaped at Shales, shuffled to the door, disappeared.

I shot the bolt and hung up the lantern. Alcohol sang in my ears as the room tilted and went hazy. There was no other light except from the fire and the glow of embers in the furnace. Shales put his hand on the mantel as if to anchor himself. The air was thick with the heat of a late May evening, the two fires and the smell of sulphur, ancient wood and father's tobacco.

I knew now that the laboratory had the power to reconstitute itself in different forms depending on who was looking; holy or hellish, orderly or ramshackle. Through Shales's eyes I saw a space without boundaries. Darkness filled the corners and smudged the angles of cupboards and shelves. The reddish light fell on curves and corners, glass, ceramic and oak, and there were four dimensions because all that had ever happened here was present in the pages of our books, the dust trapped in crevices and the hollows worn in the floorboards and seats of chairs. But mostly the light pooled on the alembic in which pearly moisture droplets had collected, on my father's alchemical notebook open at the page marked *Palingenesis* and on the glass containing the dead rose.

A burst of laughter penetrated from the library and a carriage rolled away outside, followed by the squeal of our rusty gates.

What with the fire and the furnace, the warm night and too much wine I felt stifled so I opened a high central flap in the shutters. The moon had come out and its white face, squashed like a grapefruit, shone directly on to the cloud of vapour collected in the receiver. There it was, exposed. Palingenesis.

Shales leaned on the mantel, arms folded, one side of his face in darkness, watching me. There was such tension between us that I think if I'd put out a finger and plucked the air it would have quivered like the string of a lyre.

I moistened my dry lips. 'Palingenesis,' I said.

He made no move.

'The distillation.'

Still he didn't seem to understand though he glanced at the receiver and crossed the room to take a closer look.

'Alchemy. All this time I've been working for my father.'

He perched on a stool and ran his hand over his face.

'You disapprove. You think I'm mad.'

He shook his head.

'What then? What do you think? Shales?'

'You know what I think.'

'Tell me.'

'I think this is a terrible waste of your gifts.'

'Gifts.'

'Your father knew he had an extraordinary daughter. He told me that you were the guiding force in his work on the nature of fire. That's what I thought you were doing. If we knew more about air and fire we might change the way we think about the world.'

'Well, as you see, my whole being is fixed on this.'

'You must know this work is fruitless.'

'No. No. If palingenesis can work with a rose it can work with any once living thing. I want my father back.' I stopped, appalled by the boldness and truth of this statement. 'I broke his heart so I want him to come back and be made better.'

'I think, Emilie, he broke his own heart.'

'It comes to the same thing.'

'Do you really think you can raise the dead?'

'I don't know.'

'And if he did come back, what would you do then?'

'I'd tell him I'm sorry. I'd help him put everything right.' I saw my father standing on the terrace with his coat-tails afloat and his staff in his right hand to drive away Harford and Osborne, and the menace of their measures and maps; I saw Sarah scuttle through the trees with her apron strings flying and her hair pulled loose from its immaculate cap; and I saw Aislabie gallop away in a cloud of dust and then a slow settling of silence on Selden. Except there was something so deadly in the silence that it made me shake. 'I can't stop working on this. He is directing me. I can't stop. I feel him watching me. When he was alive he kept a notebook and he wrote me down in it, every move. I believe he planned my life minute by minute as if I were a flask into which he could drop one substance after another until I was full up. And he's plotting me still. I'm part of his design. But if I make him come back I'll be able to show him how he failed. He taught me to listen and copy and learn and deduce. He taught me to experiment with the material world and to make bold hypotheses about why things happen and then to prove them again and again. But he didn't teach me how to make choices. He didn't teach me how human beings are or to understand the complication of feelings. He didn't teach me . . .'

More laughter came from next door. Shales reached out, stroked the warm receiver with the back of his finger and watched me with his steady, odd-coloured eyes. I thought that this was the first and last time he would ever set foot in here so I tried to memorise him, the many planes of his nose, cheeks and chin, the shadows and textures of his skin, the caress of his finger on glass. 'He didn't teach you . . .'

'He didn't teach me that with some people what seems to be real, isn't real at all. I used to trust what I saw. He taught me that if I could see a thing and touch it, and if it behaved as I hoped it would, then these were true qualities. But I find that men aren't like that so how do I know what I can trust? Even my father, when I had offended him, even he didn't love me much, when the test came.'

'Your father loved you, Emilie. I'm sure.'

'Not enough to forgive me or to talk to me about my mother whom I can't find however hard I try.'

Another long silence. 'He should have said more about her, I think.'

'You tell me.'

'How can I? I never knew her.'

'You spent night after night with my father before he died. I don't believe he never talked about her.'

'Mostly he talked about you.'

'No, that's not good enough. What do you know about my mother?'

No reply.

'Please. Please tell me.'

His hand went still.

'Shales?'

'I gave my word.'

'Dear God, Shales, you stand there judging me but you won't help me. You won't bend one inch. Well, then take what you want and go.' I began to snatch things off shelves and out of cupboards. 'Take it all. Take it. Silver, nitrate, mercury, potash, copper, verdigris. Scales, test tubes, alembics. Take them. The clocks, the measures, the balances. The books. The lot. Have them. Bacon, Libavius, Sendivogius. I'll never read them again,' and I slammed the books one on top of the other until the air was cloudy with dust. 'I have no time for them now. Take them. Or Gill will pack them in crates and bring them in the cart. Sell them if you like. Send them to London. Use the money to mend a few thatches in the village.'

'Palingenesis,' he said suddenly. 'How will it happen?'

'You don't want to know.'

'Help me understand.'

'It's a mystery. It happens through the application of centuries of experience and learning, through ritual and heat and natural philosophy. It combines the alchemist's belief in a vital force with our knowledge of how matter behaves. It is a mix of what we see with what we believe.'

'Then it is no different from my religious faith, except that in religion the agent is God and in alchemy the agent is man or woman.'

'But your religion, which after all is yet another leap in the dark, you think is sane and permissible. Alchemy, you think, is absolutely wrong.'

'What I think doesn't matter, Emilie.'

'Without alchemy what other way forward do I have?'

'You'll find a way.'

'I can't.'

'You haven't told me yet what help you need.'

'I need to put right the past. I was a fool to marry Aislabie.'

I spoke so low I wasn't sure he heard. There was a long silence. Then he said, 'I thought that this experiment with palingenesis was about regeneration, not rewriting the past.'

'I can try. I must try.'

The laboratory was changing and it was as if we were in a bubble of glass, like the alchemical mixture, and everything else was melting away. 'What has happened?' Shales said.

I couldn't tell him. The shame of what I'd seen in the furnace shed was too terrible.

'Emilie?'

I studied him, his sombre black coat, the tilt of his head, the concentration in his eyes. Meanwhile the water in the bain-marie hissed, another carriage set off outside and faintly from a distant corner I thought I heard my father's cough. Now I knew why I had been led through the labyrinth of the miscarried embryo, the bleak homecoming, the dead babies, the furnace shed – it was all to show me this.

This, Emilie, is the life you could have had. This is the man whom, in the end, I would have chosen for you.

I put my hand over his and felt the tension in his muscles. Then I leaned so close that I heard his heartbeat and how his breathing was rapid and shallow. Minutes passed and I turned inwards so that his cravat brushed my nose. When he put his hand on the back of my neck it was like the moment when a substance first breaks down and becomes another, ice to water, liquid steam. The clocks began to tick in harmony, the mice scuffled in the empty cages, the flames leapt in the hearth and my father turned the page of his notebook.

'Do you really want the dead to awaken?' Shales said.

'You had a wife. Wouldn't you want her back?'

'When she died, yes. I remember the night after the burial as the most terrible I have ever experienced. I couldn't fathom my loss. You see, it wasn't just that my wife had died. It was also that . . .'

His hand was tense on my neck. I couldn't bear for him to be frail and struggling so in the end I said, 'And now?'

'Now I've changed. It's nearly three years. I still grieve, of course. But I wouldn't go back. I am different now.'

'But if you could turn back time in some way. If you could go back to how it was in the months before she died . . .'

Inside the furnace hot charcoals hissed and shuffled and the room was so close, despite the open window, that sweat ran down the back of my knees. He stroked my neck and spoke into my hair. 'Still I'm not sure. My memory would not be erased, I assume, and I would therefore know too much. I would rather be as I am now, here in this place I have come to since then.'

I stood in his arms and thought: This is how love could be. I do believe that however much I argued or cried or made mistakes Shales would still hold me. But there was a sudden change, he drew a shuddering breath, put his hands on my shoulders to set me upright and took a step back. 'Perhaps we should find a way of living in the present rather than the past.'

'But the present is intolerable.'

'Then we must change the way it is, if we can.'

'And if we can't?'

He touched my face, just my cheekbone, but said nothing.

'Please, Shales.'

His face was suffused with pain and longing. 'I don't know. I don't know. I don't know. Endure, I suppose.'

Faintly, through the double thickness of the doors again came laughter. In a trance of despair I picked up the lantern thinking: Please, please don't let this be the end. We didn't speak and we didn't touch as I led him back through the cellars and up to the stables, and by the time we reached the open air the long, aching silence between us had made me sick with the knowledge that by marrying Aislabie I had burnt every last bridge and there were no words and no actions that could undo that fact.

My husband was standing under the arch, waving to some departing carriage. He caught my eye, glanced over my shoulder at Shales and gave me a knowing wink. Shales bowed and would perhaps have kissed my hand but I withdrew sharply, stepped past him and went back to the laboratory.

8

Next day in the late afternoon I went up to my bedchamber to dress for dinner. *She* was there, packing my combs into a wooden box. She looked up and went very still. Her back was to the window so I couldn't see her face but I could smell her fear.

'What are you doing, Sarah?'

'Packing, Madam.'

'Don't.'

'You are going to London in the morning.'

'I shall be staying here.'

She shuffled the contents of the box so as to fit in more combs and ribbons. Only my mother's pink ribbon was still draped over a hook. Sarah despised it because it was faded and crumpled. 'I think you have to go,' she said.

I tied the ribbon round my throat and told her to fetch my green gown. She looked surprised but didn't argue though it was the first time I had worn a strong colour since my father's death. She handled it with great caution, as if the unlucky fabric might scorch her fingers, and stood behind me as usual to tie the strings. I could see our faces in the mirror: mine dead white, eyes black and blank as obsidian, cheekbones sharp as knives and a twist of black hair falling over my shoulder; she very pale and intent, her lower lip caught in her teeth.

Her fingers were ice-cold on my back. When she knelt in front of me to reach under my skirts and straighten the hoop I saw the panicky rise and fall of her bosom. I couldn't bear her to touch my head or face and when she tried to comb my hair I knocked her hand away and sent her out.

Downstairs the house was stripped bare and at dinner there were just Harford and Aislabie, who occupied my father's old place at the head of the table. He wore a lilac waistcoat and an amethyst jewel in his neck pin, his eyes flashed iridescent as his silks and he was in expansive mood. Mrs Gill, perhaps in defiance of the London cook, had produced a fricassée of duck along with fowl and a side of beef which my husband sliced with his usual neat enthusiasm. He exploded in and out of my consciousness so that I caught only fragments of what he said but I was transfixed by the bloody liquid that dripped from his fork and puddled under the meat.

'So, Em. What have you been up to all day?' I said nothing while Harford crammed food into his mouth and Aislabie filled my glass. 'Thank God we're off to town in the morning. This place won't be safe after tomorrow. I hope your bags are packed.'

'It's best to be out of the way,' said Harford, helping himself to more sauce. 'Everything will begin quietly but how deceptive that will be. The first job is to mark out the lake and start digging. The rubble from the demolished house will be used as lining.'

'Brilliant,' said my husband. 'Economical. That's how I like things.'

'I'll be off tomorrow to see about hiring the right kind of men. It's delicate work. There is a chance that the house won't withstand the pressure of having interior walls demolished so this will be a dangerous place for anyone to live in for a while.'

'Shore them up. There must be a way. The Romans managed a dome with no fuss. Why can't we?'

I sensed a degree of calculation behind this energetic conversation. 'I shall stay here,' I said.

'There'll be nothing for you, Em. You'll be in the way.'

'I've told Sarah she can leave. I don't need her. You can take her with you.'

'Lord, Em, what would I do with a lady's maid?'

There was a moment's silence, then Harford snorted with laughter. 'What a question for the lady to answer, Aislabie.'

I stared at my untouched food and the snail's trails of grease on the edge of the plate, then shoved it aside so sharply that a spoon clattered to the floor. Aislabie separated a sliver of breast from the broiled fowl and filled his mouth. 'You come to London, my dear Em. We'll be aboard *Flora* by the end of the week. She's twitching away in that dry dock of hers.' Another mouthful, a change of subject. 'Your friend Sir Isaac Newton never touched meat, I understand. In fact, as far as I can tell, he would have nothing to do with the flesh, beastly or human.'

This unwarranted attack on Sir Isaac got my full attention. 'Very fond of his unusual niece, I understand,' put in Harford. 'The girl has done well for herself by all accounts. Did not model her approach to amours on that of her celibate uncle but proved herself a calculating little miss. Just as well because she won't inherit huge amounts from Sir Isaac. He wasn't a great business-man. Lost thousands on the South Sea business.'

'You see, Em,' said Aislabie. 'Genius ain't enough. As witness the mess left by your late pa. I've had to come up with all sorts of schemes to repair the holes in the Selden finances. Good old *Flora*, for instance. There's a lot hangs on that ship.'

The door behind me flew open. Mrs Gill had come to remove the plates. I said again, 'I'm not coming to London but please take Sarah.'

A blancmange, another new dish, swayed on a pewter salver. 'Can't have you risking life and limb here, Emilie. Your place is with me. We'll see how we get on crossing the Channel, then who knows? The West Indies. A successful merchant should know the destination of his goods and how his ships are run. He has to be bold. There's money to be made if you send your ships far enough. I may even sail with her when she goes halfway round the world.'

'I didn't know you called yourself a merchant these days.'

'Whisky and guns to Calabar, then a new cargo to the Americas.' He beamed at me across the table and took a spoonful from the side of the blancmange, which keeled over.

'I don't want Sarah and I'm not going to London. Please take her with you.'

But their conversation had moved on. There was talk of an estimate made at Jonathan's. Twenty-three pounds a head. Six hundred to a ship. Even if a third were lost that would be profit in the region of . . . Then a name that had me wide awake again. '. . . ask Reverend Shales,' said Harford. 'He's something of an expert on the movement of air.'

'That's it. Have a word in his ear. Trouble is he's gone off. Called today to let me know he'd some urgent business in Norfolk. But if he ever comes back, obviously, get something useful out of him.'

Shales had been introduced into the conversation as an alchem-ist might add nitre to cause a violent reaction. Gone away? Why?

Aislabie pushed back his chair and lay in a diagonal line, feet far extended, wineglass against his belly, watching me. 'Didn't he mention it, Em? I thought you two were thick as thieves. He's been summoned to Norwich by his father-in-law. Apparently his skills are needed to improve the ventilation of the local prison. Too many felons dying before they've served their time. Wouldn't surprise me if he stayed and took a living there. I've hinted often enough that I can't stand his politics.'

I was suddenly so sick that I retched. There was a hasty scraping of chairs, a ring of the bell. 'Sarah,' I said.

'We've sent for Sarah. She'll take you to bed. She'll look after you.'

9

When Aislabie came up to the Queen's Room later I was waiting for him. I had lit a couple of candles on the dressing table and was enthroned in a cream upholstered chair, still dressed in my green silk. The windows were wide open and the tassels shivered on the bed curtains. He looked surprised to see me but went to the mirror and began unwinding his cravat as he eyed me through the glass. 'What's the matter, Em?'

'I want to know what you're going to do about Sarah.'

He plucked off his wig and adjusted it meticulously on the stand, removed some pins from the tiny cupboard in its face, wound up a couple of stray curls and fixed them in place. Then he scratched the back of his head vigorously with both hands. 'Good Lord. Could this be a touch of jealousy? Glad to see you've got some human feeling, Emilie, but rest assured, Sarah's nothing but a frolic. You're the one. Come to London. I lose you in this godforsaken place. We'll have a new beginning.' He knelt down, put his hands on the arms of the chair and kissed my neck, but I was limp as a doll.

'Take Sarah with you to London,' I said.

'Not without you.' He gave me a little shake. 'Get it into your head. She's nothing. She's not the point.'

'How long has she been your mistress? Since she came to our house? Before you married me? Is that why you employed her, to have her conveniently on hand?' He laughed, leaned forward and gave me a smacking kiss on the cheek. As I didn't move a muscle he began to unbutton his waistcoat, shrugged it off and hung it up. 'How did you think I felt last night when I saw you with her?'

'I never know how any woman feels, my love. I know that you all seem to be happy to open your legs if a man hits the spot with a kiss on the mouth or a tweak in the right place.' He sat down on the edge of the bed and removed his shoes, untied his garters and unrolled his stockings. There was no reaching him in this mood. I had seen it a dozen times before, this fatal indifference of his once he could get no more from a situation. 'Listen, it doesn't have to be so complicated. Come with me to London. Forget about Sarah. I need you.'

'But Sarah. You can't just pretend she doesn't exist.'

'She doesn't really. She's small as a gnat in the scheme of things. Look. Look at the state of this place.' He took my upper arm and pulled me over to the window where we could see the broken terraces and ancient woods. I smelt him, my husband, exactly as when he first came to the house, the heat of him, the scent of his skin, a hint of alcohol and leather. 'I can't be doing with hanging around this bankrupt estate while my wife messes with the black arts and produces nothing. Did you know I once had high hopes of you, Emilie? I thought there might be something in the rumour that you and your pa had the key to endless riches. I hoped it would be just a matter of time. At least, the fanciful bit of me hoped that – fortunately the rest of me was somewhat more worldly. But I can't be waiting about here any longer. It isn't the life I want. I need a healthy son. I didn't marry to be chained to some ancient pile and a woman whose whole self is wrapped up in the life she once had with her father. I didn't marry your father for Christ's sake, Em.'

'I don't know why you married me.'

'How could I resist? Black-eyed Emilie, the alchemist's daughter, with her pockets full of mystery and beauty to take a man's breath away. My God, when I first clapped eyes on you I thought this was the one legend that hadn't been a lie. Everyone knew that the old alchemist John Selden had a lovely daughter hidden in his laboratory. An untouched pearl for some lucky man, we said, so I set out to woo you.' He kissed my neck again, and my ear. 'What can I do to convince you I love you?'

'Nothing. You don't love me. I want nothing more to do with you. But take Sarah with you to London. I don't want her here.'

'Can't be done. She'd be in the way.'

'You can't just leave us both here.'

'Then you come. Good Lord, the solution is very simple. Come and astonish London again with your brains and beauty. Maybe you'll even bear a son at last.'

'You deceived me. I thought you loved me but what you wanted was Selden, the name and the land. You were never prepared to be faithful. You never wanted me to be as I was, with all that I knew. You have wasted me.'

'No, Madam, I have tolerated you. I should tie you to my horse and drag you to London by the hair for what you have done in defiance of me. No other man would have put up with so much.'

'There's no need to put up with it any more. I don't wish to be known as your wife.'

'Your wishes have nothing to do with anything. You're my wife and you'll do as I say. To the letter.'

But there was something going on I couldn't quite grasp. He lacked conviction and wouldn't insist on me leaving tomorrow. Perhaps it was because *Flora* was his passion now and he would rather sail on her alone. So it was no surprise when he gave me a dismissive little push. 'Then stay. See how you like it with the house pulled down about your ears.'

'And Sarah?'

'I've told you. Sarah is a minor irritation. She'll disappear soon enough if you give her a couple of sovereigns. Don't bear a grudge, Em. Forgive your old Aislabie. All will be well, you'll see.'

I watched him untuck his shirt and unbutton his breeches, the hairs on his calves, the thrust of his buttocks. The odd thing was he was no different from the way he'd ever been and really did have as much affection for me as when we first met. It was simply that his feeling was of the kind that he might have for his horse or other slightly cherished object that delighted his senses from time to time. Whereas I had loved him so much that I had abandoned myself to him utterly. And because I had loved him so, the reverse of that feeling was not indifference or contempt but the coldness of stone. I saw him now as an agent of destruction bringing havoc in the wake of his irresistible smile.

As I left the room I glimpsed the flicker of a skirt and a whiff of Sarah's floral perfume. Though I couldn't forgive her I did pity her for what she had surely overheard.

Chapter Eight

ST EDELBURGA'S FAIR

I

When the clock in the tower of St M. and St E. struck five I stood in the entrance porch to watch Aislabie go. I wanted to be sure. He might be careless and leave bits of himself about, a dimple on the landing, a satirical twinkle in the gaps between the flagstones. I wanted to be rid of him, a clean slate.

It was the kind of May morning when everything shifts: grasses, leaves, clouds. I wasn't alone. Sarah had got up early too. Somewhere on the edge of it all a dove-grey skirt fluttered, there was a breath of her fragrance and a shiver of animosity.

Then a clip-clop of hooves on cobbles and Aislabie broke into the morning like a fist through parchment. He and his horse were tight-packed with energy; the brilliance of harness and glossy flank, the sheen of fabric, the stamping impatience to be gone. I stepped forward and he doffed his hat, bowed very low and came up smiling so that his teeth flashed white as his cuffs. 'Wish me bon voyage, Em, and you be good. Harford will be keeping an eye on you.'

Then the smile froze and his eyes slid away from the damson tree where Sarah must have been waiting. He shrugged and looked to the open gates, the lane beyond and in the distance London, *Flora*, a new adventure. The horse hooked up its tail, a stream of dung thundered on to the gravel, Aislabie lifted his hat one last time and then was gone. The carriage rolled, Gill put his shoulder to the gates, the dust settled and there was quiet.

All this time, through the crimson party and beyond, the distillation had continued; the water in the bain-marie simmered and a cloud of condensation gathered on the still head, trickled down the delivery spout and dripped into the receiver. When there had been a period of four hours or more and no moisture was collected Gill or I poured the cloudy distillate from the receiver back into the flask containing the crusty alchemical residue and began again.

No two alchemists agree when the distillation phase should stop. Some search for planetary, occult or meteorological signs. My father was even more inexact. *The sign of fire* was what he waited for. When I asked him to be more definite he said, 'We will know, Emilie.' And lo and behold there was always something: a comet, an eclipse, a streak of lightning, a fire in a haystack or even the unexplained guttering of a candle to show us it was time to finish distillation.

In fact, the next phase was the most lethal of all and had always marked the end of our alchemical adventure. Whereas the distillation is a delicate stage of the process, the next requires the addition of volatile saltpetre to the mixture and this causes an explosion which results at worst in the sudden death of the alchemist and at best an end to all his hopes. Mayow says the combination of fixed salt with nitro-aerial particles causes nitre to fly off like smoke. And Sir Thomas Browne says the explosion of gunpowder is due to the generation of a large bulk of air by the antipathetic reaction of saltpetre to sulphur.

My father, needless to say, always took the most elaborate precautions before embarking on this dangerous stage by muttering a series of conciliatory incantations, banishing me to a far corner and making Gill stand by with pails of water. Then he held the flask deep within the emptied water bath and added a meticulous measure of white powder one speck at a time. And little Emilie, wide-eyed behind her sheltering barrier, hands over her ears, saw the flash of light, smelt the delicious, acrid, wonderfully right scent of burning and knew with sinking heart that this was the peak and the end of our alchemy because all that would be left was broken glass and some charred, useless substance. The explosion, which invariably ended in disaster, marked a headlong slide to disappointment.

But that little brick furnace, the gently steaming water bath and the fine glass delivery spout, were the warm heart of Selden, my pivot in a spinning world. It seemed to me that the end of distillation was the precipice towards which I was now racing. Beyond that I had no goals and no expectations. All I knew was that I must be ready at the sign of fire.

3

Beyond the laboratory a deathly hush fell. Harford went away to assemble a team of labourers, the hired girls disappeared into the village and Mrs Gill and her new familiar, Annie, retreated to her cottage to prepare for the annual fair held at the end of June in honour of bookish St Edelburga. As for Sarah, at first I had no idea what had happened to her except that she certainly never came near me.

The fair was a time of great bustle for Mrs Gill because her reputation as a herbalist had spread far and wide so people queued at her stall for hours. To satisfy the demand for lotions and potions she spent the early summer in her kitchen where she ripped and boiled, fermented and ground the contents of her garden while Gill was sent out to gather more elusive specimens from the woods and hedgerows.

I intended to help. One evening I stepped outside into a slanting blue and green world of shadows and sunlight and had a sudden childhood memory of pounding mint in Mrs Gill's kitchen, of tipping dried camomile flowers, airy as dead bees, into little bags, of watching the fruity simmer of rosehip. I had a yearning to go back there so I hurried across the lawn to her garden gate and fought my way through the currant bushes along the brick path to the open kitchen door. I thought I would be gladly received and put to work.

The kitchen was tiny and crowded with furniture. A door on one side of the hearth led to the front parlour, on the other to the ladder-like staircase. The flagged floor was heaped with greenery, berries and flower heads.

Mrs Gill's back was to me as she heaved a great pot from a hook above the range and Annie sat at one end of the table tearing elderflowers from their stems and tossing them into a pail of water. I was about to go in and imagined that Mrs Gill would turn to me gladly and make some caustic remark: 'Well, I never thought you'd stoop so far . . .' but there was another figure, a neat body in a pale-pink frock, seated at the table, sewing muslin into bags with flying fingers and a flashing needle.

I could scarcely take it in. I thought that Sarah and Mrs Gill despised each other and that of all people Sarah would most hate to spend an afternoon with gormless Annie. But she looked more contented than I had ever seen her. A bee near her left hand nuzzled from one lavender head to the next and her little foot was buried in a cloud of heartsease.

I backed away, reeling from the shock of seeing her penetrated so deep into my world. And I was ready to weep with self-pity. Is there no end to what that girl will take from me? I thought.

4

I should have been glad to be alone. I should have enjoyed the tranquillity of the laboratory, the smell of sunlight on old wood, the meditation over the alembic, the opportunity to delve deep into near impenetrable texts. Alchemy, after all, is altogether a safer and more predictable art than life. Alchemy involves no physical journeys, no interaction with living human beings. The alchemist suffers heartbreak and disappointment but not often betrayal.

But my mind wasn't on alchemy. Sometimes I remembered the furnace shed, the bee orchard or the dead babies; sometimes I thought about Sarah and the way she had been insinuated first into the Hanover Street house and then Selden; and sometimes I thought of my father, how right he had been about Aislabie and how my punishment, which had begun the moment I plucked the rose, apparently had no end because most of the time what I thought about was Shales.

I paced the laboratory, packed away some of our best alembics and instruments and tried to convince myself that I was fickle;

that I was haunted by the memory of Shales only because he had gone away, just as I had once been tormented by thoughts of Aislabie and so I had no right to trust what I felt.

But it did no good. I was plagued by unanswered questions. Why had he left so abruptly? Why hadn't he told me on the night of the party that he was going? Didn't he care for me at all, that he could just disappear when he knew I was so unhappy? I should never have told him that I was still engaged with alchemy. He despised me for it. Or he realised that I had fallen in love with him and was amazed and frightened by the knowledge. Even repulsed. In any case he'd put a distance between us. But why hadn't he at least said goodbye?

One morning I went to the library and began packing books, boxes and boxes of them, and I remembered how Shales had brought me Sir Thomas Browne as a peace offering, and how before that he had come to warn me against Aislabie. I stared at the little table by the window where I had sat to make notes on the day my father invited him to hear about palingenesis, and with horror I remembered the smell of toasted bread, my greasy fingers and tangled hair, the bruises on my neck when he first came to call on Aislabie. I tore the books off the shelves with frantic haste in an effort to exorcise these memories.

Then I got disheartened and sat in my father's chair. His smell hardly lingered at all now, just the slightest hint of tobacco. The hearth was empty and the doors to the laboratory wide open so that I could watch the still. Everything was bathed in honey light dispersed by millions of dust particles raised from the books. I had a dazed sense of the laboratory being out of reach, like a looking-glass world.

Between me and the door was my chair, plain oak with curved arms; the chair also used by visitors. That chair, set at an angle to the hearth, spoke of absence. I associated Shales with quiet rooms, with moments of sudden calm. I decided that when he came back I would visit him in his little study, sit in the chair by his desk and direct him to collect the airs from his plants so that he could try out Mayow's experiments. I would offer to work with him on the extra chapter of his book. After all, I would soon complete my work on palingenesis and therefore be free to undertake a new project. We would test to see whether those exhaled airs were the same as common air. And then we would collect the air that is left when a candle has been burnt under a flask, the so-called phlogisticated air, and discover its qualities.

We would be restrained. There would be no need to touch. We would talk only about air and fire. There could surely be no harm in that. And I dozed, comforted by this dream of spending time with Shales.

5

I was jolted wide awake. Someone somewhere had dealt Selden a shattering blow. Immediately afterwards came not just one hammer blow but half a dozen, wallop, pause, wallop, that rattled the lattices and made jars clink on the shelves.

I felt the blows the length of my spine and rushed to the laboratory to check nothing had been damaged. The water in the bain-marie was lapping the sides and the cellar door burst open. 'It's begun,' moaned Gill.

'Where have they started?'

'The furnace shed is nearly down already. And the roof passage.'

The roof passage. I remembered that long-ago procession with the owl up the main staircase, past the Queen's Room, into the creaking passageway of the most ancient wing where the floorboards slanted and I had to duck the lowest beams. And then I realised the danger. My mother's room would be lost.

Another shattering blow, a slide of tiles from the roof and I was out of the laboratory, across the hall, up the stairs two at a time to the door linking the new wing with the old but my way was barred by heavy planks criss-crossing the threshold. I pounded with my fist and tore at the planks but they were held in place by three-inch nails.

Down I went, this time hurtling along the kitchen passage, across the stable yard where grit blew into my eyes and I was struck by the smell of newly broken stone, and out on to the terrace. There they were on the far side of the house against the backdrop of a heavenly blue sky, strange men stripped to the waist swarming across the roof and breaking Selden open as easily as if it had been an eggshell. Already the attics were exposed and ancient chimneys had crumbled in on themselves like sand. The men flung bits of tile and stone, plaster and oak beam down a canvas chute. As I watched a sledgehammer struck the roof above my mother's ceiling and further along a chimney – a spiral of interlocking brick – teetered and fell.

I screamed, 'No,' but my voice couldn't reach them. 'No. No.' A sledgehammer lifted again and another shower of roof tiles came shivering down. 'No.'

'Madam.' Sarah's hand was on my arm. 'Madam.'

I wrenched my arm free and ran along the side of the house. 'Stop.'

A lump of stone came spinning from the roof and landed near my foot. Then a bearded face peered down at me and there were shouted orders to stop work. In the sudden silence stones rattled, there was the rhythmic fall of a distant axe and then the resumption of birdsong.

'You can't break up her room,' I cried.

'What room's that?'

'I haven't cleared it. I wasn't ready.'

'It's all clear up here.' My eyes were blinded by the brilliant sky. Other heads appeared among the broken rafters. Sarah stood at my elbow. There was a moment's impasse and then Harford came panting round the side of the house.

'What's happened? Mrs Aislabie, come away, my dear Madam, you have put yourself in terrible danger.'

'You must stop them. They're destroying my mother's room. I hadn't been up there to prepare. It wasn't empty.'

'Madam, we cleared everything. Come away.'

'I won't. I won't move. I can't bear this.'

He gave a tut of irritation and pressed a handkerchief to his forehead. The sun burnt on our backs. 'I thought you understood what was going to happen,' he said, as if to a child. 'That's why we suggested you went to London.'

'I hadn't said her room could be taken,' I said obstinately.

Another tile slithered and fell perilously close to Harford. He looked up uneasily. 'Would it help if you came inside with me and told me what you wanted preserved. I'm sure we could keep a little of the wall-covering. The fireplace, even.'

'There was a bed and a chest,' I said.

'A bed and a chest. But they will have gone on the bonfire if no one wanted them. We cleared all the rooms, as I said.' He offered his arm. 'We'll go along to the bonfire, if you like, and see if there's anything left but I wouldn't hold out much hope.'

'Only if you stop the work.'

'I can't, Madam, funds are short. These men are paid by the hour. I can't have them stopping and starting like this. Now you come away.' He took one elbow, Sarah linked her arm through the other and I was ushered off between them like a puppet. I was in no state to resist but kept straining backwards for another look. As soon as we were safely on to the terrace the work went on again.

It was my fault, I knew. I had been so absorbed by what was happening in the laboratory that I had lost track of events in the rest of the house. I deserved to lose my mother if this was how I behaved.

We came to the bee orchard and found that the bonfire had long ago gone cold and there was only a circle of charred soil, carefully raked over. 'There now,' said Harford, 'why don't you walk about with your maid in the shade of these trees. That will do you good. But you stay away from the house, Mrs Aislabie. We can't have you hurt.' He backed to the gate and closed it carefully behind him.

The trees were in full leaf and tiny fruit had formed. Underfoot grass was long and silky even in the hot sun but all I could think about was the black circle where the bonfire had been. I was wearing a pair of London silk slippers under my old cotton gown and I dabbed a dainty toe in the ashes and uncovered lumps of charred wood, a metal hinge, a door latch.

Five minutes must have passed and still I hovered by the site of the bonfire and listened to the shattering of Selden's roof. Somewhere in my mind a little ship with white sails floated on a blue ocean and in it, Aislabie.

'Madam, I must speak with you.' I thought I was alone but Sarah was still there, a few feet behind my left elbow in the shade of a twisted crab apple. 'Madam, would it be convenient to speak with you?'

I flicked my hand to send her away.

'Madam, please.'

'Not now, Sarah.'

'Madam, I must.'

'I have said not now.'

'It cannot wait, Madam.'

'Another time.'

'Please. I have tried before but never been able to find you.'

I walked away from her but when I came to the gate and looked towards the neglected rose garden I had another shock. Harford had gone panting down the terrace steps, pulled off his wig and was now flapping a coil of paper at another team of workmen. They had pegged out the shape of the lake like a giant lozenge with a smaller disc in the centre which would be the island. A tree was being felled on the far side where the rope boundary wound through the woods and digging had begun on the old lawn.

Sarah stood so close that I felt the hem of her skirt shift against mine. Blows were falling one after another on the roof so that the whole of our conversation was punctuated by violent assaults. 'Mistress Aislabie, I need your help. I am going to have a baby.'

A baby.

Another blow fell on the roof and again I was distracted. If only I had gone to my mother's room – they wouldn't have dared touch it if I'd been there.

'Madam?'

A baby.

And then I thought: My father is behind this and he has a cunning far more devious than I had ever suspected. I looked down at my hands resting on the cracked wood of the gate, blotches of paler skin where acid had splashed, the calluses from old burns. Sarah presumably had no idea that she was just a spoke in the alchemical wheel.

In a gap between blows to the roof she persisted: 'Well, Madam?'

'How long?'

'I'm not sure.'

Her fingers were knitted together and her crooked eyes cast down. 'Turn round,' I ordered.

'She didn't move.

'Turn.'

She turned sideways so that she was facing the hives.

'Put your hands by your sides.' The pregnancy was obvious. Her belly was swollen under the gathers of her apron and her breasts strained against her bodice. I was transfixed by the plum shape of her. How could she have kept it hidden? Except of course she hadn't. It was simply that since the night of the dead babies I could hardly bear to look at her.

'What am I to do, Mistress Aislabie?'

'Surely my husband should answer that question.'

'He said it was up to you.'

I laughed because this was so exactly what he would say. Her head drooped further. The ground juddered underfoot. 'How long have you been his mistress?'

'Three years. Not any more.' A tear fell on to her bosom. I was ice and fire. I thought I didn't care now about my husband but I did care that on the August day when he stood in the porch all covered with enchantment, when he smiled at me and let his seductive eye linger on my loosened ribbon, he had lately slept with her and had doubtless gone straight back to her.

'I'm surprised my husband is so casual,' I said. 'I thought he'd be glad to father anything, even a bastard.'

'He said it was for you to have his child. He said it was a pity you never had one but that he hadn't given up hope. He said I should get rid of it.'

'And why didn't you?'

'I tried. I did my best while you was in the Abbey that time. She ripped me half to pieces but it wouldn't budge. She said I'd come to her too late.'

I put back my head and looked at the sky. Not a cloud. How convenient for Aislabie that Newton had died and I could be lured to London with Sarah as escort. I was glad that the baby had held fast despite their efforts, a small triumph of nature over Aislabie's calculation.

'Well you're free to go at any time,' I said. 'I'm sure my husband will set you up in London. I wish you well.'

'What would I want with a baby, Mrs Aislabie?' She couldn't keep contempt out of her voice for long. 'I have to go back to the old life now he's done with me. What would I do with a child?'

I opened the gate and rubbed my hands free of dust. 'When I saw you together last month he seemed to be as keen on you as ever. I suggest you follow him to London. If you're short of money I have a few guineas.'

But she sprang forward and grabbed my arm so that the hard bulge of her stomach touched my waist. 'Let me stay here until the baby is born. That's all I ask. Mrs Gill said you would be kind. She said you might take the baby – or she'd find someone who would have it but she wouldn't lie to you, she said, or go behind your back while you was at Selden. She said I must ask you. Please, Madam, don't send me away. If you'd gone to London with your husband like you was supposed to you would never have known about it. I'd have had it quietly here and that would have been that. It was all arranged. But you wouldn't leave and she promised me that if I told you she would take care of it all.'

'There is no question of you staying here. I want nothing to do with you or your baby. I'm amazed you should ask after what I saw. You must be mad to ask.'

Her eyes glittered in her pale face and she spoke so violently that her saliva fell on me. 'I ask because you owe me. You took him from me and you didn't want him as he really is. You don't care for him like I do and never have. You came here and brought me with you and it has half killed me to be buried here so far from him and you never saw what was going on because you never cared.'

I wrenched my arm away but she seized my hand. I twisted out of her grasp and began to run towards the woods. She followed. 'Mrs Gill said I must tell you. She said for the baby's sake I must tell you. I knew she was wrong. Don't send me away. This baby will be the death of me.' She clawed at my clothes – I unclasped her fingers one by one and tried to fight her off but she found another hold. 'I had a good life before he found me and talked me into going with him. I had a good business. He has left me with nothing. You have no idea.'

Down I went, dragging her with me past the rose garden and into the water garden where the fountain was dry and the grass crowded with dandelions. There I had to stop else we would be upon the lake diggers and Harford's greedy gaze. 'You have taken everything I had, you and him both. I had built myself up so far when he came. A trade, girls working for me. But he offered me a home and I couldn't resist because even after you came he said he loved me and not you. And then this baby.' She released me at last, tore at her apron and beat her stomach. Her face was contorted with fear or hatred or panic – perhaps all. 'You and him. You have done for me. I have seen you day after day how you were full of pity for yourself because your father died and then because you thought your husband was unkind to you and you have no idea that you are the luckiest woman on earth.'

'You're mad. You're at the root of all my misery and you blame me. How dare you? Get out of here. Get away from Selden. You're a whore.'

We stared at each other. She had her head up and one hand in the small of her back in the way of pregnant women, as if she had permission to show it at last. She was probably the same age as me though I had always thought her far older because of her pinched mouth and deft fingers. My hair had come down and I was half a head taller than her in my shabby dress and dirty apron, and as always in her presence I felt unfinished, badly put together. Once again she had trumped me and though she seemed to be the loser she was stronger because she had been everywhere before me. The look in her eyes was oddly familiar. I knew it from some distant corner of my past. My father, was it, when he threatened me with his notebook?

And then the fight went out of her eyes and she started to sob and plead again: 'I have been waiting all this last month for an answer. Since he went away. Say you'll take the child. Don't send me away 'til afterwards.'

'I've given my answer. There can never be any other. Have you thought about my feelings?'

'Feelings. Feelings. You and feelings have nothing to do with this. This is my life. I have been so sick sometimes that I have been half dead but I could never let it show. Instead, I had to go on and on with your life until you chose to say you'd had enough of me. I swear if you send me away and I have the child it will die. I've spent my life waiting to be picked up and fucked up and tossed aside. And I know you, Mrs Aislabie. Jesus Christ you have no idea how I know you. I know you to the very core. And you are stone cold. You had him and you lost him and you're sending me away out of spite. You're no different from all the rest despite your strangeness, despite you pretend to be better . . .'

'That's enough.'

She had lifted her skirts and was toiling up the steps away from me. I glimpsed her little ankles in my cast-off shoes. Then she turned, the she-cat. 'You took him and now you don't want him. Any proper woman would have wanted him but not you. I hate you and I hate this house. I hate the dark. The dark kills me. You drove him away. You didn't want him.' But at last she went, dragging her suddenly heavy frame up the steps, still sobbing, leaving me to stare down at the embryonic lake.

6

After a while I walked back to the bee orchard, past the hives where the bees were agitated by the din of demolition, and into the woods. A strong breeze scuffled the underside of leaves but whenever I emerged into a clearing the heat was scorching. Aislabie had vowed to make these woods fit for hunting again, to breed pheasants and manage the undergrowth but for now all was tranquil, though the old paths were tangled and my ankles got scratched with thorns. By the time I reached the oak tree I was so hot that I tore off my apron, dropped it among the nettles, stuffed my cap into my pocket and pressed my forehead against the ancient bark.

A baby. An Aislabie bastard. A baby and not my own.

I felt the warm trunk under my pin-thin body. A baby.

There were other creatures moving in the woods. I heard the quiet breathing of the deer. Well, watch out, I told them, watch out because one day soon he'll come crashing through the trees on his great horse and he'll be after you. Just you see.

I stumbled on and all around me there was a cracking of twigs and rushing of feet as they leapt away. The bracken had grown to thigh level and I beat it aside until I came to the broad track that led to the bridge and the village of Lower Selden. I hurried on, regardless of the heat, until I reached the river. A few yards along the bank was a willow shading a little gravel beach. I plunged my face in the soft water, bundled my hair back into the cap, washed my hands and drew a deep breath.

The lane leading to the church cottage was silent in the afternoon heat. Even the birds had stopped singing. A gust of wind drove me in a funnel of hot air to his worn steps. The door to his house was wide open and I felt a surge of joy. He was back.

I knocked and called, 'Hello. Hello,' but nobody answered. The doors on either side of the passageway were closed. My voice shattered the calm of the afternoon. When I knocked and shouted again the door to the kitchen was pushed open at last and the sour-faced maid appeared. She obviously took me for one of the girls from the village because she folded her arms and leaned on the newel post: 'Yes.'

'I'd like to speak to Reverend Shales.'

She recognised me and straightened up. 'He's not here. He's far away in Norwich.'

'When will he be back?'

'Lord knows. Ask the curate. I'm sick to death of people knocking here for him.'

I was dizzy with sudden disappointment after the long walk. 'Might I have a glass of water?'

She peered at me: 'Of course, Madam.'

'May I sit down?'

'Of course.' She opened the door to Shales's study and shuffled away.

I sat in the chair by the desk and closed my eyes. In a minute she came back with a jug and glass. 'Are you all right, Madam?'

'Very hot. Perhaps I could rest for a while.'

'I'm sure.' She hovered for a moment so close that I could feel the heat of her body, then she went back to the kitchen. The front door had been left open and a draught blew into the room. I sipped water, earthy and ice-cold. My head throbbed. A window was open and greenery spilled in from the garden. A robin began to sing throatily and a small spider dangled from the casement.

I sank down a little on the hard chair, adjusting my weight so that one knee was pressed against the desk and my other foot stretched out almost to the hearth. The robin went on singing and a shaft of sunlight shone directly on to my hand. I breathed the scent of embers, dust and beeswax and became aware of the ticking of a clock, deep and rhythmic, with a faint click between each movement of the pendulum. My hand slid away from the glass and dropped into my lap.

When I woke up the light had changed and the sunbeam shifted on to a blotter on the desk. Pain still jabbed my right temple. The two distinct sides of Shales's life lay either side of me. On the windowsill was the row of maimed plants and on the desk the apparatus for measuring airs, including a covered pot of some brownish seal – beeswax and turpentine judging by the smell.

Beyond the desk, in an alcove beside the mantel, were his books of natural philosophy, some of them – Lemery's *Cours de Chimie*, Lefevre's *Traite de la Chimie*, Beguin's *Tyrocinium Chymicum* – so familiar that I could have opened any page and recited a paragraph or two almost verbatim. A pile of notebooks had been tidied away on to a shelf and I recognised his upright, bold hand on one of them: '*The Imbibing of Water through Branch and Root*'.

On the side of the room facing the church there was a glass case of sacred texts including a shabby Bible, prayer books, a copy of the Holy Office and the work of other writers largely unknown to me because my father never bought books that weren't concerned with natural philosophy: Locke, Defoe, Milton, Dryden, La Fontaine. Above was a plain wooden crucifix, another aspect of Shales's life I couldn't comprehend.

I listened to the clock and the robin. Until now I hadn't worked out what I would have said if Shales had been at home, if he had come to the door in his shirtsleeves and smiled that wonderful, quick, kind smile, taken my hand and brought me in. Now I knew.

I knew.

I stayed as the afternoon deepened and the room cooled. I even kicked off my torn silk slippers and planted my stockinged feet on the rough boards. The clock struck six and a whiff of woodsmoke breezed in from some nearby chimney. When I bent my head I could see the church, squat and ramshackle, sinking into the graveyard and if I looked the other way through the curtain of ivy and wisteria I saw the varied greens of the experimental plants in his garden. His servant stirred; I heard her shuffle across the garden, pull open the privy door, close it behind her. A few minutes later she came back and there was the clatter of a bowl on the table and the thump of something soft, meat, possibly, or a loaf.

Then I realised I wasn't the only woman in the room.

Apart from the candlesticks, the other ornament on the mantel was a miniature in an oval frame. My skirts rustled shockingly, an unstructured sound in that orderly space, as I went to pick it up. The woman in the painting had a strong, plain face with a longish nose, small mouth, steady eyes and light-brown hair drawn back straight from the forehead. Her throat was bare but a muslin scarf was tucked into the square neck of her bodice. She seemed tranquil but it was not the most skilful of portraits and I could read nothing into the angle of her chin or the slight smile. When I turned the miniature over there was a slip of paper stuck to the back written in a neat, sloping hand: *For Thomas, on his birthday. Hannah Shales. Twickenham. April 1724.*

The handwriting told me more about the dead woman than the portrait. It was an elaborate, careful hand, very unlike my workaday lettering. I stared again into her eyes and tried out her name. Hannah Shales. A good name, balanced. Hannah Shales.

And then I noticed, pushed back on a shelf, a faded pincushion of pink velvet in the shape of a heart. It bristled with pins and needles threaded in white or black and beside it was a sewing case embroidered with the initials H. B. A couple of the needles were so fine that only the steadiest, daintiest hand might have threaded them. One, filled with cream silk thread, had been in the cushion so long that there was a rusty mark where it pierced the velvet. From the edge of the sewing case poked a narrow strip of crumpled lace.

I replaced the miniature Mrs Shales exactly on the same sliver of dust-free mantel and sat down again, this times in Shales's chair on the other side of the desk. From here I could see the whole room including Mrs Shales but not her sewing case. This is what Shales must see every day: the row of religious texts, the window overlooking the street and the stone wall supporting the graveyard, the ticking clock, the miniature of his wife.

How he must love her, I thought, to keep her portrait so close.

A cold voice in my head added: Nobody ever had your portrait painted. Nobody loved you enough.

I looked across at the empty chair, my chair. All the time I sat there Mrs Shales had been watching me. I imagined my own drooping head, my untidy black hair, my faded gown. Suddenly I heard myself speak quite loudly into the quiet room. 'No,' I said: 'No, I can't. I won't. Don't ask me.'

The kitchen door burst open and the maid came puffing in. 'I had no idea you was still here. Are you all right? Will there be anything else?'

I stumbled to my feet. 'Thank you, I feel much better now. I'll be on my way.' She stared in astonishment as I trod my feet back into the slippers, took a last look at his desk, the pincushion, the shifting shadows on the white walls and fled the house.

7

The next morning I was woken at dawn by the workmen. Nobody brought my breakfast and my clothes were in a heap where I had left them. The chamber pot hadn't been emptied since the previous morning so the air was sour. I put on my crumpled gown and went looking for Sarah. Her room was bare, not just of her but of all her things. The bed was stripped and the sheets neatly folded.

On the far side was an open door leading to the closet in which she kept my clothes. Last time I looked a few months ago this closet had been tight packed as a dressmaker's shop, half a dozen gowns billowing from their pegs, shelves piled with starched linen, shoes arranged on racks, hats on stands with the feathers straightened and the ribbons washed, a cascade of petticoats and hoops. Now the closet was empty except for one old petticoat heaped in a corner and the green silk gown. Every other item was gone, even the feathered monstrosity.

Those gowns were worth a small fortune; in fact, now I thought about it, had probably been my greatest financial asset. Their bulk would have filled at least two large chests. How on earth had she spirited them away?

The house vibrated with noise as I raced through the down-stairs rooms and looked in the pantries, the kitchen and the dairy – no sign of the Gills or Sarah, though Harford was under the arch, his sleeves already soggy with heat. He doffed his hat: 'I hope, Madam, that you haven't been too discomposed by all the noise . . .' but I rushed past him across the lawn and through the gate to Mrs Gill's garden.

The plants were ravaged, their seeds and blossoms harvested. The cottage door was wide open but the kitchen was empty. I walked through the neat parlour to the front door, lifted the latch and found myself in the packed village street. The fair was in full swing and I hadn't even noticed.

I knew that Mrs Gill would have set up her stall under the churchyard wall and I made my way there, picking up my skirts to avoid heaps of dung. A couple of youths were in competition to tip flagon after flagon of ale into their mouths; I passed stalls of cheeses rank with mould, gingerbread swarming with flies, over-ripe strawberries seeping juice, a heap of gaudy neckerchiefs, and raw-timbered ladders ranked against a cottage wall. But it wasn't until I was deep in the crowds and had paused a moment to peer over someone's shoulder at a couple of farmers arguing over the price of a calf – the creature rolled her tender brown eyes and defecated into the mud – that I became fully alert and realised the danger I was in.

Shales had given us plenty of warning that there was unrest in the village but I had assumed they were angry with Aislabie, not me. Now I noticed that nobody smiled and wherever I stood a ring of silence formed around me. I was afraid of the absorption in the eyes of people who usually led lives rigorously ordered by the rising and setting of the sun. They had abandoned themselves to strange fascinations and cruel pleasures: gawping at a pig-faced lady with a huge silver ring through her nostrils, at a sly-eyed mountebank selling cures for toothache. I had seen this possessed look in the face of Aislabie when he lay with me in the orchard and in my father when he was nearing the end of an experiment and it terrified me because it left me out.

I couldn't get close to Mrs Gill because a little throng of people was waiting for a consultation and on the table, held down firmly by Annie, lay a purple-faced baby with eyes weeping yellow pus. I stood aside while Mrs Gill dropped salve into the child's furious eyes, then I went behind the stall and touched her elbow.

She eyed me coldly. 'I haven't time,' she said, turned her back and beckoned the next customer, a boy with a putrid boil on his neck. Bewildered, I drifted over to a nearby ribbon seller and fingered some lengths of material. I was conscious of shifting and whispering behind me as I held up a pink strip and smiled. The ribbon seller seemed to smile back, though she didn't pay much attention to me because she was gossiping to a customer.

The ribbon was cheap and soft, not like the glossy silks Sarah had stolen but of another texture, dull on one side, shiny on the other, which for a moment made me yearning and dreamy so that I forgot where I was and touched it to my lips. This pale-pink ribbon was the precise width and texture of the frayed scrap left by my mother and which now hung round my neck to hold the laboratory key.

Another woman had joined the conversation: '. . . this place was too small for him. They say he's got short of money.'

'Nobody of his sort of standing would stay in such a god-forsaken hole for long,' said another.

'I'm disappointed in him. I thought he'd see us through this.'

'Never trust a man of the cloth,' said the ribbon seller and laughed. But when she saw that I was listening her eyes hardened so I let the ribbon fall on the table and turned away but was pressed so close by the crowd that my thighs were bruised by the table edge. I smiled again and fumbled at the waist of my gown as if searching for money but the ribbon seller's lips were now pursed together and for a moment I thought she must have some disfigurement. Then I realised she was gathering spittle.

The crowd behind me went quiet and a man turned his bearded face to mine so close that I saw flaking skin caught in his whiskers, cracked flesh at the corner of his mouth, broken veins in his cheek. He looked through me, his muscles slack with malice.

'Let me pass,' I said but nobody moved. 'Let me pass.' My voice rose and wavered. I took a step back from the table and my foot landed on someone's toe.

The bearded man clutched my elbow and spoke hot in my ear: 'Mistress Aislabie, I'd like a word if you please.'

Where was Mrs Gill? Surely she wouldn't let them hurt me. A flock of sheep was being driven up the street behind the crowd and there was a great confusion of frightened animals. The man kept his hand on my arm and drew me along. People stepped aside one at a time until we were in an alley where there was a bit of shade and I was pressed so near to him that I could smell his sweat and feel the heat of his skin. 'You probably don't know who I am. Barton. Blacksmith. My daughter Annie sometimes used to work up at the house.'

'Yes. Yes. I know.'

'I should like to show you what we've come to at Selden while you've been drawing up plans for your great house.'

He kept such tight hold of my elbow that my flesh ached. I tried to form the right words to explain that he'd got it very wrong but my hat had fallen back and the ribbon was tight round my throat. Meanwhile the blacksmith was hurrying me along the main street and I was conscious that a little crowd of children followed behind.

We were soon out of the village street and among a cluster of tumbledown cottages with glassless windows and ragged thatch. He pushed open a warped door and urged me in. The sun had baked through the broken roof and made a reeking oven of the place but some poor creature lay in the corner huddled under a heap of blankets while a baby mewled in its crib and a hen pecked at the earth floor.

'Nobody's been paid since April for all the labouring that's gone on to get your house emptied and the crops weeded,' said the blacksmith, who still had tight hold of my arm, 'and there's rumours that this year's will be a bad harvest. The likes of this widow Mrs Moore and her grandchild are dying for want of decent nourishment. What will you do about it, Mrs Aislabie?'

The heat pressed hard down on me and flies buzzed in the chamber pot. The smell was very bad, perhaps worse than the dead babies.

I looked him in the eye. He didn't seem a bad or violent man, just angry. But he frightened me because I had no answers for him so I tore away and got back into the main street where I was worse off than ever because the crowd had gathered again and stood in a semicircle, waiting. Some faces I recognised from church, some were strangers, probably from neighbouring villages. They were led by the ribbon seller with her bitter mouth and staring eyes.

There was no way past them. The sun burnt down on my bare head. I smelt manure and gingerbread, my own fright, excrement and sick human flesh from the cottage behind me. My skirts crumpled in my fists and I thought of my quiet laboratory, of my husband sailing away before a strong wind and of Shales who wasn't coming back.

They came closer. A child had found his way through the forest of legs and stared at me as if I were part of some show. I backed away a little and found that others had crept round behind me and I was hemmed in.

The ribbon seller spat in my face – it was almost a relief to feel the soft saliva on my cheek. Perhaps this was enough punishment and it would end here. I thought if I met her eye all would be well but her mouth was working and another gob of spittle darkened the skirt of my gown. I thought: That will sponge off, Sarah will deal with it. From far away the blacksmith's voice said, 'Now, now, that's enough,' but the crowd shuffled closer. Then something small and hard hit the side of my neck and fell to the ground with a rattle. 'Bastard,' someone shouted.

A little murmur went through the crowd, like the wind in my oak tree. The blacksmith said loudly, 'That's enough. She's had a fright. I'm sure she'll speak up for us now.'

I turned my head to thank him and from the corner of my eye saw another stone, much bigger, hurtle from the crowd. I twisted my neck but it got my cheek and breast and then a dead weight cracked against the back of my head. The blacksmith had me firmly by the arm and was pulling me backwards, the crowd was yelling, some were backing away, others pressing close enough to get a fistful of skirt and yank hard. My other hand was grabbed and the fingers wrenched apart so violently that pain shot up my arm and then suddenly through it all I heard Mrs Gill's voice come in fits and starts: 'Stop this. Stop. Are you out of your minds? Are you savages? What is this?'

The crowd parted and I was hauled along the street, thrust through a gate and pushed down on something hard. 'She'll be safe here. I'll see to them.' Then the click of a heavy latch and sudden quiet.

There were shouts on the other side of the wall and after a while other noises came back, the fiddle again, cows lowing, poultry. I clutched my injured hand and stared down at the mucousy stain in the lap of my gown, at swept cobbles and, a little distance away, a pair of small feet in heavy boots.

Mrs Gill said, 'Fetch some water for Mrs Aislabie, if you please.'

The boots moved away. She knelt in front of me and fumbled with my hat strings until they fell from my neck and allowed me to breathe more freely. 'Let me see your face.'

I shut my eyes and felt her dab at my cheek with something soft and run her hands over the back of my head where the stone had got me. 'Tell me where it hurts, Emilie.'

The hobnails rang, there was the clang of a pitcher, a beaker was held to my lips. More cold water trickled on to my stinging cheek. 'Emilie, show me that you can hear me.'

It was weeks since I had looked at her properly and it was a shock to see the fright in her eyes and the sweat on her brow. 'You must be out of your mind coming here,' she said. 'Do you really have no idea what's going on?'

I was still dizzy from the blow to my head. 'Were they talking about Shales when they said he wasn't coming back?'

The blacksmith's boy had been leaning on the wall with one foot propped behind him. When she gave him a nod he levered himself forward and ambled away into the smithy.

'Lord knows what they were talking about. Why can't you pay attention?'

'Why are you so angry?'

She stared at me until her eyes bulged. 'Have you really no idea?'

'What have I done? God knows I've done nothing.'

'Then who sent that wretched girl away?'

'She was carrying my husband's child.'

'Have you no mercy?'

I shook my head to clear it. 'She was my husband's mistress. She had been sleeping with him all through my marriage. She stole my clothes. Why do you side with her?'

'It's not a matter of siding with her. I told her you'd be kind. I trusted you.'

'She's a whore.'

'Did you ever think why she lives like this? Did you ever ask her?'

'No. Why should I? She was scarcely forthcoming.'

'Dear God, it's uncanny how he trained you up in his likeness. I have never known anyone as ignorant of life beyond the laboratory as that man. Or as incurious.'

'He had a great deal on his mind.'

'He was mighty choosy about what he thought about. Same as you.'

'What has this to do with Sarah?'

'Good Lord, Emilie, you had only to look at her to know what a state she was in. She was sick with misery apart from anything else. It was a wickedness to bring her away from London in the first place. I don't think she slept for the first month.'

'Sarah is tough. She'll survive. She stole my clothes.'

'She came to us beside herself and said you had been hard. Gill took her up the lane in the trap and she caught the stage at dawn. If he hadn't agreed she would have dragged her boxes up there herself. We helped her.'

'She could be hung,' I said.

'She had nothing, worse than nothing.' The blacksmith's boy re-emerged with a rusty hod and began shovelling bits of slack from a heap in the corner of the yard. She waited until he'd gone back into the forge. 'I noticed way back what was up with her but she would have nothing to do with me. Then at last she came to me and said she was in trouble. I said how much trouble? She said four months. I took another look and thought seven more like. When she let me touch her I found out what had gone on while she went to London with you. She's lucky to have lived this long. She must have been well past four months when they tried to get rid of it.'

'I had no idea. I didn't know.'

'You mean you chose not to see. You asked no questions.'

'But why should I? She was so cold with me.'

'That girl told me that she was apprenticed to a petticoat maker at three and by seven she'd been sent to run errands at the great houses. Then one day a couple of footmen got friendly with her, plied her with cakes, plucked her off her feet and took her to some place called Stonecutter's Yard – that name sticks in my head, I find – Stonecutter's Yard, where there was an empty attic with bird muck on the floor and they took it in turns to cover her mouth and hold her by the hair while the other had her till she was awash with blood and tears. Afterwards she couldn't walk so one of them carried her back to her mistress and said he'd found her like that and they paid over some money so the woman wouldn't go to the magistrate. Instead, she stitched her up and said Sarah was on the road to a much better career than she could offer if she so wanted. But Sarah wouldn't speak or work so after a while she was released on to the streets and she got work with a dressmaker and was sent as a model for the gowns to entice great ladies to buy, and soon she had gentlemen sniffing round her. She was careful and gave herself only to the richest and in time she had her own house and her own girls to manage, but she never smiled or kissed until Aislabie came. She was known for it. So now she has gone back to London and she will have that child all unprotected by anyone who cares for her and it will be a terrible birth.'

From inside the forge came the scrape of ashes and the rattle of coal. Next the boy applied the bellows, little puffs at first then, as the charcoal began to glow, long, wheezing gasps. Rusty horse-shoes were piled round the edge of the yard, bits of iron, cartwheels, spades, pickaxes.

I visited here with Aislabie, I remembered, dressed in silk, my hand tucked under his arm. There was heat enough in the forge that day to make an iron horseshoe flexible as clay. 'She won't be destitute,' I said, watching the first little flames dart blue and yellow. 'Those gowns are worth a lot of money.'

'I have had many girls like her at my door over the years. Believe me, that infant will die one way or another. The mother too, most like. And you could have saved them. You could have made one good thing out of this unholy mess.'

But I wasn't listening any more. I drew breath and stood up. The yard spun round but I headed for the door to the forge. Inside the air was dense with smoke. The boy added bits of coal one by one as fresh flames darted up from the new fire.

I was drawn to those flames as if I had been a moth. Some-where deep inside me I felt release.

I took another step.

The sign of fire. There it was. Lapping flames, fierce at heart. Beautiful fire. Pure as water.

The sign of fire.

Chapter Nine

FIRE AND AIR

I

Mrs Gill walked back with me to Selden as far as the gates, pushed me through and shut them firmly after me. The ground shook with the pounding and crashing on the far side of the house. My head was full of red noise but I was very clear about what to do next.

Once inside the laboratory I tied on my canvas apron and began the ritual of preparation. I was in a tunnel and saw only the chink of light at the far end as I shuffled half-packed crates through to the library and locked the two doors behind me. I wrapped glass vessels and the delicate scales in bits of cloth and linen, boxed them up and carried them down to the cellar, cleaned the work-benches and swept the floor. Then I lit a candle and closed the last shutter. The dead rose stood in its glass on the window seat, head hanging. I gave it a tap. Be patient. Just a little longer.

My father's notebook suggested that a pinch or at most a salt spoon of saltpetre was sufficient but I would be content with nothing less than conflagration. I'd had enough of caution and pain and slow revelation. I climbed on a stool, took down a full jar, perhaps a pound and a half of the stuff, and placed it on the workbench.

Then I sat at my father's desk with his staff in one hand and my mother's pink ribbon in the other. I looked at the furnace, the cloudy glass vessel, the pool of distillate, the rose on the window-sill and the alchemical notebooks. I felt no regret for what I was about to do, merely a kind of weariness that I must pass through the next few minutes.

The only item in all that room that I would miss, I decided, was my mother's ribbon. Just that. I stroked it gently, then hooked it carefully round my neck so I could take it with me. I thought of her peaceful plot in the shady churchyard. Perhaps I would be allowed to lie with her. Surely Shales would take pity on me to that extent.

My head emptied itself of prayers and incantations. Instead I remembered how I had walked down the brick steps to the hot garden and found the rose hidden among the leaves with one drop of dew on its pink petal.

I got up, took a knife and chipped away at the seal joining the receiving flask to the distillation tube. Once they were separated my clammy hands put the neck of the jar of saltpetre to the receiver. My heart thudded. I was committed. The jar tilted and the white powder began its slide downwards. Then one vessel was vertical over the other and the saltpetre was plunging into the distillate. I saw the rose again, deep pink among its inverted crown of sepals. I remembered that Shales had once been in the laboratory and that he had stroked my neck.

The explosion turned me over and over until I was a ball of fire gathering heat. Somewhere in my white centre there was a tiny conscious part of me but the rest was flame and I was consuming the air. Lightning crackled across the workbench and my head banged against the edge of my father's desk. My spine hit the floor and the breath was knocked out of my lungs.

I lay smouldering under the desk, cradled by charred floorboards and my hands shrivelled like leaves in a bonfire. Flames lapped at my feet. I was wearing – I had been wearing – a cotton dress under my apron. Just a matter of waiting, I thought. The air is trapped in my gown. Fire and air, the perfect combination. I will flare up like paper. Why does paper burn so freely? Because it is insubstantial, because it is full of phlogiston, because it is made of wood, and wood . . . and wood and paper . . .

The light again and another echoing boom in my ears. I lay in dappled shadow under the apple tree and my legs spread wider, wider.

The light. I tossed my head and fire ripped across my cheeks and into my eyes like the bodkin Newton had used to distort the shape of his eyeball. I saw my father sink in his chair and let his old head drop into his hand. I saw his staff roll on the floor.

The jagged light exploded again in my head. The dung heap. Sarah's knowing eyes in the dark of the furnace shed. A spillage of red silk.

Shales, who wasn't coming back.

Alchemy deals with opposites. It is concerned with the marriage of pairs: air and earth, sun and moon, male and female. A brace of babies. My husband, my maid.

Glass smashed and there was a sudden draught. The room burnt brighter – a fresh dispersal of light as the witless little Wepfer would have put it.

Overhead there was a tearing and crashing as old brackets collapsed under shelves and glass tumbled down. A beam was on fire, I saw a frill of flame on either side and I thought that the ceiling would fall on top of me, followed by the Queen's Room itself, bed included. The air should have been full of phlogiston but I could breathe quite easily. A shutter burst open and a fragment of burning wood fell on to the workbench above me. My father's notebook caught fire, brilliant flames licked the pages until one floated free of the workbench, down, down to the hem of my skirt. There was banging on the cellar and library doors, voices.

My ankle was burning. I heard a yelp that was my voice. A ruffle of orange spread along the edge of my apron.

I watched the flames. They were beautiful, irregular, eager and pure. They yearned up and up to the air and climbed towards me round the edge of my apron. Another gust of air wafted from the window and the flames burnt brighter still and the pain was so intense I felt my stomach turn to water. I thought: It is the air, it is the air that the fire needs and whatever is in the air is also in my skirts and in nitre and gunpowder.

And then I turned my head to one side and saw something so amazing that I rolled over and began to drag myself towards it though in doing so I crushed the flames, and pain seared along my legs and knocked my breath away. There was a green feather floating above a dark space where before there used to be floor-boards. The fire crawled up my arms and thighs but I scarcely noticed as I picked up the feather and peered into the hole. I saw a bundle of letters tied up in a piece of the red tape my father used to bind his papers. And under the letters deep in a cavity in the floor, a book, and notebooks bundled together, leather-bound, the first one labelled in my father's youthful hand:

Emilie Selden
The Alchemist's Daughter

I covered the cavity with my body and thought: I'd like to read those notebooks if I have a moment, but the next breath I took was fire. I gasped and my mouth was dry heat, and I gasped again but this time my throat closed up and my lungs ached and heaved, and I tried to open my mouth but my head was black and I knew it would burst apart, blood, tissue, bone.

Then I was tumbling into the dark space among my father's notebooks, the pain and panic fell away and I was a comet rolling in the velvety vacuum of space.

2

There was a high-pitched whining in my ears and, from far away, Gill's voice: 'Wait 'til she gets here. Never touch her until then.' I felt the boards move under his weight and the next moment I forgot about him.

My legs were on fire. I cried out but no sound came. I tried to lick my lips but had no tongue. A weight pressed on my back so I couldn't move.

I thought I must have died and soon would enter my mother's world, the silent, cold-fingered world of the dead. I yearned for the underside of fallen leaves, damp, peaty.

Voices again. Harford, was it? '. . . have put a stop to this.'

I thought my eyelids had been burnt open but all I could see was the domed shape of my skull and the blood pumping across the vessels of my inner eye. I smelt the excited chemical scent of combustion.

'. . . not safe. Keep the men . . .'

'. . . another set of explosions . . . combustible materials . . . close the . . .'

They faded into the fire. I thought in a rage of pain, why don't they put out the flames? My legs are still on fire. Haven't they noticed?

Then more bustle, another shifting on the boards, the soft pressure of a body against mine. Liquid fell into my eyes and the weight was lifted from my back. I saw a blackened hand lying near my face. Something cold damped down the fire in my legs.

'You did well.' Mrs Gill. She can't have been talking to me or Gill. She never praised us.

I was lifted up and the pain made me croak. Gill held me at arm's length with my head and arms flung back, supported by Annie on one side, Mrs Gill on the other. I saw everything upside down, the entrance hall, Annie's nostrils, an open door, the sudden dazzle of sunlight, grass. As the air touched me pain shot through my legs and sucked away my vision. Blackness again. Then a garden wall, the softness of a blanket. Ah good, I thought, here I'll sleep.

'Deep breath, Emilie,' and Mrs Gill took me by the hair and thrust my face down in a tub of ice-cold water. My world went effervescent blue and grey and red, and I was wide awake. Alive. Water streamed across my eyes and I opened my mouth to shriek: No. But she hooked me up and plunged in my arms and shoulders too. Down I went and water gushed to the back of my mouth and made me choke. When she brought me up I heard her say, 'Breathe, Emilie, deep breath. Now.' There was time to notice a rattle of a chain and a clang of metal on brick as the well bucket hit the sides and then I went under again. Fire and water, water and fire, somebody, who is it, the German, Stahl, says that water is necessary to combustion. We were going to test . . . We must find out why water . . . I could make notes . . .

The nightmare went on. I found that I did have some strength after all and lashed out at Annie as she plunged me down but she was stronger than me and in I went, snorting and gaping. Now I was kneeling in one bath while my head and arms were immersed in another. I shivered and ached but the fire in my legs was put out, that terrible sound of the well bucket scraping on brick came to an end and Mrs Gill drew me into her arms and wrapped me in a warm, soft cocoon. I turned my head into her bosom and for the first time smelt something other than ash: essence of Mrs Gill, herbal, floury. She pushed the wet hair back from my cheek and held the side of my head for a moment.

Then I was lifted by Gill and flung over his shoulder so that all the fires in my flesh were lit again. He took me out of daylight into the dim cottage, up the narrow staircase and deposited me in the bed. Mrs Gill hung me over her arm while Annie unbuttoned the remnants of my gown and cut the ribbon from my neck. I glimpsed it for a moment, a crisp brownish scrap that crumbled in her hand. They laid me out naked, swabbed my skin with ointment and dropped bitter liquid between my lips. When I stared up at their two faces, one old, one young, I saw such fierce concentration that I thought: I can't fight them. They are too much for me.

Then the fires came back and I went hurtling away under the haphazard beams of the cottage roof. Fever turned my bones to dust and jostled the hot coals in my head.

3

When the clock in the nearby church tower struck five I woke again and tried to remember Shales. I could see the Selden pew under the empty pulpit, my father's slab, the ruffled grasses on my mother's grave but not Shales. I saw grit blown along the aisle and a wasp tap-tapping against the coloured glass, a pot of dead flowers but no Shales.

Perhaps I moaned. The air above me moved to and fro and when I looked up Annie's face was there. She dripped water between my lips and moved a fan that must have been found in one of the old, doomed rooms of the manor. I thought the flowers on its papery silk would drop one petal at a time. She sat so close that her knee was against my thigh and I could hear her laboured breathing. Her top lip was drawn up over irregular teeth so that her mouth never quite closed. Occasionally she paused to swat a fly or give me water. If I could have wept I would have shed tears at her immeasurable kindness.

Then my fever rose and I streaked flame as I flew through the dark woods gripped in the claws of an owl or crashed down through the branches of the oak tree. Every thought I had was a surprise and always a bad one, so one minute I rummaged through a dung heap and came up with a tangle of baby limbs, arms and legs and clammy trunks, the next I buried my fingers in my husband's wig and off it came in my hands to reveal another false head of hair more elaborate than the last, and beneath that another and another.

'Marigold oil,' I heard Mrs Gill say. 'It should soothe her. Valerian so she sleeps.'

'. . . poor legs,' said Annie.

'. . . fool. Fortunate to be alive. She deserves . . .'

4

I woke one day to find my head was clear and there were people shouting close by outside the window. At first I was afraid that the ribbon seller would come and abuse me but then I remembered I was in Mrs Gill's bed and therefore safe.

As a child I used to hide away in this bed when I was lonely during my father's absence or because I had disgraced myself by breaking a crucible in the laboratory. I was hemmed in on three sides by an alcove and on the fourth by planks which partitioned the bed from the rest of the room. In a drawer underneath were kept what Mrs Gill called her precious things: her mother's wedding ring – paper thin and misshapen, clipped open because they had to cut it off when her finger swelled with arthritis – a lock of my dark baby hair, a paper of dried flowers, 'given by him when he came after me,' she had once explained, referring to Gill in an unlikely state of youthful ardour.

I lay between the rough sheets, watched the light seep along the uneven ceiling and listened to the half-hearted remnants of the fair, the occasional gush of water from the pump nearby and every quarter of an hour the chime of the bell in the tower of St M. and St E.

'How long have I been here?' I asked Mrs Gill.

'This is the fifth day.'

'I thought I'd die.'

'So you would had it not been for that apron I made you.'

'What damage have I done myself?'

'Your feet and legs are bad up to your thighs. Your hands and face have lost a layer of skin.'

'May I have a mirror?'

'I've no mirror.'

'Was much of the house destroyed?'

'Only the laboratory. The rest stands. It's got good thick walls, that house. A wicked shame to tear them down.'

'Is the work still going on?'

'The work goes on. Lord, Emilie, what were you thinking of?'

Annie spooned broth between my lips and plumped the pillow so I could see the sky through the tiny window. 'Is the fair still not over?' I asked.

'All but. It drags on for ever, it seems.'

'Does everyone know about the explosion?'

'They've talked of nothing else for days.'

'Annie, is Reverend Shales come home?'

'Not that I know of.'

In the afternoon I woke when the church clock struck five. With each chime motes of dust throbbed against the window. Then the clock went silent. Mice scratched under the floor and a couple of birds trod the roof. My heart cracked open.

Shales.

I remembered the hours I had sat in his study and thought I should have stayed there for the rest of my life. Except that Hannah Shales would have been watching me. *For Thomas, on his birthday* is what she had written on the back of her portrait. I thought what a joy to sit in the morning light and have an artist (even if not a good one) take a likeness. I imagined this Hannah poised over a scrap of paper, a thin, tidy woman who would certainly have practised the inscription many times before writing it out in her neatest hand. Was it just economy with words that made her omit any mention of love? Or was it perhaps that such a word wasn't needed between a devoted husband and wife? She should have written *with love* even so. I would have done.

Anyway, what did it matter? Shales had gone and here was I burnt half to death but still dragged along by the silken cord binding me to Aislabie's embroidered breeches.

When Mrs Gill came up I said, 'Thank you for healing me.'

She snorted and beat the pillow with her fist. As she turned to go I said, 'I found my father's notebooks under the floor.'

Silence.

'Did they survive the fire?'

Silence.

'Perhaps they were burnt. Do you know?'

Silence.

'Mrs Gill.'

'I thought you'd forgotten,' she said.

'Were they burnt?'

'They were not.'

'Where are they?'

She shrugged and went downstairs.

So of course I remember that evening as being the evening of the notebooks. It was one of the hottest of a hot summer with the air soupy in the confined room and the sky oatmeal-coloured through the little window. Annie's face was blotchy with heat when she brought my supper – they were stewing berries downstairs – and even the birds had stopped singing. My burns itched so I pulled away the sheets and lay with my flayed legs exposed.

There were times that evening when I was so full of waiting that I had to remind myself to breathe. I knew Mrs Gill would bring the notebooks. Once set on a course of action she was an unstoppable force. I had been waiting to read them all my conscious life because what I expected to find, besides a record of my own flawed alchemical progress, was my mother.

5

Mrs Gill came soon after eight with a flat basket normally used for collecting mushrooms. Inside was the green feather, bright as the day I had picked it up from the bottom of the parrot's cage, a bundle of letters, copies of Boerhaave's *Institutiones Medical* and *Experimenta Chemiae* and the notebooks, twelve in all, three piles of four.

I slid out the first of the letters. The parchment was brittle, desiccated perhaps by the heat of the flames, and the ink had faded. The creases were so well pressed, in fact had worn almost transparent in places, that the letter must have been unfolded many times.

14 December 1725

Dearest Father,

    I am writing to you from our new house in Hanover Street. Robert has bought me a parrot and I thought you would like to see one of its brilliant green feathers.

    I have not been able to write until now because I have been ill . . .

I knew that letter about the lost baby off by heart. Hadn't I written it a hundred times in my head before I picked up a pen? I folded it carefully and slid it back into the bundle; each letter a pipingly cheerful record of my marriage to Aislabie, each ending with the same plea: '*I miss you, Father. I hope you will write soon . . .*'

Then the notebooks. I weighed the first in my hand, sniffed. The leather was darkened by the fire and smelt scorched.

Mrs Gill said, 'If he'd wanted you to read them he wouldn't have hidden them away so careful.'

'Perhaps.'

'They were private, Emilie.'

'He could have destroyed them. He must have known I'd find them in the end.'

It was already growing dark as I opened the first book at the first page. Mrs Gill sighed heavily but didn't go away. Instead, she sat down on the only chair, planted her legs wide and folded her arms.

Chapter Ten

THE EMILIE
NOTEBOOKS

I

31 May 1706

So now I have a daughter named Emilie after her mother. A good name. Looked it up; probably from Amelia, meaning labour.

She is, according to Mrs Gill, a healthy infant though I can get little response from her. If I click my fingers she doesn't blink, if I smile she doesn't smile in return. One promising sign. When I pinched her upper arm she did cry. She is too young to do much else, said Mrs G. She is like a new pup, all instinct at present. But give her time.

A girl sent for from north of Buckingham to feed her. Mrs G. thought it best to avoid someone from the village because of talk. I don't care, but Mrs G. says we must bear in mind the baby growing up.

1 June 1706

The funeral. Rev. Gilbert made a fuss about the graveyard. She was my wife, I said, she'll be put to rest where I choose, and that silenced him. Buried her late in the evening. A decent enough ceremony, given there must have been Catholic blood somewhere in her past. Fine weather. Pondered the inscription for some time. Mrs G. said the babe should be christened while we were about it and then I wouldn't have to go near the church again. Allowed it for the sake of peace and quiet though hated to hear

Gilbert's talk of original sin. Any fool can see that the infant is without any thought, let alone a sinful or original one.

7 June 1706

Babe makes slow progress. Hear it crying a good deal though thankfully not when in the laboratory. The pace of its development puzzles me. Cannot be in proportion to size. Necessity, more like. A calf, for instance, lacking claws or the instinct to attack and with only a lumbering cow to protect it, is on its feet within hours of birth. A kitten, on the other hand, is dependent for some weeks. This human child is utterly helpless and I confess I am impatient with it, even wonder if I was not too rash in believing I could shape it.

Was I rash? If so, not a common fault in me. In any case, this was not a decision that might have been postponed.

It was the moment when her head fell back on my arm and she slept. I bent my head and sniffed her warm damp breath. That was the moment after which it did not seem to me that I had a choice.

Mrs G. says it will be six weeks or so before the child will so much as smile.

4 July 1706

Emilie caught hold of my finger again today and I laughed at the sudden strength of her. Saw that she was smiling back at me. Distinct light of intelligence in her black eye and her mouth opened wide with joy. This is not instinct but recognition. Clearly a forward girl, as I suspected. Mrs G., as noted above, said it would be six weeks before she smiled. This is barely five.

Mrs Gill was still sitting at the top of the stairs. She had merged into the shadows since I started reading but I knew that her gaze was fixed on my face.

'He doesn't mention my mother, except that you buried her,' I said.

'No, I thought not.'

'Only you. You are written about a lot.'

'That's because I was there and she wasn't.'

'But she must have been on his mind.'

'There was only one thing on his mind at that time. Nothing else existed but you. I had to remind him to eat.'

'But didn't you think it strange that he never seemed to grieve my mother or talk about her?'

She was silent a moment, then said, 'It's common, I think, for some men to become so enamoured of a baby girl that all other thought goes out of their heads. Gill was the same.'

'Gill?'

'He used to take off his boots for fear of waking you, even if you were a dozen rooms away. You have no idea, Emilie, what a stir you caused in that great empty house.'

12 July 1706

She grows strong. The muscles harden in her back and neck. Her eyes shine. She laughs and waves her hands. I carry her about and lie her amidst cushions in the library so she can watch me work and grow used to the sight of books. Talk to her all the time. Have explained to her that am currently seeking to replicate Hooke's experiments with condensed air. In fact, intended to perform his experiment in which he placed a bird under a receiver until it was at the point of death, to see if it might be revived when the air from distilled vinegar was admitted. However, find myself unable to perform said experiment at present even though I have a cage of three finches ready for the purpose. Captured one and put it under a bell jar but when its bright eye looked at me through the glass I began to sweat. Was reminded of Emilie and couldn't bear to see the bird's black eye go dull so released it.

Besides, she likes birds. She lies and watches them. It is good for the quickness of her eye to follow their movements.

NB Have begun the education of other senses.

Take her to the orchard and let her hear birdsong and watch the movement of shadows. Dip finger in honey and see her tongue lap it up. Give her whiff of menthol and she pouts. Told G. he might carry her to see and smell bonfire.

This is the start.

Am in great fear of leaving E. Must of course go to London but what if anything should happen while I am away? She seems robust though on Tuesday and Wednesday last she had a cough and rheumy eyes and nose. Questioned the girl they brought in to feed her and learnt she has three healthy infants of her own, left with their grandmother. Her eyes are clear and her cheeks blooming but I confided in Mrs G. the hope that intelligence is not passed from nurse to nursling through the mother's milk as this girl is very dull. Mrs Gill said you'd know about the internal workings of the human body more than me, Sir, but I would imagine that whatever goes on in the head is somewhat separate from the other organs. Cannot be sure. In cases of fever where the contents of the stomach are evacuated, the head may also ache and be prone to faintness, which suggests to me that the good of one part of the body is dependent on the whole. Certainly this would accord with Harvey et al.

There is so little of my Emilie. She fits into the crook of my arm and her fingernails remind me of fish scales. Mrs G. says she is still too young to spend much time in the laboratory with me, though I would like to keep her under my eye constantly. Thinks I should stay in London the usual length of time. Says that Emilie will thrive in my absence and that I will be pleased with the change in her when I get back.

Cut short my visit. Found I could not sleep at night. During reading of a paper by N. about particles in elastic fluids thought only of Emilie. Seemed impossible that some terrible accident had not happened to her; a candle left alight by a careless girl or the babe forgotten as she lies under a tree in the orchard. The bees.

Journey home very long and when Gill at last threw back the gates Mrs Gill came running out to meet us — thought my worst fears confirmed — could not speak.

I hadn't expected you for weeks, she said. Good Lord, she is sleeping, Sir, and led me up to the little bedchamber overlooking the garden, and there lay Emilie, plumper than I remembered, with her fist against her cheek and her lips moist, suck-sucking as I have noticed she does in sleep sometimes, as if remembering the

*nipple. Sat down beside her and watched and decided this
watching must become a habit of mine, because isn't it my life's
work now as much to study the growth of this human child as
the alterations to a mineral heated in the test tube?*

It was now so dark that though I tilted the book to the window
I couldn't make out any more words. 'I need a candle,' I said.

'Certainly not. You must rest your eyes.' She got up, took the
notebook and packed it away in the basket.

'He still says nothing about my mother.'

She was already at the top of the stairs.

'Or my birth. Are you sure there isn't an earlier notebook?'

But she'd gone.

2

The next morning there was no sign of the mushroom basket
or the notebooks so I sat up and swung my legs off the bed,
intending to look for them. My calves flamed, my feet turned to
powder, the room crackled. I had to wait.

'So,' said Mrs Gill when she came at last, 'you're feeling better.'

'Curious more like.'

'I assume this is all vanity, makes you so fond of reading about
yourself.' She examined my feet, put her fingers under my chin
and turned my face from side to side. 'You're doing better than
I hoped. I've small experience in the treatment of burns, thank
the Lord, but I believe the air is the best cure, as it is for most
things.

> *30 May 1707*
>
> *Her second birthday. We must begin. Long arguments with Mrs
> G. I accept that Emilie must have access to the fresh air and
> have undertaken to allow her outside for two hours every day.
> Accept also that she must sleep during the afternoon and have
> some recreation appropriate to her age.*
>
> *Will adopt the experimental method advocated by Newton
> which has not failed me yet, though I have puzzled how to apply*

it to this child who will not keep still for long. Have reflected upon the following for some time, studied it from all angles, and it now seems to me a fair plan, which should produce desired result.

<u>Herewith the proposed method</u>

The hypothesis I propose is that it is possible to take an unformed infant, of whatever sex or antecedents, and mould it into any shape or type desired. The type I desire for Emilie is that of natural philosopher and alchemist, like myself. I want her to be as I am, as soon as possible.

I am fifty-two years old. Time is running out and I am only at the beginning of what I need to do. If I could give Emilie all I know, say by the age of eighteen, what might she not achieve by the time she is fifty?

There is much that I can't foresee. According to Mrs Gill, E. behaves as any infant her age might, although she is quicker than most. It is possible, however, that there are hidden properties in this child that may not be present in others. This is true of most animate beings, it seems to me. In a litter of pups one may be easily trained, another wild, another affectionate. There seems, on the face of it, no reason for these differences although who knows what influence one pup might have upon another, given that I have noticed that in nature and in natural philosophy no thing, provided it has capacity for change at all, is left unchanged once it has come into contact, however slight, with another. Thus mercury will be dissolved in aqua fortis, expand on being heated, contract in the cold and be precipitated in calomel to form a useful purgative. Similarly a plant, say a sunflower, will flourish according to the amount of water and heat that is applied and to the exact quality of the soil in which it grows, the proportion of acid to alkali etc.

So, Emilie. I must supervise her growth exactly. After I had written the above I realised how every last thing that happens will make a difference to Emilie – the hours she sleeps, the temperature in which she wakes, the constituents of her diet, all she sees and hears. I am awed by the responsibility of this and wonder how anyone else goes about the business of bringing up a child. They seem so careless, the mothers I have seen with children roaming about outside the gates.

These are the tendencies in Emilie most likely to lead to evil, and the resolutions I have made

1. _Distraction._ She is a flighty little thing and in this I see her mother's influence, I assume, or the wet-nurse. Certainly I can't see any tendencies to distraction in Mrs Gill or myself. Emilie will not settle for more than a few minutes at a time to any task. Mrs Gill says this is her age and I must be sure to let her move about freely or she will come to hate the laboratory and the library. She says that all infants dislike confinement. So I have thought that the answer to this must be sufficient variety to ensure that Emilie does not realise she is confined, but not so much that she expects constant diversion.

Thus I allow her to watch the mice and birds in the cages, and to play with water, which she loves to do. Fire also attracts her. Gill has devised a wire cage that enables her to approach a candle safely and to blow its flame without in any means endangering herself. I have given her slate and a chalk so that she may write though she has broken several pieces of chalk and makes only meaningless scrawls on the slate. She likes best of all substances such as clay and sand, which she has a tendency to eat but seem to do her no harm. I have noticed that almost from birth she has used her mouth to test the qualities of a new substance and this shows promise.

2. _Tears._ I have experimented with how to deal with this business of tears. When she fell against a chair leg and cried I beat her, thinking that she might thereafter associate tears with more pain, but she only cried louder until Mrs Gill came and carried her off. When the child was at last returned to me Mrs Gill said that if I beat her I would make her afraid of me. Besides, have no heart to beat her more. The shock in her eye was very terrible to see. Next I tried distraction to prevent tears but I found that she quickly associated pleasure with wrongdoing and thought that if she cried I would reward her with a trip to the bee orchard or a spoon of honey. Now I ignore her tears and I find this works best of all. When I withdraw my attention she soon grows weary of weeping and climbs into my lap instead and tucks her head inside my waistcoat, which I confess gives me great joy.

3. _Clumsiness._ Have made her a series of boxes out of paper and I show her how to hold them so they don't crumple. Mrs Gill

says I may not experiment by giving her flasks or alembics to carry, these being too dangerous for the child, and with this I concur, alembics being costly.

4. And of course the question of affections or the lack of them. Will the child be prone to flirtatiousness, to an ill-developed sense of right and wrong? My answer is to instil a degree of reserve, both physical and emotional, so that she in time curbs her instinct to embrace, to turn to others for comfort. If she is sufficient to herself, if she depends only on her own good opinion, she will not be easily led.

I find this a hard resolve, indeed I break it every day, but this is my plan. I resolve not to touch her except in the morning and last thing at night when I may embrace her. She is inclined to run up and clasp my knees or pull off my wig and cover me with kisses at all times of day. This I cannot allow because of where it may lead. Shall ask Mrs Gill to refrain likewise. In a similar way I shall not use verbal endearments, and I shall not encourage singing and childish games. I want her to have a serious mind untroubled by thoughts of superficial pleasure. Mrs Gill resistant to this and inclined to argue and it pains me to write that I don't trust her to keep to my rules.

5. Worldliness. I fear that Emilie will be seduced the minute she leaves Selden, that there may be a part of her that will recognise vice as being intrinsic to her nature. So I resolve to keep her enclosed until such time as I believe her strong enough to know good from evil. In this again I struggle with Mrs Gill who sometimes is so troublesome I wonder I keep her here. In the end we have agreed that she will take her to church on one Sunday a month, and visiting in the village when appropriate. The reason: to instil in Emilie a sense of her place in the world. Furthermore, Mrs Gill insists that the child has a natural curiosity that must be satisfied and that she must learn to recognise evil, which she never will do if she is hidden from it. Mrs Gill points out that Emilie now has an appropriate respect for the damage a flame can do because I have brought a flame up close to her hand and shown her how it may burn.

Conclusion

These then are my plans for the child and these notebooks will keep a faithful tally of her progress and in them I will note down

not only her lapses but my own. I find that the child has a way of
undermining my best intentions and this must stop.

3

I read the notebooks piecemeal because my mind was still fuddled by the explosion. I would fall asleep suddenly mid sentence or if the book dropped from my hand I lacked the strength to pick it up. Besides, I was afraid of those notebooks and the truth that glimmered just beneath the surface so I couldn't bear too much of them at a time. Though my knowledge of prose other than of the alchemical or natural philosophical variety was very limited, even I could see that an extraordinary metamorphosis had taken place during the writing. While my father had set out to record an ambitious experiment, what he'd actually produced was an account of falling in love.

I recognised this because I knew how blind love was: hadn't I played exactly the same tricks on myself when I first set eyes on Aislabie? My father had convinced himself that I was all good and that any failing in me must be due to him. If there was a flaw he patiently set out to correct it, if I was slow at learning he plotted a different way of teaching me and the selectivity of this process drove me wild with frustration. I wanted the truth. I wanted to see myself as I had been, not as he saw me. At the very least I wanted him to look at me and see my mother. But my mother was as absent from the notebooks as she had been from my childhood.

The second surprise was my father's softness in writing. His alchemical notebooks were formal, concise, passionless. Whenever I had speculated about the Emilie Notebooks I thought they would be written in a similar vein – a series of observations, analyses and hypotheses. But instead I found a torrent of words and a voice that spoke of me with a vividness and tenderness he had never allowed himself in real life. In fact, he wrote about me with the same attention to detail, the same quest for the exact expression of what he saw and felt, that I associated with my feelings for Shales whose study I could revisit in my imagination inch by inch, and whose speech replayed in my head.

14 April 1716

Still working on Pascal's Traité de L'Equilibre des Liqueurs
. . . I won't allow the translation so Emilie is struggling with both language and concept. I explained that water cannot be pumped up from a depth of more than thirty-four feet due to the density of the air. Then make a more effective pump, she said. She is never limited by what seems possible, my girl.

Thought she'd be delighted by von Guericke's experiment with the vacuum pump and indeed she was. Showed her the print in the book of how two teams of horses couldn't pull apart the copper hemispheres from which air had been pumped and explained how amazed the Emperor Ferdinand had been that the air outside could exert such pressure. She said: Why was the emperor there?

To prove the experiment, to give it authority, I said, but already I had misgivings. Knew where this would lead. Have learned not to give her any opportunity to direct the lesson away from its true purpose.

She said: But if the emperor hadn't been there the experiment would still have worked.

The world wouldn't have believed it, I said.

Does the world always believe an emperor?

She takes me in directions I don't expect; saw things in the background of the picture that I never noticed. She wanted to know who might have lived in the castle perched on top of the hill, whether I had once worn an old-fashioned coat like the emperor's and whether the domed building in the little town was a church or observatory. Was suddenly tempted to visit mountains with her or even to travel with her across the sea. Thought how wonderful to see her face when she set eyes on the ocean. Found myself justifying such a trip by contemplating all the learning we might do on the way.

NB Will make enquiries into cost of some such trip when next in town.

When later we went walking in the woods she remarked how the engraver of the von Guericke experiment had chosen to watch from the shade so that he was in darkness and the amazing events with the copper hemispheres in the light. Astounds me with what she sees. Wonder if this tendency to think tangentially is common to other females or whether it is something she perhaps inherited from her mother.

Picked up a fistful of dead leaves and made her smell the peat while we waited to see if a deer might come. All the time I watched her face. I see traces of her mother, yes, in her wide forehead and the shape of her ears, but my Emilie is so fine, so quick, so unlike anyone in the world except herself.

19 September 1721

Back from London with the pus in a phial ready to engraft on to my dear child. She has grown while I was away and is more graceful. Her figure is almost a woman's. In London I took the opportunity to study other women and none is as marvellous as she. None can talk as she does about the quality of air and fire. None has such clear white skin or such black eyes sparking with intelligence.

She wanted to know everything that I had done and seen but was sharp with her and sent her early to bed. Cannot bear to see her so healthy, knowing what I must do. My misgivings give me great pain. Have seen the evidence with my own eyes. All but one of those felons inoculated with the disease survived and it's not clear whether he died of smallpox or some other infection but in this one case I mistrust the experimental method. It is not proof enough.

Am therefore in a terrible quandary. If I should be mistaken it may cost her life. I consider other errors I have made, as when in 1689 we blew the chimney off the large furnace shed, or when a delegation from the village came to complain about the smell when we failed to achieve the correct temperature for the making of phosphorus. These were unfortunate only, but this projected experiment with the smallpox could be fatal. And if I don't engraft her she is also at risk. London is full of smallpox. There are cases in Buckingham. It will very likely come to Selden again.

20 September 1721

This morning I engrafted her. Took her round, bare arm, scraped a little gash in her skin and dropped in the pus. She scarcely flinched but watched my face intently. Her eyes watered when I made the wound but she didn't say a word. Trusted me. We had earlier revised Harvey's work on the circulation of the blood, and I described in detail the experience of the convicts. After an hour or so she seemed to have forgotten what had happened. Kept her beside me constantly and checked that the wound has not become infected, but she has gone to bed in good health.

25 September 1721

These days are the worst I have ever lived. Watch her all the time. Am often angry with her for no other reason than that my worry is taking all my attention. Every time she puts her hand to her head I think she is sickening. Have asked Mrs Gill to keep a record of what she eats, her excretions, her patterns of sleep. All seem normal.

27 September 1721

The critical time. She seems distracted. Perhaps she is worried too, though she says not a word, my brave soul. To take her mind off the engrafting I told her that today we should release the owl. Gill has been pressing me for the last week to let it go but Emilie has grown fond of it and I saw no harm in keeping it confined a little longer. And we have begun work on phlogiston. Can hardly bear to see her so eager when at the back of my mind is the knowledge that I may have killed her. When we were together this afternoon she seemed dull. I thought it was the illness coming upon her and was very sharp. She is better this evening. There are times when the worry of this girl is such that I wish she had never been born.

Tonight took the owl to the roof. Not once did she flinch as we watched it fly away, though I knew she had grown attached to it. Lapsed and held her by the arm. Could feel her warm, breathing body next to my hand and I thought there, there, she is so strong, nothing can harm her. She will be well.

Emilie has eight spots, four out of sight, but she tells me they are on her chest, belly and hip, two on the back of her left knee, another on the crook of her elbow, another on her wrist. Definitely smallpox and I watch the most visible, on her wrist, all the time. Will not let her scratch it. This morning in the laboratory she complained of dizziness. Would not let her out of my sight even though she asked to be allowed to lie down. Would not let her lie down. Have a dread of her not getting up again. This evening she seemed tired but a little better.

Danger is past. Have never lived through such in my life. Nor hope to again.

4

By now the fair had ended and the village street beyond my room was quiet except for the occasional flurry of conversation, the movement of sheep or goats, the squabble of hens and the insistent striking of the clock. Meanwhile in the kitchen they were still bottling fruit and I was half stifled by the smell of boiled sugar.

My days in the attic room were numbered. I could get out of bed on my own now and walk a few steps. Mrs Gill said so much enclosure was bad for me and I should be out in the air but I wouldn't leave the house. I was afraid of getting better and being sent back to Selden because of what I might find there. Besides, I had grown attached to the attic room and to being so near other human beings in the village. The ability of people to rub against each other in ways different from those that had operated at Selden and in the Hanover Street house intrigued me. Mention of anyone except me was rare in my father's notebooks and it struck me that this exclusivity had made me singularly unfit for other less devoted men – notably Aislabie. My father had brought me up to expect that pairs of people should be everything to each other. No wonder I had found it so bewildering when Aislabie went sauntering off each day to spend time with people who weren't me.

And then I came across a name in my father's eleventh notebook that put Aislabie out of my head completely.

6 March 1725

Banished Shales. Fool that I am – didn't see the danger. Regarded him merely as a colleague but when he came into the library sensed a withdrawing of her attention from me to him. Twice he suggested that she might visit his laboratory.

When he and I were witnesses to the experiment with smallpox he had seemed sober and reserved. But with Emilie he was different and she became unlike herself. Her pupils widened, her mouth opened, there was colour in her cheeks.

I know that some male animals, once they have lost their partners – swans, for instance – can, after a period of grief, be predatory.

After he'd gone she was withdrawn. Fortunately he proved to be duller than I expected. Was mistaken in him. There is no reason for him to come here again.

So have banished him. This is what comes of attempting to include others in alchemy. In any case, acted partly out of pride – had a peculiar idea that I should try and convince Shales.

Told Mrs Gill he was not to be allowed in the house. Said I cannot have that girl's head turned by any male who walks in here and we'll have no more trips to the village. She was very sharp with me. Said I was a fool to myself, that if I sheltered Emilie she was bound to be vulnerable to the first young man who came and made eyes at her. Said she is like the young of any species and bound to seek a mate. I argued that this was instinct, not intellect and my Emilie is pure intellect at which Mrs Gill shouted at me and said you must give some thought for the girl's future, Sir, we none of us will be here for ever and then what? You have left her without defences. What good will all her learning be if she is alone? Ordered her away. Have never known her so insolent.

Since then have done nothing but ponder the problem of Emilie's future. There is the palingenesis to be sure but I cannot

235

rely on it. Wish I could. She will have Selden but I don't like to think of her alone here, as I was alone. But what is the answer? I won't have her marry. Who is worthy of her?

12 February 1725

Well. Well. So I shall take the following steps, and I have come to this decision reluctantly and after many hours of thought. From henceforth she will be allowed to meet up to three men per year (Shales being the first) but they shall be of my choosing, and when she is twenty-one I may take her to London and introduce her there. In this way I hope to teach her discernment. Shales, on reflection, has too many traits that might endear her to him; he is bookish and a natural philosopher and has a certain gentleness of manner that she might well admire. Such a man, with such sceptical views, is out of the question. He is too plausible.

In this way I hope she will learn to recognise the good from the bad, the true from the false in mankind, as I have taught her to be discerning in all other matters.

18 April 1725

Might Shales be sent away from the parish? Plagues me with notes about the state of fences and asks permission to try crop rotation at his own expense and to set up a fund for the sick and destitute. Is currying favour in the village. Says a school is needed. I haven't time for any of this.

He is very young. Unlikely to die. How to get rid of him.

13 May 1725

Must a woman marry? Emilie has me. Shall probably live another decade at least, if I take care. There is no man to equal her. A man would confine her intellect.

24 June 1725

I believe she has been infected by this Shales. Is restless and refuses to give her mind to palingenesis. Wants to pursue her own experiments on air and says she would like to meet him again. Whenever I think of that man I grow sick at heart.

On the day of the picking of the rose an omen. A visitor. There is a connection, clearly. Emilie returned to the laboratory with a perfect bloom. Truly I have seen nothing like it. She held it against her bosom, my girl. Her hair was caught on a thorn and a lock fell among the rose petals, black on pink. Her eyes were on fire with excitement because now we could begin. She was, at that moment, all I have ever hoped of her. At long last she is convinced of the truth of palingenesis.

The visitor is a merchant from London. I thought at first there was a great deal to him. He talked of phlogiston and applied it to his own business with shipping. He has attended lectures at the Society. Then I realised that he is a sham. After a very few minutes he stopped listening to me and his eyes strayed to the laboratory door. He is here, I believe, because he has some passing curiosity about alchemy. Emilie doesn't see that he is shallow and so I am reluctantly forced to concur with Mrs Gill that the girl is vulnerable. Am amazed that her wisdom in all other things does not extend to this. But I cast my mind back to my own youth and a predilection I once had for a young chambermaid. Margaret. I remember the toss of her head as she threw back her heavy hair and how a glimpse of her ankle or wrist used to excite me so much I couldn't study. I longed to hold her earlobe between my finger and thumb. I thought that it would feel warm and succulent. My father pointed out that she was a distraction and I should learn to curb my desires. But I could not. When she was sent back to the village I spent night after night yearning for her. She had an empty mind and a large, troublesome family. I saw for myself that she would bring me nothing but grief but I thought of her constantly and was in physical pain until my father took me away to London. When I came back she was married and I never went into the village after that. I have often thought, however, that if I had been allowed to spend time with her, if I had spoken to her at length I would have been repulsed by her coarseness and all my desire for her would have gone. So I have allowed this Aislabie to return and trust Emilie to see for herself how worthless he is in relation to her. I believe in this respect he is far less of a danger than Shales.

He came again and I have sent him away. Emilie took him to the orchard and they spent a few minutes together, according to Mrs Gill. The corruption has set in quickly. Now she wants to go with me to London, presumably so she can meet him there – or another like him. I believe Shales to be the root cause of all this restlessness. He began it.

She is not ready to face the temptations of the city. Am not convinced she would withstand them. Shall buy her a present. An alembic, perhaps, or a book. This must suffice. And then another time will take her to London, when she has proved herself to be a little wiser. Perhaps there would be no harm. Could take her to a lecture or two. My fellows at the Society will be amazed at what I have achieved.

22 September 1725

She
   She
   She
   Monstrous
   She
   Well, I will not

23 September 1725

I do not deserve this.
   I am an old man. I have given her every last ounce of myself.
   I trusted her.
   I should never have gone away.

26 September 1725

Called Gill. Said where were you when this happened? Don't tell me you didn't know what was going on. He stood with his hands hanging. I said: Gill, she was in your charge. You witless . . . You ungrateful . . . Brought staff down on his head and shoulder. He scarcely flinched. Stared dumbly. He was there at her start. Had he no remembrance of that? Brought it down again on his shoulder and he took it from me, placed it on the bench and walked away.

The misery that she has brought upon us all.

Mrs Gill came in with my supper. Said: You must eat, Sir. I said: After all I have done for you. You have been negligent. She was weeping. Weak tears. She said nothing at first. Then she said: She is a woman, Sir. She will make her own choices. I am not her gaoler and neither are you.

She said: There is no turning back time, for all your art. You stand to lose her if you won't forgive her.

Every hour or so the girl has come to the door and knocked. I hear her skirt brush against the wood. I hear her breathing. So I keep the library door locked and I go into the laboratory where I won't be troubled any more.

30 September 1725

He came.

I weep. Can't stop. Saw him so clearly for what he is. How could she be so foolish as to fall for him? Of all people. He is nothing. He is like Flamsteed at the Society, caring only for his own ambition.

I see it all. It is her mother. And, fool that I am, I only realise now that since her birth I have been fighting not one enemy but two – mother and father.

This Aislabie is perfumed and smooth-handed. Have lain awake at night and thought of how he must have touched her. My Em . . . I had speeches ready. I thought I would say to him I know you through and through. I found you out while I was in London, the slave-trading, the South Sea dealings, the false story about your father and his farm. You are nothing. I thought I might send him away and keep Emilie with me and look after her and forgive her but I saw it was hopeless. She will have him because she can't resist him. He comes from the world that is in her blood. He's been there all along and I never noticed. And he knows too much. He is full of veiled threats. I won't have him hurt her like that. It seems he has uncovered all our secrets.

In the space of a few weeks he undid all I had achieved, every last shred of sense, because something in his flesh called out to her. My life's work is over. The experiment has failed.

5

There was one more notebook but I stopped reading. I had my answers and I thought if I read about my father's suffering after I married Aislabie his words would haunt me for ever.

Annie came as usual to swab me with ointment, dress me in a clean shift, wash my face. Mrs Gill was away delivering twins in Lower Selden and not expected back until morning. I said, 'How can I repay you, Annie, for all you've done?'

'I'm paid well enough by Mrs Gill.'

'Nevertheless, I should like to thank you.'

I expected her to ask for money – I had won ten guineas at the gambling table on the night of the red party – but instead she crept back towards the bed and stood with her hands clasped and her tongue showing. 'There is something, if you mean it. I should like to know how to read.'

I wondered how someone as stupid as Annie could be taught to read. And I was strangely resentful that she should want such a thing. I think I saw her, just for a moment, as a rival. But then I told myself that between them she and Mrs Gill had saved my life so I promised her that we would begin as soon as I had the strength.

I was rewarded by a smile reaching almost ear to ear. 'I've always wanted to read,' she said, 'since I saw you in church following the prayers in the book.'

'You remember me from when you were a child?'

'Of course.'

'And what did you think of me, Annie?'

'I don't understand.'

'When you saw me, what did you think?'

'I felt sorry for you, of course.'

'Sorry? Why?'

'Because you had no mother. Because you was alone with him in that great house and there seemed no way out for you.'

6

The next morning when Mrs Gill came I was sitting up with a shawl wrapped round my shoulders and my hair brushed. 'I should like to get up now, so that you can sleep in your own bed,' I said.

'Don't worry on my account. I can sleep anywhere. I still have my room at the house.'

'What's happening there?'

'They've been taking it apart, bit by bit. But for now they've stopped. I slept late as a result.'

She uncovered my burns and said I would soon be well. I touched my face and felt the hard skin on my cheeks. When I asked for a mirror again she said she'd bring one from the house. She was in a great hurry and wouldn't meet my eye. I think she knew what was coming.

I said, 'Mrs Gill, was there no affection at all between my parents?'

She shrugged.

'Why did my father suspect that my mother might have Catholic blood in her? I thought you said her family were Huguenots.'

'I may have done.'

'Why does he keep writing about my mother's nature as if it was foreign to him?'

'She was foreign. She was French.'

'Yes, but what about his own nature? Why does he never talk about his own blood and how I have inherited his nature?'

She was about to fasten the neck of my shift but her hands went still. Her face was so close to mine that I could see the veins in the thin skin of her eyelids.

'So,' I said, 'I'm not my father's child. Then who am I? Wasn't my father married to my mother?'

'Of course they were married. You are his child.'

'Did she deceive him with another man?'

'She never deceived him.'

'Then what?'

She buttoned the shift, quite a struggle as Sarah had sewn such tight little buttonholes. Sarah. I'd scarcely given her a thought since the explosion. Where was she now? The last I remembered was a pair of trim ankles retreating up the terrace steps, a slight stagger to accommodate the weight of pregnancy. Of course that was another thing wrong with my father's notebooks. 'He began writing about me when I was a day old,' I said. 'That's not right. He would have begun at my beginning.'

'Leave it, Emilie.'

'I can't. You know I can't.'

She was white-faced. 'You tell me this, Emilie, is it always best to know everything, as you and your father insist on doing? Or sometimes is it best just to be quiet and let things lie as they are?'

'If it's possible to know, I have to know.'

'Is that why you nearly killed yourself in that laboratory? Even if the finding out kills a person, is that still best?'

'Yes. Yes. The truth is everything. If we can only know. That's what he taught me.'

'Then that's your choice,' she said, 'but it isn't mine.'

7

I heard nearly every chime in the church tower that night. The swallows stirred in the eaves before four o'clock and then at last I slept but only fitfully because I knew I had set something in motion I couldn't stop. And sure enough in the morning Mrs Gill stormed up the stairs and said she'd had enough of me being in her bed and I must go back to Selden soon, my brooding and waywardness were making her cordials go sour. So she and Annie wrapped me up and helped me downstairs and through the steamy little kitchen to the garden where Gill had laid out a mattress and a heap of cushions from the manor. He hovered at the end of the garden to catch sight of me and when I waved and called his name he nodded vigorously several times and picked up a spade as if he had no time to linger. Then I was left alone to watch the play of sunlight on the leaves and the headlong plunge of a bee into the trumpet of a foxglove. At eye level with dandelions and camomile buds I followed the business of ants and leafhoppers, ladybirds and woodlice, and I stared so long at a stem of fennel that I swear I saw it grow. A robin hopped over my still hand; I felt its slight, brief weight, saw the dust on its feathers. There was so much going on that I thought I would lie there for ever with my head to the ground and never have to involve myself with my own kind again.

Mrs Gill came back with the last – or as it turned out the first – volume, more worn than the rest with swollen pages and bruised corners. She hung over me, still holding the book. 'You'll blame me for what you'll find in this but I have always done what I was told. Gill and I spoke about it. He said what she doesn't know will plague her more than what she does. So here it is, given you've asked for it. But remember, Emilie, whatever you might read and whatever you might think, you have been loved.'

I looked up at her shiny, inscrutable face and knew as I took the weighty little volume and felt its cover, soft as moss, that she and Gill were the only solid things left to me and that I must hold tight to what she had said.

30 May 1706

I had spent the day investigating the nature of green vitriol that Digby believed has healing properties and can knit wounds. (Discussed same with Mrs Gill who says the essence of healing in a wound is clean air and as little interference as possible.) Consulted Glauber for his expertise on irons and read how he recommended the same for treatment of some ulcers and cancers.

It was early evening but very windy and wet from heavy grey clouds and I worked by the light of a single candle. When seven struck I took up my staff and prepared to enter the laboratory and it was at that moment, as I moved away from the fire, that I saw a woman's face at the window. She was very low in the glass, just her head visible, with the rain streaming from black hair and one hand held flat to the pane so that at first I thought she must be a chimera. I snuffed the candle to see her better and her hand again fell against the glass, then slid down as if she hadn't the strength to hold it there. I summoned Gill and told him to bring her in and meanwhile went so far as to light four candles that I might see her properly. I then prepared this notebook so I could write her down, and put away my other books and eyeglass in case she proved to be a thieving girl.

Gill was half carrying her and she was wringing wet and huge with child. We put her in my chair by the fire and looked at her. There was a great deal of flesh exposed at her breast and neck, and her feet were bare. She was sodden, head to foot, and filthy from the mud she had picked up in the woods. Her ankles, from what I could judge, were swollen to twice the normal size for a woman of her age. By comparison the wrists were thin. Her skirts were torn and ragged, and there were bits of ribbon and lace hanging down. As I have written, the bodice was gaping so that one breast was entirely exposed. I noted that it was veined like a cow's udder and the nipple was dark and wide, and rested on the high swelling of her belly. She was white and shivering and moaning a great deal. She smelt of the river and mud, and something else, somewhat fishy, which I took to be a woman's smell. Her fingernails were bitten and black.

I asked where she had come from but she didn't reply. Nor when I asked her name. Then she jolted her knee up and put her hand on her belly. Her face contorted and it occurred to me that Mrs Gill should be brought.

But she's sewing upstairs and I daren't disturb her, said Gill.

I ordered him away, and meanwhile tried again with the girl. Then it came to me that she was actually mumbling not in English but French. My own French is fluent for the purposes of reading rather than speech but I managed to make her understand when I asked her name. At last I heard her say: Emilie. But then she moaned and arched her back and almost jerked herself out of the chair.

Mrs Gill came in and made a great fuss, as was to be expected. Lord, she said, what have you got there, Sir? She fell on her knees and touched the girl's hand and then her belly. She's crawling with lice. What were you thinking of bringing her in among your books?

She told Gill to fill a bath in the stables and then they went off with her. Mrs Gill asked where she should be put and was surprised, I think, that I said any room in the upper, most distant part of the house. I hardly know why I answered that. Perhaps the knowledge of what I was going to do had already formed in me.

Well.

Well. It was fortunate that I lay on the ground under the elder because I had no distance to fall.

There she was, my mother. I had her at last. The old image of her all dressed in swirling green silk rustled away among the mint and feverfew, and instead I saw the rain dripping from my new mother's black hair and the wild night reflected in her black eye. And Emilie Selden sloughed off me like an old skin and I was my mother's daughter with an ancestry as impenetrable as the vast distances in space. It was like standing on the rooftop at Selden and staring down giddily.

. . . the knowledge of what I was going to do had already formed in me.

While she was being bathed I sat by the fire in a state of considerable agitation. I knew what she was. I had seen her sort often enough in London. It was, on the face of it, hardly my business that she had come to Selden. Mrs Gill would find a place for mother and child if I gave her a sovereign or two, I thought.

And once again I made for the laboratory doors with a view to working until supper time. It occurred to me that my meal would be very late that night and I could use the opportunity to work with the green ferrous sulphate. But I found I couldn't get myself through those doors but must sit down again by the hearth and think about how a child would be born at Selden and it might be a living child, and the more I thought of this the more I was filled with a most distracting excitement. I began to wonder how it would be if I were to keep the child as my apprentice, because this is a lack I have often felt. Gill is willing enough but slow and has no aptitude for books. Besides, he's nearly as old as I am. And finally I thought I will consult my texts and let them decide because it cannot be by chance that she came to my window in the wind and the rain, so I went into the laboratory, and I noted that now at last I was allowed to enter those doors, and in the dark I put out my hand and seized the first book from the shelf and opened the page and put my finger on a line, and this is what I read:

'When the spirit of darkness and of foul odour is rejected, so that no stench and no shadow of darkness appear, then the body is clothed with light and the soul and spirit rejoice because darkness has fled from the body. And the soul, calling to the body, that has been filled with light, says, 'Awaken from Hades! Arise from the tomb and rouse thyself from darkness! For thou hast clothed thyself with spirituality and divinity, since the voice of the resurrection has sounded and the medicine of life has entered into thee.' (Archelaus)

I wasted no more time. It seemed to me that I must make this child mine, and in so doing embark on an experiment never tried before. I would regard this whore's son as an empty vessel to be filled with light. Indeed, it seemed probable that he was to be my homunculus or alchemical instrument. I calculated that by the age of eighteen he would know all I knew, given that he would spend his time on nothing but learning – I had been allowed to waste so much of my early life on toys and fishing and running about the countryside – and I would teach him nothing except the arts he needed for alchemy and natural philosophy, and his mind, therefore, would be as pure as spring water, but running rich with knowledge.

I went looking for her through the house and I found that she had been brought to the most ancient part, under the roof. Her hair had been tied up so that she looked like a poor bird with her long thin nose and great eyes and she seemed much quieter, though from time to time pain threw her half off the bed and she tugged at a length of ribbon that was in her hand for the sake of familiarity, as Mrs Gill said.

Mrs Gill had set herself up to watch over her but I asked for another chair to be brought and I sat down and took her hand in mine. I had never held a woman's hand before and although this was a rough and well-used hand, I saw how different the bones were from my own and how narrow the wrist and long the fingers. Whenever she was conscious I asked her questions, very carefully and patiently, and it was as I thought, she was the daughter of a beggar family from Spital Fields come to London a generation ago and fallen on desperate times. She had long since resorted to whoring, but despair over the coming child had taken her to the river. She paid to be carried upstream where she might die in peace but after she plunged was hooked out by a couple of boatmen and deposited on our landing stage. And so she gave up dying and took to crawling instead, all the way up through the woods to the light in our window. This peculiar chapter of incidents I took to be another sign that she was meant for me.

Mrs Gill said she must examine the girl, and so I lit my pipe and walked on the terrace beneath her window, though it was still raining, and after a while I heard her screams begin. The first light of dawn was showing over the trees and I thought that I must secure the child and that to do this I must marry the mother. It was a thought of astonishing suddenness, given that twelve hours before I would no more have considered marrying than cutting off both my hands, but the thought was no sooner in my head than I saw it was part of the mystical plan.

And as all things were by the contemplation of one, so all things arose from this one thing by a single act of adaptation.
The father thereof is the Sun, the Mother the Moon. The Wind carried it in its womb, the Earth is the nurse thereof.
(The Emerald Table)

So I summoned Gill and told him to fetch Reverend Gilbert and then I went back up to the girl and sat by her and talked in French about vitriol, that being the first subject that came to mind, though sometimes she boiled with pain among the sheets. Mrs Gill took me on one side and said she couldn't live. The Thames water had poisoned her and she had all manner of sickness from her past life.

The girl was so weak that her screeches came more like those of a kitten and Mrs Gill put a cloth between her teeth to stop her biting her tongue because she was past reason, and I sat and held her hand and waited for Gilbert and cursed him for being so slow and ignorant. There was no moving me from the chair though Mrs Gill thought it immodest for me to be there while she stroked the girl's belly and thighs but I reminded her of the dogs and cows I had seen delivered.

When Gilbert came I went into the passage to speak to him. I said, 'I am determined to marry this girl, Gilbert, and give the baby a decent home at Selden. I want no argument and it must be done now.'

He was usually a pale man, liverish, but he went a shade of purple and said I should consider and it wasn't decent and I was not in my right mind but I said if he refused I would withdraw his stipend so he said I must get her consent, stipend or no. The little room was fetid now and the poor girl weaker still, hardly making a sound when the pain took her, and I found myself praying with all my heart and soul that the baby be spared at least, prayer being in this case entirely apposite and a form of incantation as over the Stone. Then I sat beside her and spoke to her over and over again about the baby and how she could make it safe if she married me, and I said her name and put my face close to hers and suddenly she opened her eyes and they were very clear and calm and I swear she nodded her head.

The Gills were witnesses and we devised a ring from a bit of wire I had in a pocket and at last we were married and Gilbert rushed away like the coward and Trinitarian he is.

Then birdsong came in through the glass, and a strip of sunshine, and I must here give credit to Mrs Gill who has always been an excellent housekeeper but this morning proved her worth because she suddenly began to work away on the girl who was no longer conscious, and whose hand lay limp in mine. And then the baby came in a gout of blood and I felt the hand grow colder even while Mrs Gill packed her with cotton and her pulse failed and I saw the last breath.

Mrs Gill picked up the baby and wound it in a sheet and put it in the crook of the dead mother's arm where it lay with its fluff of black hair and round dark eyes staring up.

But it's a girl, Sir, said Mrs Gill.

I have never wept in my life that I remember, but I wept then, with disappointment, I think, but also some kind of relief that the night was over. Then I took the baby and was surprised at her warm, living weight. Her eyes were steady and full of intelligence and I carried her downstairs to the library where her mother had sat the night before, and held her on my knee and tried to prevent her head from flopping on my arm. After a

moment she opened her mouth and wailed. The inside of her
mouth was dry and I saw the cartilage joining the tongue to the
floor, and the arc of the roof, and I noted that her fingers were
curled like ferns, thus supporting my theory that there is the life
of all living things in each one of us, and I thought this is a girl
and a whore's daughter, but I will fill her with knowledge and
enlightenment, I will write on her as on a blank page, and at
the end of my life I will reveal to her that alchemy is stronger
than nature.

8

Sir Isaac Newton's greatness lay in his ability to uncover truths
that people know at once are so right that it is incredible to
believe anyone ever thought any differently. Gravity, for instance,
to anyone with a little learning, is unarguably right and makes
sense of the movements of a million stars. So with me when I
read my father's first Emilie Notebook.

It was as if all these years I had been clinging to Ptolemy's
model of the universe in which the earth is the still centre around
which all the other planets and stars rotate. Because Ptolemy's
model seemed right but was actually wrong, ever more complex
mechanisms had to be introduced to force in all the other pieces
of the jigsaw. So, as soon as the story of my father's sudden
meeting with M. De Lery and his family of Huguenot silk
weavers was replaced with this new explanation so many things
that had seemed a puzzle became wonderfully clear.

For a while I lay in a trance of revelation and was almost smug
that palingenesis had worked after all because hadn't the addition
of saltpetre to the alchemical mixture revealed the notebooks to
me, and thereby restored my father and my mother in their true
colours? And I thought: Now I can forgive my father his hardness
because I understand that the sacrifice he made was for a whore's
bastard daughter rather than his own flesh and blood.

But when the implications of this began to dawn on me I went
rigid, covered my mouth with my burnt hand, stared up at the
dancing elder leaves and thought: That's what I am, a whore's

bastard. In fact, I am lower than Sarah because she at least had some knowledge of the streets from which she came.

Dear God, Sarah.

When my mother crawled up through the woods and knocked on my father's window he let her in. I, on the other hand, sent Sarah away.

Now I saw that my treatment of her had been inhuman. Wicked. From the moment she came to my room and offered to lace me into my pink gown I had been frightened of her and shuddered away. Aislabie had treated her as a scrap of linen to be used and discarded but I was almost worse – she had performed the most intimate services for me, spent days embroidering my petticoats, starched every tuck and pressed every inch of lace, failed only once to wake me in the morning and prepare me for bed at night, and yet I had never really engaged with her at all.

I tried to blame my father. This is what he taught me, I thought. He was cruel to me. He sent me away when he thought I'd betrayed him. Of course I would do the same to Sarah.

So I opened the last notebook thinking it would reassure me because in it I'd read more about his feelings of rage and hurt once I'd told him of my pregnancy. I'd learn of the process by which he had hardened himself against me and I would thereby discover how much in his likeness I had become.

5 October 1725

Began the alchemy. Why not, thought I? But I was disheartened. My wrists ached after a very short time of grinding. In the end decided to relent. Thought I would let her back for one day, just for the grinding.

Went looking for her through the house, opening door after door until I found her in her mother's room. She lay asleep on the bed with her dark hair fallen across her cheek, hand on stomach, breast rising and falling. Was afraid of the feelings I had. Gripped my staff. Would have beaten her. Would have taken her in my arms. Would have lain on the bed and buried my face in her hair. Torture myself by thinking of her hair and how when I used to stand close to her in the laboratory I smelt the rain in it and liked to follow with my eye its coils to the nape of her neck.

I surprise myself. I am not myself. These violent feelings that she has thrust upon me. Came away. But now whenever I think of her it's in that room, on that bed, above me or along the corridor if I'm in my own bedchamber. She infects my sleep. I hear her breathing. And I see the bastard within her. I imagine it squirm. I imagine it unfolding.

She is her mother's daughter.

13 October 1725

Hid the copy of the Boerhaave I brought back from London for her. Can't bear to look at it, but nor could I burn it so I thrust it away under the floor. All wasted. Wept again when I touched that book. On the journey back from London had planned how I would argue with her. Knew that she would be triumphant when she read Boerhaave on fire. Looked forward to seeing her smile and thought I would tease her. She has become an excellent advocate. She could stand up before two hundred fellows at Trinity and hold her own.

14 October 1725

And so to work. And so to the grinding again. Thought: I used to do this on my own, before she came. But the tools fall from my hands. She is everywhere. I listen for her step outside the library. Even though I've locked the door against her I imagine she will cross the room to me. I am so used to her here, with her head bent over a book and her hair dropping from under its cap. I am used to her kneeling by my chair. She has broken my heart.

I should never have allowed her in.

How did that happen? She burst through. She was the merest chick, another experiment. Why grieve? Why not cast her out like the end of every bit of alchemy. I will devise a method for exorcising her.

16 October 1725

This is what I do. She comes to my mind. I hear her voice calling me Father, the way her black eyes smile into mine when she has a question or has been especially clever, the way she tilts up her head when she is angry. Or I imagine I see the hem of her gown as she springs off her stool and runs to the workbench and leans on it in that way of turning her hands outward and gripping the *edge of the bench with her thumbs. She has the most beautiful thumbs, slender, long, white, strong. I hate her to be careless with those thumbs like that time she plucked a crucible from the flame and burnt herself. She has elbows that bend both ways, I've noticed. The hinge is not fully formed so when she leans she is not like other people. But she doesn't know this thing about herself.*

She comes to mind and I turn her round in my head. I look at the back of her, at her little cap that is so often crooked, and I imagine her walking away. That's how I get rid of her.

17 October 1725

Or I conjure up an image I dislike. Emilie in the garden, yawning, bored, Emilie grey-faced as she told me about the child. And I think good, good, you're rid of her.

26 October

The calcinations.

She is still in the house. I welcome the roar of the flames because it drowns the rustle of her skirts. I can't hear her knocking any more. I waste so much time.

(Shales called. Refused him.)

1 December 1725

She is gone.

Mrs Gill came up first thing and said: You should say good-bye.

I will not, I said.

You are a fool, Sir. This is the second time she has called me a fool. Stood at the window, well back, where no one would see me. Saw the plume of his hat and on the far side of him the carriage taking my Emilie. Watched Gill close the gates.

I walk through the house and I don't know where I am. Don't recognise the rooms. Found myself in her bedchamber. A maid was there and ran away. I went to the bed. The pillow still bore the shape of her head. I put my hand between the sheets and there was a hint of warmth.

Emilie. For the first time since her birth when I called her name she wasn't there to answer. And I think I cried out when the thought came to me: What did I do that was so wrong?

Mrs Gill came up to me later and said: Sir, you must eat. I didn't know I was kneeling with my face on her pillow and my hand between the sheets.

Shales called. Refused to see him.

20 December 1725

A letter from my girl. A letter and a green feather. A parrot's feather. She has a parrot. I would have bought her a parrot, had she asked for one.

The baby is miscarried. I can't stop weeping. I have tried. I am not myself.

I think of Emilie lying ill in some foreign bed. I think of her picking up the feather and twisting it round in her fingers and thinking of me and writing the letter, with her lips pressed together and working as she writes, and the smear of ink on the joint of her third finger because she is always clumsy and wasteful of ink as I have often told her. I imagine her wiping the pen on her apron and enclosing the feather, and clasping the seal in her thin fingers, which have always reminded me so much of the mother's.

21 December

Wrote a long letter in reply. Burnt it. Wrote: I am glad you are alive.

I can't keep warm.

Shales to call. Received him this time. He spoke very sensibly about the village. Can't help blaming him for all this.

8 January

Shales to call. Said: You don't look well, Sir. Offered to write to Emilie, was sure she must miss me. I said nothing at all. I could not. I had her and I let her go. I did her a terrible wrong. I tried to own her. When I look at Shales I see how I might have kept her close to me still but for my jealousy. I see it. Too late. Obtuse. Obstinate. Wicked old man.

I would give every last drop of blood to turn back time and have her here with me again, just as she was a year ago, full of hope and brilliance and pent-up energy.

My dearest Emi . . .
My dearest love.
My dearest child. My love. My love.

9

In the afternoon there was a commotion at the far end of the garden and Annie and Mrs Gill appeared bearing a weighty oak mirror from the Queen's Room at Selden.

They stood it in front of me. 'It's safe to look,' said Mrs Gill, her eyes bulging with challenge, 'you won't have too much of a shock.'

I pulled myself up, stared across at my image and saw a mass of greenery glinting and bouncing in the sunlight, a backdrop to a still figure dressed in white. Her black hair, singed at the front, stood up wildly round her face and fell almost to her waist, cloaking her shoulders. Her eyes were staring and black, and her cheeks and chin were blotched with patches of new skin. Her body was formless in the voluminous shift and she looked as if she was rising out of the earth.

'Well?' said Mrs Gill.

I collapsed back on the cushions. 'Get back to that straining,' Mrs Gill told Annie, who helped her lay down the mirror, gave me an agonised look and darted away into the kitchen.

'You know it makes not a blind bit of difference where you came from,' Mrs Gill said.

'You lied to me.'

'It was a story. It was a picture we gave you of yourself. Is that so different from the way anyone else lives? You are Emilie Selden and don't you forget it.'

'I trusted you.'

'Stop that. Stop it. Foolish girl. We made a choice and we stuck to it. Why not see yourself as blessed rather than cursed? That mother of yours was nearly drowned with you inside her. You might never have lived. You might have been turned on to the parish. Instead your father made you his own child.'

'But I failed him.'

'I knew we'd come to that. He failed himself. He treated you like one of his wretched caged birds. That was the failure. He had no sense.'

'Nevertheless, if I'd known I would have been more grateful. I would not have let him down like that.'

'You were the apple of his eye. When you broke into his life you brought such sunshine. He doted on you. You gave him nineteen years of joy.'

'What about my husband? What would he do if he found out?'

'It seems to me he married far above himself. In any case, I'm sure he knows. Lord, Emilie, anyone with a mind to probe would find out from the village something of what had gone on.'

'Reverend Shales? Did my father tell him?'

'And if he did, what difference would it make?' She gave me one of her blank-eyed stares.

'Of course it makes a difference. If he knew all along. He must think me utterly pitiable.'

'Nonsense. Why would he pity you? He would see you for what you are.'

'But I am nothing. I came from nowhere.'

'You are your father's daughter. He made you his. He chose you.'

'I can't bear to think that Shales has known the truth about me all this time.'

'Well. I see. That's your first thought, is it?'

'No. No, my first thought is Sarah.'

She folded her arms and was silent.

'Tell me what you remember of my mother, then,' I said.

'I remember little except her suffering. She must have been a tough girl to go through so much. I remember her black eyes. I remember thinking when I put her to bed that she must never have slept anywhere so clean or so comfortable before. She gave me such a look. Fear and then gratitude, I think. She did seem foreign to me with her ribbons and her dark skin.'

'Was my pink ribbon really hers?'

'Of course.'

Of course. Why hadn't I noticed? It was a cheap ribbon, not silk at all but some shiny cotton stuff. Sarah must have known straight away.

'I must go and find Sarah,' I said.

'In your state?'

'I've already wasted too much time. Will her baby be born yet?'

'I should certainly hope not.'

'Will you come with me?'

'To London. How could I?'

'Then I'll go by myself.'

'Take Annie. She's a useful girl.'

'Annie.'

'No need for that look. She's worth fifteen of you. And she'll never complain or do rash things like some.' She adjusted the front of her apron and I had the distinct impression that this conversation was not a surprise to her, indeed had been anticipated. 'You'll need money,' she said.

'I have ten guineas.'

'And I have some saved. You can use that.'

'You'd never get it back. No. I must be like Sarah, take something to sell.'

'Well, there's not much left in Selden that would attract a buyer.'

'I'll find something. I'll go home and take a look tomorrow.'

'You won't like what you see.'

There was a peculiar lightness between us, almost hilarity. One great change that came about after I'd read the notebooks was that I was readmitted into the faint warmth of Mrs Gill's good graces.

Chapter Eleven

LOOKING FOR SARAH

I

The next day I limped up the village street and waited while Gill unlocked the gate to Selden. Though the weather had broken at last and it was a cloudy, cold morning a little cluster of villagers gathered at a distance. Mrs Gill said that it had been rumoured that I would never recover. Children, still scantily clad after the long heatwave, pranced about in the skittish wind or waved and stared.

The gate groaned as Gill pushed it back. It was not until I had stepped through and heard it clang shut behind me that I realised there was an absence of other noise. Not only had the demolition stopped but there were none of the usual Selden background sounds of hens and horses or bustle from the kitchens. No smoke rose from the chimneys but the entrance door stood wide open.

Inside was a new smell of damp earth recently uncovered. Apart from a dense coating of dust everything looked much as ever except that the suit of armour and pictures of Selden ancestors had disappeared, leaving pale rectangles on the panelling somewhat more interesting than the portraits themselves.

While I walked across to the library Gill remained in the porch, blotting the light. 'Take care,' he said.

I threw open the door and my first thought was that I had stepped out of Selden and into some other house altogether. The air had a whitish sheen like in church and the wall between library and laboratory had been replaced by a forest of props so that the space went on and on to the double tier of windows at the far end. The side of the house gaped like a toothless mouth because although the structure of the bay window was still intact the shutters had been pulled off and much of the glass was broken, probably by my explosion. Underfoot the oak boards were covered with grit and dust and all the furniture, my father's chair, the little table for his pipe, my own chair, had disappeared.

As I crept forward the air changed subtly and I caught the first whiff of combustion. The laboratory walls were streaked with black and the floor was mushy and charred where they had doused the flames. My father's workbench lay on its side, my own desk was ruined but the medium furnace was intact in the centre of the room. Piles of rubble and broken glass had been swept into the far corners and when a gust of wind blew the air smelt of ash, and sap from the woods outside.

I looked round at Gill but he had been replaced by Harford wearing a hideous mustard waistcoat and soiled shirtsleeves. He bowed with elaborate care: 'Madam, I am glad to see you have recovered.'

I turned again in that vast space. Harford now was at my elbow and I was struck first by a waft of stale alcohol, then by the realisation that this was a very different man from the obsequious vassal who had planned the destruction of Selden. His shirt was grubby, his waistcoat soiled with plaster dust and his large face seemed to have been pumped up like a bladder so that his lips, eyelids and jowls bulged.

'As you see, Madam, there have been great changes here.'

I walked through the ruined laboratory, examining the rubble for something I might recognise.

'You helped us out,' he said. 'Expedited the work no end. For that we thank you.'

I had found the cavity in the floor where my father's notebooks and my letters had been. It was empty and blackened, licked by the fire.

'We have retained all the existing foundations,' said Harford, 'and it was considered best not to disturb the cellars, which may be five centuries old.' He paused. The door to the cellars, I noticed, was shut fast.

'Shall I explain, Madam?' Harford, who stood exactly on the spot where the double doors between the laboratory and library had once been, now threw out his arms and gazed up at the temporary beam. 'This will be a central chamber for music and dances. We plan a marble floor with tessellated blocks in white and black, although it may be that if we have to tighten the purse strings scagliola could be used – a type of plaster. The overall design wouldn't suffer and the colours can be very subtle. Then of course a new white marble fireplace with a mirror in the over-mantel and egg and dart moulding and, above, the gallery which will house the library and various artefacts brought back from foreign climes by your husband – he aims to start a collection, he tells me. And then the dome itself. There's to be a ring of windows round the base and a ceiling painted by some notable artist – William Kent if we can get him. Your husband will be a central figure and yourself of course, Madam, in some lustrous gown, with at your feet I'm sure . . . perhaps by then . . . a host of cherubic infants.'

I marched back towards the entrance hall and he dodged ahead of me to open wide the door. He added, 'Building the dome will be a difficult engineering task because the roof and supporting walls will have to be strengthened and the staircase that currently occupies the middle of the house will have to be demolished.'

I swung round so suddenly that he nearly barged into me. 'This all sounds very ambitious considering nothing at all seems to be happening at the moment.'

'Ah, Madam. At the moment work has stopped.'

The sudden exertion after days of being an invalid had made me faint. I stood at the bottom of our oak staircase and wished I could retreat upstairs to my bedchamber but instead I sank down on the bottom step and supported my shoulder on the newel post. *Vide Mara* . . . 'Why has it stopped?'

'Are you well? You look very . . .'

'Why has work stopped?'

'Money. There is a temporary shortage of funds.'

'Does my husband know?'

'I have written to your husband at every stage of the proceedings but as I'm sure you're aware he's only just back from France. He had promised to send the profits from his journey but there are none forthcoming at present. It seems he must use them to refit the ship for her next voyage.' He lowered himself on to the step beside me and sighed. I hated him to be this close; he smelt bad and his gaze roamed freely over my burnt face. 'Your husband is very sanguine about the prospects for that next voyage. Indeed, he has become so enchanted with seafaring that he is determined to go with *Flora* to West Africa. But I'm sure you already know all this.'

His hand had strayed too near my thigh for comfort and it occurred to me that he perhaps knew about my mother or he would never have taken such liberties.

'And what are your own plans, Mr Harford?'

'Somebody must stay here and keep an eye on the place. And as I've not been paid myself, I am in a very awkward position regarding my contract . . .'

'How much are you owed?'

'Something in the region of a hundred pounds. I'm afraid I had to sign promissory notes for the last weeks of work to all the labourers.'

'I assume you have kept careful accounts.'

He patted his many pockets. 'I don't have them about me just now. But yes.'

'If you leave a forwarding address I will send the money.'

He leaned back on his elbows, legs spread, thumbs loosely joined. 'I've taken a liking to Selden, Mrs Aislabie. I think I'll wait here until such time as the money materialises.'

I left him sprawled on the stair and went up to my bedchamber where things were uncannily the same as usual; my bed was made up and the floor newly swept. Next I peeped into Sarah's room, which was exactly as she had left it. I went to the closet, gathered up my green silk gown, retreated to my own bed and lay down.

The green silk subsided with a rustle into a puffy bundle beside me. Where my skin touched it the fabric grew warm and smelt faintly of Sarah's perfume. The old association with my mother came to my mind and I pushed it quickly aside. No, no more, and the white-necked lady of my fantasies slipped away into the creases of the fabric. But my flesh gave a twitch of recognition at the memory of stays and petticoats, and I wondered if Annie would manage the tapes and whether the dress would stand a journey to London, given that it was the only armour I had.

That night I slept at Selden, with Annie in Sarah's bed next door to keep me company. Some time in the small hours it began to rain and the house was full of strange noises as if it had lost part of its anchorage and was likely to be washed away.

Next morning I leaned on Annie's arm and went outside to view the extent of the damage done by the workmen. My mother's wing had gone except for traces of ground-floor walls and fireplaces. Already a few weeds had grown between cracks in the flagstones and there was no barrier for the wind, which gusted up from the woods across a desert of broken stone. The furnace shed, along with an assortment of other outbuildings, had also disappeared except for a bit of broken chimney and the blackened stone plinth on which the furnace had been built. I stood on the old foundations, breathed the clean air and thought how quickly a dark and secretive space had been burst wide open.

Then we walked on through the bee orchard where what had once been a grassy path was now a rutted track made by carters taking rubble to the lake. The bees were restless in the damp wind and the hives were peppered with agitated little bodies.

Beneath the orchard was more destruction. Instead of ancient trees the track was marked by a regiment of sawn-off trunks. The lake, which had been dug in places to its full depth of twelve feet or so, was lined with all manner of rubble from the house, much of it unbroken so that I recognised bits of barley-twist chimney stack and brick from the furnace shed. We climbed up the broken steps, past the rose gardens, which were littered with debris as if someone had shaken a giant sieve above them, to where Gill waited on the terrace to take us down to the cellars.

Here at last everything was as it had always been. It seemed to me that in any case these chambers had a fluid quality; there was no shape or end to them so who could tell if they were changed or not? Gill's lantern shone on the usual collection of broken furniture, tools, sacking and barrels, and I wondered if Harford had found his way down here and sniffed out the wine and cider. At one point the light reflected ghoulishly from the suit of armour rescued from the entrance hall, and on a stack of Selden portraits.

At the bottom of the steps leading to the laboratory Gill gave me the light while he tugged at a mound of canvas sheeting. Underneath were piles of boxes. Some I had carried down on the day of the explosion, others he must have transferred from the library afterwards. He prised up the lid of the nearest. Across the top was my father's staff, still intact though blackened by fire. I held it with shaking hands and pressed the brass handle against my cheek. Underneath were a series of linen packages. I unwrapped the first and discovered my prism, then my father's spyglass and a vacuum pump. In my frenzy to get on with the explosion I had packed these things haphazardly but now each had been parcelled up meticulously, tied with string and nestled into place.

Gill's eyes were lost in their deep sockets and his mouth was a slit. I perched on a step and held the lantern while he and Annie packed three boxes full of my most precious possessions so that we could take them to London and sell them. I allowed myself no sentiment. First in went the parrot bowl, present from my husband, then the spyglass and our delicate scales. I chose fifty or so leather-bound volumes, the most modern or the most rare, a little globe that used to stand in the library and one of the more impressive Selden portraits.

The plan was that next day at dawn Gill would drive us up to the stagecoach along with these three crates, and off we would go to look for Sarah.

<h1 style="text-align:center">3</h1>

In the evening, supported by my father's staff, I walked to the church. Despite recent rain the graveyard was parched although a few daisies struggled up among the scant grasses and a pair of blue butterflies darted close to my mother's grave. I scratched up a couple of dandelions and cleared weeds from round her headstone.

Emilie Selden
Died 30 May 1705

For a while I sat with my back to the stone. She lay a few feet beneath me, a neat arrangement of bones, and if she was dug up nobody would be able to tell from the shape of her skull or the length of her fingers what she had been. But I knew. When I thought of her now I saw Sarah big with child, in fear for her life.

I imagined that I had been conceived during some frantic coupling like in the furnace shed or under the apple tree. My blood father's identity seemed an irrelevance – what did it matter whether he had been young or old, rich or poor, kind or vicious when I owed nothing to him except existence. The notebooks made it clear that I had inherited my dark eyes and uncomfortable gift for survival from my mother. So I picked a handful of daisies, slit the stalks, wove a little crown for her headstone and promised her that I would find Sarah and bring her home. Then I stabbed my father's staff into the hard soil, using it as a support to pull myself up, and limped across to the church.

The interior was cool and quite dark. My slippers lisped on the stone slabs as I made my uneven way up the aisle to the side chapel and stood over my father's grave. St Edelburga gripped a book in the window above me, the ragged remains of a painted St Christopher strode across the plain white wall with the infant Jesus on his arm, a couple of priestly stone heads peered down from the top of a pillar. The silence reminded me of the laboratory in the evenings, another place where stillness had been deceptive because it was composed of so many little noises: the stirring of a mouse, the creaking of a board, the mechanism of a clock and the wind knocking on glass. I liked the fact that there were live things in this church, the flowers, a beetle ticking in a beam, a candle waiting to be lit. I liked the way the light drifted in from a second tier of windows beneath the roof and the dust hung softly in the air.

I laid my staff beside reclining Sir John, the Bosworth Selden, and rested against his side. 'I am here, Father,' I said.

The door opened suddenly. Footfall. Male. My fingers gripped the knight's stone hand. I knew at once, perhaps by the shape of the displaced air, that it was Shales. When he reached the chancel he tore off his wig and pressed his face to the stone arch. He was in his shirtsleeves and there was mud on his boots.

My breath came in quick gasps as I took in the fact that it

really was him: his shoulders, his back, his long legs. But after so many weeks of yearning to see him I wished myself a thousand miles away. This was too sudden. My face was wrecked. I was ashamed. And I was an intruder in his space. It was terrible to watch him kneel and put his arm across his face as if in great distress.

I thought perhaps I could creep away or that he would leave without noticing me but he turned his head and looked directly at me. The colour drained from his cheek, his eyes were blank and I could see the bones in his knuckle where he gripped the arch. 'Is that you?'

Sir John Selden's leg took my weight as my knees began to shake.

Shales said, 'I thought you were dead. Good God, Emilie.' He went on staring as if afraid I might be a phantom, then came and took hold of my upper arms, drew me into the nave and turned my chin towards the light. Over his shoulder I saw the Lamb of God prancing across a yellow window, carrying a flagstaff. My scarred face and whorish eyes were all exposed and I was trembling with shock as he crushed me against him, rocked me, held my head: 'I thought you were dead.'

'I had an accident. I was working in the laboratory.'

His thumbs brushed the scars and scaly patches of skin on my hands. A tear left a trail across my wrist. 'What kind of accident?'

'Just a mistake. There was no question of dying. Anyway it all happened weeks ago. Didn't Mrs Gill tell you I was well?'

'I haven't seen her. I came straight here. My curate agreed to send me a report punctually once a month and didn't think an explosion at Selden was significant enough to write sooner. I came the minute I heard.'

'Well, there. You see. It wasn't significant.'

'How did it happen?'

'Alchemy. It was to do with palingenesis. I added too much saltpetre to the mixture.'

'But you know the qualities of saltpetre. You know what is likely to happen. Isn't there enough pain in the world without inflicting this on yourself?' His hands were tight on my arms and his wet eyes were full of rage. Love, like a falling leaf, flipped over and over inside me.

Appalled by his suffering I started to babble, 'Anyway it was worth it, that explosion. I advanced my understanding of fire because I discovered that the theory of phlogiston is a nonsense. I saw a sudden expansion of the air. It couldn't be contained when I threw in the saltpetre so it burst out of the flask. The air burnt but not all the air; I felt a draught, a sucking.'

Shales tucked my hand under his arm and we began to walk across the front of the nave into the side chapel, back to the main aisle, down to the door, as if we were in Westminster Abbey and he was moving me apart from a crowd of people. 'This was an explosion,' he said more calmly, 'a violent reaction between two or more volatile substances. It is not the same as fire.'

'But there must be a relationship. And something else. The fire sought the higher part of the room. I fell back on the floor and saw it race above my head and that's why I wasn't badly burnt. Mayow says that animals die and flames go out faster in the upper part of a vessel because the air that is expired is lighter once deprived of the dense, nitro-aerial particles needed for life. I believe he was right about air consisting of different types of particles.'

'Then prove it. Write your paper on the nature of fire.'

'No. No, I can't prove it. My days in the laboratory are over. I'm about to join my husband in London.' We walked on in silence. By mentioning Aislabie I had brought my husband into the church and now there he was, lolling against a pillar, sardonic, watchful. I withdrew my hand from Shales's arm. 'I was wondering why you left so suddenly on the day after the party. Aislabie mentioned that you had business with your father-in-law.'

We had reached the high, empty space under the tower where the coloured bell ropes were looped overhead. 'Duty, Mrs Aislabie. Your favourite word. My father-in-law had been pressing me to visit him for some time. He's a justice of the peace and too many prisoners in his gaol were dying before they'd served their sentences. He thought that with my knowledge of airs I might be able to show the authorities how best to ventilate the place.'

'Did you succeed?'

'To an extent. I think the wretches may live longer thanks to me though it's debatable whether prolonging their miserable lives is actually doing them a favour.'

'Will you go back?'

'The work is not quite finished.'

'You should perhaps look for a living there. My husband doesn't like the influence you have in Selden.'

He laughed. 'My father-in-law can't abide me near him for long either. We don't agree on much; in fact, are opposites. I did him this one favour because I thought I owed him.'

'Owed him what?'

'I suppose I feel the duty of a son to his father. He is a lonely man.'

'Is your mother-in-law still alive?'

'She died some years ago and Hannah was his only child. It's a pity we're not better friends but I'm afraid when Hannah died we quarrelled. I can't like the old man so I try to make reparation in other ways.'

'Why did you quarrel?' He'd never spoken her name before. Now, twice. Hannah. It seemed to me he named her with great tenderness.

'There is often recrimination after a death. We all look for someone to blame. He and I are theologically a thousand miles apart. He sees me as a radical. Where religion is involved everything is connected.' But as usual when his wife was mentioned evasion soon followed, an opaqueness in his eyes.

It struck me how unequal our knowledge of each other was – that he had always known everything about me while keeping his own history dark. 'You probably thought it didn't matter that you left in a hurry,' I said. 'After all I'm nothing to you. My father was right, by the way. Palingenesis was successful. I found out who my mother was and how I came to be born at Selden. You must have thought me such a fool all this time, behaving like a great lady taking the front pew in church, sharing my father's life when really I am nobody. You should have told me the truth, Shales. You might have spared me a great deal of trouble. And as you probably know my maid, Sarah, is pregnant with my husband's child.' He nodded. Of course he knew. I began to limp back down the aisle. 'In a fit of rage I sent her away. I didn't know what I was doing. So now I have to go to London and bring her back, if she'll come, or at least offer to adopt the baby.'

'You shouldn't travel in this frail state,' he said with cruel formality.

'It's my duty. Of course I'll go. It won't be the first time an unwanted child will find a home at Selden.' I could barely speak. All these weeks I had longed just to see him again but now it was as if a fatal wound had reopened. We were trapped as ever by the reality of our two separate lives.

St Edelburga's little chapel was so dim that I couldn't at first make out where I had left my father's staff. Everything was grey with the greyness of a cloudy evening: the stone floor, old Sir John Selden with his book and his sword, even the stained glass. My legs hurt when I stooped down and the staff rolled away from my stiff hand. Shales picked it up and pressed the handle into my palm. 'I never thought you a fool,' he said.

'Well, good.'

'But I did think about you constantly. Since I first saw you scarcely an hour has passed when you haven't been on my mind. Your father did me a kindness by offering me the living here. I was running away from my old life; I thought that as there was no chance of happiness I might as well be at Selden as anywhere. I remember taking Communion for the first time in this church, my thoughts as I picked up my book, the weariness I felt that I must start everything again. The doorway from the vestry was very low and I was afraid of cracking my head. Then I crossed in front of your pew and saw your face and by the time I reached the altar everything had changed because already you were unforgettable. It was that look of burning interest you gave me then – I'd never seen such intensity in a woman's eyes. And when you greeted me in the porch you smiled. I thought to myself that is a rare smile, perhaps not used often, and it would be worth a great deal to win another. I met you and your father in the forest one day and I still remember how I walked home blindly afterwards, hardly knew how I got home. I have never been able to walk through those woods since without remembering the mist of your breath in the air. You were in my blood after that. You haunted me. When your father asked me to call at the house all I could think about was meeting you – in fact, I was so distracted that I was caught off guard and drawn into an argument with him. It's my greatest fault to be too rigid, far too rigid in what I think I know about right and wrong. Afterwards I cursed myself for being so outspoken. What did my views on alchemy matter, I thought, when if I'd agreed to work with your father I might have met you every week? So I never stopped calling at the house even though I got turned away first by your father then by Aislabie.'

The saints in the wall paintings, the Selden clan under their tombs and brasses, the priestly heads on the tops of pillars, the Green Man and assorted gremlins in the bosses in the roof and my poor father under his slab were all listening to Shales. 'I promised myself that I'd never unsettle you with a hint or a word. I could only justify staying at Selden because I told myself that for your father's sake I should watch over you. But when you brought me to the laboratory on the night of the party I knew that I was on the inside of your life where I have wanted to be all along but that I could only do you harm by being there. So I left.'

In the sudden silence there were hurried footsteps in the porch outside and a rattling of the iron door handle. 'How could you harm me?' I whispered. I knew the answer, of course; it was his duty as a clergyman not to seduce the wives of his flock, even if a member of that flock was the faithless Aislabie.

Annie's voice called, 'Mrs Aislabie. Are you there? Mrs Gill sent me to find you.'

Shales said, 'You don't know me, Mrs Aislabie. I don't have a gift for love. I have done terrible wrong in the past.'

'Mrs Aislabie,' Annie called again, with less certainty. Shales and I were tucked away out of sight in the chapel, a little apart from each other. I thought if I had to walk away from him now my flesh would tear. Annie's wooden soles came clacking up the aisle and she called again, 'Mrs Aislabie.'

I said, 'I'm here, Annie,' and there she was at my elbow. We had no more time. Her hair straggled across her face and wind gusted from among the gravestones through the open door. She gaped when she saw Shales, then grinned at him and he was suddenly the clergyman as he shook her hand distractedly and asked after her family. Then she offered me her arm, he and I nodded at each other and I was led away down the aisle.

The threshold was worn to a deep curve by centuries of Selden feet and there were two steep steps down to the porch so I had to lean on her for balance. I didn't look back as I waited for her to close the door but leaving that church so abruptly to go and find Sarah was the hardest thing I had ever done, harder than holding out my arm to be engrafted with smallpox, harder than adding saltpetre to the alchemical mixture, harder even than telling my father that I was pregnant with Aislabie's child.

In the churchyard the clouds had lifted suddenly and the light had turned golden and dusky, the twilight was laden with bird-song and from a field beyond the village came excited shouts of children. Annie fastened the lych-gate behind us and we walked the few yards to Mrs Gill's cottage.

'You have overdone it,' she said when she saw me. 'You are very pale.'

'I'm well.'

'I'm not at all sure you should go tomorrow.'

I kissed her cheek and went on through the hot little kitchen and along the brick path to the gate in the back wall. Selden in this light was transfigured, honeyed, eternal. I knew that what-ever happened I would remember every detail of the past hour including the walk through Mrs Gill's workaday strip of a garden and standing with my back to her gate. In those first, sudden moments after leaving Shales I stood in a trance of love and grief thinking when I see him again there is only one certainty, that everything will be changed.

4

Next day I got up in the rainy dawn and stood shivering in my shift while Mrs Gill and Annie manipulated me into the green dress.

Annie hardly seemed a promising companion what with spare clothes spilling out of a bundle, food stowed in a fraying basket and eyes huge with self-importance under a flapping hat brim. Her entire family came to the gates to wave us off, countless siblings who clung to her legs as if she'd be away a year rather than weeks, as well as grandmother, mother and the blacksmith himself who patted her shoulder with fiery pride. I kept my distance though he tilted his head at me in what I took to be approval.

In a few minutes the village dropped away altogether and we were swallowed up by dripping hedgerows so tall that we could see nothing of Selden along the valley behind us. I looked back one last time but the lane was empty. After that there was little to see but Gill's backside clothed in an ancient leather garment that wrinkled like a second skin. Annie's mouth dropped open and her eyes swivelled to right and left as if she'd never seen a gate or hedge before. When we plunged into dense woods Gill pulled his elbows tight to his body and the horses flung their heads from side to side to shake water from their manes. Annie gawped up into the canopy of leaves and water plopped into her mouth.

At the inn Gill unloaded our boxes into the care of an ostler and stood in the wet with his hands hanging and the rain dripping from his hat brim. Then he climbed back into the cart, whistled to the horses and disappeared. Annie and I sheltered under the gallery and stared after him, then went inside to watch the rain and an occasional burst of activity. I was conscious that Annie was a keen observer, eager to embrace every second of this rare escape from Selden. And she was not distracted and aching like me.

The servants seemed to do a great deal of hanging about and yelling at each other from one covered place to the other. I thought of Sarah who had come here with her heap of boxes filled with my gowns and I wished that living things did have a signature of some kind as my father had believed, so that she could have left something of herself for us to gather up as a sign that she was still alive.

There was a sudden bustle, the thud of hooves and a bark of instruction as the stage thundered under the arch and into the confined space of the yard. We clustered in the low doorway and in a few minutes were swept into the coach. Despite our shortage of funds I paid for Annie to sit inside, thinking she would die of fright if her first sight of London was from the precarious height of the roof.

And there I was in a world far removed from the intensity and isolation of Selden, pressed close to a hook-nosed mother and her three daughters, one wriggling and straining in her nursemaid's arms, the others loudly disputing the right of a place near the window. The mother began a speech, supposedly for the benefit of her girls, about how the family was moving to a house in Audley Street, a very new and exclusive part of London south of the Oxford Road, and how they would see little of their father due to his importance to the world of print now that his machines were turning out three broadsheets daily. She sighed and patted her chest, rolled her eyes and mourned the loss of her quiet life in Buckingham, though with a self-satisfied smile on her lips.

It was near midnight when we were set down in Bread Street by which time she had chosen furnishings, colours and wall coverings for her rooms, pots for her kitchen, flowers for her garden, planned a month's menus, decided that she and her girls must be fitted with the latest striped gowns, and listed every sight in London they would visit by the autumn. She was met by her browbeaten husband and his coach while I had to spend a precious half crown on a hackney carriage. The driver was bad-tempered already because of the rain and furious when he saw that there was a heap of boxes to load in after us but I remembered one of the valuable lessons learned from Sarah, tossed my head, averted my eye and drummed my toe until the boxes were safely stowed.

When we were inside Annie spoke for the first time in five hours: 'The lights,' and I realised how full of lanterns the streets were and how brilliant the London night compared with the dark of a cloudy night in Selden. The rain formed a sheet of yellow specks in the lamplight and I felt a rising panic at being in the place of dead babies again, and of meeting Aislabie who belonged here and had been sucked back into the city and all its temptations. It was also quite possible that the house would be closed up altogether. What would I do then?

But the Hanover Street house was ablaze. Lights shone from every floor and when I peered into the basement I saw a servant stooped over the hearth and the parrot's cage hanging in the open window. There was music, laughter, the chink of glass – a card party.

I hammered on the door and a footman opened it, dressed in a new livery. He looked at me disdainfully and then over my shoulder at Annie.

'Mrs Aislabie,' I said and swept past him followed by Annie and the driver with one of our precious boxes. Ladies were clustered on the staircase like overblown roses. One of them was Lady Essington – blond hair, swelling bosom, staring blue eyes. She put a hand on her companion's forearm, the other on the head of her little native servant. 'Lord. It's the mad wife,' she murmured and took in every inch of me – creased skirts, badly dressed hair, scorched cheeks. They all watched in amazement as the heap of boxes grew.

I ordered the footman to take the boxes to my bedchamber and told Annie to ensure they were safely stowed away. When I faced Lady Essington again I noticed that one of her eyelids had lowered slightly and a little of the radiance was gone from her cheeks. 'We were about to join your husband for a hand of cards,' she said so I took her offered arm and sailed into the card room, which had already gone quiet in anticipation of my arrival.

Aislabie was draped across a small chair, all the generous expanse of him sprawled in an inverted arc of blue and primrose. He clasped a fistful of cards and there was a glass of wine at his elbow and coins on the table. A grin spread from one side of his mouth but stopped at his eyes.

I had time to note that he wore a trim new wig with curls gathered at the nape before he unfurled himself and sprang across the room. 'Well, dearest Em, here's a thing,' and he kissed my hand and cheek. 'My wife, ladies and gentlemen, a refugee, I don't doubt, from the building site that is our estate just at present.'

He held tight to my hand, instructed a servant to bring me wine, asked if I'd eaten – 'Then we must find you some supper' – and bowed us out of the room and up the stairs. People gathered for a better view and there was a frantic waving of fans, high-pitched laughter, a fuzz of horsehair, satins, raised eyebrows.

I looked on this crowd with the detachment I used to feel for mice in the laboratory although Aislabie squeezed my burnt hand so tightly that he hurt me. He placed me in the middle of a dainty sofa, offered to send up a plate of cold chicken and abandoned me to the company of Lady Essington who peppered me with question and comment: How long was I staying? Wasn't I brave to travel alone? Was I still working away at my wonderful experiments with what was it . . . ? But she'd heard there'd been an accident at Selden recently – did I know anything about that? And did I know that I had started quite a trend with my natural philosophy, which was now all the rage. She herself had recently been to a lecture given by John Desaguliers, a close friend of the late Sir Isaac Newton, all about mechanics and mathematics. Push and pull, that was the essence.

I answered in monosyllables and smiled across at her little servant who watched me throughout with huge, lustrous eyes. 'What's your name?' I asked when his mistress was silent at last.

'He answers to Samuel,' she said.

'And where were you born, Samuel?'

'He doesn't know. He was a gift from my husband.' She rubbed her fingernails through his curls. 'Such a sweet, good boy, eh Sam?' and she took his little hand in her white fingers and led him away.

The night wore on and the more I sipped champagne the more amazed I became that I had ever tried to belong here. When I went downstairs again I found Aislabie up to his old tricks: smoking with a special crony, keeping him apart by leaning his elbow against the wall and thereby cocooning them from the rest to exchange schemes and secrets.

He pulled me to his side. 'Here she is, my little alchemist. We've been talking about you, Em, or rather that dear friend of yours, Thomas Shales.' The name cracked about my head like a pistol shot. Aislabie's arm was on my back and his hand kneaded my shoulder.

'Ah, you know the tragic Reverend Shales, Mrs Aislabie?' said his smooth-faced, smooth-voiced companion.

'Tragic?'

'Is what his friends call him. Your husband might have another adjective.'

My husband caressed the side of my neck. 'Poor Em. There's not much choice of companion in the country. But the Reverend Shales strikes me as a little too high-minded even for you, my love. A whole barrage of articles by him has hit the press about the evils of absentee landlords, how the current system of parish support is failing, rents are too high and on and on . . .' His fingers strayed across my collarbone. 'Good Lord, doesn't the man understand the meaning of the words *moderation* or *progress*? The Selden air obviously ain't doing him any good, turned him sour, in fact.'

'He was formerly rector at Twickenham, so he's not always been so far from the centre of things,' said the other man, whose gaze was following the path of my husband's fingers as they caressed the dip between my breasts.

'Ah, Twickenham. The height of fashion, in fact. But despite his vast experience with dandelions and crab apples, and an excellent reputation among his cohorts at the Royal Society for measuring airs, the man will have to leave our parish. Can't have people thinking he's voicing my opinions. How would that be for business?' said my husband. Our companion flung back his head and showed his yellow teeth. 'So next time you see him, Em, a word in his ear. Tell him to keep quiet, at least until he's found another living.'

I was given a little push which sent me reeling on to the stairs but I stood my ground and refused to go to bed though my body was humming with fatigue and my mind too full to allow sensible conversation. At one point I stumbled down to the basement in case Annie was there but was told she'd been sent to bed, her being no use whatever to anyone. The maids were white-faced and limp, and the sulky parrot had lost shine from its green feathers and wouldn't fix me with its cloudy eye.

Upstairs people were leaving but Lady Essington hung back while my husband held her hand a very long time, kissed it passionately, turned it over, kissed her wrist, leaned forward and whispered something in her ear. She wished him a safe voyage and it dawned on me that this must be a farewell party because she was pleading with him to take care and telling him that she would be waiting for him. She let her blue eyes dwell fondly on his bent head, then turned her gaze on me, not bothering to veil her look of possession and resentment. Then she stooped down for Samuel to fasten her cloak, patted him on the head, waited until he had swept up her train and sailed out to her carriage.

As soon as she'd gone the effects of alcohol, kept at bay by her fragrant presence, took Aislabie from the inside, thickened his lips, drained the warmth from his eyes and made him lurch on the stairs. I followed and spoke his name but he didn't reply, only climbed on and on until he came to the door of the red bedchamber and shut it in my face.

Below me the servants gathered glasses and blew out candles. I sensed that they were hoping to witness an argument but I took a candlestick and opened the door of my own chamber, which was not, as I'd anticipated, all bundled up in dust sheets but fresh-smelling, with roses in a little glass on the table. The Selden boxes were piled in a corner unopened – hardly surprising as Gill had nailed down the wooden lids with considerable vehemence. I hadn't the heart to summon an exhausted maid to unlace my gown so I removed my hoop, averted my eyes from the hearth where I had knelt with a lapful of dead babies, and lay down on the bed, not between the sheets because of what had probably been planned to take place between them.

I listened to the house and wished that I could turn back the clock and hear Sarah on the back stairs, even if it was in the course of an assignation with my husband. Then I relived my precious conversation with Shales in the church, every word, every gesture, and wondered for the hundredth time what would have happened if Annie had not come. The noises of London filled my head and the house swam through the teeming night towards morning and heaven knew what developments.

5

Next day the skin around Annie's eyes was greenish with exhaustion. She said she hadn't slept much because of the din in the streets outside, though her face was animated with excitement at the prospect of the day ahead. Of course she was not sufficiently hardened to the ways of the fashionable world to wrench properly at the laces of my stays so I had to call in a London maid.

'Could you tell me what time my husband will be up?' I asked.

'Oh Ma'am, he went out at eight.'

'And where is he likely to be?'

'I couldn't say.'

I slid her a sixpence and her lips pursed with self-importance. 'At his ship perhaps, or in a coffee house?' I asked.

'Either of those. Anywhere. He takes an interest in all sorts, I'm told. Down towards the Strand, I think he often goes.'

'And where is the ship moored?'

'Lord knows. Wapping, probably.'

Another sixpence. 'Do you remember a maid called Sarah Holborne who worked here last year? Have you seen her recently?'

'Not recently, not since last month when she called a few times but the master wasn't home to her.' A knowing smirk. Presumably the whole household, except for me of course, had known the exact nature of Sarah's relationship with my husband.

An hour later Annie and I set forth into the filthy morning to find a trader who would give me a fair price for my possessions. We took the parrot bowl and my father's spyglass as samples. Annie wore her stable-yard pattens and I carried an ancient umbrella found in the stand by the front door, a tattered silk affair which knocked against her uncomplaining head as we walked.

Though I had been away barely three months London had swollen and the streets near Hanover Square were full of scaffolding and loud-mouthed labourers. We went east to Soho in search of the kind of dealer who might appreciate the perfection of the parrot bowl. Each time I unwrapped it I felt a pang for the buttery glaze and the bird's gold-dusted feathers but London buyers were astute enough to note my desperation because the most I could raise was eight guineas. Meanwhile Annie dragged her feet at every shop window, goggling at the displays of locks, laces, porcelain, silverware, candles and silks. But it was the bookstalls that slowed her down the most. She ran her fingers over the spines, picked up a volume as if it were a fragile piece of glass and stooped to sniff the pages. 'Could you read every one of these?'

'Unless they were in German or Hebrew or some other language I don't understand.' She replaced the book reverently but would have stayed there for hours searching the pages for a key to their secrets so in the end I said, 'We'll start reading lessons tonight,' and that made her move all right. She hitched up her skirts and clung to me like a bloodhound.

We were by now near St Paul's and the air was thick with a fug of smoke combined with the wet of a most unseasonable August. Filth clogged the streets and the press of carriages, carts and chairs thrust us against more humanity in a hundred yards than had crowded into Selden Wick during the entire run of the fair. But perhaps the map of the city had been engraved on my mind on the day of the dead babies because I was the expert leading Annie into the labyrinth and she was full of wonder at my assurance. We found an instrument maker, a Monsieur Cheret, whose French name endeared him to me and who handled my father's spyglass with great reverence and said he would take anything else of similar quality.

Next we returned to the Strand where coffee houses had opened up in every alley and street corner. We hovered outside each in turn until a gentleman on his way in or out happened to catch my eye, when I would ask him to go and shout for Aislabie. Each time the door opened I smelt tobacco, spirits and burnt coffee beans. Each time, after it had shut in our faces, we stood for several minutes waiting for the gentleman to come back or my husband to appear. Usually no one came but one or two put their heads round the door to give me a leer or a shake of the head. Only at Jonathan's did a man walk past me almost without pause but held the door open while he called 'Aislabie' as if he expected a response. I saw long trestles, male heads bent together in conversation, male hands holding up newspapers, smoke winding from their pipes, coffee cups pushed aside. 'Aislabie,' he shouted again and one or two looked up and then across at me but there was no sign of my husband.

6

After supper Annie reappeared in a clean apron. 'I've come for my reading lesson,' she said.

I had no idea how to begin. Until that moment the transference of knowledge from my head to hers had seemed a straightforward matter but now I didn't even know whether to start with letters or words. Nevertheless, I lit a candle and we sat on either side of *The*

Castle of Knowledge, one of the few volumes in the house. 'First I'll tell you what the book is about, so that the words you read will not be too unexpected or mysterious. *The Castle of Knowledge* concerns an old argument, which until recently was so hotly debated that it lost people their lives – whether the sun or the earth is at the centre of the universe. Hence the subtitle: *A Reader on the Progress of the Heliocentric Argument*.'

We then began to spell out word after word but it was a tortuous process what with her drooping lip and laboured breathing. When I learned to read, I seemed to remember, I made rapid leaps between letters and words so that books were revealed to me all of a sudden, complete and lucid. Annie staggered over each new letter and even when she spelt out the words they made no immediate sense to her. I had to remind myself that she, despite being the legitimate daughter of a respectable family, had received none of my early privileged education. Besides, I owed her a great deal and I remembered that when my father taught me something which I failed at first to understand he would try again using a different method or example. Even so, by the end of half an hour I was on the brink of losing patience so I set her to work out the phrase: *As the World Turned* . . . and to copy it on to a slate.

At which point in came my husband. Annie reverted to her customary limpness and my hands went chilly but he seemed in a good mood as he sauntered over and picked up her work. He winked at her and shot me an amused glance from under his wig. 'Highly commendable, Em, but is it wise? Words equal aspirations, as you well know.' He jerked his head towards the door and watched Annie scuttle away, then flung himself down on her little chair, extended his legs and pulled at the ruffles on his shirtsleeves. 'Well, you have become quite a gadabout, dear Em. You'd best explain yourself.'

'I have been showing Annie the city.'

'So I gather. I heard you had been asking for me at Jonathan's. Can't have that. Makes me look a fool.'

'I needed to speak with you urgently and you disappeared this morning. I have no money.'

'Lord, I'm amazed you came all the way to London if that's the case. Nowhere gobbles up money like London.'

I took heart from the fact that he obviously hated me to be there. 'Your friends seem to think I am mad anyway.'

'They do. You are. I gather that since I was at Selden you tried to blow yourself to kingdom come.'

'An experiment. And I think I was justified in being reckless since I had just discovered that my maid was pregnant by my husband who had subsequently abandoned her. I don't want money for myself so much as for her and for the tenants who are starving.'

'I've no money to spare. None. So if I were you I'd go home this minute.' He took his watch from his pocket and stood up. 'I'll give you a couple of crowns. Should get you home. And this time stay there.'

But some time during the past few weeks, possibly in the explosion or while reading my father's notebooks, I had found some courage. I sprang to my feet, got between him and the door and leaned against it.

He sighed and folded his arms. Up close he seemed massy and immovable, and I could see the stubble on his chin and the slight coarsening of his complexion. 'I've told you. I haven't a bean. That's why I'm off on *Flora*. It will save a fortune to be on board her – escape the bailiffs for a bit. You could come with me but I'm afraid I've discovered that the crew might kick up. Some think it's bad luck to have a woman on board and there are hazards enough without that. We're all reliant on old *Flora* sailing home weighed down with gold and rum and mahogany. Real gold, just think. Then we'll be laughing.'

'What will she carry on the voyage out?'

I had touched on his current dearest love and for a moment his eyes sparked. 'This and that. Gunpowder and weapons mostly. There's a great hunger for modern guns out there.'

'And where do you sail to?'

'Calabar, in Africa, as I've said, then on to Southern America.'

'Where I presume you will sell the slaves you bought in Calabar.'

'Exactly so.'

'And how long will this take?'

'Eight months to a year. Depends on the winds. But I shall need your help, Em, if we're going to make a go of it. You'll have to behave like a proper lady while I'm gone so that when I come back I can make a name for myself.'

'If behaving like a proper lady means I may behave like you, a proper gentleman, I have a great deal of freedom.'

'You've been in the country too long, Emilie. That's not how a wife should speak to her husband.'

'This wife will speak any way she chooses.'

He bowed and put his hand on the doorknob. When I didn't move he gave a snort of laughter and took hold of my shoulder to edge me out of the way. 'Truth is I want to be left alone, Em. Happy to have you down at Selden but can't abide you being here. I have to be free to make a life without you – even considered a divorce but it's so damn hard to get the knot untied. I'm hoping you'll oblige with madness or adultery sooner or later. The world won't take much convincing if you carry on like you did last night, turning up off the streets like a beggar. See, Emilie, the world is shrinking. You think the lens of a microscope shows you everything but you're wrong. Speculation is more lucrative than fact. People imagine better roads, faster printing presses, cheaper textiles; they imagine them and the next thing is, they exist. Bit like your late lamented pa who thought he could make gold from a lump of old metal, only my method is obviously more foolproof.'

'If you tell me where Sarah is and give me some money and an undertaking that you won't pull down the cottages at Selden Wick I'll go back to the country and leave you in peace.'

'You can rest easy on the last point. No chance in the near future of building new cottages to replace the old. If you want money you'll have to wait for *Flora* like the rest of us. As for Sarah, haven't the least idea. You'll leave tomorrow, Emilie.'

'I need money now, not in a year. I must make sure Sarah is safe.'

'Don't worry about her. That little bitch could survive in any gutter.'

'And your child?'

'She gave you the chance to claim it. Seems you turned it down.'

'Don't you care what happens to the baby?'

'I've no idea if it's mine or not, although she says it is. If it was conceived at Selden I'll have to admit it was me – don't know of any other candidates except Gill or Shales. Can't see it, can you? In any case, I can't be doing with a whore's bastard for a son and heir. I needed you to make it your own. It was the only way I'd take it on.'

'I've changed my mind. I will acknowledge the child. At least tell me where Sarah is.'

'Too late. She's gone crawling back to the gutter, I assume.'

'All the more reason for me to find her. Why won't you tell me where she is? It won't cost you anything.'

'Except my good name, for Christ's sake.'

'Your name. And what about when people find out whom you married? Perhaps there are things about me you'd also rather I keep quiet about.'

He laughed out loud. 'Dearest Em. You do what you like and say what you like. I don't care. Marrying you was the worst bit of business I ever did, as it turns out, but don't think I didn't have my eyes wide open. I've always known exactly what you are.'

7

Far from being defeated by this spat I felt all the more determined. It seemed to me that Aislabie and I were entirely on the level if he had never been deceived in me. So the next day we gave the footman a shilling to carry one of our boxes and off we set in procession to Monsieur Cheret's shop where we parted with the spyglass, the globe, various alembics and my prism. The old dealer was clean-fingered and delicate in his dealings. He was also a pipe smoker and the scent of his tobacco made me weaken for the first time so that I suddenly picked up the prism and told him I would keep it after all. There was a spark of kindness in his myopic eye as he handed over twenty-five guineas and told me the address of a dealer near St Paul's who would give me a good price for my books.

Then we walked down to the river by the church of Magnus the Martyr and hired a boat to take us downstream to the *Flora*. I was possessed of the kind of energy that used to carry me through our most complicated and painstaking investigations.

Hypothesise, experiment, observe, record, conclude. In the present circumstances I thought my best chance was to wear my husband down by making a nuisance of myself in the world he had constructed without me. In any case, it was high time I met *Flora*.

So Annie and I sat side by side huddled against the wind and nervous of so much water beneath and around us. We passed the Tower – once the home of Sir I. N. during his spell as Master of the Mint – and I thought it incredible that these choppy grey waters could have flowed under the bridge at Selden where there were woods on either side, willows dabbled their branches and the only sign of a dwelling was a spiral of smoke from a chimney in tucked-away Lower Selden. I told Annie to look out for Sarah on every wharf, alley and warehouse jetty because there was no telling where she might be and after a while I almost convinced myself that she would appear suddenly in her neat white cap and cast-off slippers.

And then we were among towering ships, so many that I thought it impossible the boatman would find *Flora* and I got a crick in my neck from gazing upwards at the hefty masts and jutting prows, and marvelling at the way the timbers had been bent and made watertight. The water amidst these giant vessels was dense with rubbish and we dodged between sailing boats and barges, each so purposeful in its business that it seemed everyone knew where they were going except us.

Suddenly we were under the bows of a frigate with three masts and furled sails. Her figurehead bore an uncanny resemblance to Lady Essington, particularly the exposed bosom and leering red lips. I asked the boatman to shout for Aislabie and we were told he was not on board but was expected any minute so we were helped up on deck where we stood about for a while, watched by the seamen who took such considerable interest that one of the officers suggested I might shelter in my husband's cabin.

'First I should like to be given a tour of the ship,' I said.

'We're loading as we speak, Mistress Aislabie, it's not entirely convenient.'

'Nevertheless.'

His name was John Minshall, rank supercargo, in charge of trade. Minshall was a narrow-faced man with wolfish teeth and thick lashes, something of a flirt and vain enough to want to show off his knowledge to a lady. So he led us down a steep stairway to the gun deck in which were ranked twenty great guns ready, he said, to protect the *Flora* from privateers, pirates and other foreign brigands. Annie followed so close she trod on my heels and nudged against my back.

The ship smelt of familiar things, timber, varnish, cooking and also, bizarrely, of Gill, his unwashed body and old sweat. As we went deeper she swayed and juddered because weight after weight was being loaded into her and rolled forward. Altogether I was rather taken with her at first and began to understand my husband's enthusiasm for this orderly microcosm. *Flora* straining at her ropes reminded me of the owl we had once captured and then set free, and she creaked and rattled like Selden on a windy night.

Our guide showed us the neat little galley and crammed storerooms. Meanwhile I fired questions at him – it was a long time since I'd had such an opportunity for learning.

'When do you sail?'

'At the end of a fortnight, all things being equal.'

'How many of you will sail on her?'

'Up to thirty-eight.'

'That includes officers and crew, I suppose, and my husband.'

'Correct.'

'And where do you all sleep?'

'Officers in the cabins. Men down in the hold.'

'What about the slaves when they join the boat? Where will they go?'

'Some will sleep in the same quarters as the officers and men.'

'And the rest?'

'They go in the hold, where the cargo is currently. One lot of goods is replaced by the other. The space down there always has to be full or the ship isn't economical.'

'And how many slaves will you carry?'

'Six hundred, probably.'

'So many.'

He turned to me suddenly and his long lashes veiled his eyes. 'Down this hatch we go, Mrs Aislabie, if you're not afraid of spoiling your skirts.'

I lowered myself down a wide-runged ladder to the next deck, which was lit by square vents in the ceiling and crammed with barrels and bundles, very orderly, each labelled and pressed in tight. Minshall's face hung over my shoulder. 'We have to pack things close, else they roll about in the swell.'

'Does that rule apply to the slaves?'

'Of course. We have to build in a percentage loss, you see. We'll likely lose between a quarter and a third even on a good voyage.'

'One third.'

'The crew suffer more. It's all down to the disease the slaves bring. Dysentery and suchlike. And they're terrible for the smallpox.'

'You should have them inoculated.'

'Ma'am?'

The smell was so oppressive I couldn't draw breath. 'And in those bundles are weapons you say, and powder.'

'There are. The average slave costs perhaps twenty-five kegs of powder and two muskets, a few gallons of brandy and four cutlasses.'

He was laughing at me. Meanwhile Annie had tight hold of the gathers in the back of my skirt. Perhaps she, like me, was thinking of the shining eyes of Lady E.'s slave child and wondering how he would be treated when he grew loutish and angry with his lot.

'If you didn't cram them so tight they would survive better,' I said. 'A healthy body needs plenty of fresh air – not recirculated air breathed out by someone else. Experiments have been done which prove that our lungs take part of the air when they inhale so that the blood can be refreshed and revitalised. A mouse will not survive for long under a bell jar, even though not all the air will be gone from it. If so many bodies are breathing so much stale air they're bound to suffer.'

'Fresh air is expensive. And our other cargoes, gunpowder and weapons for instance, they don't need fresh air so it's a dilemma. In fact, too much fresh air and sunlight might cause trouble of an explosive variety.'

I remembered how Aislabie had come to Selden and talked so knowledgeably about phlogiston and the combustible nature of shipping. 'I assume you transport the gunpowder unmixed,' I said.

He shrugged. 'Your husband is one for being economical above all, Mistress Aislabie, particularly in those areas that are least in public view. In that he's not unlike many shipowners who as a breed, in my experience, tend to apply their own rules.'

We plunged down yet another hatchway so that we must have been far below the water level. Here I couldn't stand upright and I put my handkerchief to my mouth. The space was already half loaded with row upon row of small barrels, gunpowder, judging by the smell, and there was a scurrying among the boards under-foot. And beneath the acrid, familiar smell of powder was another, the press of dirty, sick bodies. Here there were no vents in the side of the boat or gratings giving on to the fresh air. I suddenly had a sharp, sad memory of Shales and what he'd said about the gaol in Norwich and the dubious merits of prolonging a prisoner's life. 'We'll go up now,' I said, 'and wait for my husband.' So we climbed the ladders to the main gangway and were shown from there into my husband's cabin.

When I first knew Aislabie I had found his desire to surround himself with all that was fashionable very touching, and his approach to the furnishing of *Flora*'s staterooms revealed this same exuberance. His cabin was fitted out in crimson velvet and equipped with what I took to be the latest in nautical instruments and charts. Long-lashed Minshall couldn't resist the opportunity of handling these toys – all of which were untarnished by any contact with the elements – and showed me a quadrant for measuring the height of the sun, parallel rules for marking a course and a celestial globe to plot the night sky. There was even a little walnut writing desk with a bound notebook open at the first page and the words *Ship's Log* inscribed in my husband's curling hand.

'But surely to use the sun as a measure is dangerous?' I said. 'How do you withstand the glare of the sun at noon?'

'Exactly, Mrs Aislabie. Hence this new type of quadrant, or backstaff. We turn our backs to the sun, thus, and measure the shadow it casts. It's all about finding our position. Latitude and longitude. Latitude we can find by using the compass. Longitude is trickier and very complicated.'

'I noticed that some of the ships on the river were painted white underneath. Why was that?'

'Barnacles. They latch on to the boat and can affect her seaworthiness in time. Some people believe that a mix of tallow, resin and sulphur will protect the hull from barnacles.'

'*Flora* isn't painted though.'

Minshall said nothing and I wondered what other dubious economies had been employed by Aislabie. Meanwhile Minshall had sidled closer and seemed to be snuffing the air near my neck so I thanked him for his time and said we would wait here for my husband.

When he'd gone I sank on to a velvet couch and indicated that Annie should do the same but she refused and instead peered anxiously out of the large windows as if afraid we might be cast off and on our way to Calabar.

One way and another *Flora* had been a shock. I realised now that I had thought of her as a kind of whim, like the projected dome and cascade at Selden, but I had discovered she was in deadly earnest. And Aislabie had transferred his most treasured possessions here. He'd even hung the landscape by Lorrain which used to be in Hanover Street between two of the portholes, and mounted copies of the plans made by Harford and Osborne for the house and garden at Selden under glass on a little side table.

We waited half an hour or so and I played with the instruments and fathomed how to use the quadrant but I was distracted by those plans for Selden. I kept going back for another look at that gracious mansion with its twin flights of steps, pillars and porticoes until in the end the sight of it made me so angry that I pushed the glass aside, unfastened the plans, rolled them up and tucked them into a pocket.

It was time to go. The more time I spent on board *Flora* the less I wanted to be there and it occurred to me that Aislabie must have been warned of our presence and chosen not to come aboard. In any case, one of my main purposes in paying this visit had been defeated. I had wanted to be part of *Flora*, to give myself an entitlement to her profits and the good things she could bring back, but such was my disgust for everything aboard that I wanted nothing to do with her. I shuddered to think what my father would say if he could see me amidst such nautical luxuries, or spending money earned from the sale of other human beings. So I told Annie sharply we should leave and suddenly in a great hurry we climbed over the side and into the waiting boat. Shivering we set off, and shivering we sat in silence until we got back to London Bridge.

8

The next day was Sunday and any respectable business was closed. I should have waited in Hanover Street to discover the outcome of my visit to *Flora* but instead I set off on another foolhardy and extravagant journey. Although I was ashamed of spending some of the precious parrot bowl money on an excursion which would bring us no closer to Sarah my feet carried me down to the jetty, with Annie of course in tow, and my hand released five shillings into the palm of a boatman who promised to get us to Twickenham and back by evening.

This time we went upstream and there was hardly any traffic on the river. The temperature had dropped still further and there was a distinct whiff of autumn in the air. Yet I was glad to be on the move again, especially as we were rowing away from *Flora* and towards Selden. And this expedition could do no harm, I argued to myself. It was only to fill the time.

Annie trailed her hand and stared at London as it tumbled down to the river bank and then further upstream unfolded itself into gardens and scrubby fields. When last I made this journey I had been sick with longing for a glimpse of my father. Now when I thought of Selden I saw broken walls, the laboratory blown apart and Shales stooped to enter the homes of his parishioners or at work in his leafy little study. I had thought, as I travelled home in January, that I was significant. Now our boat seemed a mere speck, an irrelevance to the great onward rush of time. And this made me understand the imperative of palingenesis. My father, sensing approaching death, had wanted so badly to live again.

At Twickenham I told the boatman we would be an hour at most and he shipped the oars, hauled his boat up the jetty and left us on the pebbly beach. Annie stood patiently beside me but I couldn't move. It was as if I was trespassing on private property. This was the view Shales had seen each time he came down to the river; maybe this same pair of swans though with a different clutch of cygnets dipping their scruffy necks, that far view of poplars on the opposite bank, that same farmer holding the same carthorse by the reins.

I turned away at last, walked up the beach and crossed the lane. Here was the rectory with a smart front door that Mrs Shales must have stood at several times a day to receive visitors, the gabled porch where Shales would have left his boots, the garden battered by recent rain but full of beans, cabbages and fruit trees. I noted that one or two had been lopped or engrafted, a sure sign that Shales had once lived here. And to the left, set well back in an orderly graveyard, was a low church with a slatted wooden tower.

The congregation was just spilling out and we hung well back, watching a portly cleric greet his parishioners. His alb fluttered in the wind and at one point he put his hand on his wig to prevent it blowing away. As soon as the last person had walked by he scurried back into the porch and a few minutes later I saw him blow across the graveyard towards a little gate admitting him to the rectory garden.

The church door stood wide open. Inside was the familiar perfume of cool stone, summer flowers and the lingering breath of the congregation. Annie crept over to a side chapel and spelled out the inscriptions on the memorials – poor soul, she was not yet able to tell if the words were in Latin or English – while I sat in a pew and stared. The hexagonal pulpit was a touching affair with carvings of squirrels and rabbits running through the panels and I imagined Shales climbing the four steep steps and standing before the congregation to address them with moderate words of praise and commitment.

After a while I got up to read the plaques but none was to his wife, although his name was inscribed at the bottom of a list of former incumbents: *Thomas Shales 1710–1725.* I thought of Mrs Shales arranging greenery in glass jars or polishing the brasses, a calm, small-mouthed woman, as unlike myself as it was possible to be.

The churchyard was windy but well kept with the gravestones

in neat rows, the yew clipped, the paths clear of weeds. I found her at last in a far corner under a young medlar:

Hannah Margaret Shales of this parish
Departed life 30 August 1724

Aged 30 years

Wife to Thomas Shales, Rector.

And Thomas, their only son, aged two weeks
On the same day.

Annie was at my shoulder, ploughing her way through the spellings. 'No,' I said. 'No. Oh no.'

'Mrs Aislabie?'

I read the inscription out loud: '. . . *And Thomas, their only son, aged two weeks* . . .' then I turned my head and covered my face with my elbow.

Voices called from across the graveyard: 'Is your mistress quite well?'

A couple of elderly women moved across and stared at me. Annie took my arm. 'That was a sad affair,' one of the women said, nodding towards the grave.

'Knew her, did you?' the other asked.

'We know about her,' said Annie. 'We are visitors here. Reverend Shales is our rector at home.'

'Very fortunate for you. It seemed hard on us that we should lose him as well but he couldn't bear the place once she'd gone.'

'We haven't taken to the new man half as much though he's very clever,' put in her companion. 'Rattles away about heaven and hell. Our Reverend Shales spoke only of this life. We liked that. And we all wanted him at our sickbed because he had a gift for cheering us up. He talked about all sorts, caterpillars and other bugs even. Nothing was too low for him. But then she died, and the baby, and he wasn't the same.'

'How did she die?' said Annie, and this was one of the few questions I ever heard her ask.

'She died of the smallpox. Caught it from the doctor her father insisted be brought from London though Reverend Shales said the local midwife was good enough for the rest of the village and ought to be for his wife.'

'Should have been inoculated,' said Annie. 'We all was. Our Sir John insisted.'

'Ah, but there's the terrible thing. The Reverend wanted her to be. He had all the household and anyone else in the village who wanted it inoculated but Mrs Shales refused. There were differences between them and this was one of them. Her father was a cleric, too, very strict and opposed to interfering with the work of God, which is how he saw the inoculations.'

The smaller of the two women was so thin that her neck was stringy as a chicken's but her eyes were a bright brown. 'I remember that time,' she said. 'Do you remember? A terrible time. We used to see him carry the baby down to the river to show him the swans. It was a warm August and he thought the sunlight would do the child good. We used to meet him, do you remember, carrying him about so that his sick wife wouldn't hear the child's cries. I'll never forget the sight of that great man with that tiny babe. But it couldn't thrive. Anyone could see that. It was a sickly little thing from the start. And so they were both buried in one grave, and he stood there and prayed over the single coffin. Do you remember?

'We wanted him to stay but he never got over his grief. He used to go night after night down to the river and never visited us in our homes any more. He blamed himself for the arguments that had divided them. She hated the work he did with plants and wouldn't be convinced, you see, of the rightness of any modern thing. His sermons got shorter and sometimes he forgot himself in the middle of a prayer so in the end he had to go.'

Her companion was staring into the distance with her watery blue eyes. 'We met him here one evening. I said to him, "How are you, Reverend?" And he gave me that nice smile of his but I could tell he was all wrought up. I said, "I hope you're feeling a little soothed now, Reverend," and he said a terrible thing, he said, "I feel as if I shall never be soothed. How could I be? Our child would have lived if we had cared for each other a little more and not been so obstinately set on being right." I said, "But you are a good man, one of the best I know, you shouldn't be tormenting yourself," and he shook my hand and smiled so tender at me and walked away.'

'How is he now?' asked the other. 'Is he better?'

I didn't answer so after a moment Annie said, 'I'd say, yes.'

She thanked the women and they told us to send Shales their best wishes. Then we went back to our boat. We were early so there was time to be on the beach again and look across at the poplars and the swans sailing indifferently by. Annie stood close to my shoulder and after a while I put my hand through her arm and leaned on her.

The boatman came back full of ale and good cheer. On the way downriver Annie and I were pressed against each other and the boatman winked at us and cracked jokes because he said we seemed gloomy but he gave up after a while, sighed deeply and pulled strongly on the oars to get us back as fast as possible.

Chapter Twelve

A U R E L I E

I

The next morning Annie played the lady's maid and brought a tray of chocolate to my room with a scrap of paper scrawled in my husband's hand: *Sarah Holborne. Powder Yard. Off Red Lion Street.*

I was somewhat suspicious of such a rapid capitulation but wasted no time. Annie sewed twenty guineas into the hem of my petticoat and off we set. The weather had changed and the morning was full of stench and steam under a hot sun. As we got further from the more opulent streets we linked arms and entered a maze of overhanging walls – old houses deserted by their rich inhabitants and infested instead with street sellers and silk winders living four or five to a room, in cellars and attics or shacks put up in courtyards, in rookeries teetering crookedly in former gardens so that one street led to another, a yard to an alley, an alley to a dead end. And in every bit of open space, in gutters or gaping windows, Londoners and immigrants fell over each other to earn a penny or two, to get some air, to be anywhere that was not inside the foul buildings where they slept.

The summer warmth heightened the stink and there were more animals on the streets than in the spring, more country people with their pigs and donkeys, more children too weak to work but not too young to beg. We were jostled like marbles, leered at, pleaded with, cursed, teased, pushed aside until at last we turned into a lane behind Red Lion Street where a whiff of gin belched from a distillery hidden in a row of cottages and then at last we came to a courtyard that was overshadowed by an inner block of temporary dwellings. The bricks were shiny with last night's rain and there was a reek of juniper and raw alcohol, but also the poignant touches of someone taking pride in this once gracious place, geraniums in pots, polished brass. I thought it a sure sign we had found Sarah who had such a gift for small things that give a show of elegance.

On the far side of the inner alley was a house three storeys high which retained, somewhat chipped, the ornate masonry of its former glory. A woman stood on the step tapping a closed fan against the door frame and shifting from foot to foot as if she'd been waiting a long time. My heart missed a beat because she was wearing of all things my feathered gown, embellished here and there with knots of blue ribbon, patched up at the bodice and skirt but otherwise much as when I had last worn it in the cellar with Aislabie.

For a moment a sense of dislocation made me speechless, then I asked for Sarah Holborne. She looked at me as if I were vermin.

'Sarah Holborne,' I repeated, 'I believe she lives here.'

'She might. Why, who sent you?'

Annie breathed in my ear while I stared stupidly. The woman spoke as if to a couple of idiots. 'We sent for her man Aislabie. Where is 'e?'

'I don't know. But he gave me this address. I'm his wife. May I see her?'

'I doubt it. She too sick. She's in no mood for visitors.'

'The baby?'

'The baby is still unborn.'

'Please can I see her? I have come to help.'

She stared past my left brow until I produced a shilling whereupon she came to herself and turned into the house. We followed and found three or four others lolling in the hallway with their skirts pinned up and their bodices cut beneath the bosom. They were dull-eyed and listless, rather like their wealthier counterparts at the tail end of my husband's card party. Draperies covered the doors and there was a smell of the privy under the fusty scent of sex and perfume. A very young girl with a country bloom on her cheeks darted forward but was pulled away.

The woman at the door had disappeared so what with the bare nipples and fleshy nymphs disporting themselves in prints on the wall I was hard pushed to know where to look. The other women stared and whispered behind their hands. I recognised a pair of pink stockings with gold clocks I used to wear before my father died and an embossed silk slipper kicked aside so that its new owner could pick at the skin between her toes. The little country girl had by now been shoved out of sight altogether.

When she came back the feathered woman had thrown a shawl round her shoulders and her painted features were slack with dismay. 'You can come up if you like. She hasn't said you can't because she's passed saying anything.'

One of the women drew a tearful breath as Annie lodged herself behind my left shoulder and we climbed the creaking stairs. Our guide had hauled her skirts above her knees, exposing veined calves and the whiff of menstrual blood. Up we went to a landing festooned with yet more crimson draperies made from the stuff that had once adorned Selden for my husband's birthday party. From behind a closed door came the slap of flesh and a creak of bedsprings. Our guide slid me a look from under her mouse-skin brows as she led us up another, narrower stairway and opened a door at the top. There, in a sour, airless room, propped against pillows, her hair trim as ever in her little cap but her huge body spilling from the crumpled sheets, was Sarah.

I pushed back my hood and went closer. She was too weak to lift her head but for a moment we stared at each other. I'm not sure if she recognised me, perhaps I imagined a glint of the old hostility, but after a moment her eyes closed. If I'd met her in the streets I would have walked past her she was so unlike herself. Folds of flesh covered her once delicate wrists and her face was so swollen that her pointy chin was submerged in her neck.

Annie stepped forward and pressed Sarah's hand. A white patch formed.

The feathered woman said, 'She's been like it for weeks. We told her to get a doctor but she refused until today. At dawn she sent me for her man Aislabie.'

Trust Aislabie, I thought as I stood helplessly by Sarah's bed. Of course he wouldn't pay for a doctor so instead he sent me, thereby discharging all responsibility. But I was no use whatever to a sick woman.

Then I realised that Annie had shed her usual air of diffidence and inertia, turned back the bedclothes, exposed Sarah's mountainous belly, laid her hands on it and put her ear to the navel. Then she replaced the sheet and led me to the door. 'I seen this. Mrs Gill showed me. She will die, and the babe if it's not already dead. She will get so sick that she will have fits and then go into a stupor. She's bound to die.'

The strangeness of the house bore down on me, the thumping of bedsprings now reaching its crescendo, the little gathering of silent women in the hall below.

'What can we do?'

'If Mrs Gill was here she'd know what to do. Get the baby out.' She chewed a flake of dry skin on her lower lip and frowned with concentration.

'Have we time to get Mrs Gill?'

'I couldn't feel the baby move. We have no time. She will die.'

'She's alive now, Annie. We must act. What would Mrs Gill have done?' I couldn't allow Sarah to die. Harford could engineer a cascade of water; Newton could split light; Harvey could transfuse blood; surely we could prevent a simple death in childbirth. And I wanted not just Sarah's life but the baby's too. I wouldn't allow it to be dead. Now that I was within inches of it I longed for that child.

'Mrs Gill would bring on the baby,' said Annie.

'How?'

'Don't know. Some herb. Something.'

'Think, Annie.'

'We must get a midwife.'

The girl was a genius of Newtonian proportions. We extracted a guinea from my petticoat, summoned the feathered woman and told her to go with Annie and fetch the best midwife she could find.

Which left me alone with Sarah. The other women stayed downstairs though I sensed they were watchful and anxious. Perhaps they were afraid of Sarah's state. I certainly was. I had something of the old fear of her superior knowledge – she had entered an experience far beyond what I had ever known – but I was also terrified that she might die on me. Sometimes her body twitched, sometimes she snored or moaned, generally she was quiet. From below came a yelp of pain, then a scream and a sudden rush of feet and hammering on a door. I thought about my mother and wondered whether she had resembled the blowsy feathered woman or the bright-eyed country girl. Sarah stirred and turned her head from side to side while I bathed her face and adjusted her cap because it was unthinkable that her hair should get untidy, though I was cautious as if she might bite my hand off at any moment.

It was by now late in the afternoon and still Annie didn't come back. Flies buzzed on the chamber pot and the walls billowed with my stolen clothes – I recognised the wrap-over party gown, the dark-blue dress I had worn sometimes as I came out of mourning, and my embroidered petticoats. The sight of those bodices, let out to accommodate Sarah's girth, made me weep, as did a swathe of crimson draped on the back of a chair – my ill-fated cloak. I prayed to the God of Shales, the reasonable God of the wider picture, the divine architect who had set all in motion, please to save this girl so that we might make amends. I would have given everything, my own life I think, to have had the old Sarah back with her trim waist and annihilating shrug.

After two hours more a midwife came, not unpromising despite her size. The stairs and the summer heat had worn her out and she sat fanning herself by the closed window while Annie introduced her as Mrs Jane Calder. There was a faint air of Mrs Gill about her, certainly competence and a care for her appearance that Sarah would have approved; she wore a clean apron and gown, and her face was kind under a layer of paint. When she'd recovered she performed the same checks as Annie whom she seemed to regard as a worthy colleague. Then she went to the door and called out in a voice that must have cut through even the most frantic coupling, 'Bring me savin.'

'Rue,' whispered Annie. 'That's what it is. Mrs Gill will give it to girls sometimes if they're late.'

Of course there was a plentiful supply of that particular drug in the house. A bottle was brought and a spoonful poured between Sarah's lips. Clean water was ordered up and the midwife washed her hands. 'Lord knows what I'm doing here,' she muttered, 'they're both done for but at least if we get the baby out we can say we tried.' Annie and I were instructed to hold up Sarah's knees while Mrs Calder greased her hand from a tub of fat and pushed it hard up inside, worked away energetically and gave a sudden stab that made Sarah screech and come wide awake for an instant. A yellowish, bloodstained fluid gushed from the ruptured membranes so suddenly that for a heady moment I thought the baby would follow, ripe and pink and perfect, but instead Sarah gave a deathly moan and woke up again as pain took hold.

We shuttered the windows, ordered candles, clean sheets and a tray of toast and gin for the midwife, and settled down for a long wait. Annie became a bustling professional; massaged Sarah's belly, stroked her hands and wrists, bathed her face and spooned water between her lips, while Mrs Calder dozed and ordered more gin and I watched as if just by paying attention I could make a miracle happen.

When at midnight the contractions began in earnest I wished myself in any hell but that. I tried to transpose myself to the woods at Selden or to Shales's quiet study but I couldn't escape that hot room which stank of excrement however often we changed the sheets, where the light flickered up the walls and made devilish shadows, where below us men came and went to spend themselves inside some overused woman or another, or, presumably if they had the cash, to pin down the country girl and jab at her tender flesh. Meanwhile Sarah was roused time and again and flung into a cage of pain so that her eyes flew open in terror and her hands clutched the air. We whispered endearments, stroked and soothed her but the contractions contorted her into a howling beast whose nails gouged the wall and teeth closed on the pillow as she disappeared into some hideous place where we couldn't reach her until she came panting out, looked into my eyes and at last recognised me. I saw a most welcome hint of the old hatred and her lips formed the word, 'You.' Then she lay gasping and sucked on the sponge Annie put to her lips. 'Will he come?'

Before I could make up an answer a distant look came in her eye and the pain swallowed her up again and tossed her about and that dreadful cry came from her throat.

This went on until it was bright daylight and then, as the room grew hotter and hotter and the sun shone brighter on the window, Sarah began to fade. Either the contractions slowed or she no longer noticed them. I stared at her face and willed her to survive. Though it was such an unsymmetrical face, as if drawn in a hurry, there was a delicacy in repose that was strangely endearing. I thought if she woke one last time she might forgive me.

The midwife had lunged forward and thrust in her hand again. 'This is very bad. She's barely opened the womb a couple of inches. We'll let her rest for a while and then give her another dose.'

'A doctor?' I said.

She snorted. 'You can throw your money away if you like but he'll be nothing but trouble and expense. This sort of thing has to take its course,' and she dozed in her chair with her hands folded.

Every hour or so a woman peeked in to see how we went on or to bring us tea. All day Annie and I took it in turns to sleep and watch, and it occurred to me as I put my head back on the hard chair, pillowed by the lining of my old cloak, that I had never spent any significant time with women before and that I had no women friends or expectations of women beyond Mrs Gill because I had been taught that women were frail and incapable, except for me. And I thought of Sir Isaac inside his crimson-draped coffin, and Aislabie with his grand ambition and greater greed who had masterminded my courtship, the purchase of *Flora* and the rebuilding of Selden, and I wondered how they would fare in this room, in the face of a dying woman and her dead baby. In their mechanical universe, in their scheme of things, when it came to this essential matter of birth itself they would be at least as helpless as me. Only Shales would have understood.

Sarah died in the small hours of the following morning. Her breathing had become more laboured until she exhaled and simply didn't breathe in again. Then there was a deep silence in the room, like the silence in the laboratory when the fire went out and the clocks stopped.

The midwife leaned forward, listened and put the back of her hand to the dead mouth. Her other hand fell heavily on Sarah's belly and she suddenly sprang to her feet and spread her fingers. 'Jesus Christ, it's alive.'

She dived into her bag, produced a knife, wiped it on her skirt, had Annie bring the candles close, made a swab of Sarah's shift and the soiled sheets and drew a neat incision with the blade. Then she spread open the lips of the wound and lifted from

Sarah's body a curled foetus which seemed to me still and hopeless until she tapped it sharply on the back and breathed in its mouth, whereupon it gave a little cough and then a feeble cry.

Annie fetched a cloth, bundled up the baby and thrust it into my arms where it lay with its head thrown back, its tiny mouth gaping and a tuft of hair, dark as my own, sprouting from its little skull. When I kissed its forehead I smelt new bread and blood. It lunged its head to my breast and mewled again and again until the midwife left her work with the body, picked up my hand and showed me how to let it suck on my finger. For a moment the baby looked at me with intent, dark eyes, then fell asleep with its mouth latched on so tight I thought it might swallow me whole.

2

Mrs Calder said that for a small fee she could recommend a butcher's wife with a brood of healthy infants who would fill in as a temporary nurse, so I walked up and down the cramped attic corridor jigging the baby against my inexpert shoulder while Mrs Bess Gardner was fetched.

The baby, who had a remarkable ability to unravel herself from a cocoon of blankets, astonished me with her urgent needs. Her spasmodic cry twisted my heart and she nuzzled my chin with her pink mouth. From time to time one of the women came up to offer advice or take a peek but I wouldn't let them hold her. I thought it might damage her to be transferred from one set of arms to another.

At last Mrs Gardner arrived, well-scrubbed and agog with curiosity. Annie had cleared the room next to Sarah's and the woman unbuttoned her gown, planted herself on the edge of the bed, spread her knees to receive the baby, pinched her dripping nipple into a teat and thrust it between the little gums.

I couldn't take my eyes off that child's bobbing head and frantic mouth. My breasts ached in sympathy when I saw Mrs Gardner's flesh compressed as the nipple was milked. All that was visible of the baby now was the back of her dark head, while the woman gave me a look of great ease and self-congratulation as if the baby was lapping away at the heart of her.

In the next room Annie and Mrs Calder were laying out Sarah's body. When it was done I went with the other women to stand beside the bed. We were a ragbag: Mrs Calder the smartest and most respectable; Annie composed as ever but the rest of us wild-haired and crumpled. The house was closed for business and the shutters fastened so the room was very quiet with the racket of London kept at a distance and a pair of candles burning at the head of the bed. Some of the women were weeping, others looked anywhere but at the body. They were restless and uneasy and soon filed out past the little brown-eyed girl who hovered by the door.

Sarah was shrouded in white wool, her swollen hands folded on her breast with a sprig of rosemary between her fingers. I studied her face which was still puffy but with the neat features clearly visible again, especially the fine arch of her brows and the soft curve at her hairline. The country girl crept forward and put her finger on the shroud. I smiled at her but she was blind with fear.

I wished that Shales were there so that he could tell me where Sarah had gone because gone she was, completely, with not a hint of her battling spirit left behind. I called to her from the bottom of my soul: Sarah. Sarah. There was no answer. Sarah. The gulf between the living and the dead gaped fathomless in front of me as I looked at her shut eyes and mouth. Another thing you never taught me, Father, that death is the one field of knowledge we can never explore.

After a moment I went to the door and slipped a guinea into the young girl's hand. I thought it would give her a chance to leave if she wanted but she went on gawping at Sarah as if she couldn't comprehend what had happened to her. So I pushed her towards the head of the stairs and then went back to the baby who had been expertly swaddled by Mrs Gardner and now lay fast asleep in a basket. And there I sat, hour after hour, watching over her fiercely and committing myself to the protection of every corpuscle of her being.

*

Meanwhile the life of the house went on. It was now the afternoon and occasionally a customer came to the door and got turned away; I heard low voices on the stairs, then the arrival of the undertaker come to measure up. I thought about the country girl and wondered whether she'd escaped with her guinea or if it had been surrendered to the woman in my feathered gown, who now seemed to be in charge.

I told myself that I was on my mother's territory and this is where she perhaps would have felt most at home, and I listened more intently in case something in the house stirred a secret memory. Then I crouched beside the baby's basket, wrapped my arms round my knees and willed her heart to beat strongly so that the blood might flow through her arteries and carry each new breath of air to her tiny organs and make them grow strong enough for me to take her home to Selden.

3

Mrs Calder decreed that the baby would be able to travel when she was a week or ten days old provided she was well fed on the journey. Annie had a married sister who she thought would nurse the baby once we were at Selden so I wrote to Mrs Gill asking her to prepare for our return. I was troubled by the cost of all this and saw my precious funds drain away in the hiring of the carriage and the paying of Mrs Gardner, who would have to come with us.

And then there was Sarah's funeral. Her women were ambitious to give her a fitting send-off and seemed to think I had a bottomless purse of guineas. I wrote to Aislabie, care of his club, informing him of his daughter's birth and Sarah's death. I suggested that he might see his way to providing immediate support for one and funds for the other. It was a brief note, somewhat half-hearted because I didn't expect a reply.

Given Sarah's dislike of churches the funeral had to be planned with considerable skill and the priest instructed to say the briefest of prayers. We buried her in the evening so that we could carry torches through the dark streets, which the feathered woman said would suit Sarah more than anything. The women, including the young girl who seemed to have gained confidence and status, were sumptuously dressed, mostly in my cast-off or stolen clothes, and wore smart mourning rings engraved with her name. Annie and I followed at a discreet distance as if Sarah might appear catlike from an alley and hiss us away.

The women were right to choose darkness. Sarah had lived in the shadows. When she hadn't been in the room with me twitching my laces or brushing my hair I had no idea where she was. The inside of her head had been a foreign country. The glimpse I had of her other life, the house in Powder Yard, was as alien to my own at Selden as Calabar or the Americas. But as I followed her coffin, watched the torchlight flame over its embroidered shroud, saw strange faces spring out of the darkness and fade away again, I knew that she would always be inside me, a gritty reminder of what I might have been.

Of course there was no sign of Aislabie. At Sarah's graveside I stepped forward and threw in a sheaf of pink roses tied with half a yard of the finest Mechlin lace, in deference to her great skill with the needle. It had been a day of yet more wind and rain and our skirts were heavy with mud. Rain pattered on the coffin and ran in little channels from the top of the grave. My flowers opened their petals wider to receive the moisture and it seemed a terrible shame when the first handful of mud thudded down on them. We stood in a tight little bunch and felt the warmth of each other's bodies. Sarah would have fretted over the damage to the fabric of our gowns, taken mine away and restored it to me later in perfect order. Not once had I thanked her properly for all the little services she had done me.

The next day we moved the baby to Hanover Street where the air was cleaner and there was less disruption. It must have been bad for trade in Powder Yard to have a crying baby in the house. Hanover Street had been transformed in the five days since I was last there and was half stripped of its furniture and hangings. One huffy maid had been left in charge of the house, the parrot hung dolefully in a near empty kitchen and our feet echoed on the bare staircases. There was no sign at all of Aislabie. I sold my remaining books and instruments to the bookseller near St Paul's and raised sixty guineas. Given the debt still owing Harford, it seemed a small enough sum.

4

The morning we left London was grey and drizzly. First into the carriage went Mrs Gardner, next the parrot, then Annie. The baby, lovingly dressed in the tiny bonnet, gown and shawl that used to be at the bottom of my mother's chest, was tucked up in a basket. I was about to hand her to Annie when a familiar figure came swinging round the corner of the street, waved a gloved hand as if astonished to find us there and quickened his pace.

I realised that my husband's arrival was impeccably timed. As usual Aislabie had paid minute attention to sartorial detail and had achieved a look of charming, somewhat nautical dishevelment – a blue morning coat draped at the waist with a scarlet sash, matching satin slippers, a bob wig and loosely tied neckcloth. He bowed over my hand but his gaze slid down to the baby. 'A word with your old man, Em, before you go?'

I brought the basket back inside and we went into the former dining parlour, now empty of every stick of furniture except the table which was presumably too badly marked with tobacco and drink stains to be of any value to the bailiffs. We stood either side of the dirty window looking out on to the street and the waiting carriage. Aislabie was very ill at ease, chinking the change in his pocket and darting anxious looks into the basket on the table as if at any moment his daughter might reach out clingy tentacles and wrap them round his throat.

'*Flora* sails tomorrow,' he said.

I nodded.

'Ain't you going to wish us well?'

'I have no idea what to wish for that ship. I can't help feeling it would be better if she went down with all hands before she reached her destination.'

'That's very ungrateful of you considering all I've done to fit her out. And your well-being depends on her, remember, like all the rest of us.'

'I want nothing to do with *Flora*. She will be trading in human misery. My father once said that if you dissect two dogs – one black, one white – they will both be the same under the skin. I have thought about it a great deal since visiting *Flora* and I believe it must be the same with humans. And in any case, the chances of anyone coming home safely from such a voyage seem remarkably slim. I've seen her and heard about the type of combustible cargo she'll be carrying.'

His blue eyes flickered. 'There are risks but nothing out of the ordinary. And at least I'll be living. I'll see the other side of the planet. I've had enough of this little corner of it. London confines me, shrinks me down. Anyway, you've no choice but to take an interest, Emilie, since every last penny we have is invested in *Flora*. As well as half of Selden.'

'What do you mean?'

'Fitting out a ship is an expensive operation. I had to mortgage land to raise the funds.' He drifted across to the basket and peered at the child's face. Then he touched her forehead with the back of his index finger. I nearly cried out in fear: She's not yours. Don't claim her now.

When he looked up his eyes were moist. 'Does she have a name?'

'She does.'

'Well?' He touched her again on the ear.

'We called her Aurelie Sarah. Aurelie because she arrived with the dawn. It comes from the Latin word for gold. And because it's a French name, after my mother.'

'Aurelie.' He nodded approvingly. 'Aurelie.'

'So I hope you've found some means to support her,' I said coldly, 'if not even Selden is safe from your creditors any more.'

He leaned back on the table, crossed his legs, produced an envelope and a folded paper from his pocket. 'I sold a picture for you. Broke my heart but it raised nearly a hundred pounds. I've brought you fifty. And then there's this. Your father was a wily old sorcerer. He wanted a clause in the marriage settlement in case I died or abandoned you and left you short of money. Seventy pounds a year. So there you are. A little nest egg in the event of my not coming back.' His attention wandered to Aurelie again. 'She's got a good face, I think. She'll be a beauty. You take care of her, Emilie.'

The amazing thing was there was so little self-knowledge in the man that he truly believed in the veracity of each moment. When he took my hand and pressed it to his lips I think he really did feel every inch a brave seafarer setting out on a hazardous voyage for the sake of his wife and child. And the touch of his fingers, which were clammy, convinced me that he actually was afraid. 'Give me your blessing, Em. Wish me well.'

I was silent.

He threw back his head and gave me that sliding look down his cheek that used to make me tremble with desire. 'Dear God, you're a cruel woman.'

I took the papers he'd placed on the table, picked up Aurelie and went out to the carriage. Aislabie sprang ahead to help me in and dabbed Aurelie's forehead with his thumb as if in benediction.

The coachman closed the door and I looked for the last time into my husband's face. His smile was exactly as when I first saw him, boyish and full of promise.

5

Although the journey home to Selden seemed very long the baby, rocked by the lurching of the carriage or clasped to her nurse's breast, made few murmurs of complaint. Annie stared wistfully out of the window as if she was etching the streets into her memory; then as we plunged away from the straggle of houses and smallholdings marking the edge of the city she took out *The Castle of Knowledge* and began to fumble her way through the second page. Sometimes the parrot fixed me with a beady eye and squawked. Mrs Gardner dozed. Meanwhile rain drummed on the carriage roof, the horses plodded on and on through the miry lanes and the baby sucked and slurped at the nipple.

I had tucked the envelope of money into my bodice but held the parchment, folded in three and sealed with red wax, in my lap. My father had addressed it in his tremulous hand: *For my daughter, Emilie.* I thought everybody in the carriage must be struck by its significance but they took no notice. After we had driven well beyond London I slid my finger under the flap and broke the seal. The paper was somewhat bent where it had been in Aislabie's pocket but otherwise undamaged.

30 September 1725

For my daughter Emilie Selden, in the event of her being left alone, under any circumstances. The sum of seventy pounds per year, the capital of which has been deposited . . . the name of a lawyer in Buckingham. Then a phrase typical of my father: *seventy pounds being more than sufficient, I have found, for the proper running of Selden.* Finally his signature.

I refolded the paper and pressed the seal together. On 30 September my father had closed the library door in my face when Aislabie called to discuss our marriage. And yet, that same morning, he had written this note for me which I now held to my breast like a love letter.

The first I saw of Selden was a thin plume of smoke from the kitchen chimney and an uneven cluster of roofs huddled into the side of the valley with a jagged space where the oldest wing used to be. Near the woods was the scar left by the excavated lake – apparently no work had been done in our absence. Then we rounded a sharp bend, I saw the church tower and the first cottage, and Annie craned out of the window to catch a glimpse of the forge. My heart pounded with excitement because I was coming home with Aurelie and the world was therefore utterly changed.

At Selden we dashed through the rain into the entrance hall and suddenly there was a crowd, the first since my husband's party: the Gills and Annie's vast family turned out to welcome her back, the parrot and Mrs Gardner who said she had a terrible headache from all the green air. There was no sign of Harford. According to Mrs Gill he'd got sick of the silence and taken himself off days ago on a drinking bout in Buckingham. No one mentioned Shales. I received a kiss on the cheek from Mrs Gill, another from Annie's mother who was overwhelmed with relief at the safe return of her daughter and a bone-crunching handshake from the blacksmith. Aurelie was admired, the parrot exclaimed over. The joy of such a homecoming made me dizzy.

After supper Aurelie, who had slept most of the day, was wide awake despite being brimful of milk. Mrs Gardner by contrast was dropping with headache and exhaustion so I sent her to bed, swaddled Aurelie up tight and took her on a tour of the house.

Her arrival changed my view of Selden utterly. I no longer saw it as a place of broken memories but as a refuge for her. The rooms would have to be sealed against the coming winter, the derelict parts closed down, the remaining chimneys swept. When we went out on to the terrace I pointed to the moon as it came dashing from among the clouds and shone on the window of my bedchamber, where she would sleep. Tomorrow, I told her, we will begin work on the gardens. We will restore the rose garden in memory of my father.

I carried her into the stable yard and showed her how the water came gushing from the pump and then we peered into the pantries and still room, and admired the thickness of the walls and how the air circulated through the high mesh windows. In the kitchen we studied the embers in the hearth and their reflection in the brass pots, and I chatted to the parrot whose cage hung under the high window and who had stuck his head under his wing as if disgusted at being consigned to servants' quarters yet again.

By the time I reached the entrance hall and the library door Aurelie's head was lolling against my neck and her breath came in even little puffs.

Aurelie. What will we find? I remember the library in its heyday when a fire always blazed in the hearth and light flickered on the rows and rows of ancient books, on the bowl of my father's pipe and in his astute little eyes. But the library then was a place more of shadow than of light, a reminder of all the books that I hadn't yet read, the things I didn't know, the reasons I hadn't discovered. And it was a place where time was suspended, an ante-room to the laboratory.

I picked up a candle and flung open the door. The room was

very quiet with a slight draught winding its way through the forest of iron props and up the yawning chimney. Supporting Aurelie's sleeping body with one hand, with the other I shone the light on to the empty shelves and the swept hearth. Then we walked through the screen of scaffold to the laboratory. I held her tighter, lifted the candle, took another step.

There were great changes here. The shutters had been repaired and nailed into place, the furnace cleaned and a fire laid. My father's workbench was in its old position, the top planed smooth and polished, his staff propped against it. Even more intriguing was that some form of experiment had been set up; a long tube of metal from what looked like a gun barrel had been bent into an S shape, one end of which was connected to a retort, the other to an inverted flask.

I put down the candle and its light pooled on the waxy surface of the wood. The bowl of the retort, I realised, could be filled with a substance to be heated and placed above the furnace. The air produced would then run down the gun barrel and be collected in the inverted flask above water. And once collected that air might be tested to see if it had the same properties as the air around us. We could try to light a candle and thereby establish whether it would sustain fire and life. We could test its solubility in water. We could introduce the air produced by heating saltpetre to discover whether we might make so-called phlogisticated air elastic again. There was no end to what we might do with that separated and stored air.

And there was something else, a gleam of parchment at the far end of the bench, an invitation in the form of a new notebook open at a blank page, and a freshly cut quill.

Aurelie was now deeply asleep against my neck, a concentrated, warm weight as I swayed from foot to foot, hung over the open notebook, looked up at the closed cellar door, listened. Shales was so present to me in the careful setting up of the experiment, the exact placing of quill and inkstand, the open notebook, that I half expected him to appear. I thought of what I would say when I met him again: So, Shales, despite all I've said, you expect me to pursue my investigations into the nature of fire . . . I imagined the expression in his eyes when I smiled at him.

I wondered what would be my first words in the notebook.

After all, it was many months since I had written anything of substance. Perhaps I would draw up a chart or a record of what happened when I tested the air collected at the end of the gun barrel. Perhaps I would devote the book to Aurelie, an account of her birth and childhood so she could read it when she was older. Or perhaps I would tear out a page and write a letter to Shales.

I took a few more turns about the room and thought how beautiful were these dark, empty spaces and how intimate the arrangement of candle and notebook. Finally I shifted Aurelie's weight to one side, picked up the light and walked away through the laboratory, the old library, across the entrance hall and up the stairs to bed.

6

The next day, the first of September, was fine and warm again. All morning I worked in the rose garden with Gill, pruning the bushes and sweeping away the debris left by the workmen. He brought a barrow to the bottom of the steps and we piled in the diseased cuttings so that he could wheel them to the bee orchard and build a bonfire.

I brought Aurelie out to watch the flames. Her lips made little sucking motions and her eyes, which I thought had something of her mother's uneven quality about them, fixed on my face. She took in every word as I told her that the air above the fire was quivering because of the heat and it wasn't often that we could see the air like this but I, Emilie Selden, knew for sure that air was complex, made up of at least two gases, and when Aurelie was older she and I would find out the properties of those gases and astound the world.

But the sight of that bonfire made me restless. All day I had worked with great energy to hold myself at Selden but now I couldn't wait any longer so I took Aurelie inside and handed her to Annie's sister.

'Do you know if Reverend Shales is home?' I asked.

'For all I know, Mrs Aislabie.'

'You don't think he's in Norwich.'

'I'd say not. I've seen him often in the village and he was up here these last few days working away to clear up that room that were taken by fire.'

I went to the laboratory and collected my father's staff. Then I tied on my old straw hat and walked past the dying bonfire where Gill was raking together the embers, past the new lake already pooled with water from the recent rain, and into the woods.

The leaves were tinged with brown, the bracken collapsed and beaten down. The air smelt of sulphur as if saturated with smoke from Gill's fire. Sometimes I ran, sometimes I slid on the muddy track and had to jab in the staff to balance myself. Sometimes I held the staff at arm's length or used it to swipe at a snake of bramble and once I threw it far ahead of me and watched its brass tip catch the sunlight as it turned over and over. I stooped to pick it up and as I came upright saw creatures on the path, a doe and her fawn, watching me with grave brown eyes. We stared for a while, utterly still as the sun baked down on us, then the mother kicked up her hooves and disappeared into the dappled shadow with the fawn lolloping in her wake.

When I reached the river I found it unlike its usual calm self; instead it gushed and foamed under the narrow bridge and was full of twigs and fallen leaves. Further along the bank trailing branches of willow were dragged along in the rush of water.

The lane beneath the churchyard was empty as ever and my feet were silent on the damp ground. The front door of the church cottage stood open and halfway down the passage Shales's study door was ajar. I propped the staff against the wall and waited to catch my breath. Then I heard the chink of wood on glass.

Next came more definite movements from upstairs, the rhythmic thump of a broom and his maid's heavy footfall. My feet took me across the threshold and into the hall.

He was sitting at the far side of the desk, bare-headed, rule in one hand, pen in the other. In front of him was a glass vessel inverted over a dish of water and quarter full of what looked like coal, with an unlit candle on a platform above and a siphon running into it, presumably so that he could measure and test the expelled air. Near me was the chair he kept for visitors.

Upstairs the broom hit a piece of furniture, his bed probably. I took another step and I could see the hearth, the clock and the miniature of his wife. Footsteps crossed the floor above.

I put my hand on the back of the chair. 'Shales.'

He went utterly still, then laid down his pen and rule, blotted his work and sat for a moment with his head bent. I became aware of the peculiar, hesitant tick of the clock. Then he looked at me and I heard my own sharply indrawn breath. He got up, crossed behind me and shut the door. We were so close that the brim of my hat nudged his chest. I took it off and laid it on the desk.

'There is a child at Selden in need of christening,' I said.

With special thanks to the following for their help and advice: Dr Patricia Fara, fellow of Clare College and author of *Newton, The Making of Genius*, Dr Andrew Szydlo for his advice on alchemy, the keepers of Dennis Severs' House, 18 Folgate Street, London, and Professor Tim Hitchcock of the University of Hertfordshire.

Also thanks to Charonne Boulton, Cheryl Gibson, Mary Groom and Barbara Luckhurst, and to Steve Cook and the Royal Literary Fund for their imaginative encouragement and support. Lastly, my love and thanks to Martin, Jenny, Charlotte and Jake Rainsford, without whom the book could never have been written.